Blow Happy, Blow Sad

Growing up poor in New Orleans taught him never to pass up easy money, but gradually the work increased as Olsen began using him to smuggle documents through the waterfront and to gather information from loose-lipped soldiers. Once, Chops had even hidden a German refugee, a man with a vague past: anti-Nazi scientist, engineer, or perhaps writer.

Tonight, Chops had killed.

As they sped toward downtown, Chops envisioned whom he would sneak to Sweden aboard a stolen fishing boat. Kaj. His band. Tapio. Naturally Svenya. He could never leave without her. Suddenly, all the pieces came together. He could not stop his resistance work until she was free from the Gestapo's clutches. And if he quit, Peder Olsen would have no way to send his stolen information to his superiors in London. "You don't plan on springing Svenya, do you?"

Blow Happy, Blow Sad

by

Wm. Ellis Oglesby

Commonwealth
Publications

A Commonwealth Publications Paperback
BLOW HAPPY, BLOW SAD

This edition published 1996
by Commonwealth Publications
9764 - 45th Avenue,
Edmonton, AB, CANADA T6E 5C5
All rights reserved
Copyright © 1995 by Wm. Ellis Oglesby

ISBN: 1-55197-321-9

Printed in Canada

With peace and love to my parents, Richard and Lamar Oglesby

Chapter One

Two dark, wary eyes peered through the slit in the thick oak door.

"Yes?"

"V is for Viking," Chops said. When the door opened, he placed his hand on the small of Svenya's back. She stepped over the threshold. He followed behind her. The tension in his neck and back eased when the door closed again. Somehow, all the indignities of the Nazi occupation disappeared. For a few hours in the evening, freedom and defiance replaced the fear, the helplessness, and the anger which had dominated Denmark since the German invasion in 1940.

Smukke was already packed, and more people would come as the night moved on. The air was thick with smoke and laughter. The club was in the basement, under a haberdashery between the Tivoli gardens and the waterfront. Only a little sound escaped to the streets. It was pretty safe. What would bring a soldier to that area of Copenhagen after dark?

Chops placed his cornet case on a table and shook his friend's hand. "You ready for a big night tonight?"

"Always," Tapio replied. As usual the small,

dark-haired barkeeper looked elegant in a white dinner jacket and a thin bow tie.

Svenya was busy digging at the walnut-sized buttons on her fraying wool coat. It had been old before the last war. The coarse cloth didn't give easily. When she'd unfastened the last one, she let it slide off her shoulders, revealing the blue satin dress underneath. It too was old, but the fabric was stunning. New clothes were impossible to find, so Chops had bought it even though it seemed a bit frumpy. Yesterday, Svenya raised the skirt, darted the waist, and lowered the neckline. With some pearls and a touch of red fingernail polish, the night was hers.

"Last I heard, the Nazis were still demanding sartorial austerity," Tapio said, taking Svenya's coat. "Goebbels would put you in the stocks for wearing that."

"If he could catch me." She shook her head and let her curly, blond hair fly off her shoulders. Chops reached over and took her hand, his dark, cornet-playing fingers wrapped around hers. She said, "My man looks pretty sharp himself, don't you think?"

"I dress up for her," Chops said, fluffing the red silk handkerchief in his light-gray suit pocket. "Are the boys here?"

Tapio nodded. "When are you going to start up?"

"We'll get there when we get there. Don't break your watch." He picked up his case and led Svenya to the bar. What a night. Everyone was dressed to the nines. He spotted several tuxedos. Christian was even in tails. Chops noticed the light touches, too; brass-handled walking canes and top hats, an ascot or a rose on the lapel.

Tonight the ladies were flaunting the fashion

of twenty years past, wearing short sequin dresses and carrying twelve-inch cigarette holders. The thin ones wore baggy sweaters and drew them in with a necklace around their waist. Arial was leaning against a steel support beam, draped in acres of green fabric. Chops stopped for a double-take. It was a choir robe.

"Airs, can you dance in that?" he called to her over the crowd. "'Cause if you can't dance, you might as well go home."

She blew a funnel of smoke toward the ceiling and turned her rounded face toward Svenya. "Was that an invitation?"

"He's not going anywhere until he puts that horn to his lips," Svenya said, tugging on his hand. She positioned his palm on her hip. "But you better kiss me before you kiss it."

"Yes, ma'am." He slid his hand to the small of her back and pulled her close. As their lips met, he felt her rub against the inside of his thigh. She tasted like chamomile.

"Blow it through the roof, Chops. I want to swing tonight."

"That's what I'm here for." He stepped back and took a small bow. He straightened slowly. Although he was only two feet away from her, he could already feel the caldron of nerves begin to churn inside his gut. It wasn't stage fright. He'd been around too long for that. It also wasn't the swarm of dashing men who would dance with Svenya while he played. The anxiety came from his nightmares.

Joseph Goebbels had started his crusade against jazz in the mid-1930's, labeling it *entartete*—decadent or degenerate—and by now the Nazi regime had completely outlawed it. The military had left the definition vague so they could treat violators as they pleased. Those with influential friends might walk, but Chops and Svenya didn't have friends like that. They might be sent to the camps for dancing in a club like Smukke.

Suddenly, the smile on Chops' lips felt forced. Despite his fear, he'd never asked Svenya to stay at home. And he never would.

"See ya' on break," he said kissing her hand. Spinning on his heel, he weaved his way through the back-slapping crowd.

His dressing room was small—not much more than a closet. He could hear the regulars calling for the band to come on stage. They would have to wait. As the seconds crept by, the whistles grew louder and the voices rose. Soon they would be beating on the tables and singing their own songs. Because the crowd risked so much for their entertainment, they demanded a lot. And they got what they wanted. Jazz. Burning hot and lots of it.

He heard a hesitant knock. "Are you ready, Chops?"

"In a flash, Dragor," he said to his clarinet player through the closed door. He straightened up and craned his neck in a circle. Reaching down beside him, he wrapped his pinkie around the finger hook on his cornet. He lifted the horn a few inches from his face. As he ran the valves, he dripped a shy dose of oil on the chrome shafts. Just enough for speed. He stood, buffed the bell with his sleeve, and tossed his gray derby onto his head.

He moved to the door, then turned sharply and backed against the wall. The reflection of his round, ebony face filled the small mirror on the dressing table. With a gentle tug, he straightened his double-breasted jacket and once again fluffed the bright-red, silk handkerchief in his pocket. Yes, a black man looked more elegant in a gray suit than anything else. He winked to the mirror and strutted out the door.

He joined the rest of the Backbeats in the small anteroom behind the stage. In the hot, sticky air, little beads of sweat began to appear on his forehead. The audience seemed louder here, and he could see the excitement on the other musicians' faces. Chops eyed the door to the stage and flashed his band a jovial "You ready?" look. After puffing some warm, moist breath through his horn, he began, his Danish raspy and heavily accented.

"We'll swing on the *Tiger Rag* for starts. Dragor, you take the first chorus and drag it out all you want. We'll run the turn-around twice and then I'll hit them with the tag end. Sticks, when it's over, count to ten. Then take an eight bar rumble, and we'll shoot straight into *Skid-Dat-De-Dat*. From there we fake it. When you boys start wearing thin-"

Svenya's voice topped the roar of the crowd. "Chops, we're tired of waiting."

He started to laugh. After shaking his head he looked up. "Changed my mind, Dragor. Why don't I take the first chorus on the *Tiger Rag*? You get the tag." He didn't wait for approval.

When Chops stepped onto the stage, the audience erupted. He strutted on up to the edge, took off his hat, and bowed at the hips. He stayed doubled over for a three-count. Then he straightened up and raised the cornet to his lips. He started low and then blew step-wise through the roof, holding the last tone until his eyes began to vibrate in their sockets. When he cut the note, the audience paused, spellbound. Then they exploded once more.

After this "warm-up", Chops stole the chance to rest his gaze on Svenya, holding it there just long enough to see the curve of her smile, the sheen of blue silk draped carelessly over her shoulders.

He would have looked at her for hours, but while performing he followed the laws of the stage. Here, he loved everyone equally. Chops strutted behind the drum set while the rest of the quintet tuned their instruments. The audience continued to murmur as their impatience grew. Just before the first man started to complain, Chops nudged the drummer who then struck off into the *Tiger Rag*.

As the band glided into the song, the couples flooded the floor. No one waited to see who else was dancing or what the band would play. Anything the Backbeats did was good enough for them, and they could jitterbug to it all. Their frantic steps gave the song an underlying rhythm that no drummer could have produced. As the first chorus approached, Chops shimmied to the edge of the stage. The platform only elevated the performers two feet above the floor, but it seemed much higher. He looked down and saw the blur of couples dipping, turning, and colliding into one another. And he saw Svenya.

As the chorus hit, he cocked his head to the side, put the horn to his lips, and started to blow. Where other front men played jazz solos, Chops played stories. He swayed back and forth with the band behind him and told a tale that could touch any listener. And everyone in the crowd knew he was talking to them. But he knew he was talking to her.

He had said "I love you" with his cornet long before he said it in his actions and even longer before he spoke those words. Tonight he said it again. He started with rich, morose notes and told her how happy she made him. He tilted his horn to the ground and slumped a bit, putting an edge on his tone. His melody told how cold and mean his world had been before he had met her. The band slid into the bridge, and Chops raised his cornet towards the ceiling, rocketing the high notes. Svenya smiled; she understood.

Chops lowered the cornet and a contagious grin crept across his face. He reached into his hip pocket, pulled out a handkerchief, and wiped the sweat off his forehead. The band galloped through the tag, ending with Dragor squealing the lead on his clarinet. They stopped on a short-count.

After continuing their wild gyrations for several bars a cappella, the dancing crowd realized the song was over and turned to face the stage. Over the plaudits and whistles, Chops heard the drummer counting to himself, and he chuckled softly. He bowed low again. When Sticks hit ten, Chops straightened up with his horn already poised at his lips, and they headed straight into the next number. This thrilled the audience, who commenced dancing as fervently as before.

The brass ship's bell above the door chimed one resonant, cutting tone.

The musicians stilled their instruments, and the dancers ceased their movements as the chilling, metallic sound swelled through the air and then faded. The cord yanked taut a second time and then a third. Again and again the knocker hammered out its warning. Fear descended rapidly on the club.

The bell cord led to a lookout on the third story. If the Danish police hit the block, he'd ring the bell twice. But if it were the Germans, he'd yank the cord as long as he could.

The bell stopped.

Everyone looked to the bandstand. Chops smiled nervously. He craned his neck to look at the band and snapped his fingers slowly. "One, and two, and one, and two." The Backbeats began playing a traditional German polka. Oom, pa, oom, pa. Everyone scurried to their seats and began sipping on their drinks, eyeing the door and trying to make conversation. The Smukkies began to link elbows and sway back and forth to the music. A small group near the front began singing to the familiar tune.

"I sing for my homeland and days of my youth."
Oom, pa, oom, pa.
"I drink for salvation and long for the truth."
Oom, pa, oom, pa.

The oak door burst open and the dark tobacco smoke swirled as a half-dozen soldiers poured into the basement. Their boots clicked on the stone floor as they made their formation, keeping their weapons close to their chests. Like everyone else, Chops recognized the Gestapo's black uniform and red armband. They had come for him. Why hadn't he left Denmark right after the invasion, when the borders were still open? Now there was nothing he could do. The officer in front pointed towards the band. Then he drew his finger across his throat.

Chops lowered his cornet.

Tapio emerged from behind the bar and approached the officer, dusting off the sleeves of his white dinner jacket as he walked. "*Guten Abend, mein Herr*," he said in school book German. "Welcome to my humble establishment. Please, you and your men should have a seat. Allow me to bring something refreshing from behind the bar."

For a moment, the German said nothing. He was half a head taller than Tapio, but his shoulders were thin and downward slanting. After pulling off his black leather gloves and folding them into his pocket, he shook his head slightly and said, "That won't be necessary."

Tapio swallowed and took a step back.

The officer turned to his men. His voice was soft but clear. "*Einsatz. Vorwärts.*"

The line of soldiers began to fan through the room, scrutinizing the overdressed men and women around the tables and against the walls. No one spoke. When the commanding officer reached the front of the club, he looked up at the bandstand. Chops stood on the lip of the stage and stared down at him. He seemed younger up close. Pale and underfed. But he had a gun and a uniform and a squad of soldiers to back him up. This was it.

The German muttered something under his breath, turned, and pointed at Svenya. Two soldiers jerked her out of the chair. She gasped as they pulled her to her feet. Her eyes burned with fear.

The officer snapped his fingers. "Take her away. She is a spy."

Chapter Two

The gray light of a misty day filtered through the wooden shutters and cast a thatched pattern on the cold, rugless floor. To the left of the window, a tiny door opened, and a red silk bird poked into the room. Without formality, it chirped once and then retreated into its antique, hand-carved abode. The simple messenger provided little solace. There one moment...gone the next. Lingering only long enough to say that afternoon had arrived. Outside, the world still moved as it had for millennia. As it would for millennia to come.

On the right side of the double mattress Chops lay on his back, staring at the ceiling. Sometime during the interminable morning his bedclothes had metamorphosed into a suffocating restraint. His neck ached and the muscles in his legs began to cramp. He had not slept last night. Every time he closed his eyes he saw the Gestapo hauling Svenya out of Smukke, her hair flying and blue eyes round with panic. And he saw himself on stage, cornet in hand, doing nothing to help the woman he loved. A coward. He tried to think of what he could have done to save her. It would have been suicide to jump off the stage and attack the German officer. Even if a barroom brawl had taken place, the soldiers would have called reinforcements and thrown everyone in jail. Besides, Smukkies were not fighters. They dressed up in fancy clothes and thumbed their noses at the Germans, but they went to Smukke to forget the war, not to wage it.

Somehow it was his fault. When Svenya moved from Skjern, the small bay city on the west side of Denmark, to join the Royal Orchestra in Copenhagen, he had introduced her to his circle of friends, brought her to Smukke, placed her next to the shadiest elements of the waterfront, always thinking that he could protect her. She came from a small town, attended the best schools, and had private viola lessons since she was a child, enough to find a seat in an orchestra dominated by men. Chops had been surprised how quickly she became comfortable with his friends, not just the intellectuals at the Conservatory, but also with those on the underside of society. Smukke was an insider's group, but everyone had accepted her, not as Chops' girlfriend—a title she would not tolerate—but as herself. Once when she arrived before Chops, an acquaintance asked her where her shadow was and she snapped, "We're not always joined at the hip, you know." Today, Chops felt like a part of him had been severed.

In a vain attempt to find comfort, Chops clasped the corner of his blanket and heaved his body on its side. Once again he faced the wall. The off-white paint could not conceal the texture of the plaster patches. A crack ran from the baseboard upwards, reaching the ceiling, probably even the roof. He coughed several times and rolled over again, unintentionally casting the blanket to the floor. He couldn't even find the energy to pull it over him again.

At least he didn't have a lecture this morning.

Shortly after the Germans invaded Denmark, they restructured the curriculum and the faculty, aligning the Conservatory to reflect Hitler's New Order in Europe. As a Negro, Chops lost his position as did the Jewish professors and the liberals. Piece by piece, the Nazis were taking everything he had. His job. His lover. What would they want next?

Only a thin technicality kept the authorities from deporting Chops after they suspended his job indefinitely. Seven years earlier he had fallen in love with a lady named Marie, a seamstress in a downtown men's clothing store. After a short courtship, they were married in the chapel of the Nicolaj Kirke, and they honeymooned on Laeso, a small Danish island off the coast of Sweden. The pastor who performed the marriage buried Marie only three months later, after a taxi's brakes had failed and she and another pedestrian had been hit. The coroner said she had broken her neck and died instantly without even knowing what had happened. Chops, age twenty-five, was a widower. In his grief he destroyed anything that would remind him of her: the photos, the chatty letters, even their wedding certificate. Only his Danish passport remained as evidence of their brief relationship, but that was enough to allow him to stay in Copenhagen, even after the United States declared war on Germany in 1941.

Chops' back began to needle him, so he strained to sit up. He coughed again and leaned against the wall, unintentionally thudding the base of his skull against the plaster. The dull ache in his head expanded in waves, like the ripples of a stagnant pond after a stone is dropped. He extended his legs one at a time, trying to ward off the paralyzing stiffness, although he knew nothing would help.

After climbing out of bed, he walked naked across the room and drew back the shutters. The muted light flooded into the room, and Chops shielded his burning eyes. Today, out of habit, he counted the ships floating through the Inderhavn. Three trawlers, two barges, and one fishing boat that had been damaged when her drunken skipper had tried to moor her last week. By martial decree, all ships flew the Nazi flag. Slightly gratified to see no military vessels, he closed the shutters again.

Chops stepped into some pants and began flipping through his album collection. Strictly jazz originals. In trade for a jazz record in good condition one could demand anything from gasoline to leather shoes, and Chops had refused many lucrative offers, swearing that he would never part with even one record of the collection. He valued no other possession except his cornet.

He slid Bessie Smith out of her cardboard sleeve and held her between his index fingers, blowing the non-existent dust out of her grooves. He carefully placed her on the Victrola and turned the crank several times. Gingerly, he dropped the needle, and she began whining the "Lou'siana Low Down Blues." Yeah, Bessie understood.

He blotted a tear and crumpled on the straight-backed chair in front of his desk. Swaying back and forth in his chair as Bessie sang the blues, Chops grabbed a Lucky Strike cigarette, the kind only available on the black market. Clenching it between his teeth, he leaned back and propped his feet on the desk, feeling the slickness of the lighter in his hand. He popped the cover and flicked the flint. Wavy fumes rose from the soft, golden flame. He lit the cigarette, inhaled deeply, and blew a blue-gray stream of smoke at the ceiling. Bessie sang on, and he took another puff. It did not help.

He cast a glance in the mirror and saw the face of a corpse. His skin had drawn in around his low cheek bones and the creases on his forehead cut deeper than ever before. His eyes burned, swollen and red. When he reached up to scratch the stubble on his chin, he noticed his hand shaking uncontrollably.

"I gotta do something."

He showered with icy water to clear his head. As he toweled himself dry, he walked to his wardrobe to grab a blue suit with silver chalk-stripes and a red and silver polka-dotted tie, the one Svenya liked best. "Dress up when you feel low." His mother had said it one million times when he was young. But Chops' rakish attire provided more than an emotional boost. It served as protection.

In Chops' eyes, everyone in Denmark looked basically the same, with their hair the color of straw and their faces paler than bleached flour. Although black sailors frequently visited Copenhagen, few had settled there. Occasionally he bumped into other colored people, some from Africa with British accents and others from the States, but there wasn't a black community. He would probably have avoided it if there were. Since he could never blend in, he tried to maintain a high profile on the waterfront. He wanted the Nazis to view him as a harmless ornament of the port. So far, they had left him alone.

Chops put on his coat and left his house, gratified to discover that the clouds had thinned to let the sun's rays peek through. He angled his hat down over his left eye, unlocked his bicycle, and headed off towards the dark side of Copenhagen.

Once over the Knippels Bridge, he passed the huge, eight hundred year-old stone castle

Christiansborg. Ever since the Swedish royal family left at the end of the eighteenth century, the Danish parliament had ruled here. The constitution theoretically allowed any Dane to bring grievances before the King, and Chops wished he could invoke that right to petition for Svenya's release. In practice, however, King Christian only left his Amalienborg residence once a day to ride his horse through the streets as a sign of Danish unity.

Traffic was light as he rode over the small canal to the fish market on the Gammel strand. The fishermen had just moored their boats after their morning trips and while some swabbed the deck and secured the lines on the piers, others prepared their catch for market. Glassy, silver eyes stared helplessly at the haggard fishermen who swung their knives as carelessly as a janitor swept away old cigarette butts. After the blade fell, the gills flopped open a few times and the tail flapped in futile protest against the mighty, sea-worn hand which held the scaly body in place. With blind accuracy, the fishermen tossed the gutless creature into a basket and grabbed another. Every few minutes they swept the carnage off the block, where it fell between the planks and was devoured when it returned to the sea.

The Widers-Pladsgade brought back a flood of memories. He closed his eyes, and he was eight years old again, running towards the Rue de Esplanade in New Orleans. The fish he had stolen from the market threatened to slip from his hands as he darted between the carts and stands, searching for a place to hide. Now, almost twenty-five years later, Chops was still looking for hiding places.

Once on Vingardestraede, he passed the Nicolaj Kirke where he and Marie had been wed, but he did not stop. He continued around the rotary at

Kongens Nytorv, past the Royal Theater where Svenya played with the orchestra, past the Charlottenborg Palace, and he turned left down the Nyhavn. In the sailor's district there was almost no traffic.

On the Nyhavn even the Nazis felt vulnerable. Ever since the Vikings reigned the seas, the piers and canals had intimidated the weak and the unwelcome. As the centuries passed, the actors and the props changed, but the setting remained menacing. The true character of the waterfront emerged only at night, when the drunks brawled and the harlots flaunted themselves. Now, in mid-afternoon, the sailors labored and the girls rested. As he rode along the canal, Chops watched his tires roll over the ageless cobblestones and listened to his bike's even cadence. Looking up, he saw Svenya. She had just emerged from the alley fifty feet ahead, smoking a cigarette, and now she motioned to him. Chops' throat tightened, and his eyes misted as he hopped off the bike and rushed toward her embrace.

"The bastards, they cut her hair," Chops muttered as he drew near. She had stayed in prison only one night, and the jailer had already cut her shoulder-length curls, but they would grow back in time. Then Chops saw her pull a lipstick from her pocket, and he realized she was just another tart, hoping to hustle an afternoon john. Chops swallowed hard, thinking that Svenya would never be on the waterfront alone.

"Hold on tight," he said, loud enough to be overheard. "We got us a kitten here."

The woman turned and winked. Dragging on her cigarette, she strutted towards him. "Hey, Mister. Feeling lucky?"

"My, my, my," he said, eyeing her haughtily.

Usually he enjoyed meaningless flirtations with the prostitutes, and on more than one occasion he had spent evenings with them. Though Svenya had never demanded his fidelity, he had abandoned his red light visitations after she came into his life. Today, the hooker's approach lashed him, reminding him that he might soon return to his old habits. He wanted to tell her to take a running leap into the canal, or to throw her in himself. No one could substitute for Svenya. However, he knew the value of appearances. People in Copenhagen called him the best cornet player in Europe because he acted the part, not because they could judge his talent. "I'd love to cha-cha with you, sexy, but I'm afraid you couldn't afford it."

She laughed. "If you change your mind..."

"I know where to find you." He tipped his hat and continued down the canal. He wondered if she knew about last night's raid. News traveled like the wind on the waterfront, and although he had not publicized his affair, it was no secret. In the beginning, Chops had insisted that he and Svenya keep their relationship discreet. Despite the liberal attitude of the Danes, Chops could never completely shed the racial creed he learned as a child, and he always felt awkward openly displaying affection to the white girl. Behind closed doors she excited him more than any woman he had ever met, but the eyes of others made him nervous. Svenya agreed to the inconveniences of secrecy because of her parents. Her father, in particular, would have objected to her seeing an American for fear that she would marry and leave the country. He wanted her to be happy with a nice Danish gentleman. But as time went by the rumors started, and although she had never introduced him to her parents in Skjern, their relationship was widely known.

Chops looked over his shoulder to reassure himself that the prostitute was not watching him. Good. She had retreated to a storefront and turned her back as she spoke to a potential john. Chops wanted to see the man's face, but the prostitute blocked his view. Odd. Usually the girls stood against the wall so they could watch the street. It was almost as if the customer positioned himself so he could see Chops and still remain hidden in the shadows. Was someone following him? No. He was being paranoid, shaken by Svenya's arrest.

As Chops moved farther down the canal, the condition of the red-brick buildings deteriorated. Rotting garbage lay in the streets. Shards of glass jutted out of windowsills where beer bottles had been hurled. He pulled his bike up under the tattered blue and white awning of the Cafe Kakadu and locked it to a post. After straightening his tie, he opened the door, and the smells of the coffee shop assaulted his senses. The bitter aroma of coffee mixed with the sweetness of fresh-baked pastries. Smoke drifted toward the ceiling. Six or eight patrons sat scattered throughout the establishment, regulars who came to sip coffee and to play chess, to swap gossip or to trade contraband. Some gambled and others dealt. When a merchant wanted fresh vegetables or red meat in his store one week, arrangements could be made at the waterfront. If a Dane needed to book secret passage to Oslo, and take his valuables with him, he might find a willing mariner at the Cafe Kakadu.

Chops stepped to the bar, perched himself on a wobbly stool and called, "Louisa."

A loosely dressed woman behind the bar stepped forward. Her black curly hair hung in strands over her face. She smiled. "Hey, Chops."

"How're things?"

She unconsciously brushed her curls behind her ears. "Could be better. The Germans have cut the coffee rations again and that's pinching my ass." She paused. "I heard there was trouble last night."

He nodded. After the Gestapo took Svenya out of Smukke, he had packed his horn and disappeared, too upset to talk to anyone. This was not the first time he had come to Cafe Kakadu to pour his troubles into Louisa's ear. Ever since he had known her, she had given him sound, straightforward advice.

Eight years ago he had come to Denmark, playing second cornet for Guy Sherman's big bands on a ten-week European tour. They were one of the first racially integrated bands and they had been well received in almost every city. The musicians themselves started out enjoying the trip, acting like tourists in the day, playing shows at night, and then partying until the early morning. However, after two months of revelry, tempers began to flare. On the afternoon before the band was to leave Denmark for the Netherlands, Chops had an argument with the lead trumpet player, which almost led to blows. In a rage, Chops yelled, "I quit," and stormed off to the waterfront bars. When he woke up the next morning, the Guy Sherman Band had sailed.

He roamed the city all morning not understanding a word of Danish. He had 130 dollars to his name, half of what he needed to get back to the States, but he had his horn, and the audiences all over Europe had loved the stuff the Guy Sherman band had played. He figured he'd hang around and hitch up with the next American band that toured Denmark. Around noon he wandered into Cafe Kakadu for a bite to eat, and he instinctively liked the warmth, the smell, and the slightly suspicious people sitting at the tables. One man looked up as he walked in and, from that glance, Chops knew something was up.

He walked over to a small table, sat down, and glanced at the menu. Complete gibberish. A woman came out from behind the counter and came to his table. She was a tall woman, sturdy, with a direct and purposeful look. As she approached, she said something he did not understand, set a cup of coffee on the table, and looked at him expectantly. Picking up the menu, he pointed to item number thirteen, not because thirteen was his lucky number, but because at fifteen crown it was one of the most expensive things on the menu.

After a few minutes, the man he had noticed came over and sat down across from him. "You American?"

"Yeah."

"I have been to New York. Good place."

Chops nodded.

"I learned a game in New York." With that, the man reached into his pocket and pulled out three walnut shells and a glass bead. He placed the bead under one of the nuts, and then rearranged them. "Where is it?"

Chops pointed to the shell on the left, and when the man picked it up, the shell was underneath. "You good. Try again." He repeated the process, this time moving the shells more deftly. When he asked where the bead was, Chops pointed to it again. "You very good."

The waitress behind the counter called out something, and the man turned his head and screamed back at her. Chops watched the woman shake her head and then return to the grill. "What's she want?"

"Nothing. Here. We play again. Maybe make some money. We bet ten crown."

Chops chuckled, thinking this might be the chance he was looking for. "How much is ten crown? What's that in dollars?"

"Two or three."

Slowly Chops reached into his back pocket and pulled out his wallet. He pulled out a fifty dollar bill and ran it under his nose like a Havana cigar. "So that means this is worth somewhere between 150 and 250 crown. Is that right?"

The man looked at him slowly. "It is a lot of money."

"Want to play?" Chops said, his smile widening. If his luck kept on like this, he wouldn't even have to wait for the next American band. He'd have enough money by the end of the week to ride home first class.

The man reached into his breast pocket and pulled out a thick wad of bills. He pulled two one-hundreds off the top and set them on the table. Chops dropped his fifty on top of the pile.

The guy blew some breath into his hands, rubbed them together, and placed the bead under the center shell. Starting slowly, he moved the middle one to the outside, to the inside, to the far side, weaving a complicated braid. He began moving faster, and then he would lift a shell to give Chops a glimpse of the bead. His hands were a blur, and Chops saw him pass the bead quickly from one shell to the other. He heard footsteps approach, and he could smell scrambled eggs, but he did not take his eyes off the game. Suddenly, the man clapped his hands together and raised them high off the table in a dramatic action Chops appreciated. "Where?"

Chops scratched his chin and looked at the

line of shells. He reached out and fingered the bills on the table, fanning them out. Then slowly he brought his eyes up to meet the guy in front of him. He spoke very slowly. "The ball is in your right sleeve. Right by the elbow." Just in case the man didn't understand him, he reached over and pinched the man's sleeve so he could see the shape of the bead.

Chops had seen that game so many times in New Orleans it was almost juvenile. And this character was by far not the best he had ever watched. Now the fellow just looked at him stupidly and dropped his hands by his side. But when Chops moved to take the money, he heard the metallic click of a pistol being cocked.

The bottom dropped out of Chops' stomach, and he almost pissed in his pants, knowing no one would care if he ate a bullet in this dive.

"Hans," the waitress said, as she placed the plate of eggs on the table. She spoke in a steady tone, never raising her voice and never taking her eyes off the man. He tried to interrupt her, but she wouldn't let him. After two or three minutes he shrugged and turned to Chops.

"We forget it. I buy you lunch and it's OK." Then he folded his two hundred crown, dropped his three shells into his pocket, and walked out of the cafe.

"You are crazy fucker," Louisa had said in English and patted him on the shoulder. Then she had walked behind the bar laughing.

The cup and saucer clinked together when Louisa set them on the counter. Chops thanked her and took a sip. The strong drink brought his thoughts back to the present. To Svenya. Louisa had moved down the counter to refill another patron's cup. She returned with a roll and he said, "Yeah, Louisa. You missed one hell of a show last night."

"I'm damned lucky they haven't called my number. We all are, you know."

"But why Svenya?"

"No one knows."

"But she hasn't done anything."

"Come off it, Chops. Everyone has done something." She took a drag off her cigarette and looked at him carefully. "Is she involved?"

Chops knew she was talking about the resistance. Rumors of the fledgling underground ran wild along the waterfront, with everyone speculating at who might be involved. Since Louisa knew everything that happened on the piers, most people suspected that she was a key figure, but Chops didn't agree. She hadn't survived on the waterfront this long by taking unnecessary risks, and acts against the government, such as harboring fugitives and possessing illegal news flyers, carried heavy penalties. The possibility that Svenya was a member seemed absurd. "I don't think so. She certainly never said anything about it, and I guess I'd know if she was attending midnight meetings or something."

Louisa shrugged. "She never seemed like the type. But it looks like someone pointed the finger at her."

"Who would want to get her? She's lived here less than a year, hardly enough time to make enemies."

"I could be wrong, but I'll guess we'll never know."

Chops finished his coffee and pushed the cup across the counter. "If you're right, how long until they figure out she was set up and they let her out?"

"I'm sorry, Chops."

"Huh?"

"Those fuckers don't let people out," she said as

she refilled his cup. "You know what they're like. They'll get a confession out of her one way or the other. With that they can do what they want, and from what I've seen, the Germans are looking to make some examples. I hear they're getting their asses kicked in Russia, and they're taking it out on us."

Chops nodded. "It's not just a case of a bully getting mad and whipping up on a little kid. A year ago the German armies were in sight of Moscow, but last winter hit them hard, and they've been losing ground ever since. With each allied victory the Danes come one step closer to revolt, and the Gerries can't afford to send any more troops here. They need all of them in the east."

"Nip resistance in the bud," Louisa said. "At least Svenya is a lady. A dame hasn't been executed in Denmark since the fifteenth century."

"Executed?"

"Wake up, Chops. You've heard what's happened in France and Poland. The Gerries are bringing the boot down and bringing it down hard. I wish it weren't true, but look around you. It's happening. I'm not going to let you lie to yourself. Svenya's gone. And she won't be back for a long time."

"I've got to get her out."

"Jesus Christ on a fucking cross," Louisa said, loud enough for people in the cafe to turn and look at her. "What's up your sleeve? Don't go off half-cocked like you did after Marie's accident. You could get yourself and a whole lot of other people in a lot of trouble if you do."

"I won't do anything rash," Chops said, and he hoped that was true. "Could you keep your ears open? Maybe we can find out who fingered her or come up with a way to get her out. I was up all last night trying to figure it out, but it's one dead end after another. You've got more connections than anyone I know. Talk to the girls who have friends uptown. Eventually the right German will drop his pants and open his mouth. I'd sure like to hear about it when he does."

She nodded. "Don't expect anything, but I'll do what I can." A man sitting alone at a side table motioned for his check, and Louisa wiped her hands on her apron and headed over to him. She took his money, cleared the table, and walked back behind the counter. "Have you seen Tapio this morning?"

"No, why?"

"I heard the Nazis roughed him up. Is he OK?"

Chops smiled to himself. Louisa wasn't as cold and hard as she liked to believe. Tapio was her friend as well. In fact, she'd introduced Chops to him years ago. "Tapio's fine. He's a scrappy little fellow, and the Germans were just trying to make a point. They only slapped him. Just hard enough so he can brag about it next week. Nothing serious."

"Everything the Germans do is serious, Chops," she said, shaking another Lucky out of the pack. "By the way, I've got something for you." She disappeared below the counter and reemerged with a rectangular package, slightly larger than a notebook. "A sailor from that beat-up fishing boat...what's it called? The GARM, I think. He came by swearing that he almost fell overboard trying to fish this off the deck of the Swedish barge in the storm."

Chops lifted the package and shook it like a child might the day before Christmas. He had expected a delivery today, or perhaps tomorrow, so he had brought some extra money which he pulled out of his breast pocked and passed over the counter. It was a lot of money, but passing contraband carried weighty penalties. Louisa never asked what was in the packages, and Chops had not told her, more for her safety than anything else. She probably thought she was passing on forged ration cards which Chops would sell on the black market. "I haven't heard of anything else coming my way-"

"But if it does," she interrupted.

"I'll make sure you get a cut." He fished a few coins out of his pocket to pay for his coffee and placed them on his saucer. "In the meantime, keep your ears open."

"I'll put out some feelers and see what comes up, but don't count on much. As you know, the Gestapo makes people pretty nervous. I don't think folks will be talking much after the raid on Smukke last night."

"Just give it a try." He winked at her and turned towards the door.

"Be careful, Chops," Louisa muttered, but he did not hear her.

Chapter Three

The streets were busy at five o'clock, and Chops was glad to get onto them, pleased to join the flow of the living after spending the afternoon pacing back and forth across his apartment. The workday had barely ended, yet the sun had already dipped below the horizon, and dusk would hover for another hour at least. Chops did not mind the short days. Darkness afforded him an anonymity and certain protection. As a jazz musician, his life was inclined towards the shadows. What could he do to get her out? That was the question he asked himself, time and time again, but there was no easy answer. It had been difficult for him not to call on the authorities to make an official complaint, if for no other reason than to glean some information, but he knew that would be fatal. He had weathered the occupation by staying out of sight. Asking such questions could get him deported. Or worse.

Why Svenya? What would make someone denounce her? Although she did not have many friends, she was widely respected as a solid viola player in the Royal Orchestra. No one hated her. How could they, with her sly smile and her occasionally biting wit. She and Chops spent hours in playful banter, and her quick mind and her use of subtle innuendoes kept him on his toes. She had a grasp of the Danish language that Chops would never attain.

Chops knew that he must act quickly. As Louisa had said, folks rarely got out of Gestapo headquarters in one piece. But he'd been spinning his wheels all day long, and he was relieved when the time came to drag his tail back across the bridge and into town to give a lesson to his only remaining student. Most of the ships were pulled in and moored off, and the sailors were beginning to swarm around the waterfront, looking for a bite to eat and the first of the many drinks they would have before they wove their way back to the ship or up the stairs to some prostitute's bed. Turning the corner onto his student's street, he climbed off his bicycle and walked it to the nearest lamppost. As he fed his chain through the bike's frame and locked it, he looked up and saw Kaj watching at the window.

Chops pointed his finger like a gun and fired an imaginary round and the face disappeared. Kaj made no secret that his Thursday afternoon cornet lesson was the high point in his week. It was a pleasure for Chops as well. Last year he had taught at least a dozen people, young and old alike, but after he lost his job at the Conservatory, his students backed out, one by one, some gracefully and some abruptly. But Kaj had not deserted him. He still practiced more or less regularly, and boasted at Smukke that he was a private student of the lead cornet player for the Backbeats.

Chops climbed the tenement's five flights of rickety, creaking stairs, and Kaj was waiting for him on the landing, thumbs in his pockets. He was eighteen years old and, although he had not quite filled into his massive frame, he was a big boy. They shook hands firmly, and Chops noticed a new tattoo on his muscular forearm, a busty Spanish dancer in a flowing red dress.

"New tattoo?" Chops said as he walked into the tiny apartment. There was an odd stench in the room, barely noticeable, but there.

"Yeah, the boss put it on me for free so I can show it to the customers." Kaj worked at a tattoo parlor on the waterfront, sweeping up and preparing the dye. His main function was to control the sailors who invariably liquored themselves up to gather the nerve to pay a stranger to paint into their skin. More than once someone would try to leave when the tattooist was only halfway through, and Kaj was very useful at restraining them. It wasn't much of a job, but it provided what little money the boy needed.

"Look at this." Kaj held his arm out and clenched his fist a couple of times. The muscles in his forearms bulged, making the woman's hips jut in and out in an exotic dance. "Not bad, huh?"

"Yeah, Kaj. That's OK."

As they walked inside, Kaj said, "You ought to come down and let the boss put something on you. You know, a cornet or a treble clef. Hell, I bet he'd tattoo the Hallelujah Chorus across your back if you'd let him."

"Not a chance. You know tattoos don't look good on black hide. And besides, Svenya would..." His words trailed off as he bit his lip. He hadn't meant to mention her, and he wished he hadn't. It had become automatic to consider her in his decisions, to think about her constantly. Of course, he did not always do things the way she liked. Chops wasn't that kind of man. Without finishing the sentence, he set his case on the chair, flipped the latches, and pulled out his cornet.

"Is there any word?" Kaj asked. He had been dancing with her in Smukke when the Gestapo hauled her away.

Chops shook his head. "Louisa said she'll keep her ears open."

"We'll get her out. I've got a plan. The Germans are always looking for workers, right, 'cause most Danes hate them and wouldn't lift a finger to help them. So I'll go down to the headquarters and say I need a job. Once I'm on the inside, it shouldn't be a problem. If it comes down to it, we can just bop the guard on the head and take the keys."

"We'll get her out, but not like that. It's too dangerous."

"I don't care. Honest I don't. Just say the word, and I'll go over there right now, I swear I will."

"I know you would." More than once Kaj had proven himself unafraid when it came to wreaking havoc on the occupying soldiers. He would stand on the roof and heckle as they paraded by, sometimes throwing rocks or old vegetables. Once, he snuck into the Dyrkob Hotel, where the Germans were quartering their officers, and he covered all the toilet seats with lard. He had never gotten caught, but for the most part everything he had done was harmless.

Chops knew that Kaj had a crush on Svenya. Everyone knew. But it did not seem like an overtly hormonal crush. No, it was shy and distant. He hung on every word she said, and he followed her around Smukke, fetched her drinks from the bar, and danced with her when Chops was on stage. Chops appreciated her having a strong guy at her side.

"So, have you been practicing any?"

Kaj reached down and grabbed his horn off the desk, nothing more than a door stretched across two wooden sawhorses, one of the three pieces of furniture in the studio apartment. Desk, chair, bed. The walls were bare except for a large poster of Django Reinhardt, an enlargement of one of his album covers done with charcoal on a piece of cardboard. Kaj-1940 was scribbled on the lower, right-hand corner. Besides the sparse furniture, there was only the leather trunk he kept his clothes in and the wire music stand Chops had given him. Chops said he'd hurt his neck reading sheet music off a table as he played, but that was a lie. Playing crouched over cut your wind.

"What about you?" Kaj had said. He hunched over and aimed the cornet at his shoes. "You play like this at Smukke all the time."

Chops felt himself ready to explode, but he took a deep breath and tried to relax. He'd known everything at eighteen too. "If you can do it right and choose not to, that's called style. But if you just plain can't do it, that's something different entirely."

"But..."

Chops put the horn to his mouth and ran up F major scale until he hit a high, high F, which crescendoed out of the horn and stayed loud and did not wane until Chops' lungs felt they would burst. He lowered the cornet and shot a stern look at Kaj. "When you can do that, Mister, then you can talk back to me."

Today Kaj stood perfectly erect and held his cornet parallel to the ground as he played through "When the Saints Go Marching In." Chops could tell he'd been practicing, because he hit the notes with confidence. No caution or fumbling over the notes, but still something wasn't there.

"That's good, Kaj. Pretty good. You did it just like I showed you. Now play it again, and I'll stay under you with the trombone line. But this time, put some of yourself in it. Remember, this is your song. No one else's. OK. Here we go."

They only played eight bars, before Chops dropped his horn and started waving his hands.

"Why'd you stop?"

"Didn't you hear it?"

"Hear what?"

"Listen to my B-flat." Chops played the note. "Now hit yours."

Kaj did. Then his head sank a little bit forward and he shrugged. "It's gotten a little bit flat again. Here, how's this?" He pushed the slide back about a quarter of an inch, tried again, and shook his head. A little more and it was in tune. "Sorry. It just keeps slipping when I play. My cornet is kinda beat up."

"It's got personality, and a nice round tone to boot. You've just got to make sure you keep it in tune. One and two and one..." He stepped into the walking trombone line. Together they played a fairly decent duet. Kaj didn't miss any notes, and his clumsy grace notes had a certain appeal. He actually surprised Chops by harmonizing the coda, and he didn't even crack on the high note.

When they finished, Chops stuck his thumb up in the air. "I'll make a horn player out of you yet." He saw Kaj's eyes light up, and Chops knew not to make any suggestions, although there was much room for improvement. The boy would never be a great musician. He just couldn't hear it. He knew his scales and his arpeggios and could read music pretty well, but somehow he never quite got there. Maybe he knew it, and maybe he didn't, but anyone could see how much he enjoyed playing a duet with Chops once a week. Chops had taught him a lot in their weekly sessions, ideas which he hoped would transcend musical training. He had known Kaj for three years and he had enjoyed watching him mature. He often wondered what sort of adult this lumbering giant would become. Or was he already a man at eighteen?

In the second half of the lesson, Chops forced Kaj to play scales and arpeggios, the building blocks of music that students often ignored. They were boring, but without them a soloist is doomed to copy other people's riffs. Kaj did not protest.

Normally Chops would stay and chat for an hour or so after the lesson, but tonight he packed his horn immediately. Spending time with Kaj had eased some of Chops' tension, but now he was feeling the lack of sleep. "You're doing all right, Kaj," he said as he walked out the door. "Keep on practicing the 'Saints' and next week I'll bring you some new charts. Anything special you want to work up?"

"Honeysuckle Rose."

"It's ambitious, but you might be able to pull it off. I'll write out the melody in B-flat to make it easier."

"Great. And Chops..."

"Yeah?"

"We'll get her out."

He forced a smile. "You bet we will. I'll see you around."

The ride home took fifteen minutes. He quickly opened the front door and darted inside. A sense of security came over him as he climbed the five flights of stairs to his apartment. Up in his room, Chops flipped through his record collection and selected his favorite Blue Devils album. He loved the group, not only because of Hot Lips Page's fluid trumpet line, but also because of the unconventional piano part played by young Bill Basie, who later became known as the Count. Chops turned the crank on the Victrola and dropped the needle. Crackly music filled the small room.

Chops sat down at his desk. Slowly, he began untying the string on the parcel that Louisa had given him. He unfolded the heavy paper and sorted through the contents. Danish currency. A railroad schedule with several times and routes marked in red ink. Ration cards. Two sets of identification papers. If the Germans caught him with this they would shoot him without a trial. He wrapped the material in its original package, careful to tie the string in the same place. No one could tell it had been opened. He hid it in the bottom drawer of his desk, not much protection against a thorough search, but he did not want it in plain sight in case someone walked in.

Chops directed his thoughts back to Svenya. Six months and three days had passed since she had come into his life. Never before had he been so happy, so fulfilled. Before he met her, he had always felt out of place in Europe. When he held her hand, when she smiled, he belonged. Surely he could do something to get her back. He had to devise a plan. Despite what most Danes said, he was not powerless against the Nazis.

He lay his head on the desk and fell into a light sleep. He was with her again. On a secluded beach on the Julebek Strand, they lay under the burning sun. He tried to bury her in the sand and she protested, running away and laughing. When he caught her, she wrapped her arms around him and they kissed.

Suddenly he woke. He shook the sleep from his head. How long had he been asleep? Through the closed window he could hear the calls of the working girls on the waterfront. Prostitutes sounded the same everywhere, and they probably had since the dawn of time. These ladies of pleasure favored the war because lonely soldiers would gladly sacrifice a week's wages for a few hours of comfort, knowing they might never return to their wives and lovers. Chops read the night like a Swiss timepiece. The sun had dipped behind Copenhagen's spiraled horizon, and the girls had started selling. It was eight o'clock.

A sharp click interrupted his thoughts. Though Chops had heard neither footsteps nor the creaking door, he knew he was not alone in the room. He identified the noise immediately. It was the sound of a .9mm Luger, the standard German service automatic, being cocked into firing position.

Chapter Four

Chops spoke without turning around. "Put your pea shooter down or pull the trigger. I don't feel like playing games."

"I caught you sleeping, Chops. That's bad form. Your security is way too lax." The voice was Peder Olsen's, and Chops could hear him shoving his pistol into his pants.

"It's right here," he said, reaching into the bottom desk drawer and pulling out the parcel Louisa had given him earlier in the day."

"What is?"

"The package you're looking for."

"How do you know I came for a package?" Olsen strutted across the room. He hesitated before picking it up, then hastily snapped the binder's twine and tore the heavy paper.

"How do you know I came for a package," Chops mimicked. "Because you always show up right after anything comes through the waterfront. That's how." He turned and, for a protracted second, he studied Olsen, who dressed like a dock worker in a dark, wool sweater and a hand-knit stocking cap, his canvas pants tucked into calf-high boots. Several metal tools dangled from his leather belt, including a six-inch hook that could crack open a wooden crate or, if necessary, a man's skull. His thin, crooked nose jutted out from his broad face, and his dark eyes sank deep in their sockets. He shed his gloves to sort through the documents he removed from the parcel. Chops noticed his tender and uncalloused hands. "If a longshoreman saw your baby-soft skin, he'd feed you to the sharks without blinking."

Olsen laughed contemptuously. "Quite right, old chap. I'm surprised you noticed, but rest assured I kept them covered all day. I can't afford to make mistakes." Peder Olsen worked for Britain's special operations executive. For the past eleven months he had linked the Danish resistance to London. His mission: keep supplies flowing to the underground, facilitating sabotage, labor agitation, and terrorist acts against the German occupation force.

Chops pointed to the papers. "If you want to stay alive, burn those cheese ration cards."

"Did you go through this material before I arrived?"

"No, Olsen. I have X-ray vision. Didn't I tell you? Or better yet, I read your mind. I also read today's newspaper which announced that the Germans cut all dairy rations by a third and issued new tickets. If you use those, you're dead."

The agent shoved the papers into his pants pocket and looked at his watch. "Keep your nose out of my material, Chops. The more you know, the more dangerous life is for both of us. Keep risk at a minimum. That's all I have to say. It's six minutes past eight, we should get to work. I picked up an important-"

"I'm not sending any messages tonight."

Olsen clapped his paddle-sized hands together. "We don't have time for this nonsense, old boy. Of course you are going to send the message."

Being referred to as "boy" smacked of the discrimination Chops had endured in the States, and he poised himself for a fight. "When I started working for you nine months ago, we agreed I could pull out any time I wanted to."

"Any time but now."

"I won't do it."

"You don't have a choice."

"Don't threaten me." Chops pointed a menacing finger.

"I'm not threatening you. I'm just saying-"

"They bagged Svenya."

Olsen cocked his right eyebrow. "When?"

"Last night."

The agent closed his eyes, pulled off his stocking cap, and ran his fingers through his short blond hair. "This little wrinkle could be extremely devastating. What happened?"

Chops mashed his cigarette into the ash-filled coaster and recounted the details of the previous night, fighting to control his emotions with every word. He flailed himself, thinking that if he were not involved with this British agent Svenya would be in his arms instead of locked away in a Gestapo interrogation cell. Why had he not tried to save her? Were they beating her at this moment, or worse? Somehow he managed to force those crippling images out of his mind, and he pushed through his report in an almost steady tone.

"You weren't stupid enough to tell her anything, were you?"

Chops massaged the back of his tense neck. "No. She doesn't know a thing. It's been hell keeping things from her, but I just couldn't see mixing her up in this. I tried not to put her in any danger." But he had done just that.

"Good," Olsen said, reaching into his heavy

trousers. He tossed a folded piece of paper onto the desk. "Here's the message."

Chops glared at the agent. "You haven't heard a word I've said, have you?"

"Of course I have heard every word you said. The Gestapo arrested your current vamp, but she knows nothing that would compromise this operation. Though I'm dreadfully sorry, I'm sure you'll get over it. In the meantime, encode this and send it to England in..." he paused and looked at his wristwatch a second time, "...exactly forty-eight minutes. It is a long one, so you had better get to work. Hop. Hop."

"I'm not sending the message."

"We don't have time to argue. The Radio Security Service must get this code tonight. It is by far the most important piece of information I have turned up. This could mean the war."

Chops had heard that line so many times before that he could recite it from memory. Without his help, the Germans would surely conquer the world. Oh yes. And he had believed every word. But for the past nine months he had risked everything to help this agent, and he didn't see that his work had influenced the war at all. The British were fighting hard in North Africa; the Russians were holding the Sixth Army in the east, and his efforts had accomplished nothing. All he'd done was sacrifice Svenya and that, he concluded, was enough. "I'm not sending it."

"You don't have any choice," Olsen said.

"Oh yes I do. And right now I am choosing not to send your message to England. The Gestapo is on to us, Olsen. This close behind." He held his fingers a centimeter apart. "Sending a message tonight could be the last nail in Svenya's coffin. I think we should lay low for a while, wait for things to cool down, then spring my girl." He held up the paper. "Find another way to get this across the channel. You have a wireless. Use it."

"That is just what the Nazis want, you fool. The Gestapo knows that secrets are getting out, but they don't know how. And they don't know you are a part of it. If they even suspected that you were involved, would they have picked up your lady-friend? No. They would have arrested you. They are guessing, Chops. Stabbing blindly. You are not thinking like they think. Get inside the Nazi's head for once. They are just stirring up the pond to see what surfaces. Don't you see? I'm sure that every radio-detection van in Denmark has been in gear since last night, waiting for the frightened agent to send his SOS to England. And when they intercepted that transmission, they would attack in swarms like hornets.

"I am not the only agent the SOE sent to Denmark, Chops. I know of eleven men who parachuted into this country last year, and I am the only one who remained operative for longer than three weeks. The only one. Two of them escaped to Sweden, and the other eight died in the Gestapo's cellars. All because they used their wirelesses. I didn't. Instead, I found you. You must send this message."

"I can't put Svenya in any more danger. I just can't."

"If you don't go on the air, Chops, you will be killing her."

"What do you mean?" he asked.

"The Gestapo knows that information is getting through. Perhaps they have a mole in London. I don't know. But if the intelligence stops flowing exactly one night after they arrest Miss Svenya Hjorth, they will automatically assume a connection. That alone would serve to prove her guilt. And captured spies face immediate execution. There is no reprieve. Not even for Danish nationals."

Silently Chops unfolded the sheet of rice paper that Olsen had tossed on his desk and read the message. D2O IN C NOT NORSK HYDRO. "What the Hell does it mean?"

"I can't tell you that."

"Come off it. I'm risking my hide. If anyone deserves to know what it means, I do."

He forced his hands back into his gloves. "Perhaps you are right. Only, no one deserves to know. But believe me, it's big. If the Germans get away with the plan I've uncovered, no one will be able to stop them. Not the British. Not the Americans. No one. The Nazis will rule the globe. I promise. It is that big."

Chops figured that no single message could have such importance, but he had to protect Svenya. Damn Olsen and his seamless logic. As he began working out the code, Olsen walked to the door. "The paper's edible," he said before leaving. "Security is important. And don't be late. You are due at the station in..." pause, "...thirty-two and a half minutes."

Thirty-two and a half minutes. Chops would have to rush to the station and encipher on the way. The lid closed on the cornet case with a dampened thud. He snapped the latches in place and stood abruptly. After donning an oversized black and white checkered blazer and an overcoat, he grabbed his horn and walked out. The brisk, salty air stung his face, and his limbs felt heavy, lifeless. Once in the garage, he fastened his cornet case on his bicycle with two crusty leather belts and looked longingly at his landlady's Citroen sedan. He wanted to drive into town, but the tank had been empty for months due to petroleum rationing. He pushed his bicycle out of the shack and rode down the street.

He passed a park bench on which he and Svenya had stenciled the words "VI VIL VINDE." We Will Win. He had wanted to paint "Nazis can kiss my Black Ass," but Svenya had thought it too crude and dangerous. Graffiti had been commonplace in Copenhagen since June, 1941 when the BBC began airing a Danish language news program. Every Thursday, the BBC announcer urged the civilians to revolt. Every Friday, unrest spread through Denmark.

Though Chops pedaled hard over the cobblestone streets, he arrived at the station a few minutes late. Blood rushed through his body, and he felt a tense excitement. He stayed outside until his breathing returned to normal. Then he locked his bicycle to a streetlight on the Ostgebande. He looked up to the radio tower and shook his head. He still could not believe how he had landed this job.

Two weeks after the British had begun their propaganda campaign, a high-ranking official visited Chops and made him a lucrative offer to play on the radio. The Germans wanted Chops and the Backbeats to broadcast a weekly show called "The Thursday Night Exchange" to draw listeners away from the BBC. For political reasons, the word "jazz" could never appear. Instead, they called it "Danish Art Music." Although the Nazis distrusted all modern art forms, they were willing to make small sacrifices to keep listeners away from the BBC propaganda.

Chops climbed the ten marble steps and then looked out over the city's collage of lights. How many people out there would listen to him play tonight? How many would tune in to the BBC?

"Heil Hitler," barked the security guard at the front desk, pointing at the musician. "Show your papers. Open your case."

Chops produced a cloth-covered booklet from his jacket's inside pocket and handed it to the young man. He tapped the desk.

"I've never seen you here before. You're kind of young, aren't you, boy? Wouldn't you rather be playing with your dominos or doodling in a coloring book?"

"I'm a soldier of the Reich," the German said, examining the document. "These seem in order. The rest of your band is already in the studio, so you should go up. The station manager will be displeased since you are late."

"Nah," Chops said, shaking his head. "Herr Wolf's all right."

The young man looked around nervously. "Sir?"

"Yeah?"

"Would you mind playing some Count Basie?"

"I'll see what I can do," Chops said before entering the stairwell. He did not understand the Nazis at all.

As the receptionist promised, the entire band had assembled in the tiny studio. It provided much better performing conditions than Smukke. A carpet covered the floor and plush curtains hung on three walls, which soundproofed the room and dampened all unwanted echoes. Through the large window in the fourth wall Chops saw the two technicians in the control booth. Their equipment was hidden from view, but he knew that the smaller man listened to the Danish station and the pudgy one monitored the BBC to ensure that the "Thursday Night Exchange" coincided exactly with the Danish-language news show. Chops wondered whether he would be allowed to play if the British decided not to broadcast tonight. No. Not a chance.

He smiled across the room at Dragor, the tall, lean clarinet player who had been most reluctant about playing for the Nazis. "It's just not right, Chops," he had said. "I hate the machinists who manufacture small arms for the Third Reich and the farmers who supply their armies. Those guys are traitors. Why kiss the boot that just kicked your teeth in? Our talents should go against the regime, like...well, like it is at Smukke." The two men had debated the subject for over a week and finally agreed to play. They simply could not risk being labeled as agitators. The Germans kept appearances civil by paying the musicians five hundred Krone a week and by supplying them with extra ration cards. However, none of these rewards erased the specter of violence that accompanied the Nazi offer. "What's shaking, Drag?"

"A quiet day at work. Not much more."

"Don't nod off on me," Chops chuckled. "I want to hear you blow like a wild man."

Dragor flashed a glance towards the control booth. "After last night, I think I'll keep things mellow. Is there any news on Svenya?"

Chops' pleasant expression soured. He wanted to forget, to allow Svenya's arrest to seep out of his mind, if only for a moment of peace. But the vision would not fade. Chops glanced at the soldiers in the control booth. He saw devils. He knew they had nothing to do with Smukke, so he tried to cool his hatred. Lightly, he punched Dragor in the shoulder. "Not yet, but I'm sure we'll hear something soon. Come on. This is a gig."

He opened his case regretfully, foreseeing the sounds that would come from his cornet when he put it to his lips. Mournful sounds. Hateful sounds. Lonely sounds. He knew that the authorities would

BLOW HAPPY, BLOW SAD

not notice if he played poorly, but he did not play for them. He blew for himself, for his friends, and for strangers throughout the country who shared his love for jazz. In recent months, he had also played for Peder Olsen and for an Allied victory in Europe.

With the agent from the SOE, he had developed a method of encoding messages into his cornet solos, which were broadcast by Danish National Radio and intercepted by Britain's Radio Security Service. A cornet's written range spans two and one-half octaves, from low F-sharp to the second C above middle C. Most accomplished players could reach a third octave, but Chops numbered among the few who could squeeze out a fourth, reaching the highest note of the piccolo. He found devising the code extremely simple. Starting with the D above middle C, he assigned each letter of the alphabet a note on the chromatic scale. A became D. B became E-flat. C became E, etc. Ten digits fell in line after the alphabet, making the number nine the third C-sharp above middle C. The first note Chops played after a melodic break became a part of the message, unless he followed it immediately with drag-triplet figure. Choosing songs into which the coded notes fit unobtrusively posed the greatest difficulty.

Chops eyed the large wall clock. eight fifty-one. He would have to rush to encode the message. D20 IN C NOT NORSK HYDRO. Nineteen characters. Why was it so long?

A tall, lean, well-dressed man walked through the studio door. His blue eyes sparkled through his round spectacles, and he smiled thinly. "Hello, Chops," he said, extending his arm. The two men clasped hands firmly. "It's good to see you tonight. Really good. I'm looking forward to your show."

Chops grinned cautiously, wishing the man had remained in his office so he would have time to work out the code. "Pleasure's mine, Herr Wolf."

Herr Wolf worked for the Nazis. Were he not allied with Denmark's oppressors, Chops may have trusted him because he seemed pleasant and genuinely interested in all forms of music. After the Danish capitulation, the German High Command gained control over all forms of communication. They named Herr Wolf ersatz station manager. He could have completely rearranged the station's programming to suit his personal tastes, but he refrained.

Other than his rather strict monitoring of the news broadcasts, Herr Wolf let the station run as it had in previous years. He arrived at his office promptly at nine and left just after five, except on Thursdays. Week after week he spent his Thursday evenings in the booth watching the Backbeats perform in the tiny studio. Not once had he touched the controls or tried to exert any pressure on the musicians with whom he occasionally joked before the show. Once, Chops had met him on a downtown street, but he had been in a hurry and could not accept an invitation for coffee in a nearby cafe. Perhaps it was for the best.

Herr Wolf scratched his chin. "You know how much I enjoy your work."

"Yeah."

"And you know that not all of my countrymen share my musical taste."

Chops nodded. On another day he might have commented on Wolf's understatement, but he was not quite sure where this conversation was headed.

Wolf continued. "To be perfectly open with you, my superiors have been breathing down my neck for the past several weeks about the Thursday

Night Exchange.' There are those at Headquarters who would rather have the Danes listen to insidious British lies than your 'art music.' They say it is too ethnic and too dissonant."

Chops rolled his eyes.

"As long as the BBC broadcasts in Danish, I think we can keep this show. As long as you don't play too radically."

"I'll see what I can do."

"Good," the station manager replied. Then his voice dropped to an earnest whisper. "I understand that our boys interrupted your concert last night."

Chops' lungs froze and his pulse jumped. For a moment, he felt like he had last night, petrified and helpless. How had Herr Wolf learned of Svenya's arrest at Smukke? He simply worked for the Communications Directorate. The Gestapo reported directly to Berlin, to Hitler himself. Their actions were secret. Chops' throat became dry, but he commanded his eyes to remain level, trying to maintain poise. His panic intensified. He could think of nothing to say.

Herr Wolf placed his hand on Chops' shoulder. "I'm sorry. Our boys get carried away sometimes. The war makes people rash, perhaps even crazy. I don't think you have anything to worry about."

"That's good to hear," Chops heard himself say. He wanted to ask the station manager what he knew of Svenya. He must have connections in the Gestapo. Could he push for her release?

"It's almost nine," the taller man said. "You had better start preparing for the show. Oh, I almost forgot." He pointed to the ON THE AIR sign. "The bulb burned out. Don't let it bother you. Just play a good show."

"All right." Chops pressed the valves on his cornet rapidly and looked at the clock. In less than two minutes he would be broadcasting and he had not even decided what to play, nor had he encoded the message. He closed his eyes and took a deep breath. D2O IN C NOT NORSK HYDRO. He repeated the message to himself several times, feeling it absurd that he did not understand what he was encoding. The first letter of the message was D. That would be a low F, he told himself. Good. An F fit well into most blues arrangements.

Chops looked at the other members of the Backbeats milling about the tiny room, nervously glancing at the clock. One minute to go. "Boys," he rasped. "Let's start this set with, oh, how about 'Dead Man Blues' and then move into..." TWO. The next message in the code required a two, a very high F-sharp, out of the written range. What in Jesus' name took an F-sharp?

Dragor clicked his fingers. "I just heard a new cut from the Bennie Goodman Orchestra, which gave me some ideas. Can we play 'Stompin' at the Savoy?'"

Before Chops could answer, one of the technicians began tapping on the window and pointing towards the clock. Show time.

"OK," Chops muttered. "Let's swing."

Through the window, he could see Herr Wolf holding up his hand. Chops blew some warm breath through his horn and craned his neck in a circle, preparing himself for the hour-long show. Grena took his seat behind the small, upright piano and Sticks adjusted the tilt on his snare drum. Herr Wolf brought his fingers down one at a time. When he clenched his fist, the Backbeats began playing "Dead Man Blues."

The melodic line swayed back and forth, and the men behind the glass nodded their approval. When Chops' solo approached, he stepped forward

and blew a low F which started softly and then
swelled to fill the studio. The vibrato tone lingered
and then faded into oblivion. An image of Svenya
laughing in the garden had seeped into Chops'
head and transfixed him. After a moment, Dragor
nudged him and the cornet began to sing again.
The solo sounded like it had been born from mis-
ery and reared in desolation. Dissonant notes accused the world of harsh cruelty, and the simple
resolutions reminisced a strong sense of purpose.
Chops shirt became translucent with moisture as
he played.

The Backbeats finished their first song and
moved straight into "Stompin' at the Savoy." Chops
stepped to the side and let Dragor near the microphone. Of course a clarinetist would want to play
a Bennie Goodman tune. Chops listened to the
solo, enjoying the fast trills and smooth glissandos
while unconsciously adding simple cornet accents.
Whenever someone else took the first solo, Chops
played the second chorus and on into the next
verse. Peder Olsen's code needed an F-sharp. How
would that ever fit into a B-flat arrangement?
Chops cursed himself for letting Dragor pick the
song. As the clarinet solo ended, he muttered a
brief prayer.

Chops raised his cornet towards the ceiling and
attacked the F-sharp with vigor. It sounded like a
screech owl's death throes. The technician in the
booth ripped his headphones away from his ears.
He pointed at Herr Wolf and started talking, but
the station manager shook his head. His expression did not change, and he did not stop snapping
his fingers to the music. Yet somehow, his mo-
tions seemed strained. The sweat on Chops' forehead turned icy. After Herr Wolf's lecture on dis-
sonance, this note must have sounded like a slap

in the face. Or worse. Unless he somehow made the mistake sound like it belonged, the Germans might realize he was encoding secrets. He hit the dissonant tone a second time and then half-valved down the chromatic scale until he hit the F-sharp in the lower octave. Then he loosened his lips just enough to let the tone sink to an F-natural, the dominant note in the B-Flat key signature. The owl's cry became a swan song.

Chops could see the technicians talking to each other behind the soundproof glass. What were they saying? For a few measures, Chops played the richest, sweetest melody he could conjure. He felt like he was playing a nursery rhyme, so he doubled the tempo and headed to the upper register.

He finished the first half of his solo and went into the bridge. D2O IN C NOT NORSK HYDRO. Did he need a zero for D-Twenty or the letter O? He had no way of knowing, and Olsen had not told him. Quick. Choose.

Chops stopped playing.

The Backbeats continued and after three beats Chops blasted away with a high E. Since it came after a break, the British would know it was part of the code. A Zero. Chops chose it because it sounded exactly as bad as the F-sharp. A high, blaring note one half-step off pitch. This time flat. The overweight technician leapt out of his seat and thrust his hands towards the ceiling, waving his headphones in the air. Wolf, too, stood up. He pointed his finger at the sound man, who reluctantly returned to his seat. Wolf shook his head slowly and then moved towards the window.

As he had done just a moment before, Chops sped down the chromatic scale to the off note in the lower octave. This time he pried it a half-step upwards until, once again, he rested on the dominant F. By repeating the pattern—dissonant high, dissonant low, resolve to dominant—he tried to appear as if he were repeating a musical experiment instead of covering a mistake. But could Herr Wolf appreciate that?

Grena had begun soloing on the piano, and his fresh, sparkling trills lightened the air in the studio. Chops looked at the unlit ON THE AIR sign. Herr Wolf remained standing behind the technician, and Chops concentrated on the code. The next four coded notes would be low B-flat, high E-flat, low E, high E-flat. A song in D-Flat would work for all four as long as the E, a sharp nine, fit with the melody.

"What's next?" Christoph asked.

Chops had played through the final chorus of "Stompin' at the Savoy" without realizing it. He looked at his bass player. "Herr Wolf likes Hoagie Carmichael, doesn't he? Let's pay 'Georgia on My Mind' but play it in D-Flat."

"What do you mean? It's in C."

"Don't argue. One, two, three, four."

When Herr Wolf heard the first chord of the familiar tune he cocked his head. He continued speaking to the technicians, but Chops could see a smile form on his lips. For a moment, Wolf seemed to sway to the tune; then he returned to his seat and leaned his head against the wall. Unless Wolf had been born with perfect pitch, he wouldn't recognize the slight key change.

The next four coded notes fell into place and before the end of the song, Chops had planned a set that would allow him to send the rest of the message. As the minutes ticked by, the air in the room became so hot and sticky that breathing was difficult. Ellington. Basie. Waller. The Backbeats moved gracefully through their repertoire, and the hour passed quickly.

When the clock hit ten, Herr Wolf burst into the studio. He pointed at Chops. "I thought I told you not to play so racy tonight."

Chops turned sharply. "Smile when you say that, Whitey." Wolf hesitated and the musician grinned to show he was joking. "How did you like it?"

Wolf returned the smile. "Ausgezeichnet," he clamored. "You outshined even Bix Biederbecker."

"Don't get carried away, Herr Wolf," Chops laughed.

"No, I'm serious. I wish I could hear you play more than once a week." Chops felt uncomfortable in the pause that followed. "But we must be satisfied with what we get. Were I still in Germany, I would not even be able to hear your music this often."

"Do I hear a hint of dissatisfaction in your voice?"

Wolf chuckled. "We are not too different, you and I. Both doing what we must to get along, far away from home for reasons not entirely under our control. Neither completely satisfied with the land of our birth. Have you ever been to Germany, Chops?"

"I played a show in Hamburg a few years back with the Guy Sherman Band."

"You must come back. After the war. Germany is a beautiful country, though she has her limitations. I come from a small town near Freiburg, in the Black Forest. I miss the hills and the fir trees and the people I know so well. But one learns so much being abroad. You see, ever since the Holy Roman Empire my countrymen have followed rules sent from above, from the Kaiser, from feudal princes, from noble families, and now from the Fuhrer. I grew up in a series of ordered systems:

oneway streets, permission slips, and appointment books. Your playing intrigues me because you have no rules. It is complete and utter freedom. That is why your jazz music inspires me so."

"I'm glad you liked it," Chops said, packing his horn. He glanced at the ever-dim ON THE AIR sign and then at the German officer. "I'll see you next week."

Chapter Five

"The night's almost over and you haven't even said hello." Louisa's voice came from behind Chops as he sat cooling down after finishing his show at Smukke. He enjoyed playing a late set on Thursdays after the radio show because it helped him relax after encoding Olsen's message at the station. A live audience provided a different sort of tension, and it helped balance the night.

Only sixty people had been on Smukke's dance floor when the Backbeats left the stage after their final encore. Now, in his dressing room, he listened to the din of the crowd dissipate as the patrons left two by two, silently returning to the world under martial law.

"Hello." Chops pushed back from the dressing table and shifted his chair. "I thought everyone had gone home."

Louisa leaned against the doorframe, holding a drink in one hand and a cigarette in the other. Her black, curly hair hung loosely over her shoulders, cheeks red with excitement, dancing, and liquor. The blue satin material, moist with perspiration, clung to her middle-aged figure and betrayed her round waist in a way a looser garment would not have. The slit in her skirt revealed most of one stockinged leg, a habit left over from her younger, lighter days. "You must be exhausted after playing such a great show."

"Not really." He smiled. Whenever he played at Smukke, this particular sensation arose, this feeling of purpose and belonging. With the cornet at his lips he felt at home. So what if New Orleans lay thousands of miles away, if he hadn't seen his family or his childhood friends in eight years? Jazz filled the crevices in his existence. If only he could play forever.

She walked up behind the chair and placed her hands on his neck. She began kneading his shoulders, pressing her thumbs and fingers into his flesh. "Your muscles are knotted like mooring lines. I can't..."

"You've been on the docks too long."

"What?" Her hands kept moving in concentric circles across his shirt.

"Knotted like mooring lines? Pretty soon you'll start swearing like a longshoreman, too."

"Fuck you."

"I told you," he replied, and they both laughed. He swigged from the tumbler of gin and water that he drank to replenish the fluids that flowed from his pores when he performed on stage.

"Thanks for playing my favorite song tonight."

"Stardust?"

"Yes," she cooed. "How did you know it was my favorite?"

"It's all the girls' favorite. I play it because it makes me look sensitive. It works like a charm."

She ended her massage and slapped him lightly on the cheek. "You horny son of a bitch. Has anyone ever fallen for it?"

"A gentleman wouldn't answer that question."

"So what do you have to say?"

"Pretty sassy," he said, clapping quietly. Then his voice softened. "Did you really like it?"

She cleared a spot on the dressing table by brushing aside an ashtray and a bell mute. Clumsily, she hoisted herself up and crossed her legs. "You played better than I've heard in a long time. From the very first note. There was so much enthusiasm. Energy. Emotion. I'm not sure what it was, but I felt it. Everyone did. And it went so quickly. I couldn't believe it when you said 'good night.' I thought it was only about eleven-thirty."

"I'd have played until the sun came up, but Tapio cut us off at one o'clock. Last night made him pretty nervous. He's never been raided before."

"Have you?"

"Once or twice," he answered flippantly. As a young horn player he had performed mainly in dance parlors and brothels in the Storyville section of New Orleans. Because of prohibition and prostitution, everyone expected nightly police visitations. Occupational hazards.

Louisa finished her cigarette. "Did it piss you off that so few Smukkies came tonight? On a regular Thursday night this place is jammed. How many did you have tonight? Sixty? Seventy? Most people in this city are scared of their own shadow."

"Lighten up, doll. Lots of folks don't like to be scared. They stayed home, listened to us on the radio, and played with themselves. Fine with me. But the cats who did show were lightning charged. Dancing on tables. Drinking like fish. And I don't think anyone left alone." He paused. "Come to think of it, I saw some guy digging on you tonight. What happened?"

"I came here to dance. That's all."

"Then why are you all decked out?"

She straightened her leg and pointed the toes

of her black stiletto heels, scratches partly covered with magic marker, towards the wall. Luxuriously, she stroked the fishnet stockings, and her dangling earrings tinkled as she shook her head.

"It's fun to dress up. This is the only chance I get these days. Do you know what would happen if I went to town like this? The first soldier I ran into would steal my jewelry and say it was for the Reich. The second one would flash a twenty and offer to dork me. They really think it would be an honor for a Danish woman to ball one of them, just because they are German. Aryans. The master race. God, they piss me off." She flipped two cigarettes out of a pack and stuck them in her mouth. She struck a match before Chops could open his Zippo, so he sat back and watched her light up.

He took the one she offered him. "Did some sausage-head proposition you this afternoon?"

"Two of them did. One man. Ugh. Man's not even the right word. He..."

Chops patted her on the knee. "You can't let them get to you, babe."

"I can't help it."

"Of course you can. Just remember, you're just as good as any one of them. Better than most. It's just like dealing with a bully in grade school. Humor them when you must. Ignore them when you can."

"And?"

"And beat the tar out of them when you're sure you can get away with it. It couldn't be any simpler."

Though she laughed, a wounded tear rolled down her cheek, mascara trailing. "How do you know all of this?"

"Practice," he said solemnly, handing her his handkerchief. "About thirty years of practice."

Racial prejudice had permeated every aspect of his life in New Orleans, and he had accepted it the way one accepts being born blind. Not until coming to Europe had he realized that he might be treated as an equal. And not until the invasion had the Danes realized they might not be.

"I'm sorry," she said, wiping her face. "I know you're tired. And I didn't come here to complain. I've got some news."

"Business?"

"Yeah." She ground out her cigarette in the ashtray. "Bad news about Svenya."

Suddenly the air in the tiny room thickened. Chops' lungs strained. His pulse accelerated and his cheeks began to burn. An uneasy feeling fluttered in his stomach, but he forced his visage to remain calm. Knowing she could not see his hands, he grasped the chair's arm rests and squeezed them until his knuckles cramped. Early in life he had been taught to hide his feelings, to smile and say "yes sir" regardless of how severe his torment. He had learned to contain his emotions and release them later, when it was safe. Not now.

"I'll tell you what," he said softly. "We shouldn't talk around here. Why don't you go out front and get your things? I'll be there in a flash and I'll walk you home. You can fill me in on the way."

She shook her head. "You don't have to. It's late and my place is out of the way. Come by Kakadu tomorrow. This can wait."

Chops pointed to the door with his thumb. "I'll meet you out front in two shakes. Go."

"All right. All right." She plopped to the floor and fluffed her skirt. "I need to pee, so give me a minute." She walked out the door, her heels clicking on the stone floor.

As soon as the door closed, Chops squeezed

his eyelids together and sighed. "Don't let them get to you, babe," he had said. Why couldn't he heed his own advice? Whatever Louisa had to say, he could take it. Perhaps, no, almost certainly, Svenya was dead. Executed the German way. Quickly. Efficiently. But they had not gotten him. Not yet. He could not let her loss destroy him. This was war. And in war people kill. People die.

If Louisa told him that Svenya had been hanged, he had two things to do. First, he would give her the best send-off Copenhagen had ever seen. He and his friends would drink hard liquor and play sweet jazz straight through the night. Maybe even in the streets, New Orleans style. If King Christian could parade on horseback every day, why couldn't he?

"Stop it," he hissed to himself. If Svenya were dead, there would be no wake, no Dixieland funeral. He would never even see the body.

He stood and yanked his coat off the hook on the door. As he fastened the dull, brass buttons, he noticed how the hound's-tooth material sagged on his chest. It had felt snug when he bought it three years ago—back when clothes from London, Paris, and Berlin filled the storefront windows—but now it was too large. Grabbing his cornet case, he flipped off the light and walked down the corridor.

When he entered the barroom, Tapio and Louisa were talking next to the front door. As usual, sweeping hand gestures accompanied the bartender's speech. Chops interrupted him with a pat on the shoulder.

"Oh, there you are. Louisa and I thought you'd slipped out the back."

Chops shook his head. "There's no back door."

Tapio laughed, then stepped backward and held out his hands. "Get out of here so I can clean this place up."

Louisa punched the bartender lightly on the shoulder. "I'm glad you opened Smukke tonight, Tap. A lot of people were awful grateful."

"Everybody had fun and nothing got broken. It's what I call a good night."

She smiled. "Drop by Kakadu sometime."

"I will." Tapio looked at Chops, put his thumb to his lips, and waved three fingers up and down, imitating a horn. "Great show."

"The folks who came were dancing up a storm."

"Your bass was really hot tonight."

"Christoph?" Chops said, wanting only to leave Smukke and hear what Louisa had to say. Still, he did not want to seem rude. "Man, Christoph was so sharp he almost cut himself. You know, he doesn't understand a thing about music. He just feels it. Sometimes it works and sometimes it doesn't. But Tapio, don't tell him you liked his stuff. He'll try to figure out what he did right and he'll sound like a buffoon for a month."

Tapio and Louisa nodded.

"How much hooch did we go through tonight?" Chops asked.

"More than you'd expect for such a small crowd. We emptied one half-barrel of beer and four liters of gin."

Chops whistled in approval. "I guess that means I should start a new batch sometime soon. We'd be in a world of hurt if we went dry." Music alone did not make Smukke popular. People wanted to drink as well as dance, but Denmark exported most of its alcohol to Germany. Only the lowest grade beer and liquor remained for internal consumption, and the state taxed it heavily. However, bootlegging kept the bar at Smukke in operation.

"Do you have time to brew?" Tapio asked earnestly.

Chops did not want to think about beer, but he nodded to be polite. "Sure thing. The next time you go to the market, see if you can get two sacks of two row malt. Unless my yeast has died, we can cook something up early next week."

"If your yeast dies, we're in trouble."

"Nah," Chops said, thinking about Peder Olsen and his supply connection to London. "We can get just about anything we need. We'll talk about it tomorrow. It's late."

Louisa tugged at Chops' jacket. "Yeah, quit talking shop. I need to get some sleep. My shift starts damned early tomorrow."

Tapio bowed grandiosely. "Goodnight," he said, grabbing his mop.

Chops and Louisa slipped out of the door and they heard the lock click behind them. Slick moss grew on the steps that led to the surface. Silently, Chops climbed just high enough to survey the street. As his eyes adjusted to the darkness, silhouettes of trash cans and fire hydrants materialized against their velvety black background. Nothing moved. He motioned with his head and ascended to the sidewalk. Louisa followed and they walked towards the train station.

One block away from Smukke, Chops ducked into an alley where he had chained his bicycle to a lamppost. He strapped his cornet to the rear rack and, after a brief struggle with the rusty lock, he rolled his bike back to the main road.

Louisa chuckled and pointed towards the bicycle. "I thought this was a strange place for you to go to take a leak."

"I always lock it here. I can't ditch it at Smukke or someone might get suspicious. This seems safe enough. Hidden pretty well. And we can talk here."

She looked over her shoulder and then shook

her head. "Maybe we shouldn't talk in the open like this."

The street looked completely vacant, but there was no way to be sure. Every day, Peder Olsen stressed the need for utter secrecy, so perhaps it was a good idea to wait until they got to Louisa's apartment. What was the worn-out slogan? Loose lips cost ships.

"Want to ride on the handlebars?"

"Have you lost your fucking mind?"

"Just checking," Chops said. With one hand on the seat and one on the grip, he pushed his bike through the dark street. The bike's headlamp burned dimly and cast an eerie glow on the cobblestones. Other than that, the city was dark.

"Did you ever think it would go this far?" Louisa asked.

"What?"

"Smukke. I mean, at first it was just a Saturday night party, and suddenly it's an illegal dance club with a password and everything."

"It didn't start as a party. The band needed some space to practice since the Nazis came down on jazz. A fellow could get in trouble playing a record in his apartment, and we certainly couldn't jam at Dragor's house anymore. Tapio knew someone whose restaurant had just gone under, and he said it would be all right for us to practice there on the sly. Only at night, of course."

Talking about Smukke kept Chops from thinking about Svenya, and he launched into a story, although Louisa probably knew it anyway. "One day, Sticks asked if some of his friends could come and watch us. Tapio and Grena did too. Seems like everyone was looking for something to do after dark. I said it was OK as long as they showed the proper respect."

"Proper respect?"

"What I meant was that they wouldn't disturb us, talk to us while we were playing. It's hard enough to get the guys to practice under the best circumstances, and if they were flirting and showing off the whole time, it would have been a disaster. But that's not what I said. It was OK by me as long as they dressed up and didn't cause any trouble."

"Why'd you say people had to dress up?"

"No reason. It just sounded good at the time."

"You know that's why it caught on. I like to dance as much as the next gal, but there's something about dressing up that really makes night special. Especially when the government is asking everyone to wear gray flannel all the time. That first night we weren't going into an unfurnished basement to listen to your band practice. We were going out on the town. I shortened the skirt on some old mourning gown with a high collar and black lace sleeves. It wasn't just the girls, either. When Tapio met us at the door in a white dinner jacket, he was smiling like a fox. I'll bet you don't remember what you wore."

"Checkered cut-away and the ruffled tux shirt from the Guy Sherman Band."

"Damned if you didn't. How many people were there that first night?"

"A dozen or so. Everybody begged us to do it again the next week, and that night we had at least fifty people on the dance floor. Things were really kicking. Someone brought a couple of jugs of black market liquor, and we all got a little drunk, including the band. That's when we knew that something was going right."

"Tapio and I sat down the next day to talk about it. Having a dozen friends over to dance one night is one thing, but we were moving in another direction. He wanted to make it a members-only dance club, and he didn't care about licensing or any of that crap. Keep it a secret, he said. And he came up with the password and the name."

"Why Smukke?"

"You haven't heard this story?"

"No."

"Thyra Smukke was an old friend of Tapio's. A long time ago, Tapio swore he'd name his first kid after her, and that club is the closest thing to a child he's ever had."

Louisa paused and pointed towards the corner building, almost identical to Chops' apartment house. "Come on up."

"Where can I lock my bike?"

Louisa yawned without covering her mouth with her hand. "If you feel like lugging the son of a bitch up these steps, you can lock it in the entryway."

With an exaggerated groan, he bent down and hoisted the bicycle into the air. The cornet strapped to the back made it especially heavy. He followed her up the steps and waited for her as she fumbled with her keys. After two tries she found the right one and opened the creaking door, holding it for him as he crossed the threshold. He placed the bicycle in a shadowy corner under the fire extinguisher.

"Light's burned out," she said, flipping the switch up and down. "Hold onto the rail so you don't slip."

"I'm following you, babe," he said, unstrapping his cornet from the rear rack. As he took to the steps, he banged the case on the wall. "Damn."

"You could just leave it on your bike instead of banging it around everywhere you go."

"I'd feel naked without it," he chuckled. "I always have." When he was thirteen, he took his horn into the bathtub with him, and the soapy water ruined the felts. His father had to loan him a nickel to have them replaced. Years later, the cornet won him a music scholarship at Washington College in Baton Rouge, which took him out of New Orleans and afforded him a formal education. It earned him some money and a little fame.

"Musicians are a peculiar bunch," Louisa sighed. "So have you ever seen Thyra?"

"Who?"

"The girl who Smukke's named after."

"Nah. She was way before my time. I'm surprised Tapio never told you about her."

Louisa shrugged as she slid a key into her apartment door. "It must be a guy thing." She pushed it open and stepped into the dark room. For a moment she fumbled through a drawer, and then she struck a match. The warm, golden light cast deep shadows across her face as she lit the three-tier candelabra. "The place is a wreck, so don't look at anything."

Chops rolled his eyes back in his head. "If you want to see a wreck, come to my place."

"For you, it's different. You're a musician. If you're a slob, it's eccentric. I'm a barmaid. It doesn't work that way for me."

"No one said life was fair." He tossed some old newspapers from the couch to the floor and sat down, wishing she would simply tell him what she heard about Svenya. But not wanting to appear too anxious, he kept himself from asking. When something hard poked into his leg, he reached down and removed a half-eaten apple and tossed it into the air. "Dinner?"

"Fresh fruit's hard to come by," she answered self-righteously.

"True." He bit into the apple.

"And let's just say things aren't getting any better." Louisa sat down on the arm of the sofa and leaned against the wall. "Every day the Germans are squeezing us tighter and tighter, and people are starting to get angry." She bent over, pulled off her shoes and tossed them in the corner. "You listen to the BBC. 'Don't let the Germans make us bomb you.' They say it every week, and people are beginning to listen. Not only that, people are beginning to act. Almost every week there is a new, illegal flyer on the streets. The last one I saw described how to make a poisonous gas bomb out of kitchen bleach and a pickle jar."

"I don't see a lot of Germans shaking in their boots in fear of pickle jars."

"You'd be surprised. I've heard they're taking it very seriously. They've even brought in extra Gestapo to crush the resistance before it can get moving. If they even suspect someone might be involved, the Gestapo will pick them up, not an official arrest and nothing in the press. They're trying to scare the piss out of everyone. I've heard of three so far, the priest at St. Albans, a banker downtown, and Svenya."

"But why Svenya?"

"Someone pointed the finger at her. It's a witch hunt, and they don't mind burning innocent people at the stake." She put her hand on his shoulder and squeezed gently. "I'm sorry. I really am."

Chops tried to make sense of everything, but he was exhausted and he couldn't think clearly. Tomorrow he would speak to Peder Olsen, who understood the dynamics of wartime politics better than he. Unfortunately, Olsen wanted only to win a war. Chops wanted to save a life.

"Do you want to stay here tonight?" Louisa

asked. "Your apartment is not exactly around the corner, and the Germans want everyone in by midnight. You know, the streets aren't as safe as they used to be."

Chops inhaled deeply, ignoring the joke that the waterfront had never been safe. At first he thought she was simply acting overly protective by offering him a safe place to sleep, but then he wondered if she wanted more. The bathtub gin had made her a little tight. Somewhere in her expression Chops saw the word "lonely." Maybe not. He saw that word everywhere.

After struggling out of the overstuffed sofa he held out his arms and hugged Louisa firmly. "I think I'd best be getting home. And you look like you need some sleep."

"What's that supposed to mean?" Her voice turned sharp, and she looked away for a moment.

"Nothing," he said. "You just look tired, that's all."

She smiled thinly and twisted a fingerfull of her dark curls. "I guess you're right. And work starts early."

Chops grabbed his cornet. "I'll come by Kakadu tomorrow. Will you bake some strawberry turnovers?"

"We haven't seen strawberries in months. Cheese tarts. That's all I can offer."

"They'll do." He moved to the door. "And Louisa?"

"Yeah?"

"Thanks for coming tonight."

"Sure."

The door closed behind him, and he squeezed his eyelids shut. Then he forced them wide open and adjusted to the dark. He stumbled down the stairs quickly, his feet plodding heavily on the bare wood. The cornet case knocked clumsily against the walls, and the sound traveled easily through the building, but Chops did not care if he woke every tenant. He wanted only to ride his bicycle home and to crawl into bed. Tomorrow he could begin looking for the traitor who denounced Svenya.

He reached the bottom landing and paused to catch his breath. Into the shadowy corner he moved, pulling his bicycle from against the wall and strapping his horn on the back. He pushed open the door, rolled his bicycle over the stoop, and carefully lifted the frame as he descended the stone steps. He set it on the moist street and swung his left leg over the seat.

He felt the impact before he saw the body.

As he straddled the bicycle, someone dove into his chest and knocked him off balance. Chops' head hit the cobblestone walk with a crack and a blue-green blur exploded in his eyes. As his vision cleared, he felt his assailant on top of him, and he reached out to grab his hair, his clothing, anything. His fingers dug into pliable flesh and clamped down tight.

"My ear," the man howled in Danish and then hammered a fist into Chops' chest. He tried to roll away from the blow, but the bicycle frame pinned him to the ground. The second punch came at his face, but he raised his left arm and blocked it. Grabbing his assailant's sleeve, he pushed the man away, wrenching his ear towards the ground.

As the weight lifted from his chest, he kicked his bicycle away and scrambled to his feet. He raised his fists and lowered his chin like a boxer. "Leave me be or I'll kill you, Mister," he spat. Chops was at least thirty pounds heavier than his attacker and he had seen plenty of scraps.

The man did not move. Blood spilled from his

torn ear down his face, and he raised his arm slowly. His hand moved imperceptibly and a thin blade shot upwards, glimmering in the night.

Chops looked behind him, hoping to find a glass bottle or a stick. He did not want to fight a switchblade bare-handed. Instead, he saw a second man, swinging a rusted pipe at him. Without thinking, Chops dove to the ground and heard the metal whoosh above his head. The breath exploded out of his lungs as the man kicked him in the ribs.

"Let's go." The two men exchanged quick words, and Chops turned to see one run towards the railroad tracks. The other grabbed his bicycle and rode off into the darkness.

Chops climbed to his feet and ran after the thief but quickly realized he could not catch up with a bicycle. He could never run fast. Shaking his head, he dusted off his pants and muttered, "At least I'm not bleeding. What's a used bike cost, anyway? Two hundred crown? I'll bet I can buy that one back tomorrow morning on pier seven."

Then he remembered. He had strapped his cornet to the rear rack. His horn. His livelihood. It could never be replaced.

Chapter Six

In the distance, the gray sky dipped down at the horizon to meet the dark sea, and Chops could not tell where one ended and the other began. He felt like he stood in the center of some monochrome sphere. The dawn seemed only slightly brighter than the night because the dark clouds cloaked the rising sun. Cold winds heightened the waves, encouraging them to crash against the sea wall, and salty foam and water pellets sprayed upwards and fell on the stone promenade. A bright-yellow oilskin kept him dry and added a dash of color to the dull landscape, but it did nothing to soothe the pain that had been throbbing in his side since he was kicked last night.

The roar of the sea overwhelmed the din of the waking city. Chops listened intently, concentrating on the wind and waves and the scavenging gulls that hovered above the surf. One half-mile to his north the ships and barges chugged in and out of the harbor, unhampered by the threatening sky. The same distance to the south stood the four marble residences known as Amalienborg castle, but here he found peace. He loved this spot on the Langelinie Promenade, and he came here often to clear his head. Before the war came to Denmark, tourists flocked here to see the memorial to Hans Christian Anderson, who lived and wrote in Copenhagen. The city didn't welcome visitors in 1942.

Chops marveled at the sleek, bronze mermaid, sitting forever on a barnacled stone, her tail curled up beneath her. Gracefully, her arms hung beside her breasts, hands clasped in her lap as she gazed towards the promenade. She remained complacent as the thunderous waves assaulted her back. Chops did not envy her composure. He knew her suffering. Half maiden, half fish, she perched in the no-man's land between earth and sea, in view of both worlds yet a part of neither.

"You'd think the Nazis would melt her down and use the metal for their tanks, wouldn't you, Chops?"

Chops' neck tensed and his shoulders jerked involuntarily as Peder Olsen's words intruded on his thoughts. He could feel blood rush to his cheeks, and he clenched his fists, but he remained silent.

"You shouldn't let me sneak up on you like that, old boy. It's bad form."

He heard Olsen close his pocket-watch, but continued staring out to sea. Why defend himself by saying that he was not a trained agent for special operations or for anybody else? He knew about style, not about form, and he considered "good morning" to be the proper greeting on the promenade this early in the day. Casting one last glance at the bronze mermaid, he coaxed his body to relax. "I was hoping I'd see you today," he said. Perhaps the spy could help him recover his cornet or, if necessary, order one from London.

He turned away from the sea and, at first glance, Olsen seemed to have aged. Against the brown material of his work clothes, the agent's skin took on a squalid pallor, and dark stubble covered his chin and neck. His hat bore the insignia PARK INSPECTOR, and he carried a small, three-pronged rake, its points rusted to the color of dried blood.

Olsen pointed his finger at Chops. "You stand out like a sore thumb in your rain gear, Chops. There's no need to draw attention to yourself."

"I can wear whatever the hell I want to. Is that clear, Olsen?" As soon as he had spoken, Chops wished he had kept his mouth shut. He had rummaged through his closet for ten minutes to find the rain suit, although he could have just as easily worn his blue overcoat. He had sought it out to give him some exterior inspiration, some sense of well-being, and he did not want to hear Olsen's criticism. However, he felt tired, and he wanted to avoid an argument. "Forget it," Chops said, shuffling his feet.

"You should watch your temper," Peder Olsen said.

Chops said nothing, because he knew Olsen was right.

"Do you know what this is?" Olsen asked, holding out a twisted and charred piece of metal.

Chops took it and flipped it in the air several times. "Lay it on me."

"It's the handle from a freight-train door."

"From the looks, the train's had a pretty rough time."

Olsen nodded. "A bloody rough time indeed. The damage would not have been nearly so severe had the train not been carrying several tons of ammunition to Norway. Bullets that the Nazis were planning on using against the Norwegians. Of course, there were other supplies aboard the train besides explosives: food and uniforms—some of them with German soldiers inside. Replacements.

But it was the ammunition that made the difference when the RAF Mosquitoes dropped their bombs on the tracks."

"When did this happen?" Chops asked. No one in the city ever received accurate war news. German propaganda filled the Danish newspapers, and the BBC was almost as bad when it came to detailed information, so most people only trusted the underground presses.

"Last night outside of Alborg, on the North Coast of Jutland."

"I know where Alborg is. You were there?"

Olsen nodded and took the metal handle out of Chops' hand. He stared at it for a moment. "The shock was total, the timing perfect. I don't care what you say about the Germans, their trains run on time. When it passed—one-thirteen on the nose—I tossed a lighted flare on top of one of the coal cars. The Mosquito bomber sighted on the flame and ten seconds later, detonation."

Chops looked at Olsen in tarnished admiration. "Congratulations."

"It's my duty," he replied. "If you want to pat someone on the back, pat yourself."

"What?"

Peder Olsen heaved the piece of metal far out into the sea, and it disappeared into a wave. "You sent the British the coordinates. The message that you encoded and played on the last Thursday Night Exchange told the British where to bomb. And when. Without your work, the Mosquito Bomber would never have come. Your country owes you a great debt."

"I don't need America's gratitude."

Olsen tilted his head and looked at Chops in a peculiar way, dark eyes penetrating from deep sockets, lips drawn in slightly. He appeared more confused than angered, as if Chops' last sentence completely confounded him. Or he had just gained new insight into the musician's psyche. "You've got another job to do," Olsen finally said.

"You know I won't be on the air until Thursday and before then..." Chops tried a second time to tell Olsen that his cornet had been stolen and he needed a replacement, but the agent interrupted him.

"This doesn't have anything to do with your 'Thursday Night Exchange.' The boys in special operations think we should step up our activities. They want the network active."

"What network?" Chops knew many people who fought against the Germans in their own way, people like Kaj, who buttered toilet seats or threw rocks at supply trucks, but he had never heard of a well-organized group.

"Surprised? You don't know this town as well as you think you do. Sure, you still see a lot of what goes on in the port and on the waterfront, but I know Copenhagen. You even lost contact with the university after the dean sacked you. Finding people to join the resistance was easy. The trick has been organizing them, keeping them quiet, and not letting them know anything about the rest of the network. Everything is in place, and the Germans know nothing about it."

"In place for what? Are you and a bunch of untrained hot-heads planning to drive the Nazi war machine out of Denmark?" Chops peppered his voice with sarcasm, ruffled about Olsen's comment about his being fired and losing touch with the university. He seethed at the mention of the dean, that Nazi bureaucrat who knew nothing about running a school. "This is the stupidest idea I've ever heard, Olsen. Denmark surrendered two and a half hours after the Germans invaded. You can't fight a war."

"Of course we can. You're part of this now, and you're right—we can't fight a war, at least not on their terms. Not until the British and Americans invade the mainland. Then they will find an underground army waiting for them to help smash the German army. In the meantime, we're going to lash out with well-timed sabotage. Trains, bridges, munitions factories. I've already drawn up a list of targets."

"Don't bring me into this. I play cornet and make a few deals on the side. Do you know what will happen if you start blowing up factories around the country? The Germans will come down on us like rain." He immediately thought of Smukke. Only his naiveté allowed him to believe that the Germans did not know about the club, and it would certainly be shut down in a Nazi clampdown. The Danes had weathered the war better than any occupied country, but that would not last if they started shooting unwary Germans.

"That's the point," Olsen said. "The Germans will have to retaliate, and they will do it by arresting civic leaders, cutting rations, and imposing a curfew. They'll put up roadblocks on every corner and shut down all the restaurants and bars. They'll probably even close Tivoli."

Chops threw up his hands in disgust. "It sounds like your sabotage plan is really going to help this country. You'll be a real hero for getting the Germans to close Tivoli."

"You've missed the point again, Chops. My countrymen won't stand for it. They will complain and strike and riot."

"And then the Germans will drive in tanks and toss more people in the clink. It sounds good, Olsen. Really good. What will they do when they run out of prison cells? Just start shooting people on the street?"

Olsen clapped his hands cynically. "Imagine that. It would be just like a war." He put his hand over his mouth in mock surprise. "A war! Oh, that's right. We're in the middle of a war." His voice returned to its serious tone. "We can't let the Germans forget that. We need to cause as much trouble as possible and draw their attention away from the other fronts. If high command has their eye on Denmark, they may not give Rommel the support he needs in North Africa until it's too late. Then they'll either have to surrender to Montgomery, or pull troops away from the eastern front. They can afford neither.

"A year ago Hitler thought he'd capture Russia with a Blitzkrieg," Olsen continued. "He didn't even supply his troops with winter uniforms. Fortunately, the Germans couldn't fight both Mother Russia and Mother Nature at the same time, and the war has drawn on longer than anyone expected. The German pantry is bare, and their supply lines are too long. The Sixth Army has been gnawing away at the defenses in Stalingrad all fall, and it's not over yet. If Stalin can hold out until winter, then the war may be over. The Third Reich is like a rubber band stretched to its limits. If it holds, the Germans win. If it pops, they lose. The outcome of this war will be decided this winter, and we must do everything we can to sway the balance."

An abnormally large wave rolled against the sea wall with a thunderous crash, and a thin, white sheet of foamy water arced into the air, splattering the two men. If salt water had gotten into his eyes, Olsen did not appear to notice. He just stood there with his jaw protruding and his thin lips tight. A granite statue. Chops shuddered, wiped his face, and said, "Do you really think a bit of sabotage in Denmark could cause the Reich to come tumbling down?"

"Along with a lot of other things and a bit of good luck, yes." He paused. "Let's walk. We've stood here conspicuously long." He motioned with his head and moved away towards the low wall which separated the park from the seaside promenade. Chops took a step and a bolt of pain shot through his ribs where the thief had kicked him as he lay on the ground the previous night. The burning subsided into a dull ache. Perhaps he should have been thankful that the hoodlums had not broken any of his bones or injured his lips so he couldn't play, but he did not see it that way. He needed Olsen's help to find those punks but the agent only wanted to talk about his harebrained schemes for getting himself killed. He and Kaj would get along well, Chops thought.

Several paces behind, he watched Olsen leap over the three foot wall and into the park, his movements exceedingly gracefully for a man his size. Chops remembered his once saying he had been a speed skater. He would not have played a team sport. Certainly the British considered themselves lucky to have recruited him for such a dangerous assignment. He never explained why he had volunteered to work for the SOE, but he never said much outside of giving orders. A one-track mind. Victory.

Chops used his hands to help himself over the wall, and the motion hurt him so much he could not breathe. He rubbed his side, hoping he had not cracked a rib or two. His feet sank in the moist grass as he walked towards Olsen, who stood under a beech tree, its leaves afire with the colors of autumn.

"OK, Olsen. Let's assume that your plan will work. You have the men, but where are you going to get the firepower? You can't expect to smuggle guns and explosives through the waterfront like you do with your forged documents. The port authority would notice anything bulky."

Olsen nodded. "That is where you come in. The RAF is going to drop some supplies tonight, and I need you to help me collect them."

"Me?"

"Yes."

"Tonight?"

Olsen nodded.

"What about your extensive network? Ask someone else to help you."

The Dane shook his head. "It's imperative that I keep this operation compartmentalized. I don't want my resistance fighters to know where they're getting their weapons just like I don't want you to know where I'm going to store them. That way, if anyone gets caught, they won't be able to tell the Germans anything."

"When they are being tortured in the Gestapo cellars? No thanks, Ace. When you suckered me into working for you, we agreed I would just blow your magic notes on the cornet and pass some papers. I don't want to be stomping around in the middle of the night, looking for airplanes and waiting for the Germans to cook my goose. That's not my style."

The agent reached into his pocket and pulled out an overstuffed money clip. "I will make it worth your while," he said softly, flipping the bills with his thumb.

"This isn't a question of money. I'm not going to act like a foot soldier, marching in straight lines and sleeping in foxholes. It's just not my style."

Olsen shook his head. "Get off your high horse, Chops. A job's a job, and this one's important. You get it done and you get paid. You turn coat and I'll watch you die. As far as I know, those are the only rules. Since London wants us to expand this part of the operation, I think we need to enlist someone to help collect the supplies. The parachute canisters are heavy, and you're too weak to lift them alone."

"I'm not going."

"If you want help getting Svenya Hjorth free from prison, you'll help me pick up this parachute drop."

The remark hit Chops like a falling tree. Momentarily jarred, he realized that the agent might be his only chance of saving his lover, and that put him in a weak bargaining position. He wanted to hear what Olsen had learned about Svenya, but before he could ask, the spy had begun rattling off orders. "We'll meet tomorrow morning at three fifteen behind the train station kiosk. You, me, and a third man."

"Do I know him?"

"No."

"I've got a better idea," Chops said. The idea of working with a stranger hoisted a red flag somewhere in his mind because he knew how easily he could be identified, and he could not afford to take unnecessary risks. If he must work with someone else, it should be with a friend. Someone like Kaj. He smiled. "I know the man we should take."

"I've already picked someone."

"Well, change your decision. I know a cat stronger than a horse who has almost declared war on Germany by himself. I trust him like a son. Not only that, but he certainly won't endanger the rest of your precious organization"

"Hmm. What's his name?" Olsen asked.

"John Doe."

Olsen chuckled. "You learn fast, Chops. How do I know he won't turn me in?"

"You don't."

"Mutual distrust," Olsen said. "It's the only way to run an organization. Tell your friend to wear dark clothes and not to bring any identification. Make sure you tell him about the risks."

"He should get paid."

Olsen nodded and pulled one hundred Krone from his money clip.

"He should get paid more than that. You don't want him to feel like you owe him, do you?"

"I'll give him one hundred now and fifty more if he does a good job. If he won't work for that, I'll find someone who will."

"He'll do it."

"Good." Suddenly, Olsen bent down on his knees and began pulling up weeds with his hand rake and whistling loudly. "Don't look at me," he hissed, and Chops stepped back a few paces. He leaned against the trunk of the beech tree as two women rode past on bicycles without paying any attention to the black man in the yellow raincoat or the supposed grounds keeper.

The couple reminded Chops of last night's fight and his lost cornet. "Do you have any control over what the RAF puts into your supply basket?"

"The Royal Air Force just delivers the canisters. The special operations executive packs them."

"Can you say what goes in them?"

"Why?"

Chops sighed. "I need a new cornet."

"Forget it. Special operations sends us military equipment to be used for military objectives. They don't provide us with candy and toys. I would love a fresh pair of boots or a sharp razor, but I'm not going to get them from the British, and there is no way you are going to get a shiny new cornet just because you've grown tired of your old one." Olsen spat on the ground and wiped his mouth with the back of his hand.

Chops had expected the agent's reluctance but not his scorn. He hated the way this man looked down on him and how he always assumed the worst. "I'm not tired of my horn. A couple of hoods took it off me last night along with my bicycle, and they've probably already sold them. Unless I get my paws on a new ax, I won't be able to send your precious messages to England, and, if you haven't checked the storefront windows lately, brass instruments can be a little tough to find." In its early stages, the war had boosted Denmark's economy to relative prosperity which lingered even after the Germans invaded. However, when Germany declared war on the USSR in June of 1941, it began sucking Denmark dry, and by now the empty shelves in the stores had become the main staple of conversation.

"Borrow one."

"From whom? I can't get anything from the university, and all my students quit except one, and his horn is too beat up to play." When Kaj first began taking lessons from him, he told him to buy a new one as soon as he could afford it. Tattooists don't earn much.

"It won't hurt you to play on an old instrument."

"You don't understand. The felts are shot. The second and third valves are bent so they don't always close. The spit valve is held shut with a rubber band, and the top tube is cracked. It's more adhesive tape than brass." Chops could see that the man had stopped listening. Once again he dug at invisible weeds with his rake, and Chops felt like walking away. Then he remembered. "The slide is loose. Do you know what that means, Olsen?" He practically yelled the name, and the agent looked at him.

"No. And furthermore, I don't-"

"It means the cornet won't stay in tune. The slide moves out and the note goes flat. That's how a trombone works, but this isn't a 'bone. It's a cornet. I play an A, and the boys in London hear an A-flat or even a G. The RAF might drop their supplies on the wrong day. Or in the wrong place."

Olsen stood up and nodded his head slowly. His hand caressed the prongs of the rake, and he closed his eyes. "I see," he said.

He took two steps forward and returned. Chops held his breath while the man paced. He could almost see Olsen's brain at work, analyzing the situation and his possible alternatives. Chops saw only one. He needed a new cornet.

Olsen leaned against the tree. "What would the station manager say if he saw you with a new instrument?"

"Wolf? I don't know. He knows his way around music so he might notice. Then again, he might not, but if I came in to the studio with a busted up old piece of junk you can bet your sweet one that he'd say something."

Olsen nodded. "But you could explain that. Someone stole your cornet, and you borrowed the best you could find. Now, how would you explain a brand new cornet that could not possibly have been bought in Copenhagen. How would you explain that?"

"Wolf doesn't ask questions like that. He thinks I'm doing him a favor by playing at the same time as the BBC broadcast. He would not want to mess that up."

Olsen wet his lips. "Do you trust him?"

Chops thought for a moment. He had known the station manager for over a year, and he had never annoyed Chops or insulted him. He spoke fluent Danish and did not seem the least bit militant or elitist, quite the opposite actually, with his quick sense of humor and his far-reaching knowledge of jazz. Chops watched Olsen's cold face and chose his words carefully, thinking the right answer might win him the horn. "I don't exactly distrust Herr Wolf."

Olsen spun violently and smashed his hand rake into the trunk of the beech tree. The spikes stuck deep into the wood, and the handle vibrated as he let go of it and turned to Chops.

"That is what he would do to you, Chops. I know his type, and you can't trust him. Not even for a second. If he thought you had some contact with England, he would arrest you, me, and anyone else he could find. He would not think twice. This man is nice to you because he thinks he needs you, just like you said."

Without warning, the menacing expression on Olsen's face melted. He clicked his fingers. "Of course. Wolf does need you. Tell him to get you a new cornet because your old one was stolen. If anyone can find one, it is he. Do you have his number?"

"Yes."

"Ring him this morning. I'm certain he'll have you one before next Thursday. It's your best bet."

Chops nodded. The plan made sense, although he felt awkward about asking such a favor from Herr Wolf. Especially if Olsen's opinion of him was justified. "I'll ring him today."

"Now."

"All right. I'll walk straight to the box on the

Nyhavn and see what he says. But before I go, what about Svenya?"

"Your girl. Yes. It doesn't look good, I'm afraid. She was one of several unofficial arrests, and more are expected to follow. Nothing on her specifically, but the Gestapo is trying to get confessions. They will succeed, you know. They always do. Have you been through her apartment?"

Olsen's matter-of-fact report stunned him. And what did they do to get confessions? He forced himself not to think about it.

"Have you been through her apartment?" Olsen repeated in an irritated voice.

"No?" Chops stammered. "Why?"

"Because if the Gestapo search her home, they will probably find some traces of you. A photograph. Some clothes. One of your black, curly hairs on the pillowcase. As soon as she was arrested you should have cleaned out her apartment."

"You should have mentioned it Thursday when you came by."

"That would have been too early. Careless and unprofessional."

"Will they be watching?"

"Not likely. But they might search the place themselves, and we can't afford to have loose ends. They don't have any reason to suspect you of anything, and I want to keep it that way. And you know how up tight the Germans are about racial purity. I don't want anyone to throw you out of the country because you were sleeping with a white girl."

"They wouldn't do that. I'm a Danish citizen."

Olsen nodded. "So was Svenya."

Chapter Seven

"Danish National Radio. Carl Elling here."

"Station manager Wolf, please."

"Who's calling?"

"Chops."

"Chops who?"

"Just Chops. He'll want to speak with me."

"Hold the line."

Chops heard a click, and a numbing hum replaced the voice on the telephone. He placed his foot on the wooden seat and leaned against the wall of the public telephone booth on the Nyhavn, gazing blankly through the fogged glass panes and listening to the cold drizzle fall on the small, metal roof above him. Twenty minutes earlier when he left Peder Olsen on the Langelinie Promenade, the idea of asking Wolf to recover his cornet made great sense, but now he was not sure. The thought of asking a favor from an officer of the Reich, even one as innocuous as Herr Wolf, put a sour taste in his mouth.

"Hello, Chops. Herr Wolf here. How are you today?"

Chops chuckled, hoping not to sound too desperate or too flip at the beginning of a deal. "About like the weather."

"They say the clouds will move out to sea in the afternoon. What can I do for you?"

"We've got a problem."

"Oh?"

"Yeah. I was out late last night and two thugs jumped me. They stole my cornet."

"Are you hurt?" the voice quickly replied.

"Nah," Chops sighed. "I got kicked in the ribs, but I scratched one of 'em pretty good so I figure we're about even. Except they got my horn."

"I was afraid something like this might happen."

"Happens all the time."

"I don't think that was a random mugging, Chops. A lot of people want the 'Thursday Night Exchange' off the air. I don't mean my superiors who consider your music a cultural insult. I'm talking about overly patriotic Danes who despise anyone collaborating with the occupation force. Surely you know that some consider you a traitor."

"Me?"

"Don't kid yourself. You get on the air because you conflict with the BBC propaganda broadcasts. Don't you know people who'd call that treason? But don't worry. I'll see about getting you some protection."

Chops pictured two uniformed German bodyguards trying not to stand out as they followed him into Smukke on a Saturday night. He smiled at the absurdity. "I think you're overreacting, Herr Wolf. A couple of hoods ripped off my bike, and my horn happened to be on the back. Will you ask some of your friends in the police to track down the thieves and get my cornet back?" Chops smiled, listening to how smoothly the request rolled off his tongue. A simple favor. Nothing more.

"Well, I'll see what I can do. My title of station manager ought to be good for something. And if they can't find it, maybe we could pick up a new instrument. Tell me, Chops, what size mouthpiece do you use?"

"12B," he replied automatically, and then he began to wonder how Wolf always knew the right questions. Who besides a musician would care about mouthpiece sizes?

"12B," Wolf repeated. Then, after a pause he said, "Chops, do you have any plans for Sunday?"

"I'm not sure," he replied cautiously. He knew he would stay up all Saturday night to help Olsen retrieve the parachute drop and, at thirty-two years old, he no longer had the energy to function two nights without sleep. Besides, the Backbeats played at Smukke on Sunday night.

Wolf continued and cut off Chops' thoughts. "I'm having some guests to dinner, an old friend of mine named Klaus Schadling and his wife Anna. He played ragtime on the piano some years ago, actually, and he's just in the city for a few days. When you phoned it occurred to me that he might enjoy meeting you. Won't you come?"

"Well...I've...the band sorta has an engagement Sunday night." The mistake struck him as soon as he made the excuse. Why couldn't he have just replied that he had plans?

"But you have lost your horn."

"I'm the band leader. I'm not sure if-"

"The Backbeats will be fine, and I can't imagine you'd enjoy sitting by yourself offstage."

The words "by yourself" struck Chops oddly. Did he mean "without Svenya?" Or did he simply understand that Chops would feel left out? He felt himself groping for the escape hatch, but words began spilling out of his mouth before he found it. "I don't know, Herr Wolf. It might look odd."

"Come now, Chops. This is not an official function. Everyone will have a good time."

"Well...hmm. I just... What time?" Chops closed his eyes and shook his head.

"Excellent. Around seven. Do you know my house? It has a large, stone front porch so you can't miss it. Kongelundsvej, number 23."

Chops repeated the address to himself. "I'll be there at seven."

"Good. Bring a little something for my guests, a few cigars or some cognac. I'm tied up here at the station, and I really don't have time to go into town."

Chops saw the lie immediately. Wolf had all the time he needed, but one could only find certain luxuries on the waterfront, where connections meant more than cash. German laws strictly forbade trading on the black market, and Wolf clearly could not risk getting caught. Although Chops could find these things easily, he did not want to set himself up as Herr Wolf's underworld contact. "I don't know any place that has good booze anymore." It was a weak attempt, and Chops knew it.

"I'll tell you what," Herr Wolf replied in a tone that had suddenly taken an edge. "I'll ask my friends about the cornet and you ask your friends about some cognac. You can do that, can't you?"

"I'll try."

"Of course you will," Wolf replied. "Until Sunday, then."

"Good-bye." Chops laid the telephone receiver in its cradle. He reached into his pocket, felt the spare key to Svenya's apartment, and walked out into the rain.

Chapter Eight

The key turned easily. The lock opened with a subtle click. As his heart continued to pound inside his chest, Chops turned the knob and stepped quickly into Svenya's unlit apartment, closing the door hurriedly behind him. Less than a minute had elapsed since he slipped through the building's rear entrance, and he had met no one on the stairs or in the hall. If the Gestapo questioned the neighbors, they would reply that no one had snooped around Miss Hjorth's flat. Or had someone in an upstairs window seen him approach? Yes, he had passed several pedestrians on the back streets, but none of them seemed to recognize him and took no note, no more than they would have when passing a one-legged man or a child carrying a goose. His black skin made him an anomaly in Copenhagen, and that would never change.

Chops inhaled deeply and closed his eyes. Did he have the right to enter Svenya's apartment, to rummage through her possessions, and to take the things that might lead the Gestapo to him, the photographs, the books? He felt half like a thief and half like he had seven years ago after his wife, Marie, had been run down on the street. That night he sought out her clothing and her letters and burned every last bit. Despite his efforts, his memory of Marie lasted long after the wind blew her ashes out to sea. But Svenya wasn't dead, just held in custody at Gestapo headquarters. Oh God, let that be true.

The smells of her apartment—wood oil, spices, and perfume—overwhelmed him, and he leaned his back against the door to muster his strength. Then, letting his reflexes guide him, he stepped across the hooked rug to the corner table and switched on the lamp. He let his eyes wander across the small sitting room. Besides the potted plants with sagging, brownish leaves, her home seemed tidy and put away, the way Svenya always left it.

How different he was from her. In his one-room studio in the Christianshavn, clothing lay strewn about and his phonographs, sheet music, and coffee cups adorned the disarray, but here everything had its proper place. Olsen had ordered him to clean up the apartment, to remove anything he had left behind. Where would he start? Everything here reminded Chops of her.

As Chops scanned the room, he gradually allowed himself to believe what his eyes told him: the Germans had not searched the apartment. No matter how skilled the inspectors, they would have left some trace of their presence, misplaced the cushions on the sofa, tilted a picture frame, shelved a book that always remained on the coffee table. No, the police had not been here.

He pulled his wet, gray overcoat off his back and hung it on the coatrack, placing the hat on top. After Olsen's upbraiding about walking around Copenhagen in a yellow oilskin and looking like a clown, he had returned his favorite slicker to his apartment in exchange for the nonchalant garment that reminded him of funerals. As beads of water dripped off his coat and puddled on the floor, he reached into his breast pocket and removed a pair of white cotton gloves. His thick fingers stretched the material, and the fabric constricted his movement, but he could not risk leaving fingerprints. They must have been all over the apartment, but he had not visited in almost a week, and he did not know how long fingerprints lasted. Olsen knew. Chops should have asked that demanding forensic encyclopedia who knew everything about spying and spy-catching, but Chops' pride would not have allowed him to listen to Olsen's condescending answer. He kept the gloves on, hoping that fingerprints dried out after a few days.

Last week. It seemed like a former life. Svenya had invited him to dinner and prepared a smoked herring and a butterscotch pie, which his bottle of wine had complemented. The extravagant black market prices meant nothing to him when it came to Svenya. He could always make more money.

His eyes wandered over the room and came to rest on the wire music stand next to the sofa. Under it lay Svenya's viola, its black leather case untouched in three days. A neglected child. Every day she practiced at least two hours and sometimes as many as five or six, even on holidays. The calluses on her fingertips were as hard as stones, and her left grip was so strong she could crack a walnut without flinching. When they had gone to the beach, Chops had asked her to leave her viola at home, and she had exploded, yelling at him for not caring about her art. He was incensed. Hell, he wasn't taking his cornet.

"Of course you can slack off for a couple of days," she had screamed. "You're the only authentic, black, New Orleans cornet player in the whole country. Everyone at Smukke would worship you if you missed every note. They're tone deaf."

"Tone deaf?"

"And blind drunk most of the time. What would happen to me if I so much as rushed a trill? I'd be out on my ear, that's what."

Chops had conceded because she was right. The Royal Orchestra did not allow for mistakes, not from an outsider and especially not from a woman.

He pried his eyes away from the viola and looked at the bookcase. He believed one could tell a lot about a person by the way they ordered their books. Accountants alphabetized by title. Hand workers aligned their books by size, academics by subject, and hipsters just threw them on the shelves in any order they felt like. He had never deciphered Svenya's system, but he knew she had one. Perhaps she put books on the shelves in the order she read or received them, or according to things she associated with the books. The Bible might fall under W for Father Wirkkala, her priest at the cathedral. He could never figure it out.

He remembered that he had lent Svenya a copy of Mark Twain's collected short stories because she rarely read, and when she did, she chose authors like Balzac and Tolstoy whose works he had only read to fulfill a world literature requirement at Washington College his sophomore year. She had loved Mark Twain's sense of humor and biting commentaries. Chops glanced at the couch covered with a dainty flowered material and remembered sitting there with her, discussing *The Mysterious Stranger* and pondering original sin. He had said sin was his favorite part of life, and she had exploded. Her voice took on a frantic air when she was mad, and her face turned red. Chops loved to tease her. When had they discussed Mark Twain? Last March. Yes,

BLOW HAPPY, BLOW SAD   101

spring had come late last year, and after she calmed down they huddled under a down quilt, the book between them, holding hands and sipping tea. When the cups were empty, he wrapped his arms around her and they kissed. They had made love that night. On that flowered sofa.

He shook his head, reached out, and took the broken-spined book off the shelf. Scanning the other titles on the shelf, he wondered what else he should remove. What about the *HISTORY OF DIXIELAND*? Svenya had bought these herself, but it was Chops who had sparked her curiosity. Would they point the Gestapo toward him? He doubted that the police would even search the apartment, but he took those books too and cast them with the collection of Mark Twain's stories into the leather satchel he had brought from his apartment.

On the other side of the room, Svenya's small writing table stood under the window. She would spend hours there writing in her diary, studying orchestral scores, and sometimes composing them herself. Not everything she did was so serious. She also wrote silly poems and short stories that she would read to the children when she volunteered at the orphanage. "Kriegskindschen" she called them. She and Chops had never mentioned their future together, except casually saying that they would like to travel. She had even mentioned going to America.

Chops had often wondered how his family would react to Svenya. Of course they would welcome her into their homes and respect her politely, but could they accept her? None of Chops forebears had been slaves. His grandfather had been a *gens de couleur*, a free gentleman of color, part of a class that existed only in New Orleans. The French colonialists who founded the city believed in slavery, but they did not consider it a permanent condition. A man could buy his freedom, and the children of slaves were not indentured. The *gens de couleur* were cultured, respected, and many had mixed blood, but when the Union army marched into the city after the War Between the States, they freed the slaves and forced all blacks to the same caste.

Chops remembered his father recounting the time some men assaulted him because he entered an all-white bistro and interrupted their game of cards. He was trying to find his boss and tell him that his son had been thrown from a horse. They were drunk, and they broke his nose and knocked out three teeth, but he could not press charges. Everyone Chops knew had similar stories. When the government outlawed prostitution, white policemen raided the bars and brothels of the Storyville neighborhood, forcing Chops and his fellow band members to run or hide behind the stage. He knew the fear and the hatred and had learned to contain it, but could his family?

Chops pulled out the chair at the writing table and sat down. Leaning forward, he tilted the window shade so he could peer down to the street. Empty. The neighbors would stay in their downtown offices until five o'clock, so he had plenty of time to finish the job, but he wanted to leave the apartment as soon as possible. He clicked on the ceramic lamp and opened the center desk drawer that contained only pencils and paper clips and a few sheets of paper and a ruler she used to draw musical staffs when she could not find any lined paper. He then opened the drawers on the right hand side, casting only cursory glances inside. When he reached the third, he found a stack of letters, and he raised his eyebrow. He did not know that Svenya kept her old correspondence, but why shouldn't she? He did.

He took the stack out of the desk and flipped through them, looking mainly at the return addresses and the date stamp. He had written several of them himself. When they first began seeing each other, Chops always jumbled his words when he tried to say important things, and if he ever completed a sentence, he sounded crass or sarcastic, or else he came across like a high-schooler with his first crush. He mostly preferred to express himself with his music, but sometimes when he wanted to be specific, he wrote to her. Late at night, after playing at Smukke or after gossiping with Tapio, he would sit in his apartment and compose little missives to her, but they never left his desk. He only mailed his letters when he traveled with the Backbeats.

He opened one envelope and read what he had written.

Dearest Svenya,

> *I just want to jot down a few lines and say how much I enjoyed Sunday's picnic. You pack a mean basket. I can't remember you ever looking prettier than in that yellow dress, but I hope you didn't burn in the sun. Sitting in this hotel room, I miss you though I'll be back in the city in a few days. Every day since we met, I've thought about you, and I sure feel like one fat cat. I'll miss you when you're in Naestved with the chamber orchestra, but I'm sure it will be a great show (although it's straight stuff and not swingin').*
> *The show is going well. We're jamming in a joint called THE STORK. As far as I can tell,*

*the local law doesn't care, so everything's
pretty legit. Being legal is a strange feeling.
Maybe we can have dinner on the pier when I
get back.*

Chops

He shook his head, remembering how he worried about closing the letter. He did not feel like he
could say "Love, Chops." "Fondly" sounded too femi-
nine and "Sincerely" rang standoffish. Finally he
settled for "Chops", although after he wrote it he
had wished he had put "Yours, Chops." She never
mentioned the closing, she just said how much she
enjoyed his letter. "Especially the misspelled words,"
she had said, kissing him until he burned.

Taking a rubber band out of the top drawer,
he bundled the letters and let them fall into his
satchel.

He turned off the light and looked over his left
shoulder toward the bedroom door. His stomach
turned queasy, for in that room he and Svenya
had first shared the secrets of their love. After that
night they spent most of their time together in his
apartment, because it lay closer to Smukke and
to the Conservatory, but he liked this cozy room
with barely enough space for a twin bed, a dresser,
and a small night stand. White wallpaper with little flowered bouquets covered the walls and the
ceiling, giving him the impression of being inside
a gift box.

He fought to keep the memories from overwhelming him. He commanded his body to rise
and to push the chair under the desk, to walk with
even steps across her floor and to turn the knob.
What was he doing? His eyes adjusted slowly to
the darkness, but he could not risk opening the

shutters. A musty smell lingered. Svenya always closed the windows for protection when she left the house, although she slept with them slightly open to provide a draft and never understood why Chops complained about the night's coolness.

Had he left a spare suit in the closet? Chops could not remember, but when he opened the door, he saw only Svenya's clothes. She did not have many and certainly none that she did not wear. Yes, there was the yellow sun dress that she had worn to the picnic. Reflexively he reached out and fingered the material, feeling the texture of the thin cloth. Its lifelessness gnawed at him when he thought of the wind blowing and pressing the cloth against Svenya's suppleness. He remembered her in the pink dress during high mass. And the black one, required when she played in the orchestra. Only the blue dress she had worn when the Gestapo had pulled her out of Smukke was missing. The thought stung like an icy needle. What was she wearing now? A gray prison smock? A shroud?

He closed the closet door slowly, and over the soft whine of the hinges he heard footsteps and voices on the outside staircase. Chops distinguished a woman's and a man's voice but not their words. Had the landlady heard him in the apartment and phoned the police? Chops ducked into the bathroom next to the closet and closed the door as quietly as he could, but the lock required a key that had long since disappeared. He considered hiding behind the shower curtain but realized he must climb through the small window if he wanted to escape. Then he would be stranded on the second floor ledge with no way down except to jump. He decided to risk it and unfastened the latch, but before he could raise the pane the voices had trailed into nothingness.

Chops sighed and wiped the sweat from his forehead. One of the other tenants must have stopped on that landing to find their keys. Nothing more.

He opened the mirrored medicine cabinet and fingered through the bottles and tubes. Despite the small amount of time he spent in Svenya's apartment, he kept a jar of lotion there that he used to keep his skin from coarsening. Svenya had never seen a man use skin cream before, but then Chops was the only colored man she knew. He also grabbed his spare toothbrush and slipped it into his pocket. Then, as an afterthought, he took a close look at Svenya's hairbrush, remembering Olsen's words about finding a curly black hair in the apartment, but there was only blond hair in the bristles. Svenya's.

He left the bathroom door open and as he stepped toward the bed, he saw a small piece of paper on the floor behind the headboard, just out of a broom's reach. So even Svenya missed a spot or two. He reached down and snatched the torn scrap and started to crumple it and toss it into the wastebasket but stopped when he saw it was printed in German. Although Chops could not read the language, he knew it was a ticket stub, and he could make out the title: Der Ring der Nieblungen. He knew that theaters all over Europe performed Wagner because Hitler praised his work. He could not decipher the name of the Opera House, but enough of the date remained. August 11. Wasn't Svenya on a concert tour in mid-August? Of course. And she must have seen the opera with the rest of the chamber orchestra. But hadn't the group stayed in Denmark? He stuffed the ticket stub into his pants pocket and made a mental note to check the date with one of the professors in the music department.

From across the room the three photographs on the night stand glared at him. He walked to them, sat on the side of the bed, and examined them one by one, although he had seen them many times. The largest one showed Svenya and her younger brother Bjorn as children, playing in Christmas snow in front of their parents' house. Chops could see the resemblance in their faces, but he had never met her brother. The second photograph was an old promotional shot of him holding his cornet, taken years ago when he played with the Guy Sherman Band in America. He was only twenty-three when the picture was made, and he looked young and arrogant, but Svenya liked it and he had given it to her, although it was the last one he had. He suddenly thought it strange, because a duplicate of the picture sat on his mother's dressing table in New Orleans.

Instead of sitting inside a frame, the third photograph was pasted onto a folded sheet of cardboard that stood up like a lean-to. The image was grainy and flat, but the joy in Chops' and Svenya's faces was genuine. Everyone smiled in the Tivoli gardens, with its rows of flowers, balloons, clowns, rides, and restaurants so that the local photographer had an easy job. How far away the war seemed when he spent time in Tivoli. Could he even escape his concern for Svenya there? Shaking his head, Chops picked up the two incriminating photographs and dropped them into his satchel.

He had wondered if his leather bag would hold everything that he needed to take from the apartment, and now he marveled at how little he had collected. A few books. Toiletries. Two photographs. Were those the only proof of their relationship?

He paused before opening the single drawer of the night stand where she kept her diary. For years she had kept a loose record of her life, sometimes writing every day for a month and sometimes not touching for a week. He had asked her if she had written about him, and she had laughed. "Of course, you silly goose. That's part of being in love, isn't it?" But she scowled when he asked if he could read from it.

For the first time since entering her apartment, Chops felt glad that he had come. The thought of some Nazi interrogator leafing through Svenya's diary made him wince, and although it would be tempting to read a few lines himself, he would resist. He would keep it safe for her return. He curled his finger under the drawer's handle and tugged. It did not come open. He pulled again, and this time he tilted the entire table toward him and the remaining photograph tumbled.

"Shit," Chops spat as he heard the glass pane of the frame crack on the floor. He steadied the table with his left hand, lowered himself, and jerked with all the strength he could muster. The wood, swollen from the humidity, came loose, and the drawer flew open. The orange spiral-bound notebook was right where he had expected it to be, and he dropped it into his satchel, closed the drawer, and left.

Chapter Nine

As Chops walked toward Berngardspladsen, the cobblestone square in front of Copenhagen's main train station, he cast a glance over his shoulder and studied the footprints that he and Kaj had tracked in the virgin snow. The black asphalt showed through in regular intervals from Smukke's basement door to where they now stood, and the dark clothing he wore to blend into the shadows betrayed him against the now-powdery landscape.

"Fresh snow brings good luck," Kaj said.

Chops ignored the remark and asked what time it was.

"Five after three."

"We're late."

"Hell, Chops, you're always late, but these things usually run on time, don't they?"

"What things?"

"Resistance things."

Chops reached out, grabbed the back of the boy's collar and yanked hard enough to make him slip but not enough to bring him down. That would have taken a lot. Kaj turned around slowly and hung his head, a shy pupil reprimanded for running at recess, his eyes lowered and his vast shoulders bent forward, hands clasped together at his belly.

"Look at me," Chops demanded.

Kaj's eyes rose slowly.

"Don't ever let me hear you say that again. Your mouth's gonna get us both killed. There is no resistance. Nothing organized. I won't tell you again, this is business, not politics. Free enterprise."

"The black market." Kaj sounded like he was repeating the catechism.

"Right," Chops replied, although he knew it was not. When he had asked Kaj to help in Olsen's plan, he was confident enough, but now he feared he had made a mistake. "Of course I'll help," Kaj had said, but what had Chops expected? He knew how much the boy looked up to him and would do anything he said. Back in New Orleans people had considered him cool and tried to emulate him, but always from a distance. He bore no responsibility if they wore sharp clothes that made them look like fools, or said they liked jazz because it was the craze that week. But Kaj was different, and if he got in trouble, Chops would be responsible.

"Since when has the black market had airplanes?" Kaj said spreading the snow with his feet. "I thought everything came through the port."

How would he answer such a simple question? It did not take a genius to figure out that the military played a part in tonight's activities, but if Kaj said something to the wrong person, he would be signing his own execution papers. It was all right if Kaj knew their orders came from the resistance, as long as he never mentioned it, or even dreamed it. "Things change," he said and resumed his walk.

The silence made Chops uncomfortable, and he knew it make Kaj uneasy as well. He worried that the boy thought he was angry at him when he was deeply concerned. Why had he asked Kaj to help? How would he react if something went wrong?

They approached the newspaper kiosk at the west side of the station, an angular black form against a gray landscape. In the morning, throngs of Danes would whisk past or stop and purchase a paper, but now the streets were empty. Chops leaned against the clapboard wall. Did they stand out against the building? In theory it did not matter, because the Germans only requested a voluntary curfew, but some policemen had arrested people on the street after twelve "under suspicion of seditious acts."

"This is where we meet," Chops said, looking around the lonely square.

"The others are even later than we are. When do you think they will show up?" Kaj asked.

"Soon," the musician replied, although he sensed Olsen nearby, hidden in the shadows and watching. Perhaps the agent from special operations had followed them from Smukke, evaluating Kaj, the unknown element.

"Do you know where we're going?"

"No."

"Any idea when we'll be back?"

"No."

"Know what we're picking up?"

"No. I don't know anything and neither do you." Chops regretted his harsh tone. "Keep it that way. Don't hear anything. Don't see anything. And most of all, don't say anything. We don't want anyone to get into trouble."

The eighteen-year-old shook his head and rubbed his hands together to fight the cold. Chops looked at his own gloves and felt vaguely guilty that he had not advised Kaj to bring a pair, but he could not think of everything. Only the basics. Like silence.

After a few minutes of silent pacing, Kaj asked,

"Know a girl named Meta?"

"What's she look like?"

"She's a swing crazy. Lots of make-up and a big smile. She was at Smukke tonight wearing her father's red cardigan sweaters that came down to her knees. You saw her, didn't you?"

"Yeah," Chops conceded. He had nothing to do tonight at Smukke except look at the women and watch the Backbeats play without him and hope they would not fall apart. They sounded fine. Grena could patch any hole with his eighty-eight keys, and Dragor blew some pretty sweet solos near the end. They did not falter, and that made Chops sad and proud. He danced to a few tunes but felt like a hoax with new partners and returned to a bar stool and ordered seltzer-water, fearing that booze would slow him down after his rendezvous with Olsen.

"I think she wants to bump."

Chops feigned a cough to keep from laughing at the boy's expression, remembering a time when sex was new, honest, and forbidden. Kaj seemed unaware of his magnetism, his boyish good looks, his lighthearted sense of adventure, and his shyness. "With you?" Chops asked.

"Yeah, with me."

"What makes you think so?" Chops asked.

"Well, she asked me to walk her home from Smukke tonight. She said her parents are out of town."

"What'd you say?"

"Just that I had promised help Tapio clean up shop. It was the only excuse I could come up with."

"Did you offer to visit her tomorrow night?"

"Wouldn't that have been a little forward?" Kaj asked.

Chops shook his head. "Maybe for other guys, but if she really digs you, it'd be OK."

"Maybe she just wanted someone to walk her home."

"And maybe she wanted to hoist your mainsail and blow it all the way to Iceland. Don't worry, kid." He paused and stomped his feet on the snow. "I hate this cold."

"Here," Kaj replied, pulling a pack of cigarettes from his coat pocket. "A smoke will warm you up." He put the cigarette in his mouth and raised his lighter upwards, flicking the flint with his thumb. As soon as the spark flew, a whirling form appeared out of the darkness. A hand clasped Kaj's wrist and spun him around, banging his arm against the kiosk wall and knocking the lighter to the ground.

Chops recognized the tactic before he saw Olsen's face, but as he moved to separate the two men, Kaj groaned, grabbed the SOE agent by the collar, and hoisted him into the air. As the boy turned to slam Olsen into the wall, something clicked and Chops saw a flash of metal. Kaj's eyes widened. His feet six inches off the ground, Olsen grinned and pressed a thin blade under Kaj's chin. The boy's lips turned white. Keeping his jaw upturned from the pressure of the blade, Kaj slowly lowered Olsen to the ground.

As the snow crunched under his feet, Olsen retracted his switchblade and turned to Chops. "He's fast but stupid. He might have had the edge if he'd thrown me to the ground, but instead he tried to pin me to the wall. Few people make that mistake twice. What's your name, boy?"

Kaj rubbed his neck and saw he was not bleeding. "I don't have one."

"Good. Don't ever light a cigarette at night again. You can see the flame two kilometers away." As he straightened out his dark brown jacket, he asked Chops, "Did you search the girl's apartment?"

"Yeah. No one has been through there, but I took out anything sensitive like you suggested."

"Find anything?"

"Nothing interesting," Chops immediately replied. All evening he had debated whether or not to tell Peder Olsen about the ticket stub he had found in Svenya's room and finally decided against it. The spy would automatically assume the worst, and Chops had not even confirmed the dates.

"All right. Let's go." Olsen turned on his heels and headed into the darkness. His all-white uniform made him look like a medic or a ghost. The two others followed behind, and they found their way across Central Station's freight yard, ducking between boxcars and fences until they reached a military ambulance parked under a broken street lamp disabled, Chops realized, by Olsen in order to keep the vehicle unobtrusively in the shadows.

The SOE agent unlocked the rear door and motioned for the others to climb inside. "Lie down on the stretchers and don't make any noise until we get out of town. Then make yourselves comfortable. It'll be a long trip."

Chops looked at the cramped interior and wished he could ride up front where he'd get more air and a better chance to escape if things went wrong. The back had only one door and almost no room to maneuver in case of trouble, no place to hide during a search. He climbed inside and offered a hand to pull Kaj up.

The boy hesitated and then pulled himself aboard. He looked at Olsen. "Shouldn't we have a gun in case someone stops us?"

Olsen slammed the door.

Chops listened as the SOE agent climbed into the cab and cranked the ignition. After warming up for a few moments, the ambulance lurched across the parking lot and turned onto the street. Although the windows were painted and he could not see out, Chops knew they were on the Vesterbrogade. The turn, moments later, put them on Hans Christian Andersen Boulevard, which ran between the Tivoli gardens and Town Hall and continued through the center of Copenhagen. Here Olsen switched on the sirens.

"Does he want to attract attention?" Kaj asked.

"He knows his stuff."

"I sure am glad he's on our side."

"Be still, boy. Act like you belong in the back of this meat wagon or you might wind up in one for real."

Chops adjusted the small pillow under his head and tried to relax in the stretcher. The sirens blocked out the sounds of the night, and the rhythm of the road became as familiar as a mother's heartbeat to an unborn child. His thoughts wandered. How dangerous was this mission? He counted the ways that things could go wrong. A roadblock. A flat tire. The RAF plane might go down. Parachutes tangled themselves in trees. A million unanticipated events could happen. Who would have guessed that Svenya's father's union work would cause her arrest and put Olsen's resistance work into jeopardy?

Svenya.

She might be in a cell the size of this ambulance, laying on a bed less comfortable than this stretcher, trying to warm herself from the draft blowing through the barred windows. Maybe there was no ventilation at all, a stuffy, stinking room; no place for a woman. Chops had spent several nights in the New Orleans jail for playing jazz in whorehouses or for disturbing the peace. Anyone who was hip had done time in the poky and bragged about it afterwards, but Chops had heard horrible rumors about the Gestapo's detention center. Svenya would receive much better treatment if the Germans transferred her into the Danish prison, but they could not do that without leveling official charges against her. Then she would find a lawyer who would prove her innocence in front of a Danish judge. The Nazis would not allow that.

"Hey Chops."

"What?"

"Is your pillow comfortable?"

"Hell no. I think it's stuffed with rags." He sat up on the stretcher, shoved his hand into the pillow case and pulled out the knotted cloth, thinking he could fold it neatly and make it more comfortable. He noticed that the pillow case contained two pieces. Could it be? After withdrawing a pack of cigarettes from his breast pocket and putting two in his mouth, he lit his Zippo. Since the windows were painted, no one, including Olsen, would see the flame.

"Are you crazy?"

"Look at this," Chops answered, holding the burning lighter in one hand and the cloth in the other. "Surgical scrubs. White ones. Just right to blend into the snow, to make us invisible." He lit both cigarettes and handed one to Kaj. "Let's see if they fit."

"Hey, I've got some too."

Slipping into the clothes in the dark proved cumbersome. The trouser legs seemed folded to prevent him from getting inside, and he broke one of the buttons off the jacket. "I sometimes take off my clothes in the dark, but it's usually light when I put them on. And I'm almost always standing up."

"Mine are a little tight."

"Are you surprised, Kaj?"

"Not really. Thanks for the cigarette."

Chops settled back into the stretcher and found no pillow less comfortable than a lumpy one. When the sirens quieted, Kaj tapped him on the shoulder and whispered, "I think we're almost there. We're driving slower like the roads aren't too good, and we've been driving for a long time."

"How long?"

"Almost an hour."

"We could be halfway across the country by now, maybe all the way to Nykobing," Chops said, remembering the time he and the Backbeats drove to play a show in that old shipping town.

"Wouldn't you think we'd stay on the coast?"

"Safer for the airplane, you mean?"

"Yeah."

"Maybe," Chops said. "But the German Navy patrol the coast. It might make more sense to go inland. If Ol...if our driver ever lets us out, we might be able to figure out where we are." Would it matter if Kaj learned Olsen's name? Perhaps, although, for the first time, Chops wondered if the agent's name really was Olsen. Before he came to a conclusion, the ambulance stopped, and he heard Olsen climb out of the cab and twist the rear-door handle.

He stood silhouetted in the moonlight, ghoulish in his white smock. "I see you found your snowsuits. Let's go."

Kaj and Chops exchanged glances before climbing out of the ambulance. The snow covered the ground two inches deep here, Chops noticed as his pants' legs moistened. He surveyed the night. They had driven up a one-lane county road and had not bothered to park the ambulance in a grove of trees. Perhaps Olsen feared it would get stuck.

Tall, slender birch trees lined the road, and their trunks gleamed silver in the moonlight. Chops listened hard but only heard the wind. They were not near the coast.

Olsen looked at his watch. "The plane will fly over in seventeen minutes, so we need to get moving. The drop point is a field almost a kilometer from here, due south-southwest. After a prearranged signal they will eject a supply canister. We collect the package, bury the parachutes in the snow, and head back to the ambulance."

"Why bury the chutes?" Kaj asked. "They're valuable."

"Not to us," Olsen replied in a low voice. "Someone might find them and report it to the police."

Chops raised his finger. "You missed. Parachutes are made of pure silk. I can sell the stuff on the waterfront. The police won't find them."

"We're burying the parachutes in the snow. End of discussion. The plane should arrive in sixteen minutes. Try to stay together, but if we split up, follow the North Star until you hit this road and from there you can find the ambulance."

"If we get split up," Chops asked, "are you going to wait for everyone before you drive away?"

"As long as it's safe. You'd do the same, I'm sure."

"Not when you have the only set of keys."

"Just make it back to the ambulance. Now follow me."

Olsen turned his back and headed into the woods at a crisp pace, never changing direction although he did not consult a compass. Chops allowed Kaj to walk ahead of him because he knew walking in the middle would be safer for the boy. The others were less than a few yards ahead of him, and he marveled at how difficult they were to see. The white uniforms made all the difference.

Once Chops accustomed himself to the cold, he enjoyed the crisp, clean air, but it did not quell his fear that he might never leave the forest. Kaj might not either. Olsen would.

Chops noticed the woods thinning and soon he stood with Olsen and Kaj on the edge of a clearing, slightly larger than an athletic field. The agent had selected his spot carefully. The empty field would be easy to locate from the air, and there were no trees to snare the parachutes as they fell. But once they left the woods, they had no place to hide.

"Where are we?" Kaj asked, and Chops cringed at the question in anticipation of Olsen's answer.

"This is the country estate of a wealthy anti-Nazi family," the agent responded. "The manor house is on a lake on the other side of the property, but they have closed it up for the winter. Only the caretaker and his family live here all year around. Good people."

The reply surprised Chops. Olsen rarely volunteered that sort of information, and he had never said anything as complementary as "good people." Why was he acting so civil to Kaj? Was he trying to recruit him, or did he simply like the boy? Outwardly, the two were remarkably similar. Large. Athletic. Danish. Certainly, if he had been older, Kaj would have chosen Olsen's path, fleeing to England and training with the Special Operations Executive so he could return to Denmark and organize resistance against the Germans. Would the British spy-masters have transformed Kaj into an unfeeling machine? Had they done that to Olsen?

"Here they come," Olsen said.

"How do you know?"

"Just listen, boy. You can hear the hum of the engine."

Chops concentrated but heard nothing besides the wind in the trees. An owl hooted. Then slowly another sound emerged, that of a bumblebee. It grew louder, but he saw nothing in the sky.

Olsen pulled an electric torch out of his coat, whispered "stay put," and ran into the center of the field. He held up the light and flashed it several times, repeating a simple pattern—two long flashes and a short one.

Then he saw the plane, a small black spot in the sky, return the signal.

"Look," Kaj said, pointing upward. "Two parachutes. I thought we were only supposed to get one."

"Must be a bonus," Chops said, watching the two cones float toward the ground. For a while they stayed close together, but then one caught a draft and drifted quickly to the left. "It's gonna hit the trees."

"I'll get it," Kaj said as he lumbered away.

"Don't," Chops called but the boy did not hear him. Seeing Olsen move toward the first parachute, now close to the ground, Chops started in his direction. A cloud of snow rose as the torpedo-shaped canister hit the ground, and before the flakes settled, Olsen had begun bundling the silk.

Only seconds later, the entire parachute lay buried, and Olsen started toward Chops, pulling the canister by the parachute cords like a sled. "Where's the boy?"

"They dropped an extra canister, but the wind caught it and it drifted away. The kid went after it."

"Damn," Olsen muttered, but he did not have time to say anything else.

A searchlight exploded.

On the far perimeter of the field a patrol of soldiers piled out of a light truck and began shouting for everyone to freeze. *"Stehenbleiben. Alle bleiben stehen."* The search light swept the field, and when the beam caught Chops, he thought he was dead.

Without a word, Olsen dropped to one knee, pulled a machine pistol from his belt, and opened fire. The weapon rattled off five short bursts, and the light went dead. Over shouts and screams Chops heard the searchlight shatter and knew Olsen had hit the bulb. Chops dropped to the ground. More shots. More screams.

"Chops."

He looked at Olsen.

"Take these. I'll meet you back at the ambulance." The agent tossed him two hand grenades and took off into the darkness.

Chops did not think. He moved. Something in the center of his primordial self told him to run to the woods, not retracing his steps but heading to the side, outflanking the German patrol. Before he reached the field's edge, he heard bullets whizzing by and he dove into the snow. He grabbed the hand grenade and pulled the pin.

Then he froze.

Another barrage of bullets zinged past him and he bolted upright. He saw two black figures approaching, and he hurled the grenade toward them and lay down again, covering his head.

The shouts continued. He heard the footsteps nearing and pictured the boots trampling the snow. They would kill him. Oh God, he thought. I am going to die. He imagined a bayonet piercing his back as he hugged the snow, the searing blade sliding between his ribs, cutting through his muscles, puncturing his lungs, prying through his organs until it impaled his heart.

The explosion jolted him, but the footsteps stopped, their crunching sound replaced by silence.

Chops closed his eyes and sucked in a mouthful of icy air. His lids sprung open and twenty feet away he saw the line of trees that marked the end of the field. Twenty feet from cover. Digging his toes into the frozen ground, he lurched forward. He stumbled. His fingers clawed into the ice and he pulled himself back to his feet. Shouts followed him as he ran into the thicket but he did not look back. Past the first tree. The second. Chops leapt over a frosted bush and twisted his right ankle as he landed, pain searing up his calf and into his thigh. His steps continued. An ice-covered branch reached out and dragged its sharpened claws across his cheek, but his hands refused to protect him. They had a life of their own, pulling at the underbrush and pushing off tree trunks, propelling his body deeper and deeper into the forest.

Collapse.

His knees buckled, and he fell prostrate into the snow. He could feel the cuts on his face and hands. His leg throbbed, and his stomach felt as if he had guzzled gasoline. For a moment he thought he would retch, but he stilled the need. As breath came easier, his clouded vision began to clear and his mind began to churn. Where was he? Could he reach the ambulance before Olsen and Kaj drove away? Had they even survived?

The shouts from the field subsided, replaced by a voice of authority hurling orders in German. The Nazis were regrouping, and he had left a trail like a herd of elephants. He had to start moving.

Chops' legs protested as he climbed off the ground and moved further into the woods, slower now, more cautious. The ambulance lay over a kilometer away, and he realized he had to conserve the energy that the cold was sucking out of him. Step by step he penetrated the forest, pains-

takingly trying not to leave traces for his pursu-
ers. As the overhead foliage thickened, the snow
on the ground became sparse, and he directed his
steps so as not to leave tracks.

The minutes passed and, whenever he could
see the sky, he pinpointed the North Star as Olsen
had instructed. Soon he would cross the road
where the ambulance was parked.

"Gerade aus. Gerade aus."

Chops did not understand the words he heard
behind him, but his adrenaline began pumping
through his veins like liquid fire. He reached into
his pocket and grabbed the remaining hand grenade, and he wondered whether the first he threw
had any effect. Had the explosion injured anyone?
His frozen fingers could not feel the waffled texture, only the roundness and the weight. Outrun-
ning the Germans was impossible. Chops refused
to be hunted.

One quick scan over the landscape and he
noticed a clump of bushes, chest-high and thorny.
He pried his way between the thick branches and
crouched low, peering out from between the ice-
covered leaves. The sounds of the approaching
soldiers grew louder, but at first he could not see
them. The crunch of snow under their boots
slowed, and he thought they might turn back, but
they did not.

Chops saw them. Four men in combat dress,
walking in a crouch with rifles poised at their hips.
The moonlight glowed on their helmets and cast
shadows over their faces. They continued to speak
in hushed voices, and although Chops could not
hear their words, he thought he detected fear in
their tone.

The soldiers moved closer. Soon they came
within three or four meters of where Chops hid,

but they continued forward until he could see their buttons and the SS insignia on their jackets as they passed. Then he saw only their backs.

Chops pulled his last hand grenade from his pocket and stared at it, knowing he was about to kill. The pin slid silently from the explosive cap. If they heard him stand tall to throw the grenade, they might turn and open fire, cutting him in half. He did not want to die in the snow. He wanted to die in New Orleans as an old man. He wanted to live.

The Germans were about twelve meters away when Chops straightened his legs and rose over the bushes. He hurled the grenade towards them and dropped to the ground, peering towards his targets. He did not see the grenade when it landed, but he heard it impact in the snow. The Germans heard it too. *"Vorsicht,"* one of them yelled, but then it was too late.

The explosion rang in Chops ears. He watched the four men being blown apart by the grenade and heard their screams, loud at first but quickly softening as they died.

The wind blew overhead, whistling softly as it moved through the trees, and an eerie calm descended on the forest. Slowly, Chops climbed out of the bushes and walked passed what remained of the German soldiers, neither inspecting the carnage nor shielding his eyes from it. As he followed the North Star through the woods, Chops heard the sarcastic words Olsen had said that morning as they stood along the Langelinie Promenade, words which now assumed new meaning. "Imagine that. It would be just like a war."

In a few minutes Chops saw the road and instinctively knew he had overshot the ambulance. Although he felt the danger had passed, he remained in the woods for cover and walked toward the ambulance, reaching it quickly. He saw no one in the driver's seat but resisted the temptation to look up close. The woods were safe.

The minutes passed slowly and as his adrenaline subsided, Chops became cold and tired. His eyelids turned heavy, but he fought the temptation to close them, remembering stories of people going to sleep in the cold and never waking up. Many drunks ended their career in this fashion, even in New Orleans where the temperature never dropped much below freezing.

Chapter Ten

Something rustled in the bushes and caught Chops' attention. He squinted and saw Olsen emerge from the woods, moving straight to the ambulance, crossing the road like a shadow. Without stopping to survey the road, the agent jammed his keys into the lock. Once he had the door open, Chops called out, "It's me," and stumbled onto the road.

"Hurry," Olsen replied, not bothering to look up from selecting the ignition key. "Let's get out of here."

"Where's the boy?"

"He's not with you?"

The question rattled Chops, and he shook his head violently. "No. I haven't seen him since the shooting started."

"Go on. Get in." Olsen climbed into the cab and shut the door behind him.

Chops ran to the passenger-side door and placed his foot on the running board. "What are you doing? We've gotta find him."

"He knew the risks. Get in and hope for the best."

"Kaj needs our help." Through his panic Chops realized he had divulged his student's name, violated the code of anonymity he had insisted on to protect his friend.

The wind howled, blowing aside the clouds that obscured the moon and an eerie pale glow filled the ambulance. Chops could see the mist coming out of the agent's nose and mouth as he breathed. A jagged line ran from the tip of Olsen's bluish lip to the base of his ear and blood mixed with dirt as it seeped down his cheek. The agent remained silent.

"He's just a kid. There's no way he'll survive out here."

Olsen turned the ignition, and the engine sprung to life. "Think of that next time you recruit someone," he said, fastening his seat belt with a firm tug.

Chops climbed inside the cab so he wouldn't have to shout for Olsen to hear him, but inside his voice sounded hollow, as if he spoke through a pipe. "We can't just leave him."

"Want to bet?" Olsen jammed the clutch to the ground and shoved the stick shift into reverse.

Chops stared at the agent, wanting to tell him to burn in hell and to climb out of the ambulance, but knowing if he did, Olsen would vanish and he would have to face the Germans alone and unarmed. He would never see Copenhagen again and neither would Kaj.

Without thinking, Chops thrust his right hand to the key in the dashboard and shut off the engine, but before the motor's rumble stilled, Olsen reached out and grabbed his wrist, wrenching his hand in a downward arc. As Olsen squeezed, he drove his knuckle into the tender flesh, pinching the nerve that ran through Chops' elbow and sending a molten wave of pain through his entire arm.

Their eyes locked. Chops stared as hard as he could but saw nothing inside those black pits, no guilt, no fear. Keeping the pressure on, Olsen deliberately moved his free hand under the steering column, gripped the key, and turned. The engine came to life.

He released the clutch and the ambulance spun backwards into the road, tossing Chops against the unpadded door. When Olsen hit the brake, the front end slid around, and the agent automatically shifted into first and stomped the gas. They shot forward.

Chops envisioned Kaj reaching the road just in time to see the ambulance disappear into the darkness. Instinctively, he looked in the rear-view mirror, but he did not see the gigantic boy frantically waving his hands or running after them. The mirror was empty, and Kaj was on his own. "Dear God, help that boy," he prayed silently.

They drove far too quickly for the icy conditions, and Chops feared they would land in a ditch alongside the road, but Olsen maneuvered with a mechanized precision that only comes from training and years of experience. Soon, they turned onto a larger, well-maintained road and Olsen accelerated, edging the speedometer over one hundred kilometers per hour.

Sitting motionless in the cab, Chops' breathing slowed and his moist shirt began to cool, clinging to his chest like an ice pack. Inside his gloves, his fingers felt like frozen sausages, immobile and brittle. His nose began to drip and he wiped his sleeve across his face, checking to make sure that it didn't come back bloody. After twelve hours of sleep and a hot bath, he would feel human again, at least physically. What about Kaj? Tromping around in the snow, answering to Gestapo interrogation, or bleeding to a slow death in a ditch. When would he feel good again? Would he ever again come to Smukke to drink after mopping the floors in the tattoo parlor or struggle through his scales on his beat-up cornet? Chops could not force the boy's round face out of his mind. He reached forward and adjusted the heater knobs until a steady stream of air started hissing at the floorboards. The temperature remained about the same. "The Germans will set up roadblocks."

Olsen nodded. "If we're lucky, they'll assume we're headed straight to the city, and they will station check-points south along Highway Seven. That's why we're headed west. We should have enough petrol to circle around and enter Copenhagen on Route Two. Of course, they might stop all traffic entering the city, but this is the only chance we've got."

"Can't we stop somewhere outside the city and lay low for a while?"

"I suppose you know of a safe house somewhere?"

"I thought you had contacts everywhere," Chops challenged.

Olsen shook his head. "I can't just barge into someone's home, demanding protection, regardless of how sympathetic they are. Too dangerous. Too desperate."

"Isn't this desperate enough?"

"Chops, you haven't yet seen desperation."

"Yet?"

Olsen did not respond.

Chops eased himself back in the seat. He never planned to be a spy or to wage war against the Nazis, much less sacrifice his lover and now his friend to the awful regime. All he really wanted was to play his cornet and to love a special young woman whom he never quite understood.

He reached inside his coat and pulled out his lighter and a package of Lucky Strikes. He had smashed them pretty thoroughly when he fell in the field, but rolling the cigarette between his fingers rounded it out a bit. He placed it between his lips and hesitated, knowing Olsen did not like smoking. "Want a smoke?"

"No."

"Suit yourself," he said, flicking the flint. He pulled hard on the cigarette, filling his lungs with warm smoke, holding it in, and then exhaling through his nose. There was nothing like an American cigarette. Of course, one could only buy them on the waterfront, and they cost a healthy sum, but Chops always had the resources, thanks to Olsen.

His second drag tasted acrid and made him want to spit.

Chops knew he benefited from his resistance work and, until now, it had never bothered him. He took risks and accepted payment. But Svenya had never agreed to play a part or received any benefits from the arrangement. Chops had risked her life as well. He had tried to keep her out of his black-market dealings and his work with Olsen, but all along he knew he could never completely succeed. Sucking on the bitter tobacco, Chops asked himself why he had not given up the black market years ago and why he had allowed Olsen to pull him into his game.

Marie. Svenya. Kaj. He hurt everyone he touched. Who would he destroy next? Louisa? Tapio? One of the Backbeats? It hurt too much to think about.

"What time is it?" he asked.

"About twenty past five," Olsen said without looking at his watch.

"The sun will be coming up soon."

"No. The sun will rise at seven forty, and by

that time we should be back in the city." Olsen shook his head. "Don't go back to your bed until you know it's safe. It's bad form. If the Gestapo captured Kaj, then they will have a surprise party waiting for you when you get home. Go to a friend's house and get some sleep. Have someone check if anyone is watching your apartment or asking questions. I don't think you have to worry, but you should be cautious."

Chops repeated the word to himself. Cautious. If caution were in his blood, he'd still be in New Orleans saying "Yes sir" to every whitey that spit in his face. In the mornings he'd teach in the city schools, and at night he'd play leftover Dixieland standards for the tourists on Bourbon Street. The time he had spent in New Orleans as a young man blended together in a giant cauldron, days into seasons, Easters into New Years, until nothing stood out in his memory except the night Guy Sherman offered him a place in his band and the day he played "When the Roll is Called Up Yonder" at his father's funeral. When he was twenty-five years old, he only wanted to leave the French Quarter and tear up the world, and now at thirty-two he longed to clean up the shards he had scattered.

Suddenly, he heard a loud pop and he saw Olsen tense up at the wheel. The ambulance jerked and decelerated rapidly, listing to the right as it hobbled to a stop. Chops gripped the door handle, wishing he had a gun.

"Bloody hell," Olsen whispered.

"What is it?"

The Dane opened his door, stepped out, and circled to the rear of the ambulance, and Chops heard a resounding thud as Olsen smashed his fist against the rear quarter-board. "A flat."

He left the cab and saw Olsen shining a pen

light at the right rear tire, illuminating a tear that spanned one third of the way around the wheel. He could smell stale air and charred rubber. Why couldn't Olsen have stolen an ambulance with good tires, he asked himself, although he knew that all spare automobile parts went to the German war machine. Even a used tire cost three hundred Crown on the black market, if you could find one. "Got a spare?"

He joined Olsen at the rear of the ambulance and swung the door open. Among the inside shadows he could see the outlines of blankets, a first-aid kit, a fire extinguisher—the few tools trained professionals use to save a life, if that's what they're trying to do. The Dane snorted as he lifted the left-hand stretcher and tilted it back against the window. Below it in a small compartment nestled a thin tire with a jack and a few miscellaneous tools. Olsen handed him a tire iron. "Let's get to work. No reason to be here longer than necessary."

Chops wrestled the remaining equipment from its niche and dropped it to the ground next to the flat, where it clattered and echoed into the night. He knew little about automobiles, but the tools seemed to fit together without complication. After wedging the jack under the rear fender, he pushed down on the crowbar, and the entire contraption slipped out and fell apart. Mercifully, Olsen said nothing.

Chops reassembled the jack and, holding it in place with his knee, began to pump. The steel creaked as it strained against the ambulance, and the lever offered stiff resistance. Chops levied all his weight against the bar and soon the tire lifted off the ground. Despite the cold, a few beads of sweat formed on his forehead, and he paused to light another cigarette.

"No time to waste," Olsen called, pacing back and forth along the road.

"Are you going to help?"

The agent cocked his pistol. "I'm standing guard."

"Right," Chops replied. He pulled on the cigarette, exhaled, and forced the crowbar over the first lug nut. After a hard push, the nut began to turn. "Do you think Kaj will crack?"

Olsen smirked. "You're so naive. If I needed information from that boy I could get it in ten minutes, and I only trained with special operations in England. Gestapo interrogation training in Berlin is more thorough and much more ruthless. The boy wouldn't last two minutes, but I don't think the Gestapo will need to question him. I'd give that a one-in-twenty chance."

Chops swallowed hard and turned his attention to the third bolt. "You think there is a ninety-five percent chance that they killed him? That's pretty low. They didn't kill us, did they?"

Olsen glanced quickly at Chops and said, "Kaj was in on it. He set us up."

"Don't kid me," he replied, wanting to be offended, but the idea seemed too ridiculous. He loosened the final nut and removed the tire.

"Someone set us up tonight. Was it you, Chops?"

"Would I be changing this flat if it were?"

Olsen took the decimated tire and flung it far into the woods. "I've been thinking about it since we left the drop site and it makes too much sense. This operation was airtight until you brought in that boy. The Gerries didn't stumble upon us. They were waiting. Don't look so surprised. How long have you known the boy?"

"A couple of years," he said, although he could

not remember exactly when their paths had first crossed. It was long before the Germans invaded Denmark. Chops had been teaching a few music courses at the University and had instructed six students in private. Kaj had heard the Backbeats play several times before jazz went underground, and eventually he walked up and introduced himself after a set. He said he had a cornet and wanted to learn to play hot, which struck Chops as funny coming from a fifteen-year-old Dane. They talked for a few minutes, Chops sizing him up, and a week later the boy began his lessons.

"So you're not exactly childhood friends," Olsen said. "And how often do you see him? Once or twice a week? Do you know about his past? His friends? Maybe he's gone to a few Nazi rallies that you don't know about."

Chops finished tightening the second lug nut and turned to Olsen. "Lay off. He left home because his folks were selling their crops directly to the German army. Kaj hates the Nazis. That's all he ever talks about besides learning to play the horn."

"So he comes from a family of sympathizers," he muttered. "And he squawks a lot? Maybe the boy's overcompensating. Who knows? But doesn't it seem the least bit odd that the Nazis were waiting for us? Waiting for us!"

"But Kaj didn't know where we were going," Chops said, and he noticed the panicked edge in his voice, as if he feared that Olsen's absurd hypothesis were true.

"Only a slight inconvenience to the Germans. He could have told them that we were meeting at the main train station at three o'clock, and that would have been enough. He could have carried a small transmitter so they could follow us."

"A radio would be too big to hide."

"Maybe. But Kaj is a very big boy, and the German radio technology surpasses even the Americans'. He could have hidden a small radio beeper with a limited range. How else would they have found us?"

Chops hesitated, searching for the simple answer that would prove Kaj's innocence, knowing also that Olsen would blame him for bringing a traitor into the operation. He finished attaching the spare tire and moved to the jack. "Maybe the Germans tracked the plane."

"Track a solitary mosquito bomber? If the Gerries were that good, they'd have won the war by now."

When the jack went limp in Chops' hand, he disassembled it and carried it to the rear door. "Maybe there's a spy in London."

"You're grasping at straws, Chops," he said, lowering the stretcher over the tools and straightening the sheets.

"Me? You're the one trying to blame an eighteen-year-old kid because one of your foolproof missions almost got you killed."

"Think so? Then tell me one thing."

"What?"

"Why did Kaj separate from the group right before the shooting started? He never was in the line of fire, was he? Maybe he knew things were about to heat up."

Chops heard his voice rise. "There was an extra parachute. You saw it, didn't you? He went to get the second 'chute."

"No. I didn't see a second canister. Did you? Or did you just hear the boy say that there were two? At any rate, his orders were to stay put. He left the line of fire before it even existed, and that tells me he knew something was about to happen." Olsen climbed in the front of the ambulance. Chops waited a moment before following.

"You're seeing ghosts," Chops said, but he knew Olsen better than that. The SOE agent possessed no imagination.

Olsen turned the key and steered the ambulance back to the road. He accelerated to sixty but did not push it any further. "You're letting your feelings get in the way. Very bad form. Admit that he may have turned us in. And we need to know, especially if he miraculously escapes," he said, stressing the word "miraculously."

"What's that mean?"

"Let me ask you this. What will you think if Kaj shows up, safe and sound, on your doorstep tonight?"

"I'd be spinning."

"I beg your pardon?"

Chops tilted his nose upward and exaggerated an upper-crust Danish accent. "I would be overjoyed."

"You'd be a fool. Without as much as one question, you'd welcome him back to the fold? You wouldn't even suspect that he betrayed us to the Germans or that when their little ambush failed they sent him back to set you up again."

"You're on a witch hunt."

Olsen took his hand off the wheel and began to massage the back of his neck. "Think that is a bit farfetched? Try this. Assume he did not set us up and the Germans capture him in earnest. They give him a choice: stand trial for treason or work with us. Tell us everything you know—which isn't much right now—and then go back to the waterfront and report everything you hear to Gestapo headquarters. Does that sound a little more feasible?"

"Maybe," Chops said. "But as I'm sure you realize, that could work for you. Kaj tells me what's gone down, and then we use him to feed crap to the Gestapo. Isn't that how it works?"

"Applause, applause," Olsen replied, changing lanes to avoid an animal carcass on the road. "Maybe I should give you more credit. You're learning. Becoming more professional. Three months ago you would have suggested that we sneak him off to Sweden as soon as possible. Now you're talking about using your friend, knowing full well that every double-back increases the risk geometrically. How long do you think that boy could lie to German intelligence before he slipped up? A week? Two at the most? Then they would put a slug in his skull and throw his body in the sea. That's one hell of a way to treat your friends."

Chops wondered if he really were beginning to calculate like a saboteur, like a machine, like Olsen. "I suppose you think Svenya is working for the Gestapo."

"So the thought has occurred to you," Olsen countered. "You are learning."

"Up yours. She hates Nazis as much as you do," but as soon as he uttered the words, he remembered the German opera ticket he had found in her bedroom. Why did she tell him she was taking a trip to southern Denmark and then go to Germany?

Olsen did not respond. He just sat behind the wheel and kept his eyes on the road, turning left as the highway met Route Two. Soon they began passing a few buildings that marked the outskirts of Copenhagen. Downtown lay only a few minutes ahead. "I'm going to let you off on a side street behind the train station."

"That's a half hour walk to Christianshavn."

"I told you not to go back to your flat. You have some friends downtown. Stay with them until midday. I'm serious about you checking out your place before you walk into a trap."

Chops wanted to argue, but fatigue taxed his mind so heavily that it refused to cooperate. Sleep. If he could only have a little sleep. He cracked the window to let some cold air blow on his face, but the wind did make his eyelids lighter. He thought back to the night when Olsen first approached him, making the task sound so simple and so important. Just blow a few magic notes on your cornet and you could help turn the war against the Nazis, who had already forced jazz underground. Then, to sweeten the deal, the agent offered to pay five hundred Crown per broadcast and to throw in extra ration tickets, paper gold on the black market. Growing up poor in New Orleans taught him never to pass up easy money, but gradually the work increased as Olsen began using him to smuggle documents through the waterfront and to gather information from loose-lipped soldiers. Once, Chops had even hidden a German refugee, a man with a vague past: anti-Nazi scientist, engineer, or perhaps writer.

Tonight, Chops had killed.

As they sped toward downtown, Chops envisioned whom he would sneak to Sweden aboard a stolen fishing boat. Kaj. His band. Tapio. Naturally Svenya. He could never leave without her. Suddenly, all the pieces came together. He could not stop his resistance work until she was free from the Gestapo's clutches. And if he quit, Peder Olsen would have no way to send his stolen information to his superiors in London. "You don't plan on springing Svenya, do you?"

"I haven't decided."

"You have too." Chops kept his voice low, but he could feel the anger boiling under the surface. "You know that if we bust her out, we'd have to smuggle her out of the country and that I'd go with her. Then your precious system of broadcasting information to special operations would go up in smoke. That's why you haven't done anything to get her free."

"Chops, what do you want me to do? Storm the place with twenty well-armed men? Our own little Bastille? The Germans would kill every one of us and have fun doing it. You are such a simpleton."

"You haven't lifted a finger to help her."

"You're wrong. I'm actually making some progress, but these things take time. I'm certain that someone denounced her, and a certain Oberleutnant Heissen ordered the raid on Smukke. She's in cell 211 E, and so far she hasn't confessed.

"I think we've got a lever," Olsen continued. "You see, the officer in charge, Oberleutnant Heissen, has been married for the last three years to a lady of Jewish descent, and although he has managed to hide this fact from his superiors, he desperately wants this piece of trivia to remain a secret. His wife is only one quarter Jewish, and Oberleutnant Heissen would hate to see either his family life or his career ruined by what he considers ancient history.

"He's our key, Chops. When Miss Hjorth goes free, she will walk through the front doors of Gestapo headquarters in broad daylight carrying official papers, and the two of you can live happily together in Copenhagen. But these things take time, energy, and money. I'm putting out a lot for her, Chops. Don't cross me."

The ambulance began navigating the labyrinth of downtown Copenhagen, its streets still devoid of life. Olsen pointed ahead. "I'll let you out at the corner. Get some sleep and try to act as normal as possible. Let me take care of the lovely Miss Hjorth." He pulled the ambulance up to the curb. "Don't get impatient, Chops. She's been in jail less than one week. Give it some time, and we'll get her out. I'll be in touch."

Chops stepped onto the curb, thinking how much could happen in a week in jail. "You know where to find me," he said and closed the door. Olsen pulled into the street and disappeared around the corner.

He took his bearings and began walking toward the train station. A heavy weariness bore down on him as he stumbled down the street, feeling pain in his legs, back, and shoulders with every step. As always, Olsen was right. Kaj could be a traitor. Herr Wolf could be recruiting him to work for the Nazis. Svenya might be an informant. The word "trust" lost all its meaning when the Germans invaded Denmark over two years ago. April 9, 1940. Everything changed on that horrible day, although many Danes didn't realize it until later. Some still did not understand.

In a few minutes he reached Louisa's apartment building. He rang her buzzer and waited for a reply. Even if she worked the early shift at Cafe Kakadu, she would not yet have left for work. Where was she? He rang three more times. Perhaps she had spent the night with a sailor. Where would he go then? To Tapio's? To Smukke? He pressed the buzzer and kept his finger down.

"What the fuck do you want?" Louisa said as she opened the door. She wore a coarse, wool robe that hung down to her knit slippers, and her face looked bleached out and weather-beaten. "Oh Chops, it's you. You look like hell. What's happened? Are you all right? Have you been hurt?"

He forced a smile. "Rough night, that's all. Can I grab a few winks?"

She led him up the stairs. "You don't have to ask. Just don't snore."

They reached the landing and she led him into her apartment. "Don't mind the mess," she said, but he hadn't even noticed it.

They walked straight into her bedroom, and he sat on the bed. No piece of furniture had ever felt so welcome. He lay back and closed his eyes, only for a moment, before he took off his boots.

"I'll grab a warm cloth to clean you up a bit," he heard her say before he drifted into a deep sleep.

Chapter Eleven

Even as he slept, Chops missed the familiar sounds floating up from the waterfront; the chains, the nets, the ropes and rudders, the early morning noises to which he had become accustomed from eight years of living above the piers. Other sounds seeped into his head, the floor creaking in the other room, somehow different than it moaned when he walked on it, and different from when Svenya paced back and forth. So heavy was this curtain of sleep that when he tried to rise, he felt heavy and immobile, like a glove filled with sand, so he gave up and returned to his dreams, sordid, turbulent, and muggy.

The first sliver of light that seeped through when he cracked his eyelids seemed too blue, too intense. He wrenched his body over and buried his head in the pillow, but then it was too late. He was awake, lying in bed with his eyes closed and his head full of visions from the previous night. For the first time, Chops had killed.

He remembered the excitement and the fear, the bare trees contrasting against the powdery snow like a forest of skeletons, the parachute canisters floating slowly to the ground, and the German searchlights washing the field. He thought about the grenade he threw and the men who died.

Was that guilt he felt? No. This was something different than guilt, more detached. Perhaps those soldiers believed in Hitler's new European order and hoped to kill all the Bolsheviks, gypsies, and Jews. Or maybe they enjoyed racing motor cars or playing the piano or collecting stamps. Chops would never know. He had simply tossed a grenade in their direction and stood by as their screams followed the blast. He had acted just like Olsen would have.

As he lay in bed, the skin around Chops' right eye felt tight and itchy, and he remembered falling in the snow. He reached up to touch his forehead, lightly at first. Although his fingers barely made contact, he noticed something was stuck above his forehead, but his fingertips came back clean. No blood.

Still groggy, Chops pulled himself up in the bed and tried to focus on the oval mirror above the bureau. He saw a white X of adhesive tape holding a small square of gauze in place on his forehead. Louisa must have put it on him as he slept, which seemed peculiar. She had never before worried about little cuts and infections. Quite the opposite. One night at Cafe Kakadu, a crane driver got his nose broken in a fight, and Louisa wouldn't let him leave until he had paid his bill. She said bleeding wasn't an excuse.

The footsteps outside the room continued until Chops heard a glass drop and shatter, followed by a loud, "Crap."

Chops snickered. He had never met a lady who swore as much as Louisa. Neither his mother nor any ladies he knew in America besides hookers and white trash cursed. He thought of swearing as a masculine habit, but Louisa had learned well, and it fit in a dive like Cafe Kakadu. How would he explain to her his sudden arrival or his cuts and bruises? He couldn't. He could not tell her how last night he narrowly escaped capture and killed four Germans in the process, couldn't break the news about Kaj.

Kaj.

The echo of gunfire reverberated in Chops' head, and he saw the boy running across the clearing, movements slowed as if through water. He heard the German officers yell, and he saw the flames spitting out of their guns. Perhaps Kaj escaped, hid until the patrol moved away, or maybe he did not. When your number comes up, it's up, Chops reasoned, but still he hoped that the boy would come back. Either way, he couldn't change last night.

He corralled his thoughts away from the previous night and forward. What was his next step? Tonight he had agreed to attend a small dinner party with Herr Wolf, but he had no way to get there. He had not replaced his bicycle, and the station manager lived on the outskirts of the city, much farther than he could walk. Did he say that a bus ran near his home, or perhaps a tram? He had to find out.

He fell back into bed, thinking about everything he had to do. He had even agreed to bring a bottle of wine to the party, but he had not taken the first steps to get one. Finding things on the black market required a combination of time and money. The more of one you had, the less of the other you needed. At this point, when the afternoon shadows lay long across the room, he could only walk to the waterfront with a pocket full of bills and see what he could find. His best chance would be Hans, an ex-sailor, who ran a black market operation out of a knife-sharpening shop, but as a matter of protection the man never kept contraband on the premises. Some things took time.

Chops rolled out of bed and stepped over to the chair where his clothing lay in a semi-folded pile. He needed to clean himself up and to get ready to go to Herr Wolf's. The station manager knew about the raid at Smukke, and he might be able to help Svenya, especially if Chops had something to offer. And the German had no contacts on the black market, no way to get the luxuries he desired. Chops realized that Wolf would not free Svenya for a single bottle of cognac or a box of Cuban cigars, but they might be a starting place, a sign that Chops was willing to play ball.

As Chops pulled his belt tight around his waist, the door opened and Louisa stood in the doorway, holding a ceramic water pitcher. She had pulled her hair back in a neat ponytail, held together at the bottom by a copper pin. The square collar on her blue dress hung unevenly below her neck and exposed one strap to her brassière, but Chops had the feeling that if she straightened herself up, she might look presentable. "Glad you're awake," she said with a smile, raising the pitcher in the air. "I was about to resort to drastic measures to get your lazy ass out of bed."

Chops looked at the water pitcher and looked at Louisa. He smiled, not at her feeble joke but at her good spirits, which might have been a sign that she wouldn't demand an explanation of last night's events. Keep the jokes moving, he thought. "If you poured that on me, you'd tell everyone at Smukke that I wet your bed."

She laughed more than Chops' joke deserved. "Hungry?" she asked. "I picked up some bread this morning, and if you want something warm, there's still some chicken broth in the kitchen. It's not much for breakfast, I'm afraid, but for most people it's past lunch time."

"I'm more late than I am hungry. I gotta scram." He bent over to pick up his wrinkled shirt.

"Sit your fat black ass down, Chops," she said, dropping the pitcher on the bedside table, and almost spilling the contents. "You can't just come into my house at the crack of dawn looking like you lost three fights in a row, sleep till two o'clock, and then say 'gotta scram.' You owe me an explanation. You're in trouble, right?"

Chops stared at her for a moment, dumbfounded and unsure of how he should respond. He sat down in the chair, landing firmly on top of his coat. "Things got ugly last night."

"How ugly?"

"I killed four."

"Soldiers?"

"Yeah."

"Any witnesses?"

"It was dark."

Louisa nodded her head thoughtfully. "Want a bath?"

"Sure," he sighed. "I can't walk around town looking like I've been on the front. Does your water heater work?"

"When there's coal in it."

"Already burned your rations, I guess."

She reached back, pulled her pony-tail over her shoulder, and half-consciously wrapped it around her finger. Walking towards the bathroom, she said, "Not quite all of it. Go ahead and poach your ass. It'll do you good."

She turned and walked out of the room. A few seconds later, Chops followed the sound of running water to the bathroom and leaned against the doorframe.

"Go ahead and jump in while it's filling. No reason to waste the heat." When he hesitated she smiled and said, "Go on, it's nothing I haven't seen before."

He pulled off his shirt, which he had not yet buttoned, and folded it neatly on the laundry basket. Louisa stared at the rising water, occasionally splashing it against the tub, paying no attention to him, so he unfastened his belt and let his trousers slide to the floor. These, too, he folded and set on top of the hamper. "How's the water?"

She turned and he felt her eyes run over his naked body, neither arousing him nor making him uncomfortable. "See for yourself."

He stepped forward and splashed his foot into the tub. Up to his calves, his skin constricted, tingled, and burned pleasantly. "Outta sight," he muttered as he shifted his weight and brought his other leg over the edge of the tub. He sat in the scalding water and leaned back against the chipped enamel. Closing his eyes, he splashed his curly-haired chest and his shoulders.

Louisa turned to the mirror, pulled at her lower lip, and began examining her gums. "I don't like it, Chops. One day the Nazis haul Svenya out of Smukke, and the next day you shoot four of them. I was worried you'd go nuts like you did with Marie."

"What makes you think it had anything to do with Svenya?"

"Because I know you."

"Well this time you're wrong," Chops said quickly. "The shooting last night was totally random. We were walking-"

"I don't want to know the details," Louisa said, putting her hands over her ears. "People who know things get into too much trouble. It's been that way ever since I was born, and it won't change before I die. I don't want to know. Finish up in the tub, and I'll fix you some lunch," she said. She reached out and grabbed a light-blue towel hanging from a brass hook. After holding it under her nose, she grabbed the brown towel below. She shrugged. "Use whichever one you want. I think the blue one is cleaner."

"I'll be there in a minute."

"Don't rush. The soup will take a while to warm up." She reached behind her back, opened the door, and stepped into the hall.

When Chops heard the latch fall, he closed his eyes, bent his knees, and sank deeper into the tub. The warm water soaked pleasantly into his skin, and as he breathed, he felt a lightness evaporating from his stomach. Had bathing in front of Louisa made him nervous? Nonsense. He had always considered her more like a sister than a friend. Months went by when he would see Louisa every day, and others passed when he would not see her at all. It didn't seem to make any difference in the way they behaved. In the eight years Chops had known Louisa, she had changed very little. Perhaps she had a little more zest or appetite, but really she was just the same.

What was she like when she was younger? Was she fiery and impetuous like Svenya, or demure and resigned? Had she had many lovers? When she and Chops had first met, she slept around, but as she matured her escapades became less frequent. He could not ever remember her being in love with someone. Her relationships lasted more towards hours than months. Perhaps she would find a man to be happy with, an older man or a soldier returning from the war.

"Your ass get stuck in the drain?" Even through

the closed door her voice rang strong.

"No," he called, grasping onto the top of the soap dish and pulling himself to his feet. "I'll be right out." After soaking in hot water, the air in the bathroom stung and made him shiver. He reached for the towel as he stepped out of the tub and dripped water in puddles across the gray tile floor. As he dried himself with the towel in one hand, he wiped the foggy mirror with the other. He saw an adhesive X across his forehead, the mark of Cain, a flag stating, "I WAS SHOOTING AT NAZIS LAST NIGHT."

He picked at the corner of the tape, and when he had a grip on it, he ripped. "Ouch." He involuntarily squelched his eyes and clamped his jaw, and when he looked down, he saw three eyebrow hairs stuck to the tape. He shook his head, wadded the bandage into a sticky ball, and tossed it into the trash can.

Chops leaned toward the mirror and examined the cut on his forehead. Not more than a scratch, really. The scab was more than an inch long, but it was not deep. If he wore a large-brimmed hat, no one would even notice it. He was lucky to have escaped last night's ambush with only cuts and bruises. Even Olsen was hit by shrapnel, and Kaj didn't make it out at all.

As he continued to look into the mirror, he saw Kaj polishing the windows in the tattoo parlor and humming the chorus to Kansas City Blues over and over again because he could not remember the verse. Chops pictured him arm wrestling sailors at Cafe Kakadu and Lindy-hopping in Smukke, and he hoped that the boy was not gone. He couldn't be. Not at eighteen.

"Not at eighteen," Chops said aloud as he slipped into his pants. "Not at eighteen." He reached for his undershirt, but it was stained and smelly so he tossed it into the trash can beside the sink. His shirt wasn't much cleaner, but he found a cut-glass bottle of lavender water, splashed some under his arms, and walked into the hall.

Louisa spoke without turning away from the stove when Chops stepped into the kitchen and sat in a wobbly, straight-back chair. "Feel better?"

"A little."

"Some soup will do wonders." She ladled the soup into two chipped Royal Copenhagen bowls and set them down on the bare table. "I'll get a spoon."

She pulled open a drawer and fished around for some clean cutlery, and Chops savored the simple smell of the kitchen. Chicken and cabbage. In better times he expected carrots, barley, celery, and onion in his soups, but wartime rationing simplified his diet considerably.

"Smells good."

"Nothing special, just a little chicken broth."

"Marie used to cook something similar."

"Your late wife?"

"Know any other Maries?" The sarcastic bite in his voice surprised him, but he did not apologize.

"I guess not." She looked down and took a spoonful of soup. "Do you miss her?"

"Sure. Not all the time, but she's never too far away. We were just kids, really.

"And now you're an old goat at thirty-four, right?"

Chops laughed, although her reply wasn't funny, and when his laughter subsided it was replaced by an obtuse silence, only deflected by spoons clinking against the bowls. He raised his glass but it was practically empty, and he shook the last drop of water into his mouth.

"Did you hear the British pushed Rommel out of Egypt?"

"I thought that was the Americans."

Louisa crumpled her napkin, tossed it onto the table, and sighed. "I don't think so. Your boys are on the other side. In Morocco. It's not in the papers, but everybody's talking about it."

"I guess they're planning on squeezing the Gerries out of North Africa for good."

"Hitler swore he'd never surrender Africa."

Chops wiped the corner of his mouth. "Hitler swears all kind of things. He's the swearingest man I ever saw. He swore he'd let Denmark rule itself, too, didn't he? My guess is they'll diddle in North Africa through the winter and wait 'till spring to try and finish off the Russians. It doesn't matter much to me. I'll be in jail long before that."

"The GARM sails for Malmo tomorrow, Chops, and you should be on her. Why stay around and wait for the Gestapo to drag you off? Nobody gets away with killing these days, definitely not killing Germans."

"I was just joking," he said. "Sweden's too cold for a Louisiana boy like me."

"From Oslo you might be able to catch a boat back to America. Sweden's neutral."

Chops shook his head. "If I went back to New Orleans, they'd probably set a tin hat on my head and send me back to kill more Gerries. That's two long boat trips for nothing."

"Your sense of humor never goes away for long, does it?"

"Let's hope it stays that way." Chops arched his back and stretched his shoulders. "What time is it?"

"Quarter to three."

"I have to go. I've got a dinner party to go to, and I need to pick up some things before I go."

"It's Sunday, Chops. All the shop are closed."

"Not those kind of things."

Louisa just nodded her head. After a brief pause she said, "Did you hear that Hans moved to the country for a while?"

Hans was perhaps the most common name in Denmark, but Chops immediately knew she was talking about the black market trader he was counting on to get the wine for Wolf's party. His throat became dry. "Left the city?"

"Yeah."

"When?"

"Thursday. Closed up shop and left. He said that life in the city wasn't for him anymore, and he was moving to the country. Word has it that the Gestapo was about to drag him in, and he found out about it in time. That buzzard had ears everywhere and mouths most places. I'm surprised you didn't hear about it."

"I've been busy."

"I noticed."

Chops ignored her jab. If Hans had really moved out of the city, where would he get Wolf's brandy? Tapio might have some behind the counter at Smukke, but the bartender always asked too many questions, and Chops wanted to keep things as simple as possible. Perhaps he should comb the waterfront for a couple of hours and keep his ears open. Opportunities always popped up, but he did not have much time. His chair scraped on the ground as he pushed away from the table.

Louisa stuffed a piece of bread in her mouth and spoke as she chewed. "What do you need from Hans?"

"Some hooch."

"Why don't you just grab some at Smukke."

"Bathtub gin won't do. This could be important. I need a bottle of wine or some liqueur or something. I'll ask Rousseau what he's got. He always has some good trinkets."

Louisa glared at him like a nun who had caught a child blaspheming. "Rousseau? You do business with him? He's in with the Nazis. I heard he even turned in some smugglers for a percentage of their haul. I'm surprised he hasn't wound up in the harbor by now."

Chops shrugged. "If they killed him last night I'm going to have a time getting good booze."

"Don't go looking for trouble, Chops. I've got a bottle stashed away that'll do."

"I don't think-"

"Just take a look at it. If you don't think it'll do, all you lost was a minute." She stood up and shook her finger. "Stay put." Without pushing her chair back under the table, she walked out of the kitchen.

Chops reached across the table and took the half-eaten crust off her plate, soaked up the remaining soup and stuck it into his mouth. Despite what Louisa said about Hans, Chops knew he could get a good bottle of brandy somewhere on the waterfront, even if it took a little time. Rousseau wasn't such a bad risk. Louisa exaggerated everything. He listened to her plow through her bedroom closet, tossing shoes and boxes behind her. She called out a few times, but most of her words were not distinguishable. How could someone so disorganized keep such good track of who's where on the waterfront?

"Found the fucker!"

"Congratulations," Chops called into the other room. "I was about to call in a rescue squad."

She strutted into the kitchen, holding a brown bottle in her hand like a trophy. "I knew it was in my closet somewhere. You're supposed to store wine in a dark place where it doesn't get too hot in the summer."

"I know that," Chops said wiping his mouth. "Let me see it."

She placed the bottle on the table and stepped away, clasping her hands behind her back and smiling. Chops picked it up and looked over the red wax top and the lettering stenciled on the bottle with white paint. "Eighteen-ninety vintage. Port. Sandeman and Son."

"It's supposed to be pretty good."

Chops eyed her suspiciously. "This is nineteen forty-two. That makes this bottle over fifty years old. Are you sure it hasn't gone bad?"

"Port lasts longer than regular wine."

"Fifty years?"

"It should still be good."

"It must be an expensive bottle," Chops said, trying hard to be subtle while opening the door to discuss money. During the occupation it had become customary to pay for favors, even from friends.

"It didn't cost me that much, but I got it a long time ago."

"Saving it for something special?"

"Not anymore. I'd rather you have it."

"I'd appreciate it."

Louisa smiled, placed one foot on her kitchen chair, and stared Chops straight in the eye. "One question."

Chops returned her steady glance, but inside his stomach began to knot and his mouth went dry. "Shoot."

"Who's the lucky girl?"

"I'm bribing a German officer," he said without delay.

Louisa tossed her hands into the air and sighed. "I don't want to know any more. It's none of my business."

Chapter Twelve

Fog covered the windows of the tram, so Chops had to wipe a hole in the middle so he could see out. The patches of snow on the trees and rooftops looked soft and comforting, almost warm under the half moon, whereas the tram itself was uncomfortable. His back would not conform to the uncushioned wooden seats, and he feared he would catch a splinter if he shifted suddenly. The air inside tasted used, but the windows were frozen on the outside.

Chops had ridden almost forty minutes before the tram reached Idraetsplads, the closest stop to Herr Wolf's home. The doors opened, and a crisp wind struck him as he climbed carefully onto the icy platform. As the tram rumbled away, he pulled his collar tight around his ears and looked across the forlorn station, little more than a lamppost, a sign, and two crumbling benches.

Chops welcomed the solitude. When he climbed on the train at town square, he felt that every stranger was watching him, saying, *there's that colored man whose going to eat dinner with the Nazis*. He imagined what Dragor, Tapio, or any of the boys at Smukke would say if they knew what he was doing tonight. He had not even told Peder

Olsen about the invitation, although asking Wolf's
help to recover the cornet had been the Danish
operative's idea.

He walked up the hill towards Wolf's house,
clutching Louisa's bottle of wine like a football and
taking unusually long strides. His legs had tightened up on him during the tram ride, but on the
whole, his body felt fit, considering this time last
night he was preparing to go with Olsen. The cut
on his forehead felt tight, and it was beginning to
itch. Before he left he had removed the bandage
and carefully inspected the scab, picking away at
the edges. It was small enough where it might go
unnoticed. He was lucky that Louisa let him stay
at her apartment and rest.

The houses on either side of the road stood tall
and dark against the sky. Most of them had been
built around the turn of the century when stone
archways and iron fences enjoyed an upturn in
popularity. Relatively few of the windows were lit
for fear of an air raid. Bombers rarely stalked the
night skies above Denmark, but everyone had seen
the news clips of the destruction in France. Everyone was a little afraid.

Wolf's house, number 23, stood a couple of
hundred yards off the road and a thin, brick path
led up to the stone front porch, just as he had described. Large gas lanterns burned on either side
of the front door and cast lively shadows over the
potted plants. Apparently, Wolf did not worry about
the Allied bombers, and why should he? The house
wasn't even his. He once told Chops the story of
the Danish nationalist who had lived and raised
his family there. The man abandoned the property
after the invasion, and the occupation government
took the deed. The story was not uncommon.

Chops slowly climbed the seven steps up the

front door and hesitated before he rang the bell. Seated dinners with strangers and business associates had never been his type of affair. The only exception had been years ago when his deceased wife, Marie, had dragged him to a different party every weekend, and her social graces and lightheartedness made the evenings fun. Why hadn't Herr Wolf asked Chops if he wanted to bring a date tonight? Perhaps a simple oversight of native customs, or else he did not want Chops to have an ally.

His mother had warned him of being too friendly with the people you work with. As a gentleman, you must be friendly to the people at work, but that does not make them friends of yours. Chops always figured she gave him that advice because he frequently worked playing cornet in bistros and brothels, but her words came back to him now as he rang the bell.

A petite young woman, wearing a simple black dress and a white apron, opened the door. She had pale skin, and her hair was pulled back in a tight bun. She stared at him a moment with wide eyes before saying good evening.

Chops could tell by her accent that she came from a rural area somewhere to the north, as did most of the domestic help. She had probably never seen a black man in her life. "My name is Chops Danielson."

The maid curtsied quickly and began to blush. "The family Wolf is expecting you. Please come in."

A crystal chandelier cast a bright light over the large, wood-paneled entrance hall. A curved staircase descended from the left, and he caught a quick glimpse of his reflection in the mirror above the umbrella stand. This morning's newspaper sat folded on a small table, and Chops read the headline, "Victory in Africa Near." He could hear chatter from down the hall. The smell in the house reminded him of Christmas, and he realized that a goose was cooking somewhere not far away. "This way, Mr. Danielson," the maid said, opening the door on the far side of the hallway.

Moving through the doorway, Chops saw Herr Wolf standing with a man and a woman by the fireplace. Above the mantle hung two portraits in twin frames. One showed the once-proud king of Denmark, King Christian XII, atop his steed in the courtyard of Amalienborg, with the royal guard in formation behind him. The other was a simple bust of Adolf Hitler, the man who had ordered the invasion of Denmark, and who had allowed King Christian to remain in the castle as a figurehead monarch.

A lady in a long, emerald dress of taffeta and lace walked up to Chops and offered her hand. "Welcome Chops," she said in slightly accented Danish. "Welcome, welcome, welcome. I'm Gabriella Wolf, and it is a pleasure to meet you."

"The pleasure's mine, ma'am," he said. "Your husband has told me lots about you. Looking at you I can tell that most of it is true." Chops felt himself on stage again, and his mood changed from apprehension to playful banter as naturally as spring followed winter.

"*Ach Klaus. Du sagtest nicht, dass er ein Schmierer ist,*" she called to her husband, and Chops did not know enough German to know whether to translate *Schmierer* as charmer or con man. "Pardon me, Chops," she continued in Danish. "I sometimes forget how rude it is to speak German in front of guests. Please forgive me. Can I take your coat?"

"Please. But before I forget, this is a little something I picked up on the way over." He casually handed Frau Wolf the bottle Louisa had given him, and he wondered if Herr Wolf had told his wife that he had asked him to bring some booze. He slipped out of his overcoat.

"You shouldn't have gone to so much trouble," she said, glancing over the label and folding the coat over his arm.

"Chops, it's good to see you." Herr Wolf smiled and extended his hand, looking more elegant than elderly in his accented Italian smoking jacket and thin maroon tie. His slightly graying hair was short and combed back, and the warm light in the hall made him look healthier than at the studio. "I trust you didn't have any trouble finding my home."

"None at all. I understand why you enjoy living out here. It's really beautiful."

Herr Wolf laughed softly. "You'd be bored to death here. A young man like yourself needs to be in the heart of things, where the action is."

"Well...sometimes I get..."

"Look, Klaus," Frau Wolf said, squeezing her husband's arm and holding Louisa's bottle of port up like a trophy.

"What have we here?" He took the bottle and held it up to the light. Then he brought it closer, inspecting both the label and the wax top. He mumbled something and held it up to the light again. "My, my, my. Hans, come and meet the best cornet player in Denmark."

The couple by the fireplace turned and walked across the room towards them, the woman in front and the roundish man waddling just behind her. He wore round glasses and was completely bald except for tufts of curly white hair above his ears.

"Chops," Wolf said. "This is Hans Schadling and his lovely wife Anna."

"Frau Schadling," Chops said, taking her hand.

"It's a pleasure to meet you."

She returned his smile, and Chops liked her immediately. "You should call me Anna."

He nodded, and then extended his hand to Herr Schadling. "How do you do?"

"Very well, thank you." He rose up on his toes slightly and sank again, making the six medals over his left jacket pocket jingle together. "Klaus is showing us a good time here in Copenhagen. This is my first trip to Denmark since I was a child. Everything is smaller than I remember it. Quaint instead of imposing."

"Memories are like that," Gabrielle Wolf answered, and then she chuckled nervously.

"Hans, look at this," Herr Wolf said, thrusting the wine in front of his guest.

"Hmm." He squinted at the label for a moment and then he cast a sideways glance at Chops.

"That's right," Wolf said.

"Eighteen ninety?"

"Eighteen ninety."

Chops glanced back and forth at the two men, not knowing whether they were impressed or insulted. He should have known better than to bring a fifty-year-old bottle of wine to a dinner party. Louisa must have given it to him because she knew it had turned to vinegar decades ago.

"Where in heaven's name did you get this?" Schadling asked in a tone of bewilderment.

"I stole it from King Christian's private cellar."

He laughed and patted Herr Wolf on the shoulder. "Musically gifted and a patriot as well." He continued to laugh for a minute, and Chops allowed himself a small chuckle, more at the round man's appearance than anything else.

"Hans," Frau Schadling said to her husband. "Could you please tell us what all the commotion is about?"

"I'm afraid Chops is to blame. He brought a very fine bottle of wine. A port, actually, and a good vintage at that. Vintage eighteen ninety Sandeman. The early part of the growing season in Portugal that year was unusually warm, bringing the fruit..."

"Red or White?"

"Well...you see it's not...exactly..."

"Red," Chops stated, amused by her lack of pretense, and by her husband's inability to give her a straight answer. "It's red," he repeated, this time looking at Herr Wolf.

"I love red wine." She looked at Chops with an earnest eye. "I thought Americans only drank whiskey."

"Good whiskey is hard to find."

"I drank whiskey a few years ago," she continued. "The first glass was difficult to get down, but after that it got easier. A friend of Hans' brought it back from a trip to New York. I've never been to America myself, but I understand it can be rather decadent."

"Have you ever walked along pier nineteen after dark?" Chops asked with a sly smile. He had heard all of the stereotypes of America—cowboys, Jews, gangsters—and occasionally he corrected them, but he knew that tonight everyone was playing a game where you lost points by contradicting and forfeited by being silent.

Herr Wolf stepped back and turned to Frau Schadling. "This talk of foreign cocktails is making me thirsty. Can I offer you something to drink? Beer or perhaps something stronger. Gin?"

"Gin, please," she said.

"A beer for me," Chops said, reminding himself to go light on the alcohol. He would have preferred a double shot to loosen up, but he had to stay alert.

"They will be right out. If you'll excuse me, I'll go to the kitchen and make sure this port is properly decanted before we sit down to dinner." Wolf turned and walked out of the room.

As if on cue, his wife entered the spot in the small circle that he had left vacant. She wore an apron over her evening dress and smelled of expensive perfume. No flour in her hair, no smears on the apron. Chops doubted that she had actually done any of the kitchen preparation. No more than oversee the army of servants, goose-stepping right off stage. "Dinner will be along in a few minutes."

"Splendid. I'm famished."

"Do you cook for yourself, Chops?"

"Sometimes. Mostly when I want to eat something that people around here don't eat. Usually I just eat out."

"What kinds of exotic things do you cook?" Anna Schadling asked. Chops noticed that she had a penetrating look when she asked a question, which she then demurely deflected as he began to answer. It gave him the feeling of talking to an adolescent who wasn't quite sure where she stood.

"Nothing fancy. Sometimes I get a craving for jambalaya or cornbread, and I'll make some. It's not the best in the world, but it seems to hit the spot just the same. It doesn't happen much, maybe two or three times a year. Most of the time I'm over a stove I'm warming a can of soup."

"I'm sure Chops has a beautiful lady-friend who keeps him well-nourished." Frau Wolf said.

"They come and they go," he said, wanting to slap his hostess and fighting to keep the smile on his face. His cheeks were beginning to feel like premolded putty that was melting under a heat lamp.

"Of course he has lots of elegant ladies chasing him around. Klaus tells us that you are the star attraction at Danish National Radio," Frau Schadling said, gracefully changing the subject.

"I'm hardly the star attraction of the radio, Anna," he said, testing out her first name. It felt good rolling off his tongue. "My band has a weekly spot on Thursday nights, but I couldn't swear that anybody listens to it."

"Ha," Herr Wolf called, returning with a tray full of drinks. "It's the most popular show on the air. I'll bet seventy percent of the young men in the city listen to it religiously. Military and civilian alike. Even though your music is a little unorthodox, I fight like hell to keep it on the air because it takes everyone's mind off the war."

Chops knew that meant his show kept people from listening to the weekly BBC news broadcast, but he did not say anything. He wanted to keep the conversation from going political.

"That's almost like trying to keep bears away from honey," Anna Schadling said.

"Am I hearing a touch of French in your accent?"

Her laughter died quickly, and she looked at the ground. She swallowed and shook her head. "Why do you ask?"

"Because you definitely have an accent. It's very subtle, but it comes out in your 'R's.' It's not the buried German 'R.' It's French, isn't it?"

She moved her shoulders back almost imperceptibly and raised her chin. "You are very perceptive."

Chops countered her cold tone with a big smile. He had found out something that he should not have, and he had given away nothing in the process. It was a minor achievement, but it made him more comfortable. "You should not be surprised. I make my living with my ear."

"So you do. My accent never comes out when I

speak German, but I guess it slips a little in Danish."

"Were you born in France?"

"Marseilles. But Papa was a German, and he brought me to Berlin when I was still in grammar school. If you want to know the truth, I went by Anias until I moved, but Papa wanted me to change it. He said it was best for a child to blend in."

"Don't lose your Frenchness. Nous disons que la France c'est magnifique, n'est-ce pas?" He had hoped that a few words in her native tongue would warm her up, but instead, the entire room fell silent. Embarrassed eyes shifted from host to guest to carpet and back. Chops pretended that he had not noticed his own faux pas. He had wanted Anna to comment on his French so he could have told her about growing up in New Orleans' French Quarter, but he had forgotten that warfare breeds strange etiquette. In this house, French was the language of decadent has-beens.

Chops always teased Svenya when she said the wrong thing in the wrong place, and she would not have let him forget that remark. No, she would have reminded him of it for weeks. Instead of her playful digging, he felt only awkward silence, and he could not think of any way to start the conversation rolling again.

"How long have you lived in Denmark, Chops?" Anna finally said.

"About eight years ago I came with a big band and just wound up staying. You know how those things are." For some reason he did not want to go into detail about quitting the Guy Sherman band and finding himself stranded in Copenhagen.

"Do you live downtown?"

"No. I live on Christianshavn in the old warehouse district. It's more exciting and less expensive than the center of town."

"It's also more dangerous," Wolf said. "That cut on your head looks like more than a little scratch. Has a doctor looked at it?"

"Well...no. It's really nothing serious. Nothing compared to..." He mumbled, hoping to change the direction of the conversation, but Anna Schadling persisted.

"I wouldn't have noticed, but now that you mention it, it looks painful. What happened?"

"Just an accident," he said, and then realized he sounded like he was dodging the question. He had to offer a better explanation. "A sour piece of luck, you know. Day before yesterday I slid down to the waterfront, just to get some fresh air. And there I was..."

"Go on and say it, Chops. It's nothing to be ashamed of. You were mugged. It could happen to anyone."

"Mugged?" she gasped.

"That's right." Of course Wolf would connect the assault to the scrape on his forehead. Chops put his hand in his rear beltloop and slid into his storytelling mode. "It's not that the neighborhood's so bad, but I was out late, walking home after a few drinks, and I wasn't paying much attention. Some punks jumped me from behind." He sighed. All eyes were fixed to him—his previous transgression forgotten—and he let the suspense build for an instant, like pausing one blink before a kiss. "He wasn't big but he was scrappy, and he had me sort of pinned beneath my bicycle. If he'd pulled out the knife then it would have been over."

"But he didn't."

"Not before I popped him twice in the nose and threw him off of me, but when I took to my feet he knew I meant business..." He raised two fists to his chest. "That's when he opened the springer."

"Springer?"

"Spring knife. You know, a switchblade."

"Chops, you did not tell me he had a knife," Wolf said in a airy tone.

"I would have if he'd cut me." Chops could feel the train veering off course, heading off into fiction, but everyone was buckled in for the ride, and he was conducting. "When he lunged at me I had to think quick. I'm a big believer in the 'live by the sword, die by the sword' business in the New Testament, but I wasn't in any position to be teaching lessons."

"So what did you do?"

He shrugged. "I knocked it out of his hand before he could cut me. He must not have had a good grip, because the knife flew ten feet or so."

"Then?"

"Well, I certainly wasn't going to let him have a second shot at me. My luck could have run out any second. I ran over and grabbed the knife."

"And what did he do?"

Chops tossed up his hands. "That sly son of a..." He caught himself. "Son of a gun hopped on my bike and rode off. I couldn't believe it."

"So you lost your bicycle?" Herr Schadling had now joined the circle.

"Worse than that, I'm afraid." He relaxed his posture, dropped his eyes just a touch and softened his voice. "I had strapped my cornet on to the back of my cycle, so I lost that as well. That boy got a fine horn."

Wolf laughed, somewhat spoiling the effect that Chops had in mind. "Don't be so morose about the whole thing. You had that cornet for years and it's time you had a change. Look here." He marched across the room and opened the closet. Reaching inside, he pulled out an unscratched leather case.

He shoved it into Chop's arms. "I phoned Gerreth Schnur at the police department, and he said your horn had probably been melted as scrap by now, but he had confiscated some musical instruments in some police action or other. I didn't listen for details, but he said I could come down and have a look. This is what I came back with."

Chops stared at the case for a moment and then looked up at his host, not knowing what to do. Part of him wanted to throw the latch and see what was inside, but part of him wanted to read the fine print on the contract before he opened the case. It was hard to believe that a trumpet was just sitting down at police headquarters waiting for him.

"Well, open it up," Wolf said.

Chops stepped back and sat on the armrest of the sofa. He slid his thumbs outward, so the two latches sprung simultaneously. Cautiously, he lifted the lid and saw the silver Bach cornet, complete with three mouth pieces and a cup mute, lying in a bed of black velvet. It bore a few visible dents, but the pearl caps on the valves reassured him he was looking at a fine instrument. He grabbed the horn with his left hand and raised it, gauging the weight, learning the balance. A moment passed and then he lowered his fingers on the valves and lowered each one three times. Good. Just the right amount of spring in the action. Then, to prove to himself what he already knew, he fingered his way up three octaves of a B-Flat scale and down the related pentatonic. The shafts moved like pistons. It occurred to him that the valves must have been oiled that day by someone who knew their stuff, but the thought evaporated as he reached for a mouthpiece. As he pulled it out of its sheath, he remembered where he was.

He looked at his host and nodded. "It's a gracious ax."

"Looks nice, doesn't it?"

"Yeah," he said slowly. "It sure does. When does it have to go back to the police station?"

Herr Wolf shrugged. "I've had it for about three hours and that's long enough for me. You can keep it for as long as you want."

"You're giving this to me?"

"Call it an indefinite loan. Technically. I hope you will accept it as a gift?"

Chops smiled and nodded. "With pleasure. Thanks."

Herr Schadling clapped his hand. "Play something for us. Let's hear the maestro."

Chops shook his head. "The neighbors might get upset."

"I don't care if they do. Go ahead."

"What do you like?"

"Brahms," Frau Wolf said.

"Leroy Brahms and the Cookin' Five?" Chops said knowing full well she meant Johannes. "I jammed with those boys once in Storyville, but I didn't know anybody outside Louisiana had ever heard about them. What was that tune they used to do? The Backwards...nah...The Backside... No. It was the 'Backache Stomp.'" He tore into the old standard, and from the look in Anna Schadling's eyes he could tell he'd surprised her. Good. He pulled back, because the cornet's tone was richer than he'd expected, then for good measure he shot up to a high E. It sounded like a crystal bell.

Chops took a breath and smiled. "It's nice," he said, putting it back into the case. He slid the mouthpiece into its place and lowered the lid, clicking the latches back into place.

"You're very good," Anna Schadling said.

"Thank you."

The maid came and whispered into Frau Wolf's

ear. "Excellent," Frau Wolf replied. "Dinner is served. Can I show everyone to the dining room?"

"Lead on," Schadling said in a ballooning voice that reminded Chops of American parodies of British colonialists. They did not walk back through the entrance hall, but rather through a twin set of doors on the other side of the room that led through the music room and into the dining room. Inside the music room, Chops immediately noticed a baby grand piano, with the top up and a half-full glass of water on the ledge—not the kind of thing that these maids would leave standing for more than a few hours. Unfortunately, his eyes weren't good enough to read the titles of the music on the stand. What did they play in this house? Frau Wolf obviously liked Brahms. And the husband would prefer Mozart, although he would seldom have time to practice.

He noticed the plush carpet and the expansive curtains. No doubt this material was put there to enhance the acoustics—a very expensive way to do it. He remembered collecting egg cartons to line his bedroom walls when he was in high school. His father though he was crazy, but nothing absorbed the sound better or cost less.

No gramophone in the room.

From the music room, they entered straight into the dining room where the table was set and the first course—a creamy soup—sat waiting for them. Although Wolf had promised a casual affair, the room bore every sign of a seasonal event. The blue and white china sat atop a white tablecloth, and candles burned in silver candlesticks. The bowl of winter flowers in the middle of the table lent the whole room an air of relaxed elegance.

"Chops," Frau Wolf said, putting her hand on his elbow. "Why don't you sit next to me. And then

Hans, you can sit...hmm...there with Anna on your left. Klaus, that will put you at the far end." She gave the impression that she was calculating the proper seating arrangement on the spot, yet Chops knew that this had been pre-planned, planned, and rehearsed.

"Frau Wolf," Chops said. "Do you mind if I sit with you on my right? I'm hard of hearing in my left ear, and that might make things easier." He had exceptional hearing in both ears, but he considered her act a little affected, and he wanted to shake it up.

"Of course I don't mind." Her voice shook with embarrassment, feigned or not Chops could not tell. "How rude of me not to ask."

"How were you to know?" he said as he pulled her chair back for her.

Chops sat down and paid careful attention to his hostess, not picking up his spoon before she did and crumbling his crackers in the soup instead of buttering them and eating them whole. An army of servants cleared the dishes and brought out a beautifully arranged, although small, salad with broad spinach leaves and crab meat. When they emptied the first carafe of wine, a butler appeared with a second without being asked, and Chops wondered why Wolf had asked him to bring some booze. Obviously he could get anything he wanted, so perhaps he really just didn't have a chance to pick something up, or maybe it was some sort of test. As the entree arrived, he began to feel that his guardedness was unnecessary. No one seemed to be watching what they were saying, and he never felt pumped for information or compromised in any way.

Sometime halfway through the main course, he stopped eating with his knife in right and his fork in the left, and switched back to the way he had learned to eat as a child. The American way. He noticed that he had changed, but did not know when. Since no one had mentioned it, he continued in the way he was more comfortable.

"Tell me, Chops," Schadling said after finishing his third glass of wine. "Is there any hope for European jazz?"

He shrugged. "It's a difficult question."

"Some people say you've got to be colored to play good jazz," Frau Wolf said.

"What about Jean Omer, Django Reinhardt, or even Bennie Goodman? Those guys sell the records and play the big concerts. Everyone I knew in New Orleans was trying to play like them. Imitating the white cats who made it big."

Herr Wolf dabbed the corners of his mouth with his napkin. "You're right, Chops. If jazz in Europe dies young, it will be because of our politics, not our racial purity."

He continued. "I have a lot of good things to say about the New Order in Europe. We need to protect ourselves from the Bolsheviks, and it's about time we did something about the disgrace of Versailles. Look at how fast our population is growing. Hitler is politically astute; he knows what we need and how to motivate the people, but he should keep his fingers out of popular culture."

"Hear, hear."

"If he wants to support classical, Germanic art, that is his business. Build all the museums he wants. That's what I say. But to outlaw modern art and music...that's when he should have his wings clipped."

Chops had never seen Wolf display such emotion. For a moment he though his host would throw down his napkin and storm out of the room, but he did not. Instead, he eased himself back in his chair and lit a cigarette. "I'm just glad we're not in Berlin anymore to watch it."

"Ach, Klaus," Schadling said. "You're better off here. It's less hectic. You don't have parades every other day. You don't have to ask the culture ministry before you can go the bathroom."

"That's right. Here I'm my own boss."

"No," Chops said. "You're my boss." And everyone laughed.

Schadling crossed his knife and fork across the plate. "You have other work besides at the station, don't you? Teach at the University, I thought Klaus was saying."

"The University isn't offering classes in modern music this semester," Chops said as a polite way of saying that he had been all but thrown out of the department after the invasion. "But I still have a few private students, and occasionally I earn some extra money playing."

"Where do you play?"

Chops throat seemed to close up, and only with considerable effort could he swallow the crust of bread that he had just put into his mouth. Where did he play? Jazz had generally been banned from public consumption, so much so that a barkeeper like Tapio could go to jail for allowing a band to play American jazz in his pub. What had he been thinking? He took a sip of water. "We just play around town every now and then."

"Terrific. When is your next show?"

Chops noticed all of the eyes on him, waiting. "I really don't have anything on the books. Things just come up, you know. A friend of mine will get married and throw a party, or the guys just decide it's time to play. That's the problem with most jazz players. We can't plan in advance. Herr Wolf, haven't you had problems with live acts at the station before, not showing up and what have you?" Chops hoped that Wolf would go off on some tangent about a particularly colorful band from years past, but Frau Schadling did not relent.

"We'd really like to see you play sometime. Wouldn't we, darling?"

"Oh yes."

"Well, maybe something will fall into place," Chops said with a smile.

Herr Wolf stood up and filled all the empty glasses with wine, and Chops felt he frowned when he saw his glass was still half-filled. The German topped it off anyway. "What Chops is so politely trying to say, is that you are not welcomed in the places he usually plays. Isn't that right, Chops? You don't have to be so shy around here."

"It might be difficult," Chops conceded.

A big smile crept across Herr Schadling's face. He used the over-energetic tone found employed by the last person to solve the puzzle or understand a joke. "You play in underground clubs."

Chops realized he was in dangerous territory, but he did not know what to say. How would Olsen react? "Not exactly. I just mainly play at private functions."

"It all sounds the same to me. Anna, isn't this fascinating? Do you know people who sit around and plan to overthrow the regime and such? It sounds terribly dangerous."

Chops formed a gun with his finger and pointed it at Schadling. "We don't just plan. Bang." He fired his imaginary weapon.

Frau Schadling began to clap. "Touché, Chops. Touché. But you must forgive my husband. In Germany we hear exaggerated stories of people trying this or that, going to prison and such. They really capture the imagination. Still, it is a shame that we can't hear you play on that beautiful new horn."

"Do you have plans for Thursday?" Wolf asked.

"No, why?"

"Chops and his band play at the station every Thursday night. I'm sure it would not be a problem for you to sit back in the studio with me and watch them play. Chops, do you see any problem with that?"

"Of course I'll have to ask the boys," he replied. "But I don't think there will be a problem." The Backbeats would not object nearly as violently as he wanted to. Two extra pair of ears in the sound room would not make the task of broadcasting Olsen's code any easier.

"Well, that was easy enough." Herr Wolf picked up the silver bell in front of his plate and jingled it lightly. Seconds later, the maid appeared and curtsied beside him.

"Yes, sir?"

"Is the port properly decanted?"

"Yes, sir."

"We shall have it in the sitting room, please."

"Right away."

Herr Wolf stood up and helped Anna Schadling out of her chair. Light conversation continued as the group moved through the wooden doorway, across the music room, and into the living room where they had their first cocktail. The stuffed goose in his stomach slowed him down considerably, and he would have felt more comfortable if he could have loosened his belt one notch, for he had eaten several servings. He wanted coffee, not port.

He sat down next to Herr Schadling on the ivory-colored linen couch and crossed his legs. For some reason the room seemed much smaller and more intimate than when he had walked in a few hours before. Perhaps the lights had been turned down.

"Here you are," Herr Wolf said, passing out small port glasses. "Let me propose a toast. To peace and prosperity." Everyone agreed and clinked their glasses.

The port tasted warm and syrupy in Chops' mouth, and he held it there a moment before swallowing.

"It's a fine wine, Chops," Herr Wolf said, setting the glass down on the end table. "You really outdid yourself on this one. It has tremendous character. Something you'd never find in a younger wine." He pulled a cigarette out of a thin case, lit it, and flicked the match in the brass ashtray. "What do you think, Hans?"

Herr Schadling concentrated intently on the wine swirling in his glass before he took another sip. "Very elegant. It's funny, I think of drinking port after dinner as a very European thing to do. I'm surprised that you—as an American—thought to bring a bottle. If you had brought cut flowers or an elaborate cheese ball, that would have seemed more...Yankish."

The smoke from Wolf's cigarette enticed Chops, and he reached into his coat pocket for his pack, only to find it empty. He'd smoked his last one waiting for the tram in the main square. He'd thought about buying another pack, but the tram arrived and he did not have time. Damn it. Now Anna was lighting hers, and Chops knew that there was no better way to relax after such a feast as to smoke a cigarette. He leaned forward. "Herr Wolf, can I try one of your smokes? I seem to be fresh out."

Wolf and Schadling exchanged a quick glance, and Chops knew he had made some sort of mistake. But it was just a cigarette. "Of course, Chops. Help yourself."

He took the cigarette Wolf offered and lit it with his Zippo. "Thanks." It tasted just right. He savored the feeling, the slight hum behind his ears that accompanied good, strong tobacco. What had Schadling been saying? Something about him acting European. "Herr Schadling, you must remember that I've been in Denmark over eight years. Almost a quarter of my life. You shouldn't be surprised that something has rubbed off."

"I guess my interest is how much," he said, sitting forward on the straight wooden chair. "Do you still think of yourself as an American?"

Chops took another drag of his cigarette and shrugged. This sort of conversation inevitably arose in one form or another when he spoke with people he had not known long.

"What he means is, where do you stand politically?"

Chops took a sip from his glass, trying to think of a way to phrase his answer without sounding like he was skirting the issue. "I try to stay out of politics. They happen above me, somewhere on this plane where I never go and where I'm not welcome. I'm in favor of any government that keeps the streets clean and that lets bars stay open all night. That's all there is to it."

"When you hear that Rommel outmaneuvered Montgomery, don't you feel a little anger?"

Hadn't Louisa said something this morning about the British pushing Rommel out of Egypt? As far as Chops could tell, no one knew for sure how the war was going. He said, "More than a little, but not because one side came out above the other. I get mad because I have to hear about it all the time. It's everywhere, and nobody says the same thing. The radio. The news clips. Posters. Bulletins. You can't escape it, and you can't believe it either. It wears you down." Chops did not know how much of this was true and how much he said because it was a good dodge. It all sounded true.

"Aren't you interested in the news?"

"No. Why should I care? It's not my war."

"That's hard to believe," Schadling said, raising his voice just a touch.

"Hans," Anna gasped.

"Well it is."

"Don't be surprised," Chops said to Anna. "Everyone thinks 'us versus them,' except me, and I think 'them versus them.'"

"It can be dangerous to be unallied," Wolf added. "You might find yourself being everybody's enemy."

"I try to stay out of sight."

"That's hard to do when you can't blend into a crowd. Everyone at the station knows you. Everyone at headquarters knows you too, and frankly, many would rather see you sitting behind bars than playing dance music in a bar."

"I've made it this far."

"Times are changing, Chops. Changing fast. The war has gone on too long, and high command is getting nervous. A year ago our agreement with the Danish government was more or less 'don't cause trouble, and we'll leave you alone.' But the days of tolerance are over. It really is just like you said. Everyone thinks in terms of 'us versus them,' and you would be much safer if more people thought of you as 'us.' You might think about some gesture that would align you closer with the regime. I would suggest joining the Nazi Party of Denmark, but that is of course impossible."

"No one wants darkies carrying their flag, right?"

"You don't mince words, do you? The party

would never accept anyone of African decent, just like they won't accept Jews or gypsies. But I had an idea when I went to the police station to collect your horn."

Chops told himself to calm down. "Yes?"

"Everyone knows about the crime on the waterfront. Narcotics. Prostitution. Smuggling. Most people turn their backs on these petty annoyances, don't they?"

"That's because most people want to stay alive."

"Don't exaggerate, Chops. And don't talk rubbish about honor among thieves. No one believes that nonsense now and they never did. If you, as a good and upstanding citizen, discreetely reported some minor offense, your safety could be assured. It wouldn't have to be major. Anything more than purse snatching would do, although some political misconduct would be best. Perhaps something as simple as a rebellious teenager painting graffiti under a bridge."

"You want me to inform for you."

"Your self-righteousness doesn't impress me, Chops. You said yourself that you did not play on either team. That you look out for yourself. Between friends, I'm telling you how to do it. I've gone out on a mighty thin limb keeping you and your band on the air, and I'm glad to do it. You are a good musician, a good man in an unfortunate situation, but the time has come for you to act. The umbrella you're hiding under is beginning to leak, and if you don't do something, you will get soaked."

Chops did not respond, but he wondered what Olsen would have said.

Wolf reverted to his friendly tone. "I don't want to compromise you, Chops, but these are dangerous times. I certainly don't want to see you arrested with your friends. And if you help yourself, you might be able to help them as well."

Chops nodded his head slowly. "It's something to think about." Now that the contract was in the open, he wanted to exit the house immediately, but that would be admitting that he came only to deal. "Tell me, Hans. Do people make such a big deal about political appearances in Berlin, or is this native to Copenhagen?"

"Ha. This is a puppet theater compared to the extravagant political productions in Germany. Everyone growing mustaches like the Fuhrer and walking without bending their knees. Absolutely absurd."

"It's quite different in the country, though," Anna added. "I went to visit my mother in Edlestadt two months ago and everything was the same as always. The Boys' Club changed their name to the Hitler Youth, but they still play the same games and sing the same songs. I saw an occasional swastika, but farmers never liked flags much anyway."

"Yes," Frau Wolf said. "This political ra-ra seems peculiar to the city. Everything is so much simpler in the country, isn't it? I think everyone in the city should be forced to spent two weeks in the country every year. Just think of it."

Chops saw the conversation stretching toward absurdity—a sign that the evening had lasted too long. No one had anything left to say, but when faced with the possibility of silence they just started blabbering. Thank God no one was really drunk. He reached into his vest pocket and pulled out his watch by the chain. "Herr Wolf. Frau Wolf. Thanks for a wonderful evening. One day we'll drink and chew the fat until dawn, but not tonight. The last tram will be here soon, and I'd best be on it."

"Don't be silly, Chops. Stay and talk and we'll drive you into town."

"No thanks. Save your petrol," he said, and wondered whether the Germans subjected themselves to rationing or if that was a plight of being Danish. "Besides, I'll sleep better if I get a little fresh air after a big dinner like this."

"No use waking up with a swollen head, is there?" Wolf said as he stood. "Let me get your coat and show you to the door."

"Thanks." He reached down and grabbed the trumpet and followed Wolf out of the room. "It was very kind of you to invite me for dinner. I haven't eaten like that in quite a while."

"You made the evening, Chops. Hans and Anna liked you, and I'm sorry if Hans was a little abrasive. He gets that way."

"Anna more than makes up for it."

Chops slipped on his overcoat and Wolf opened the door. The German looked over his shoulder, as if to make certain that the two of them were alone. He reached inside his jacket, produced a small envelope, and handed it to his guest. "Thanks again for finding that bottle of wine. I think this should about cover it."

"That's not necessary," he said out of politeness, and, as he suspected, Wolf cut him off immediately.

"I want you to have it. Now go on and catch the tram. I'll see you on Thursday, if not before."

"Goodnight," Chops said, and he walked out into the crisp night air.

Chapter Thirteen

Chops descended the cold, mossy steps, and he paused when he came to Smukke's door. Usually, one scurried down the steps as quickly as possible and rapped hurriedly on the door to make sure no one saw you enter the unlicensed club, but right now he did not respect the habit of caution. The tension from Herr Wolf's dinner party had dissolved, and now he was on familiar ground, like a hunted hare that escaped to the safety of his burrow.

Through the sturdy oak door he could barely hear the hum of voices inside the bar, and he listened closely for strains of music. Last night the Backbeats had played without him, and he figured they would do the same tonight. On his way downtown he had imagined walking into the crowded room, crossing the floor, and stepping straight onto stage with his new cornet. He occasionally daydreamed about dramatic entrances, about stunning the crowd with a surprised appearance, which he knew was every musician's fantasy.

He continued to listen, but he heard no music. Perhaps the band was just coming back from a break. Last night he had encouraged the Backbeats to play without him, and they had performed well—a little disorganized perhaps, but their sound was good. He figured they would do the same tonight, but apparently he was wrong.

Chops' new cornet felt heavy in his hand. He had carried it from the tram stop at the main square. His palm was sweaty, and he was ready to play. With his free hand, he knocked on the oak door. Over the past few months, the code at become automatic. Three soft knocks and one hard one. Morse code for V.

Chops became slightly impatient as he waited and watched the mist come out of his nose. He looked around and saw no one on the street above him. The noise from behind the door stayed thin and constant. Had they heard him? Perhaps Tapio was filling glasses from the tap. It would take him a minute to get to the door. But Chops wanted to be inside. He wanted to submerge himself in the air of rebellion. Dining at Herr Wolf's felt like eating in a laboratory, or playing a chess tournament. Everything was clean, polished, and inspected, and every move he made was judged, scrutinized, and reacted to. Still no response from his knock. He beat the code again, this time harder. Surely someone heard him that time.

The square peep hole in the door opened, and he saw Tapio looking through. "V is for Victory," Chops said. The password was mandatory, even for Tapio's friends. It said, "I haven't been followed." It said, "Everything is OK," although it never was. Safety was relative during the occupation.

The heavy door swung open, and Chops whisked inside. He glanced around, disappointed by how few people had come. It was surprising how small the club looked when it was empty. On crowded nights you couldn't see the walls of Smukke because of the bodies, or the ceiling because of the smoke, so you had the feeling of being in an immense hall. Tonight, less than two dozen people sat scattered at tables and their flashy dress seemed out of place. Chops focused on a tall man at a table wearing a smoking jacket and a scarlet beret. The woman he was with looked more interested in her cigarette holder than the conversation, and she kept tapping the toe of her high-heeled shoe on the chair leg. She wanted to dance.

Tapio's dark eyes looked more sunken than usual, and his smile seemed wan. The silk rose on his white lapel drooped, and his sleeve was smeared with ash. His thin, black tie listed to the right. He patted Chops on the shoulder. "Glad you made it."

"Better late than never."

"You haven't missed much," he said while shutting the door. The deadbolt fell into place with a click. "Holger beat Georg Ebbesen in an arm wrestling contest, but that's been it for excitement. Maybe things will pick up with you here."

Chops shrugged. "Nothing ever happens in this town on a Sunday night. Most people have to be at work early tomorrow. I'm surprised there's anyone here at all."

"I've thought about not opening at all on weeknights," Tapio said. "But there's not much use in keeping the doors closed. I'd be down here anyway, you know?"

"Me too, so let's not worry about it." He held up the new horn nonchalantly, maintaining the air of a cool-headed musician. "Look at this."

"You got a new horn. Where did it come from?"

"Someone owed me a favor, Tapio," he said with a wink.

"Payback is hell," the bartender said, and Chops did not know what he meant.

"Any of the boys here?" he asked, scanning

the room. "They sounded pretty good last night. I figured they'd be playing again."

Tapio shrugged. "Everyone's here, but they said they didn't want to play. Not even one set. Sticks is at the bar, and he's been drinking pretty heavy."

"How bad?" he said, looking over to the bar, worried that the man would be too drunk to play. Sure enough, the thin drummer was nursing a tumbler of gin and tapping his coaster with his fingertips. He was slouching but still upright.

"I've seen him worse."

"Let's see if he can play," Chops said without smiling. On his way to the bar, he looked for the rest of the band. Christoph, the bass player, was talking to Grena as he sat on his piano bench near the stage, apparently arguing given their animated expressions. They argued a lot. He caught the piano player's eye, and opened his hand twice and then pointed behind the stage. Meet me in the dressing room in ten minutes. Grena nodded.

Chops approached the drummer, snatched the drink out of Sticks' hand, and downed the gin in one draught. All evening he had wanted to throw back some booze, and Wolf and his guests had been pushing it on him, but he reserved serious drinking for when he was around friends. "Pour me another," he called to Tapio, who had arrived at his post behind the counter. "But no more for you, my well-oiled friend," he said, draping his arm around the drummer's shoulder. "You far gone?"

Sticks sat up straight and smiled. His head rocked back and forth slightly, and Chops assumed he was trying to focus. "Chops, where'd you come from?"

"I've been on the outskirts of town. Do you feel like playing?"

"Of course," he slurred. "But I don't know if

anybody else does. Do you? Of course, you always feel like playing, except for last night when your horn was stolen. You can't play without a cornet."

Chops held the new case in the air so his friend could see it.

"You found it. Chops that's great. I was miffed when I heard you'd lost it. Who'd steal your horn, I want to know. Did you go to the police?"

"You must be drunk. Do you think the police would lift a finger to find a stolen cornet when it's practically against the law to play one?"

Tapio set the gin on the bar, lit two cigarettes, and handed one to Chops. He spoke with a sarcastic tone. "Good-sized crowd."

"Drinking much?"

"Hardly at all. A few people are putting back some drinks, but mostly everyone is just being polite."

"Cut this sailor off," Chops said, patting Sticks on the back.

"Why?" the drummer said, rearing up in protest.

"'Cause we're jamming in fifteen minutes. That is if you can sit behind your drum kit. And you better start drinking coffee quick. I don't want to play without drums." Chops noticed the marshaling tone in his voice, and he wished he did not have to use it. The only aspect of the band that he really enjoyed was playing and occasionally composing. He led the band because he had the most experience, but he hated managing and babysitting the musicians. "Tapio, make sure he has three cups before we go on stage, all right?"

"No coffee tonight, Chops. No tea either." The bartender used the tone reserved for belligerent drunks, and it surprised him.

"Are you running short of anything else? Maybe I can look around tomorrow, and..." He cut himself off, remembering his worry about finding a bottle of wine. He shouldn't promise things he couldn't be sure to deliver.

"We're short of everything. The Germans are tightening up around here. After Hans left the waterfront, everything dried up. I think he must have told the Krauts which captains haul the most cargo. Nothing's been getting in."

Chops thought for a moment about Louisa's report about Hans. How could he have missed such a major event on the piers? It had happened almost a week ago and today was the first he had heard about it. Maybe people had stopped telling him news, or maybe he just had other things on his mind. "I heard he moved to the country to get some peace and quiet."

"The jails are filling up quick. He did the right thing."

Chops mashed out his cigarette in an ashtray and looked at the tired barkeeper. "You're taking a bigger risk with Smukke than he was with his little black-market operation. Are you planning on moving to the country as well?"

Tapio shrugged. "The black market is a bigger concern to the Germans. It undermines their economic control. Smukke is just a bunch of people thumbing their noses at the war. They'll probably continue to ignore us, unless we start causing trouble, throwing rocks and that sort of thing."

"I hope you're right," Chops said with a thin smile. "This place isn't much, but I'd hate to lose her. In the meantime, I'm headed back to my room to warm up. Sticks, meet me back there in ten minutes." He climbed off the bar stool and made his way slowly to his dressing room with Tapio's words echoing in his head. "The jails are filling up quick." As he walked across the room, Chops counted the people he could turn in to Wolf in exchange for Svenya and make the jails fill up even quicker. Everyone was guilty of something. The Nazis made sure of it because it made people easier to manipulate. The guiltiest came to Smukke because it was safe, or that's what everyone believed, until the Nazis stormed the club last Wednesday and arrested Svenya. They must still think it's safe or else they would not have returned. Coming to a club like Smukke was practically a crime in itself. Chops could point his finger at anyone in the room and set Svenya free. At least that is what Wolf suggested. It would be so easy, and no one would ever know.

The thought tasted sour in Chops' mouth. Who was inside his head, suggesting he resort to betrayal? Politics aside, he hated the idea that other people were controlling his thoughts and even his actions. The people in Smukke were his friends, and they trusted him.

He imagined another raid on Smukke, and he could see clearly the look on people's faces as the soldiers dragged them out onto the street. That expression on Svenya's face had embossed itself on his mind. Bewilderment. Defiance. Fear. They should have arrested him. She never encoded messages to the Allies. She never smuggled maps of troop movements and forged documents through the waterfront. She never killed four German soldiers with one grenade in the middle of a snowy night in northern Denmark.

Chops felt a hand on his shoulder, and he turned with a start to find Louisa standing before him with an obligatory gin in one hand and a cigarette in the other. She wore a cream-colored, knee-length dress with a high neck and an imitation pearl choke collar, and she had an RAF bombers cap angled across her forehead. It was the kind of outfit Svenya loved to wear, more playful than sexy, but daring enough. She would have worn the hat back on her head, because of her height, and probably added pilots' wings as a broach, but nevertheless the similarity was striking. Tonight, Louisa must have taken extra care with her makeup. Her cheekbones looked more sculpted, and her eyes seemed deeper than usual. She smiled, staring Chops in the eyes, and she dragged on her cigarette luxuriously. Chops watched her, thinking she must be up to something, and he was curious. Relax, he told himself. It's just Louisa.

"I didn't think you were going to make it tonight."

He shrugged. "I wasn't sure I was going to make it."

"It's been a slow night. Not many people," she said, scanning the crowd, "and not much excitement. Take away the rebels, and all you have is a bunch of drunks."

Chops raised his glass and clinked it against hers. "We drunks make the best rebels."

"Cheers, I say." She took a small sip from her glass, and she smiled. "You going to play tonight?"

"The music is back," he said with a fifty-cent smile, as he raised his cornet. "In just a few minutes the Backbeats will take the stage, and we'll be dancing until the sun comes up."

"These aren't the dancers, Chops. These are the drunks and the dreamers."

Chops looked around. Most of the people in the club were in their early twenties or even younger. "Well maybe these people aren't dancers," he said. "But that isn't going to keep me from playing tonight."

"I never said it should."

"Sometimes I like playing for the sitting crowd. You don't have to stick with steady rhythms, and you don't have to play songs everyone has heard before. You can really get dirty."

"Don't talk like that,' she responded in a falsely low and airy tone. "You're giving me goose bumps just thinking about it."

"Wait 'till I do it," he said with a coy smile, letting his double entendre linger.

"I will," she replied, keeping her eyes steady like a statue. A moment passed and she seemed to relax her pose, leaning against the wall and stretching her shoulders. "What are you going to play tonight?"

"I have no idea. I mean, we haven't planned a set or anything, so we'll probably just do some standards with long interludes. Slow nights are good to stretch out your range and try something new. If we goof, there are only two dozen people in the joint to hear us."

"When is the last time you screwed up on stage, Chops?"

"Nineteen twenty-six," he said, and they both laughed, sarcastically at first and then more earnestly. Still chuckling, Chops leaned against the wall and pulled the pilot's cap down over Louisa's eyes so she looked like a child in her father's hat. He felt so light standing there in the back of Smukke, laughing at his silliness. The gin did not hurt one bit.

She flipped some ashes from the cigarette on the floor. "Another package came through the port this afternoon."

The news did not surprise Chops. Olsen usually received two packages from the British every week, and this one was overdue. He wondered if the men in the special operations executive knew that the Germans had intercepted the parachute drop. Probably not. Olsen would probably give him a message to that effect to encode in this week's broadcast. "Did you bring it with you?" he asked.

"To Smukke? I'm not that crazy. Come by Cafe Kakadu tomorrow and pick it up."

Chops shook his head. He did not like Louisa being involved with Olsen's network, especially since she knew nothing about it. He wanted to get the package out of her hands as soon as he could. "I'll walk you home after the show and pick it up then, unless you have other plans."

She smiled. "None to speak of, but you know how these things go."

He gave her the thumbs up sign. "Unless you get lucky I'll see you after the show.

"I'll meet you outside," she said. "Play well."

"OK." Chops watched her turn and walk back to the bar before he stepped back behind the stage and navigated the small corridor to his dressing room. The air inside smelled musty and stale, but at least it was cool, and he was alone. He tossed his hat on the hook, but it missed and fell to the floor. He left it where it landed. "Jesus," he said, as he plopped down in the chair and placed the brand-new cornet in front of him. The rest of the band would be there in a matter of moments, and he had some repair work to do. He opened the lid to the cornet case without ceremony, a mechanic and not an artist. At least the horn was in pretty good shape. It had a dent in the bell, which was mainly a cosmetic problem, but the crowd at Smukke cared more about looks than anything. Chops pulled open one of the drawers of the dressing table and shuffled through it until he found a small rubber mallet and a oilcloth. Most of his tools, including his soft-vice, were in his apartment, so he had to rest the instrument on his leg when he worked on it. He lay the horn across his lap and padded the bottom with the oilcloth. Holding the neck tight with his left hand, he tapped at the bell with the mallet, which produced no noticeable effect after several tries. Growing impatient, he pulled the hammer back and used his forearm as well as his wrist for momentum. The oilcloth muted the sound but did little to lessen the pain in his leg. It was worth it. He had reduced the dent to a slight wave in the metal, which hopefully no one would notice. To fully restore the shape of the bell would take several hours' work, and that could wait.

He folded the oilcloth and put it back in the drawer with the hammer. Then he stuck the mouthpiece in the instrument and brought it up to his lips. He pushed some warm air through it and jiggled the valves. Taking a deep breath, he blew a D-Flat, warm and low, crescendoed lightly and fade. The tone was good—rich and beveled, like the silver handle on the end of a gentleman's favorite walking cane. Chops closed his eyes and played the first twelve bars of *Pachabel's Canon*, slowly and precisely, polishing the notes and rolling them out of the instrument. Perhaps he was just imagining things, but this cornet seemed well-nourished, well-cared-for, cherished. It did not play like an instrument off the shelf or one that had been stored down at police headquarters.

The door opened and Grena stepped inside, followed by Sticks, Christoph, and finally Dragor. They formed a loose circle around the room, sitting on the table and leaning against the wall, not saying much. "You boys want to jam?" Chops asked, expecting a chorus of "Hell Yes" and "Damned Straight", but instead all he got was one "I guess so," from Grena.

"I thought we had the night off," Dragor said. He was leaning on the wall next to the door and shuffling his feet a little. The midnight-blue, double-breasted suit he wore made him look especially tall and thin, and his hair stuck up on top to add to the effect.

"Don't be a pill," Sticks said, and Dragor did not respond.

"New ax?" Grena asked after a brief lull.

Chops nodded and held up Wolf's cornet. "I just picked her up tonight, and I don't know about you guys, but I'm ready to blow the fool out of it. Remember, I didn't get to play last night like you did. You were playing hot while I was on the sideline watching the kittens walk by. Tonight we'll knock 'em dead."

"You gotta be kidding," Sticks said. He speech was not slurred, but he spoke loudly, and he spit more than usual. "We weren't hot last night. We sounded like dog biscuits when we got on the stage, almost an hour late, I might add, because we couldn't agree on what to play. We..."

"Only because you said we shouldn't play any Armstrong charts," Dragor interrupted.

"You wanted to play *Twelfth Street Rag* with no brass."

"I could have covered it with my pipe."

"You couldn't cover..."

"Enough," Chops yelled, and silence blanketed the room. "We'll play *Twelfth Street* tonight, right after we do *Come Back Sweet Papa*. I feel like that tonight."

"*Mood Indigo*?"

"Sure, why not?"

"Forget the flabby Ellington tunes," Dragor said. "You need a whole orchestra to play crap like *Mood Indigo*. Stick to basics." He jutted out his chin.

"Grena," Chops said, looking over to the piano player. "Do we need an orchestra to play Ellington?"

"I like his stuff. Nice progressions."

"Then let's play it." Chops saw Dragor sigh, and he wondered what had gotten into him. He usually loved to play big band stuff—especially Bennie Goodman—because they tended to have prominent woodwind runs. "What do you want to play, Dragor?"

"I don't care."

"How about *C Jam Blues*. That's about as raw as it gets."

"OK." His voice showed anything besides enthusiasm. He looked down and fiddled with the top keys on his clarinet, which clicked like falling dominos.

"Is that a set?" Sticks asked. "Four songs?"

"We can stretch out *C Jam* as long as we want, and we're getting a late start. Who knows how long Tapio will let us play. He shut you down early last night."

"Last week's surprise shook him up pretty bad," Christoph said. "I think he's still pretty nervous. He'll lose the most if the Gerries clamp down hard. He doesn't want to go to jail, and he doesn't want to close Smukke."

Chops nodded.

"So are we going to play or not?" Sticks asked.

"Let's go." He stood up and walked out of the door, and the rest of the band followed him. The corridor smelled musty, and as Chops walked through it, he could feel the excitement building in his chest; slower than on other nights, but he could still feel it. He played through all the chord changes in his head, although he had played them so many times before. Four breaks per verse on *Sweet Papa*. Minor six in the chorus of *Mood Indigo*. If you forgot that progression you sounded like a live goose tossed into the kettle. Concentration was the key. As long as you were thinking about what you were doing, you could play anything. But as soon as you started worrying about anything else, everything went to hell.

A hush came over the club as the Backbeats walked on stage, and then a few hands in the audience began to clap. From onstage, the crowd looked even smaller than it had when Chops had walked through it. Perhaps some people had left while the band was in the dressing room. Not likely. But he remembered that it was late, and most people had to be at work in the morning. Before he was released from the Conservatory, he had to lecture at eight fifteen on Monday mornings, which kept him from staying out late. These days, things were different.

Chops reached into his back pocket and pulled out a white handkerchief, which he draped over his right hand. He brought the new horn to his lips and, starting with a low C, he blew up and down the chromatic scale. Two octaves at first, and then three. Usually he went for the fourth—something that few players ever mastered—but tonight he decided against it. He hadn't played in several days, and his lips felt a little soft in the unfamiliar mouthpiece. Perhaps he'd go for the fourth octave late in the set.

He glanced at the band warming up behind him. Sticks was practicing seven-stroke rolls, hunched over the snare drum like a miser. On the last beat of every roll he would stomp the bass pedal, toss his head back slightly, and rest for one sixteenth note before moving into the next roll. On the other side of the stage, Grena flitted on his piano, seeming oblivious to his surroundings. Dragor held his clarinet by his side and spoke to Christoph, who played scales double-time as he

listened. What were they talking about right before a set? They should have been warming up
like the rest of the band.

Chops tapped Dragor on the shoulder. "You
guys ready to jam?"

"Anytime," Dragor said.

Chops moved to the toe of the stage, dropped
his left hand towards the ground, and started snapping off the tempo, humming *Come Back Sweet
Papa* to himself to make sure he didn't start the
band off too fast. He raised his horn to his lip and
snapped the four-beat with his free hand. He
pounced on the cornet solo, accenting each note
as a bright bell-tone, leaving no doubt that the
show had begun. An awkward silence followed
Chops' six-beat introduction. He stood under the
front light at the edge of the stage, alone with his
cornet, with no music behind him. The hole lasted
two and a half beats before everyone came in together at the beginning of the third measure. This
song always reminded Chops of jumping off a tall
rock into a river. You jump by yourself and you
are weightless and giddy until you hit the icy waters, and then you realize you took a big risk, and
if you don't make it up, there is no one to blame
but yourself. Suddenly, you break the surface,
breathe in warm air and sunshine, and the band
is playing behind you like there is no tomorrow.

Come Back Sweet Papa never was a hard song
to play, based on a simple melody and a straight
four-beat, but it had a lot of small solos and one
long piano break that Grena shined on. He stayed
simple, keeping the one five-chord progression
moving with his left hand and lightly peppering
the melody with right-hand trills. But for two measures somewhere in the middle he transposed into
the relative minor, banging out multiple flat five-

chords and arpeggiating drag sextuplets on the high end—just to show everyone that he could—before dropping back down the written score. It sounded to Chops like a middle-aged insurance salesman who passed a beautiful woman, grabbed her in his arms, and kissed her passionately on the lips. After this impromptu embrace, he tipped his hat and returned to his light-gray world of claims and premiums.

Throughout the last verse and the repeat chorus, Chops and Dragor played off of each other, but something seemed off. Dragor usually had more flare, and his runs were always subtly challenging, claiming he could play higher and faster, or sweeter and slower, but now he just answered Chops. Perhaps he just needed a while to warm up.

But he did not warm up. On *Mood Indigo* he played so softly that practically no one heard him. In a large band, that doesn't make so much difference if someone plays softly or not at all, but in a quintet like the Backbeats, a missing voice can show one hell of a hole. Dragor took some solos on *C Jam Blues*, but they sounded listless, so Chops took over most of them and tried to see how much sound he could squeeze out of his new cornet. It played even better than he expected, but the ultra-polished tone sounded slightly out of place with the group. The instrument belonged in a symphony, not in a jazz dive.

Halfway through *C Jam Blues* two couples in the back stood up and left the bar. The stage lights were too bright for Chops to see who they were, but he still had the feeling he had been snubbed by a close friend. Chops had planned on playing two sets, but he welcomed the end of the fourth song and did not mention playing any more. He simply stepped forward, bowed slightly, and listened to the audience clap politely. They did not call for an encore.

Louisa was sitting by herself at a table on the left side of the stage. When he caught her eye, she put her finger and thumb together in the OK sign. He wished it were Svenya there, waving her hand slowly and waiting to meet him outside the club, but by Lord he needed to talk to someone.

He turned to his band, and they looked tired as they packed their instruments and folded their music. No one said much. Chops set his cornet case on the piano after he packed it and asked the band to gather in close. Everyone shuffled together. "Let's take tomorrow off, guys. I think everyone needs a break. Plan on practicing for a couple of hours here on Tuesday. We can't go on the radio Thursday night sounding like this." He looked at each band member in succession, and he could tell by their beat puppy-eyes that they had heard him. Whatever was going on had no place on stage. "Let's pack it up, boys."

As they walked off the stage, Chops lagged back and pulled the clarinetist aside. "Are you OK?"

"Sure."

"Don't give me that nonsense. You played like a wind up toy. Mechanized. Do you even remember what we played? Sticks played better than you did and he was half drunk. What gives?" He flashed a glance over his shoulder and saw that the rest of the band had turned the corner.

Dragor turned and shoved Chops against the wall. "What gives? You tell me."

"What do you mean?"

"Where were you tonight?"

"Where was I?" Chops mocked. "I was right here, dead on, note for note. Where were you? You played the same sophomoric pentatonic run in three different solos. Once in *Sweet Papa* and twice in *C Jam*. Worse than that, you didn't even play it well. Sure you were on pitch and on time, but there was no bend, no cry. You sounded like you just didn't give a damn."

"That's not what I mean, Chops." His voice was stretched, almost a croak. He thudded his fist against the wall. "You showed up here at one o'clock. Where were you before that?"

"I was at Herr Wolf's, having dinner. He is entertaining some old friends from Germany. An old school friend and his wife who are on leave in Denmark. They are only going to be here for a while, and Wolf wanted to introduce them to some local color." Chops heard himself and realized he was talking too much. Simple questions deserve simple answers, unless you are guilty. "Since I'm the only local colored in the city, he invited me."

Dragor ignored the joke. "Where'd you get the horn?"

"He gave it to me."

"I'll see you later," Dragor said, and turned his back. He took two steps towards the main room of Smukke, and Chops felt like grabbing him by the collar and shaking some sense into him. *Why make a scene*, he asked himself. Everyone will feel better by Tuesday afternoon.

Chapter Fourteen

Copenhagen had always been known for her lights, the black iron street-lanterns on every corner, candles ablaze in church windows, and telltale red beacons above certain downtown doorways, but since the occupation, the night produced a different effect. The city blacked out for fear of air attack, which gave the town the feel of the middle ages. The darkness brought out a different side of Copenhagen, a quieter side, and sometimes, like tonight, it was a welcome change from the bustle of a twentieth century metropolis.

Chops had felt tired and irritated when he left Smukke, but walking through the lightless city with Louisa revived his spirits. They talked on safe topics, an old one-eyed sailor they knew who had died before the war, and the low quality of the gin at Smukke. They laughed a lot.

The air inside her apartment tasted musty when they walked in, but he suggested they hoist a window and let it ventilate for a few minutes. The old window stuck a little, and Chops tugged hard to get it to move, straining his side in the process. "Damn," he sighed.

"What?"

"My ribs are still killing me from where that

hood kicked me." He had started referring to the assailant as "that hood," although he had decided it might be more than a random assault. It did not really matter now that he had gotten a new horn from Wolf.

Louisa shook her head. "I'm still surprised that you got mugged in this neighborhood. The street you live on is lots worse than this one."

"I've never gotten into trouble on my street before," he said with a cynical air. "But maybe that's because the people there know me."

"Maybe so." She motioned to the sofa. "Why don't you sit down for a second? You don't have anywhere to go, do you?"

"Not really," he said, as he plopped down in the overstuffed seat. He had not planned on staying long, but she was right. There was no one calling him home.

"I'll be right back," she said.

She turned and walked into the hall, leaving him alone in the sitting room. It looked like she had cleaned up a little during the day. The newspapers were missing and a broom stood in the corner next to the trash can. Despite the makeover, her apartment still resembled a cluttered nest with too much furniture and too little room to breathe. At least some fresh air was sneaking in.

Louisa returned, carrying an unlabeled bottle and two squat glasses. "Want a slash?" she asked.

"What do you have?" Chops asked. Lord knows he deserved a drink after everything he'd been through tonight. Dinner at Herr Wolf's had frazzled his nerves, and the Backbeat's botched performance at Smukke did little to make him feel better. He felt like he had not relaxed in months.

"I put my hands on a liter of scotch this afternoon, and I guess this is a good time to drink it."

Scotch was almost impossible to get these days, but if she had some to share, he certainly wanted to be a part of it. It was late, and he found it curious that he was wide awake after such an eventful night, but he remembered that he had slept most of the day. These are the hours he had kept when he was younger, a hot cornet player in the States. There it was expected that the jazz musicians led their lives at a different tempo.

"Do you have a hundred Crown?" she asked as she sat beside him and placed the bottle on the table.

"Sounds like a lot to pay for a drink, even if it is Scotch."

"Not for the hooch, you peckerwood," she said, twisting the cap off the bottle. She reached into her pocket and pulled out a small, unmarked bundle, more of a thick envelope than a parcel. "For this. It's what you came for, isn't it?"

He snapped the envelope out of her hand and looked it over carefully. It had been sealed with lots of thin, brown tape, and he knew he couldn't open this one without Olsen noticing.

"You do have the money?" she said in a low voice.

"You know I always keep a spare hundred on me." He reached inside his breast pocket and pulled out a money clip. He freed a crisp one hundred Crown note and pressed it into her hand. "Can I have a receipt?"

She laughed and shoved the money into her pocket. A hundred Crown seemed a lot of money for passing an envelope, but that didn't count the risk she was taking. Anyone caught with material coming straight from the other side could count on standing on the wrong side of a firing squad. And Louisa didn't even know the risk she was taking. She probably thought the parcels contained forged ration cards that someone would sell on the black market. She poured two glasses of scotch. "You didn't tell me anything about your little party. What did the Gerries think about the wine?"

Chops put the envelope in his jacket pocket next to his money clip. "It went over well. In fact, Herr Wolf could not shut up about what a nice bottle it was. Something special about the growing season, he said."

"Herr Wolf? Isn't that the head of the radio station?"

Chops nodded. He had forgotten that he had not told Louisa anything about the dinner party. "A friend of his had come up from Berlin, and he invited me to come over and meet him. They talked a lot about old times and what they would change if they were in charge."

"This Herr Wolf sounds like a bore."

"Not really. At least he doesn't regurgitate the party line, the innate superiority of the Germanic peoples and all that crap. I can't stand to hear that all the time." He lifted the glass she had filled, and they clinked a simple toast. "Cheers." He took a big swig, and the strength of the whiskey caught him by surprise. He choked a little and felt like a twelve year old smoking his first cigarette.

Louisa drained her glass. "I'm glad you made it to Smukke. You didn't play very long tonight, though. Only one set."

"I wish we hadn't played that much. The band sounded as flat as a squished possum. Everything was off, especially Dragor. I don't know what his problem was, but he did not have any life at all. He sounded like an amateur." He finished his drink and let Louisa refill it for him.

"He's got a lot on his mind."

"Who doesn't?"

"Did you hear about his brother?"

As far as Chops knew, Dragor had not spoken to his brother in years. They had not gotten along since childhood. "Haven't heard a thing."

"They arrested him yesterday." She did not need to say who "they" were. "They sacked his house and found stacks and stacks of illegal flyers. All the underground rags and some foreign ones too. Even some American ones. Apparently, he kept them around as some sort of status symbol, and he must have showed them to one person too many. They were waiting for him when he came home."

"Holy Christ."

"He tried to make a break for it, and they chased him down the street. Some of the neighbors saw it, which is how Dragor found out about it. Otherwise, he probably would have just disappeared."

Chops closed his eyes for a moment. No wonder Dragor didn't feel like playing. Why had he not said anything? Chops would have understood, better than most people, although these days everyone had lost something or someone. It must have hit him especially hard when Chops said he had gotten the cornet from Herr Wolf. Dragor always had reservations about the band working so closely with the official radio station, and he had no idea that Chops was actually using the radio as a way to smuggle information to the Allies. Olsen's package burned next to his chest. How had he let the Danish spy talk him into this?

Louisa continued. "At least someone saw the arrest. There is someone to demand an explanation, although it won't do much good. If the police get you, you might have a chance, but once the Gestapo is involved you're a goner. Dragor's not naive. He knows it's over..."

She kept talking, but Chops didn't hear another word she said. He just thought about Svenya. Was he just being naive to believe he could get her out alive? Never again would she bite her lip when she played viola or cry over old movies in the theater. How she wept over Gretta Garbo and Rudolph Valentino. Chops couldn't even remember the name of the film, but he could see her tears vividly and hear her muffled sobs. Svenya knew passion like no one he had ever known.

"Chops, what is it?"

He was looking straight down at the glass of scotch that was trembling in his hand. She was gone. Chops felt his throat close up and his stomach tighten, and he fought to keep control, but his vision began to blur and his lip started quivering. He felt Louisa's hand on his arm.

"Chops, look at me. What has gotten into you?"

"She's gone," he whispered, and he let the glass fall. "She's gone for good."

He felt Louisa's arms around him, and he pressed his face against her shoulder. He told himself to stop and get control of himself, that a grown man should not cry. Tension racked his body as he fought to hold back the tears.

"Let it go," she said in a cool voice. "It's all right, just let it go."

"No," he barked, and tore himself away from her. He stood up and walked across the room, rubbing his eyes with his fingers. "I'm OK."

"You've got to let it out, Chops. There is so much hate and hurt burning inside you that if you don't let it out, you're gonna blow."

"Svenya," he said, facing the wall. "She's in prison, and I haven't been able to do a damned thing about it. I just stood there and watched them pull her out of Smukke. I couldn't even move. I love her, Louisa, and I've got to get her out."

For a moment, Louisa said nothing, and Chops continued to stare at the wall, not seeing it, but looking beyond it to an earlier place and time. Then he turned around and looked at Louisa, who was watching him blankly. She reached down and picked up the glass he had droped. "Sit down, Chops. Have another drink and we'll talk. You'll feel better."

"I don't know," he said, moving slowly toward her. "I don't know what to do. She's been under my skin for a long time, and I can't get her out of my head. I see her on the streets. I dream about her. Sometimes I think I'm going crazy."

She handed him the drink. "How did you meet, anyway?"

Chops took a long pull from the glass and wondered where he should begin. "She came to Copenhagen to play in the Royal Orchestra, but she's really a small-town girl. We met at a reception at the University, and we joked a little. She has a certain style, you know, light and determined at the same time. And smart. I know what it's like being new in town, not knowing anyone, so I offered to show her around a little.

"It didn't take long before I was hooked, but she did not make life easy for me. One minute she'd be warm and open, and then she'd close up like a shell. I was pretty determined, and I asked her out for dinner a couple of times, ending the night with not so much as a good-bye kiss. We had connected, though, and it was like I'd known her all my life."

Louisa shrugged and filled his glass. "I remember the first time you brought her to Cafe Kakadu. She was giving you shit about hanging out on the waterfront when I could tell she found it really exciting. You're right. She had style. How old was she, anyway?"

"A little younger than me. She'd be thirty in January. I was planning on throwing a surprise party for her at Smukke, but I guess that won't happen."

"Stop torturing yourself, Chops."

"I can't help it."

"You're not the only one who misses her. Tapio said something about it tonight. And what about her parents? Have you talked to them?

"No. They are the traditional type, Svenya told me, and they did not like the idea of her getting involved with a foreigner. You know, maybe she'd move away and they'd never see her again. I never met them. I guess that's one less thing I have to worry about, now that she's gone." Once he had joked that the first time he would meet her folks was at their wedding. Chops' eyes clouded again, and he responded by gulping at the whiskey glass, although he could already feel his head buzzing. Talking about Svenya made him feel better and worse at the same time, like a medieval doctor was closing a wound with a lighted torch. The alcohol only added fuel to the flame.

"Svenya started listening to the Backbeats play on the radio on Thursday nights and talking about the show with such enthusiasm. Then one day I invited her to come to Smukke and see me play. I told her all about the club, that it had become a private, underground place because of the Nazi regulations. She loved the idea of dressing to the nines and drinking bathtub gin, but I made her promise not to tell anyone about it. Not a word. Tapio put her on the guest list for me.

"We couldn't show up together because I didn't want people to start talking, and when she got there

I almost did not recognize her. Dressed to kill. She had found a red-satin frock and some costume jewelry. Put on lots of makeup. She could dance, too. Took lessons when she was a kid, she told me. I took her home after the show, and that was it. We...we...we made love all night." The tears started again, squeaking through his clenched eyelids like juice through a fruit press. He couldn't stop them.

Louisa shifted on the sofa and brought her arms around his shoulders. "It's all right," she said as he pressed close to her, needing her warmth and her strength. He gave up trying to control his emotions and surrendered to their whims. Eyes closed, he lost track of time and place. He knew only his pain and Louisa's calm, soothing voice and her arms around him.

Did Louisa kiss him or did he kiss her first? He could not answer the question, and it made no sense to try. There it was. A kiss, frantic and pleading. His arm rose up behind her neck and pressed her toward him, sealing their lips together. Tongues touched and fingers intertwined. In a wave he engulfed her, hearing her breathe, tasting the scotch on her palate, smelling the warmth of her skin, feeling her body against his. Without understanding, he knew that her pain matched his own, and her loneliness as well.

Louisa drew back, and he felt the cool air pass between them as she rose to her feet and pulled him off the sofa. Without a word she led him towards the bedroom, and he followed. When they reached the doorway, he stopped and shook his head. "This is a mistake."

"No," she answered. "This is a reprieve."

He tried to say it could not happen, that he was in love with another lady, and her life practically depended on him. He wanted to say that he was dangerous, and that the people he touched always got hurt, but she did not give him the chance.

She pulled him forward and kissed him again, pushing her lips firmly, almost painfully against his, which were tired from playing in a new mouthpiece. He tried to pull his head back, but although the effort was real, it was only halfhearted. The feeling of being desperately wanted—even needed—overwhelmed him, and he felt himself begin to respond. As she rubbed large circles across his back and kissed him in long, succulent waves, he brushed his fingers through her hair and stroked her neck.

It seemed to Chops like he was outside his body, watching Louisa sliding her hand under his jacket across his chest and then over his shoulder, prying the cloth off him. He pulled his arms out of the coat and let it drop to the floor. Her hands were already tugging at his tie. To clear his head, Chops took a deep breath, reached out, and cupped Louisa's cheeks, looking deep into her eyes and seeing a side of her that had always remained hidden, guarded, protected; a youngness and eagerness that would betray any woman on the waterfront. "I don't know," he said softly.

"I know," she replied, gripping his shirt and pulling him forward onto the bed. He landed beside her, and she rolled on top of him. She slowly unfastened his shirt, button by button, and kissed his chest as she forced the folds of cloth apart, her lips so light on his chest that he could barely feel them.

When he closed his eyes, Svenya came into his mind, and he wondered if it were too late to stand up and walk out the door. He knew he must and that he could not, for the loneliness in this room was not all Louisa's. He would allow himself the comfort of spending the night beside her. Her hand moved deep between his legs, and he reached out and began to shimmy her cream-colored skirt around her waist.

Soon the lamp was off and all their clothing lay on the floor except for Louisa's pearl choker, which she had insisted on keeping around her thin neck.

Chops lay on his side, propped up on his elbow, looking down at Louisa. Her hair spread over the pillow like a fan, and her lips glistened. When they first tumbled onto the sheets, her kisses were fierce and hungry, but now he lowered his lips upon hers slowly, so they barely touched, as if they were a blown-glass ornament that would shatter at the tiniest nudge. Her lips parted in response, and she brought her hand up behind his shoulders and kneaded the back of his neck, pulling out the tension and the worry. The war could wait. The resistance could wait. Tonight they were not alone.

Louisa's eyes were closed softly, but Chops wanted to see everything as he pulled his kisses down her neck and to her shoulder. He saw her chest rise and fall as she breathed, her hand clench the sheet when he moved his thumb over her nipple, the shadows dancing across the wall as a patrol car drove down the street. Her skin was the color of parchment, and with his thick, dark fingers he drew wild and abstract shapes across her flesh.

As he blew soft air across the crook of her elbow, Louisa rubbed the sole of her foot up and down the inside of his leg. Their fingers locked, and she led his hand past her navel to her privates, but she did not let go. Her fingers pushed his inside of her, and together they explored her folds. She was unashamedly touching herself, showing him where to go, helping him to get there, and her movements surprised him. He felt uneasy. Did she think that he did not know how to make love to a woman?

"Chops, you're wonderful," she said. "You're caviar." She rolled on her side and tugged her other arm out from underneath him. She inched forward so their chests, abdomens, legs, and toes touched. The hair between her legs was bristly against him. She kissed him, and placed her fingertips on his side under his arms. "I've had a crush on you for a long time," she said, pressing her nails into his tender skin and moving them slowly down his side. The crease she made from under his arm, to his hip bone, and then down into his crotch burned slightly, but by the time she wrapped her fingers around his sex, he was swollen and needy. Her hand was wet with her own oils, and as she caressed him he felt the burning stretch down through his legs.

He was mesmerized. Everything was going too far. Louisa's movements seemed in slow motion as she threw her leg over his, sitting upright and straddling him. Her head was back, her mouth open, and she was staring at the ceiling as she used both her hands to press him inside her.

As she rose again, he pulled himself free. "We can't," he stuttered. "I'm not wearing anything."

She giggled and mounted him again. "You're sweet, Chops, but you don't need a Frenchie with me." She bent over and kissed him passionately on his lips.

When it was over, she lay on his chest for a while and he rubbed her back, wondering what this meant, wondering if it meant anything at all. Might this be a new starting place? When he broke up with his first girlfriend in high school, his mother had said to him in her soft New Orleans voice, "Other mothers have beautiful daughters, too," and, although her words made him angry, they never left him. Is this where he wanted to be, so soon after Svenya was taken away? He held Louisa tightly and mustered his courage. "I don't know how this is going to work out."

"It doesn't have to," she said. "Close your eyes and get some sleep."

"Sleep well," he said and turned over.

Clouds settled over Copenhagen during the night and dawn came late. As usual, Chops woke with an erection, which he did not want Louisa to see. She might think of it as an invitation to repeat last night's performance, when it was just a natural reaction to a full bladder. Trying not to wake her, he rolled out of bed and walked to the bathroom. His steps were a little shaky, and his head felt swollen and heavy—the aftereffects of too much scotch that he knew well.

When he returned, Louisa was awake, lying on her back with her legs bent, her knees raising the sheets like two snow-covered mountains. She looked pleasantly natural, not made-up and artificially young like she did at Smukke. Her face seemed pale and wrinkled, and her eyes puffed out with dark crescents underneath them. Her brows had all but disappeared. It was the most vulnerable he had ever seen her, and he was glad to see this side of her. He felt closer to her than he ever had, but both of them knew it was not love. But that didn't matter right now.

"You're up early," she said. "I figured you'd be asleep when I left."

He debated returning to bed, but decided against it. Instead, he bent down and stepped into the pants that lay crumpled on the floor. "I slept the day away yesterday," he said. "I don't want to make a habit out of it."

"This is the second morning in a row you've woken up at my place. You know, the neighbors might start wondering." She sat up on the bed. The sheets fell away and her gourd-shaped breasts hung low and matronly.

"How did you sleep?"

"You snore like a fucking sawmill, but besides that I slept all right." She laughed and her morning wrinkles faded a bit.

"Are you working this morning?"

"I've got the eleven o'clock lunch-shift, but I've got some things to do before work. Pick up some groceries and such. What about you?" She climbed out of bed and walked over to the closet. There was not a big selection of outfits hanging on the bar, and she had no trouble selecting something to wear—a simple earth-colored dress with pleats and a belt.

Chops had seen her in that outfit many times. "Tapio's worried that he will give out of booze, and I promised him I'd go and help him with a new batch. Who knows what would come out of the still if he had to do it by himself." He buttoned his shirt, which was as wrinkled as used tin foil. He too looked like hell.

"Tap says the same thing about you. He said the last time you made gin it tasted like petrol. In my opinion, that's what it always tastes like. But hell, if it's good enough for a car, it's good enough for me, right?"

"Right."

She buttoned her dress, tied the sash, slipped into some pumps and, within thirty seconds, she was fully dressed. "How about a quick bite to eat before you go? I might be able to find something in the kitchen."

He wasn't hungry, but he thought that a little food would help settle his stomach. They walked into the kitchen, and she pulled a pitcher of tomato juice out of the refrigerator. "Grab the loaf in the bread box, will you?"

Chops pulled the bread out of the box, and he could tell that it had come from Cafe Kakadu. One of the fringe benefits of working at a cafe, he knew. Fishing through a drawer, he came up with a knife that seemed sharp enough to cut, and he set it down on the table. He was amazed at how normal everything felt. Usually, after sleeping with someone for the first time, he noticed tension in the air that happened when people asked themselves, *now what?* but everything seemed natural and easy.

Louisa smeared some butter on her bread and chomped noisily. "We've known each other a long time, haven't we Chops."

"Eight years or so. I'd call that a long time."

"Funny that we haven't wound up in the sack until now."

Chops had nothing to say, no response at all. He ate his bread slowly and sipped at the tomato juice, which he hated, before he came up with, "funny how things happen."

"I guess I always knew we'd get down to it sooner or later. Maybe I was subconsciously avoiding it because you're a foreigner."

"You mean 'cause I'm black?"

"Maybe, but you're foreign in more ways than your skin. You forget that a lot. Even if you were as white as a new sail you wouldn't be a Dane."

"What would I be?"

"I don't know." She finished off the piece of bread and washed it down with the rest of her juice.

Her chair scraped the floor as she pushed away from the table. "But you wouldn't be a Dane. Are you about done?"

"With breakfast? I just started."

"Shove it down quick, sailor. I'll get my things and then I'll be ready to leave." With that, she walked out of the room, leaving Chops to finish his crust of bread alone. He took the chance to pour the rest of his tomato juice down the drain, and he made it back to his chair before she returned, carrying a shopping net and his new cornet.

"You don't want to leave this behind," she said, setting the case on the table.

"I think I can manage to keep up with my things," he replied, wondering if this is what married couples sounded like after eight years.

Together they walked down the stairs and out the front door. The day was a little cloudy, but it looked as if the sun might break through soon. His mind flashed back to Svenya. "Louisa, you know I'm still going to try to get her out."

She shook her head. "There's nothing you can do, Chops. If the Gestapo arrested her, she's gone. I'd love to paint a pretty picture for you, but there is no use. Marie's death has haunted you for years, and I don't want to see that happen again. Just let her go." He said nothing, so she added, "I'd say the same thing if we hadn't spent the night together."

"I know. But I've still got a couple of aces up my sleeve."

Louisa put her hand on his arm. "Don't do anything stupid, Chops. I don't want you to get into trouble."

He looked into her eyes and smiled. "I'll see you later."

Louisa did not ask for a parting kiss, and he did not give her one before they went on their separate ways. After several blocks he passed a newsstand and he thought he might buy a paper, even though the news was heavily censored and could not be trusted. He reached into his pocket for some change, and he found the envelope that Herr Wolf had given him in return for the bottle of wine. How much had the German decided to give him for the port?

He tore open the envelope, but instead of a bill he found a single piece of stationery. Unfolding it, he saw the hastily scribbled words and knew instantly that it had come from Svenya.

Chapter Fifteen

Dear Chops,

I love you. That is most important. I love you. A man just slipped this pencil and paper under the door of my cell. He said, "Write to him quickly." Forgive my hurried words, and my cramped script. It hurts my hand to write. I'm trying to stay in good spirits. Pray they let me out. It's all you can do. Guard's back. I love you.

Svenya.

Chops clasped the note as the Copenhagen wind threatened to rip it from his hand. White and gray snow clouds drifted overhead and light traffic continued down the street, but as far as Chops could tell, time had stopped. He read the note a second time, savoring each word as a morsel unto itself, imagining Svenya's thin fingers, strengthened by years of playing the viola, directing the pen over the page. The wind continued to whisk past, and Chops' eyes began to cloud so much he had to wipe his sleeve across his face. Knees weakening, he stumbled backwards like a drunkard and plopped himself down on the uneven stone wall beside the sidewalk.

Svenya. She was alive. The note seemed like a message from beyond the grave, and it shocked him so much that he did not notice he was sitting down until the snow began to melt and wet his pants. Until now, he had only received vague promises that someone might try to solve the problem; thin words that had disappeared as soon as they were uttered, but now he held a tangible object, something he could hold onto, smell, and even taste if he wanted. A shiver snaked up his spine, and for the first time in a week he felt that he was making real progress. Had only six days passed since the Gestapo dragged her out of Smukke? It seemed much longer. So much had happened in the past few days that the world seemed transformed.

"Yes!" He meant to whisper to himself, but the word came out as if he had shouted with all his strength. An elderly man walking on the other side of the street looked over and caught Chops' eye before shaking his head and shuffling down the way.

Perhaps it was a bad idea to be sitting idly on a well-traveled street. Realizing he might be attracting attention, he stood up and brushed off his suit. Only then did he notice how much water had soaked in his britches. He looked as if he had sat down in a rain barrel. Oh well. The suit needed laundering anyway.

Chops read the note one more time before carefully folding it and slipping it into his pocket. For a moment he wondered if he should destroy the piece of paper as he would have a message from Olsen, but he knew he could not. Then it would be just one more memory. The letter did not say anything, really. Of course Svenya knew that whoever gave her the paper would read what she wrote. She was far too clever to give anything away that easily, even if she had something to divulge.

The day was sunny and cold, and Chops began to shiver. Perhaps he should take the letter to Cafe Kakadu and show it to Louisa. She was a wise bird and she had been around the block enough times to offer advice on almost anything, but he decided that was a bad idea. He could still smell her must on him. Last night had been a frantic burst of emotion; not a mistake but an anomaly, as if some colossal force interrupted the normal path of his life and placed him in another world for a few hours before returning him to his normal place. Running to Louisa now would affirm their liaison as something more than that, and expectations might grow on both sides.

Could he tell Svenya that he had slept with another woman? He did not know. Surely she would understand his weakness and forgive him. Was forgive the correct word? No, he did not think so. The whole incident seemed small and almost insignificant now when pitted against Svenya's freedom. It made no difference. Now was a time for action, not contemplation, so he stood up and moved through the back streets, headed for home. He began to feel anxious about walking around the city in a wet and wrinkled suite. In his New Orleans days he had kept a spare suit at three different ladies' houses. Those days, he had more clothes at his friends' houses than at his own, but those antics belonged to younger men.

Chops walked down the street at a brisk pace, eyeing the buildings he passed. The neighborhood was filled with apartment buildings, some of which had storefronts on the ground floor. Copenhagen was filled with sturdy brick and stone. Masons laid some of the mortar centuries ago, carrying water in buckets from the canals and hauling cement in wooden wheelbarrows, but it was as strong as the younger buildings. Maybe stronger. Only a few blocks away lay the medieval town square where the Dagmar House stood, the headquarters for the Gestapo. How would he ever rescue Svenya from such a vault? It would take an army or a battalion of tanks to storm the place, and Chops knew that would never happen. Svenya knew that as well. Was that why she said that he should not try to free her?

Chops imagined his reunion with Svenya. She would be wearing the same blue dress she wore last Wednesday at Smukke, the same costume jewelry, the same shoes. Walking out of Gestapo headquarters, she might squint in the sunlight, and then manage a smile, subtle and thin. He would not say a word but take her immediately in his arms and pull her close. With his eyes shut, he could feel her slender body against his and taste her thick kisses. Where they would go from there he did not know. If they remained in the city, the police could arrest them again on a whim, but if they left, Olsen would lose his link to London, and despite Chops' claims of neutrality, he was beginning to see his work with the underground as important. But never as important as Svenya.

Chops turned down a side street that would lead him to Hans Christian Andersen Boulevard and across the canal to Christianshavn. A few blocks down he saw a slogan, large, white letters so hurriedly painted across the brick wall that streams of paint dripped down to the sidewalk. *NAZIS GO HOME*. Rarely did such graffiti last more than a day or two before some pro-Nazi worker would sand the letters out of existence, but no matter how hard they tried, they could not erase the hatred that continued to simmer against the occupying country.

He planted himself on an empty wooden crate and pulled Svenya's letter from his pocket. Bewilderment and euphoria began to fade as he scrutinized the handwriting, asking himself if this could be some sort of trick. After all, the message had come from Herr Wolf, a high-ranking German. Were the Nazis worried that he would try something to get her loose and that this may keep him from trying anything? Or was this Wolf's way of proving that he could help?

Perhaps Svenya had not written the letter at all. Surely the Gestapo could have forged her handwriting, but that seemed like a lot of effort for such an insignificant message. Chops brought the paper close to his eyes and carefully examined the script, but he knew he was no expert.

Why would someone ask her to write to him? Had Wolf really slipped her the paper as a favor to Chops, or as a sign that he had ties to the Gestapo? Chops thought back to the previous night when Wolf had given him the envelope. So much had happened afterwards that he found it difficult to remember the German's exact words. They were alone by the door, out of earshot from the other guests, and Wolf had said something like, "Thanks for the wine. This should cover it." At the time, he thought it was just money, and Wolf was too smooth to let him think otherwise. What would have happened if he had opened the letter on the spot after drinking a few glasses of wine? He might have blurted out something the other guests would have heard, and from the way the German acted, he did not want anyone to know that he was dealing with an American.

Was Wolf really the key to Svenya's release? Last night he had said, "If you make a small gesture that would ally you with the regime, I might be able to help you and your friends." You and your friends. This letter was Wolf's proof that he had connections, but Olsen would be furious if Chops asked for Wolf's help. The agent would never permit it. Chops remembered the day that Olsen hammered the rake into the tree above his head and said that Wolf could not be trusted. It was the most emotion that Olsen had ever shown around Chops. Even now, he remembered the fiery look in the agent's eyes when they had spoken about Wolf.

Olsen claimed to have some pull inside the Gestapo as well. He had also produced information about Svenya. Relying on the Dane had one overwhelming advantage. Chops knew where the man stood. He might be irritating, even abrasive, but he hated the Nazis more than any man Chops had ever met, and the agent was not afraid to take risks for his cause. Very few men would escape from their own country days after the invasion and then have the courage and skill to return as a spy. The British subjected their agents to harsh training, both physically and psychologically, and Olsen had obviously learned a great deal to have survived so long and accomplished so much. Olsen never mentioned his home or his family, except to say he learned to shoot as a child on the farm, and everyone knew that the farmers who refused to supply their crops to the German war machine lost everything; houses burned, land confiscated. They were frequently jailed or worse if they put up any resistance. What had Olsen seen that could allow him to wager his life in such a high-risk gambit? His drive was so deep that it suffocated his humanity, transforming him into a professional killer, skilled and dangerous, but in wartime, such people were needed.

As Chops walked down Hans Christian Andersen Boulevard, he noticed a crowd gathered at one of the stores and a police truck out front. The people looked like working class Danes, wearing clumsy shoes, overalls, and coarse wool coats, who had come out of their shops to lend support to the victims. These scenes always had victims. Although Chops wanted to know what had happened, he did not want to step into a hornets' nest, so he kept his distance and listened to the rumbling mass. He reacted with the same two emotions as he did as a child, when the white policemen came into his neighborhood: curiosity and fear. The police hauled at least three people into the back of their truck, and they were threatening to arrest more. Chops noticed an older woman walking away from the group, and he fell in step with her. "Excuse me."

"Yes?" She did not stop walking, nor did she turn to look at him from under her bonnet.

"What was that all about?"

"Who knows," she replied, her upper crust accent filled with disdain. "The HIPOS are at it again." She stopped suddenly and walked across the street.

The HIPOS were a group of pro-Nazi Danes who received uniforms and a little training from the German SS. In theory the HIPOS provided a stepping stone into the Freikorps Denmark, the army of turncoat Danes who fought for the Germans in the east, but in practice they were little more than licensed hoodlums who swarmed the streets assaulting people suspected of aiding in the resistance. Being Danes with the legal power of Germans, they made the most fierce enemies.

Chops felt jittery in his stomach as he looked back to the crowd by the police van. At least if the HIPOs arrested you, you received what was left of due process of law, whereas if the Gestapo took you, you just disappeared. He picked up his pace and headed for the bridge that would lead him back to his neighborhood on the other side of the canal. The street was filled with a stream of bicyclists, moving much faster than he could on foot, and he remembered that he should buy a bike as soon as possible. He had ample money. Hell, he could buy an auto, if he wanted one, but then there was always the problem of getting petrol.

Five minutes later, Chops turned onto his street. The anonymous apartment blocks were not attractive, but he had lived here for years, and they provided the simple comfort and security of being at home. As he neared his building, he saw a large man in a well-tailored suit heading into the front door. None of his fellow tenants wore business suits. They were all dock workers and day laborers whom he knew by name or at least on sight. If he had arrived a moment or two earlier, he might have gotten a better glimpse of the man, but now he had a feeling it might be Olsen. The Danish agent always arrived shortly after Chops received a package from Louisa, and he inevitably appeared when he was not wanted.

Once he had made the connection, Chops felt sure that the Danish spy was making one of his notorious surprise visits to his apartment, but instead of rushing up the stairs to meet him, he decided to wait beside the door until the man reemerged. Olsen always said security was important.

The minutes passed slowly as he waited beside the door. The street was empty with not so much as a pigeon pecking at the stones. Perhaps he was mistaken, and it was not Olsen after all but a guest of one of his neighbors. Chops resisted the urge to take out Svenya's letter and reread it as he waited. Maybe it was a detective checking out his apartment. The possibilities were endless.

Quick steps echoed in the stairwell, and Chops breathed deeply to calm his racing pulse. The taps grew louder and then muffled as the feet left the resounding staircase and hit the worn carpet in the entrance hall. The door swung open. Peder Olsen emerged, but did not see Chops behind the door as he passed. Without thinking of the consequences, Chops yelled, "Freeze!"

Olsen spun around with his fist outstretched, but Chops had already stepped back and the swing fell short. At that moment, Olsen must have recognized him because his eyes widened and he did not step forward to attack.

"Your security's getting lax," Chops said with a chuckle.

"Don't be stupid, Chops," he said straightening his pants and slicking back his hair. "I could have just killed you. Did you think of that?"

"Lighten up, Olsen. It was just a prank."

"I'm not the man you should be joking with."

Chops shrugged, knowing that his nonchalant air would infuriate the Dane. "Come on upstairs while I throw on some new duds. You're looking pretty sharp yourself." He held the door and let Olsen walk ahead, remembering all the times that Olsen had snuck up on him and then said something condescending about security. Beating the Dane at his own game lifted Chops' spirits, although a voice inside told him he might have made a big mistake. The two men did not say anything as they climbed the stairs to his apartment, but between landings Chops decided that he would not mention the letter from Svenya. He would keep that on a "need to know" basis.

The air inside the apartment smelled a little musty, but it felt good to be inside his own pad. Chops switched on the light and headed to the closet as Olsen sat down in the straight-backed desk chair. He selected a gray, tweed sports jacket and navy blue wool trousers, but then he decided on a charcoal pinstripe because he did not want to be outdressed by Olsen.

"So what's on your mind?" he said as he emerged from the closet.

"You shouldn't be so cocky after a botched mission," Olsen said.

"You didn't come here just to bitch at me, did you?"

The Dane leaned back in the chair and crossed his legs on the desk the way gangsters did in the movies. "How was dinner with the Nazis?"

"We didn't talk about troop movements or anything. It was strictly casual."

"Strictly casual. That's an oxymoron, isn't it?"

"Describes the evening pretty well. Everyone was acting as friendly as possible, but the veneer didn't cover the fact that we're on different sides of the fence. The conversation never flowed because you had to think about what you were saying and make sure you weren't out of line. Lots of grins and nervous laughter. Herr Wolf did come up with a horn, just like you said he would."

"Did he give it to you?"

"He called it an indefinite loan."

"Typical." Olsen looked surprisingly at ease as he sat there in his business suit. The Dane always made Chops a little nervous because his size and demeanor implied a threat of violence, but today he had a different menace, that of a prosecuting attorney. "What do you think of him?"

Chops thought a moment before replying. The question could mean anything from "Is he a nice guy" to "Which side are you on," and Olsen had already said that he did not think Wolf could be trusted. "He's slippery. He tries to give off this 'friend of music' air, but I'm not sure I buy it. He could be up to something."

"Do you think he knows what we're doing?"

Chops shook his head. "He'd arrest me if he did. Even if he suspected I was involved with the resistance, he'd pull out my fingernails until I told him everything. My guess is he wants to know how deep my contacts are in the black market."

"Did he mention that?"

"No, but I brought him a bottle of wine that you couldn't find in a store."

"Why did you do that?"

"Just to give him something to chew on. If he wants to put his energy into documenting my connections on the waterfront, let him. That will keep him away from what we're really doing." Chops sounded so convincing that he almost believed it himself.

"Good thinking. By the way, do you have something for me?"

Chops remembered the envelope that Louisa had given him. It was still in his coat pocket. "I'll get it." He walked into the closet and returned with the thin package.

"Excellent," Olsen said without opening the seal. "I've got something for you as well." He pulled a slip of paper from his lapel pocket and handed it to Chops. It read *PACK RECEIVED*. Chops read it and then looked at Olsen inquisitively.

"Encode it on Thursday," the agent said.

"You don't usually confirm receipt when something comes through the port."

Olsen studied him for a moment and then said, "No, I don't. I'm not referring to this little goodie. The SOE wants to make sure we received the canisters they dropped."

Chops set the paper on the desk and pulled off his wet trousers. "Isn't that a little misleading, or is there something I don't know?"

"Just do it."

"We can't send lies to London."

Chops expected a harsh reply, but Olsen's tone was reserved. Perhaps this new air simply went with the expensive suit he was wearing, or maybe something deeper inside the man had changed. Chops wasn't sure. "I've thought a lot about this one, old boy. I don't like the idea of lying to my superiors any more than you do, but I don't see any choice."

"What do you mean?"

"If they know that the Germans intercepted the drop, then they might shut down the whole operation. My network is good. Very good. I'd say it's the best in occupied Europe, maybe the only one. From what I gather, all the men I trained with in London have been killed. Before I returned from England to build this network, I spent three weeks at security school at Lord Montagu's Beaulieu Castle. It was a crash prep course for life on the run and a last chance for special operations to find out if we would crack under interrogation. They told us that the life expectancy of an SOE operative was three weeks, but I've been active for months. I'm just afraid if we tell them what really happened they might pull the plug on the whole operation. I can't let that happen. Not now when we're really becoming important. The Germans won't survive another Russian winter. They just don't have it in them. They'll pull back, and the Allies will open a second front next spring. When they do, we must be ready to deliver the knock-out blow. We can't delay because it will take months to stockpile the kind of arsenal we need."

"You know, you're not off to a great start," Chops said, tightening his half-Windsor. He peered into the mirror on the wall, not so much to straighten his tie but to observe Olsen. His lip barely twitched at Chops' last jab.

"No, you're right. But there will be other drops."

"How are you going to keep them out of the Germans' hands? I'd think you'd be trying to figure out what went wrong instead of worrying about how to fool the guys in London. Do you still think Kaj turned us in, or have you come up with something that makes sense?"

Olsen patted his hip pocket, and Chops figured he must be carrying a pistol. "I solved that problem earlier this morning."

"You solved the problem?"

"I figured you must be right. The boy you brought with us would have had a hard time leading the Germans to us, since he really had no information before we met at the station. It could really only have been one person, besides you or me."

"Who?"

"The man I used to get the ambulance. He was the only loose connection in the whole operation, so I paid him a visit this morning. We had never met before, but his record looked clean, and I had hoped he would be a help in the future. It's hard to tell in this business. As it turned out, he phoned the Gestapo right after I contacted him, and he assumed I would be behind bars or at the end of a rope by now. That's why my appearance this morning shocked him so much. He confessed to everything."

"And then?" Chops knew what Olsen would say, but he wanted to hear the words straight from his lips. How would Olsen admit that he was a cold blooded killer?

"I solved the problem."

"You shot him."

"Yes, I shot him. Not much choice, was there?"

"I guess not." Chops asked himself what he would have done in a similar situation. At least if he had been forced to kill someone he would not have been so smug about it.

"The Germans won't find his body, so that will buy us a little time. Even so, we've got to be even more careful. One doesn't usually get a second chance in this kind of game. I've decided not to recruit any new network members for a while, which means you will have to do more work than I had anticipated.

"That's the one positive aspect of the whole disaster. I got a chance to see how you would react under fire. I'm glad I can trust you, even if things get messy."

Chops shook his head. "Don't count on me for any more stunts like that. I've got better things to do than to get shot at. I was almost shitting in my pants the whole time. No, that is not for me."

"Give yourself more credit, Chops. In the initial invasion of France, only half the French soldiers fired their weapons. The invasion of Denmark was even worse, if you remember. How long did it take to conquer this country? Six hours? Maybe eight. No, Chops. Some people can fight and others can't. I wasn't sure at first, but you've proven yourself to be a man who can stand up to the heat."

Chops pulled up another chair and sat down. "I think we should lay low for a while. Let things cool off."

"I wish there were some way to do that without letting the SOE know that we were ambushed."

"That's all the more reason to tell London the truth. It will give us some time."

"Out of the question." Olsen's tone showed no compromise, and Chops did not want to argue. This wasn't his network.

"Let's concentrate on getting Svenya out of jail, and then we can worry about how to get more ammunition. Have you made any progress on that front?"

Olsen shook his head. "Sorry, old boy, but I've had other things on my mind. You can't expect me to worry about her when the Germans are this close to nabbing us."

The question about Svenya had been burning in Chops since he entered the apartment, and Olsen's answer enraged him. He wanted to bring out the letter and yell, "Don't you think Herr Wolf has other things on his mind as well?" but instead he pointed a stiff finger in the agent's direction and said, "You don't get it, do you Olsen? I've done my part. I've played your magic notes. I tromped through the snow and almost got myself killed. I lost one of my best friends trying to help you, and if you aren't going to come through on your part of the bargain, you shouldn't be looking for any more support from me." He took Olsen's note and handed it back to him.

Olsen refused to take the paper from Chops. "I'll see what I can do, but I'm not promising anything. In the meantime, don't lose sight of the forest. There is a war going on, and believe it or not, you are playing a big part in shortening it. You can be proud of what you've already done, but if you stop now, your work will be for nothing."

Chops nodded, although the answer didn't

pacify him much. He wanted to believe that the politics were not important, but he knew that he did care. He was proud that he was fighting against the Germans. In the past months, he had begun to consider himself as an American again instead of a man without a country. He stood up and motioned to the door. "I'll be damned clear. I want Svenya out of jail before the show on Thursday night, and if you don't deliver, your precious lie isn't going anywhere. Understand?"

Olsen stood, and he suddenly seemed larger than he had when he came into the apartment. "Don't make ultimatums, Chops. I've told you before, and I'll say it again. These things take time. I know you want your girlfriend out of jail, and I want that too, but these things take time. If you quit on me, I'll guarantee you Svenya will never see the light of day again. It's not a threat. It's a simple truth. I'm the only chance she's got."

Chops thought about the letter in his pocket, and he wondered if Olsen's statement was true. Maybe if he showed it to the spy, he would work harder to press for her release, but then Chops decided that was not a good idea. Olsen might begin to suspect that he and Wolf had joined sides, and that was far from true. He was only mildly responding to the German's vague overtures, interested in where they might lead and how they might illuminate his loyalties. Chops looked at Olsen, thinking that he had ruthlessly shot a man only hours before. No, it could be dangerous to tell the man he had received a message from Wolf.

Olsen stood up and moved to the door. "I'll see what I can do about your girlfriend. In the meantime, encode the message. That's in everybody's best interest."

"We'll see," Chops said as he closed the door.

Chapter Sixteen

Chops stood by the door to his apartment and listened to Peder Olsen's footsteps fade as he descended the staircase. He was glad to be alone again with a few moments of solitude to sort out the events of the past few days. Despite the meeting with Olsen, which had been confrontational as always, he felt at ease like one does returning to home. He had not spent much time in the apartment in the past week, and he had ignored the basics of living. Clothes overflowed out of his laundry basket; dishes were piled up in the sink; the refrigerator was empty. The thought of handling these mundane chores did not sit well with him, and he decided to relax for a while. After lighting a cigarette and taking a long drag, Chops sat down in front of his record collection. What did he want to listen to? King Oliver, Bessie Smith, Bennie Goodman, Fats Waller, he flipped through the familiar records and finally decided on Sidney Bechet, a musician he felt oddly tied to. Slightly his elder, Bechet had also grown up in New Orleans, and then he had moved to Paris in the thirties where he had become an unrivaled star. As far as anyone knew, he was in France when the war broke out. Perhaps the Germans had arrested him or maybe he was playing in underground clubs like Chops was. There was no way to know.

He turned the volume up until the screeching soprano saxophone filled the room. Once again, Chops took Svenya's letter out of his pocket and reread it.

If she ever needed him, this was the time, but all he could do was wait and rely on Olsen to pull off some magic trick. He wondered if he had acted too gruff with the agent. He had made his stand, and he would stick to it: Get Svenya out or I won't play a part of your resistance network. After she was out of prison, he would do his best to help Olsen and the Allies.

Chops looked around the apartment and imagined Svenya sitting at his desk and leafing through his charts, amazed that someone could transform the simple notes and chord notations on the page into such moving music. The note Wolf gave him vaguely reminded him of the weekly letters his mother sent him before the war interrupted the postal system. Her notes were brief as well, two or three sheets of flowery note pads and occasionally a clipping from the newspaper of the church bulletin.

The morsels of information his mother sent made sense to him because he had grown up there and the news had some context. He suspected that his letters made far less sense to her. Neither the complex hierarchy at the Conservatory nor the simple beauty of the Danish Christmas Festival could have meaning for her because she had never ever even visited. Shortly after he married Marie, his mother had planned to sail to Denmark, but after the accident she never mentioned the trip again. Perhaps she simply pretended that the marriage had never happened.

Sitting in his apartment in Christianshavn, he found it hard to imagine what his life would be like if he had returned to America with the Guy Sherman band instead of staying in Copenhagen. He would have probably married a local woman by now and settled down to teach at the high school. His life would be comfortable enough, he guessed, but he would not have the excitement that he enjoyed as a professional musician in Europe, nor would he have the same standard of living. True, he did not live in a large house or drive a fancy car, but these things did not mean so much to him. He had plenty of money to buy nice clothes and to eat out at fine restaurants.

He knew this was not the main reason he stayed in Denmark. Ever since he was a child, he had seen himself as someone destined to walk a different path, someone not restricted by the world he had been born into. As a child, this played out in a fantasy world where he sailed to Africa to hunt lions and where he led expeditions to discover gold on the South Pole. His imagination led him to music, where dreams could become almost tangible. Now the wind from his cornet had blown him across the sea, and he knew that if he had gone home he would always have the nagging feeling that he had given up.

Never before had he been so happy as during the past few months when he was with Svenya. He remembered a few weeks ago when she had caught a bad flu. He had insisted that she come stay with him, and she had feebly objected, worried that she would be too much trouble. He did not listen to her protest, and she stayed in his bed for four straight days until she regained her strength. He went to the pharmacy for her and when he learned that all the good medicine went to the military, he went to the black market and bought the best pills available. Vitamins and aspirin. Decongestants and everything else he could get his hands on, including a little morphine that she refused to take. "It's only the flu," she said.

Sidney Bechet ceased to play, and the music was replaced by the strange rasping sound of a finished record. Instead of selecting another, he decided to go into town and try to find another bicycle. Walking in and out of the city took far too much time, and he might hear something interesting. He pulled out his wallet and leafed through the bills. Only one hundred Krone, enough for daily expenses, but not nearly enough to cover the cost of a good bike. Reaching into his second desk drawer, he fished through some half-finished compositions and some stationery until he found his brown leather pouch where he kept his reserve funds. Both Olsen and Wolf paid him well, and he saved most of his money. He did not count, but it looked like he had at least five thousand Krone, maybe more. He took three hundred out of the pouch and stuffed it into his wallet before closing the drawer. The laundry could wait.

He locked the front door as he left the apartment and decided to walk to Smukke and visit Tapio before he tried to find a bike. Chops had not spent much time talking to Tapio in recent weeks, and he felt bad about neglecting his friends. He did not want to get locked into spending the afternoon brewing a new batch of beer or siphoning off more gin, but if that's what the barkeeper was doing he would lend a hand.

Twenty minutes later Chops stood in front of the old oaken door to Smukke, a bit winded from his brisk walk. Yes, he definitely needed a bicycle. He knocked the code on the door, hoping that Tapio was around. The peep hole opened almost immediately, and he saw the bartender's eyes through the slit. "V is for victory," Chops said out of habit.

"Glad it's you," Tapio said and closed the peep hole. The hinges squeaked as the large door opened.

"What's shaking, Tapio?" Chops said as he stepped inside. The air smelled heavy of hops and yeast. The brewing must have started earlier this afternoon.

Tapio wore canvas work pants and a white smock that hung down to his knees, which gave him an entirely different appearance than the white dinner jacket that he wore when the club was open. He looked younger and stringier, like a tough kid on the docks. "You seen Kaj recently?"

Chops shook his head and hoped he did not look as guilty as he felt. He had tried to put the boy out of his mind, denying his responsibility and his loss. How could he explain it to Tapio, especially since he hadn't mentioned it last night?

"You're not going to believe this," he said as he led Chops past the empty tables and behind the bar. His feet stuck to the floor as he walked, and he noticed that many of the ashtrays were still filled with half-smoked butts.

Chops followed Tapio into the kitchen, which felt like a steam bath and smelled like a brewery. Steam rose out of the boiling vat on the old gas stove and swirled through the thin light like an apparition. Before the war, the building which now housed Smukke had been an inexpensive seafood restaurant, so the cooking facilities were far more expensive than the jazz club needed, but the extra space did come in handy for making alcohol.

"Hey Chops."

The familiar voice came from behind him, and

he turned quickly, eyes wide with shock. "Kaj," he cried. "How the hell did you get here?"

The boy sat cross-legged on a barstool beside the sink, wearing a fisherman's sweater and work shoes, and as far as Chops could tell, there wasn't a scratch on him. "You didn't bring me, that's for sure."

Chops walked over and put his hands on the boy's thick shoulders, assuring himself that what he saw was real, delighting in the touch, the presence. He had broken the hip-jazz-musician role which he'd maintained for so long, and he felt light enough to float. "Jesus, I'm glad to see you. I thought you were a goner. Are you OK?"

"I guess. That was one hell of a reception we got, wasn't it?"

"I didn't know whether to shit or go blind."

"I think I did both," Kaj said. "I went head-first into a snowdrift and buried myself. Deep."

"Why didn't you freeze?" Tapio asked.

"Too scared."

"I wanted to go back and look for you, but the driver wouldn't let me. We just took off and headed back to the city." Chops sighed and wondered if he sounded like he was making excuses.

"I figured you would," Kaj said. "But I was afraid that if I headed for the road, someone would see me. It only took the Germans a few minutes before they fixed the searchlights, and then I didn't have a chance to escape. I couldn't see anything, of course, but I heard a lot of shouting back and forth. There were a couple of small explosions, hand grenades I guess, but after that everything quieted down. After an hour or so, I heard the trucks start up and drive away. By the time I came out of the snowdrift, it was already dawn." He finished filling the fourth carboy, and he stood up and set the vat on the counter by the sink.

"Where did you go?" Chops asked.

"I just kept walking until I hit the road, and then I followed it to the first farmhouse. I saw an old man walking out of the barn, and I went up to him and told him I needed help. He must have been seventy or eighty years old. He smoked like a chimney, and his voice was so raspy that I could barely understand him. He was nice enough, and when I told him that my friends had stranded me out here as a joke, he offered to bring me into town. Only he wasn't going until this morning, so I stayed at his place and helped him build a loft in his barn. A nice guy."

Tapio had walked over the stove and started stirring the boiling mixture with a long wooden spoon. He fished out a net full of hops, pressed it against the side of the vat to drain off some of the malt, and then tossed it into the trash. "So, is someone going to tell me what you were doing there in the first place, or do I have to guess?"

Chops looked at Tapio and then at Kaj.

"I haven't told him," the boy said sheepishly.

The musician jumped up and sat on the counter. He knew he should keep his mouth shut and preserve Olsen's precious security, but he was tired of lying to his friends. "It's dangerous, Tapio. Capital D dangerous. I'll tell you, but you're better off not knowing."

Tapio turned off the gas burner. "Look around you, you buffalo. What could you tell me that would get me in deeper than I am already. I break the law every time I open the door to this dive, and if they decide to pull my number, I'm going away for a long time. I don't see that it makes a hell of a lot of difference what else I know."

Tapio's passion surprised Chops and he decided to open the vault. "I've been involved for several months. Resistance. The real thing, not just a couple of angry dock workers or overactive intellectuals at the University. So far we haven't done anything serious besides smuggling papers through the port. Until last week, that is. We received a message that the RAF was planning on parachuting us a shipment of supplies."

"Supplies?"

"Guns and ammunition. We're supposed to stockpile it until the invasion so we can attack from within. Only, something went wrong, and the Gerries were waiting for us."

"I call that asking for trouble, Tapio said. "Give me a hand with the funnel. The beer is getting cool fast."

Chops grabbed the funnel from one of the upper cabinets and held it over the first jug. Tapio stuck his hands into two big pot holders and tried to hoist the vat off the stove.

"Let me give you a hand with that," Kaj said. He stood up and walked slowly across the kitchen floor. His steps seemed stiff, and Chops wondered how long he had stayed buried under a snowdrift. The boy rolled his shoulders and grabbed the pot holders, and then lifted the vat off the stove, grunting slightly. He carried it over to where Chops was squatting, and began pouring the hot liquid into the tin funnel, which heated up so much Chops thought the skin would sizzle off his hands.

"Do you have a towel?"

"Sure." Tapio tossed him a towel, and he wrapped it around the funnel as they began filling the second jug.

After they filled all four, Kaj set the pot back on the stove. "Guess what I found while I was in the woods?"

"What?"

Kaj reached to the far corner of the counter and grabbed a burlap sack that Chops hadn't seen before. He untied the end and dumped the contents out onto the white linoleum. Four Colt .45's and six boxes of ammunition fell out into the light. "Do you remember the second parachute that drifted away, the one I went after? I found it in a tree and pulled it down. It took me ten minutes to open up because the clasps were frozen, but it was full of stuff. Blankets, food, compasses, guns, and all kinds of things I didn't recognize."

"And this is all you brought?" Tapio said.

"We can go back for the rest later."

"Too dangerous," Chops said. "It doesn't matter. Four guns might not be enough to throw the Germans out of Copenhagen, but it's a hell of a lot better than what we had before." He lifted one of the pistols and examined it, never having held a handgun before. A policeman let him look at one when he was a child, but that was as close as he had ever gotten. It felt heavier than he expected. "Have you ever shot one of these before?"

Both Tapio and Kaj shook their heads. "Have you?"

"All the time, when I lived in the States." He found the clip release and pressed it, and the bottom fell out of the hand grip and landed on the counter with a clank. Thank God it was empty. He pulled the mechanism back and peered into the empty chamber. Even in Denmark, the Colt .45 was legendary. "These things kick like a horse, but if you get hit by one, you're a goner. Even if you just nick someone in the shoulder it will knock them down."

"Big bullets, huh," Kaj said, taking one of the shells out of the cardboard box.

"Have you shown these to anyone?" Chops asked the boy.

"No. No one."

"Good. Don't. You neither, Tapio. I'm serious. If word gets out that we have some heat, we could find ourselves in the slammer before we could blink." Chops spun the gun around his trigger finger like the cowboys in the movies did, and he almost threw it across the room. He put it on the counter. "We sure could have used these the other night, huh?"

"Yeah."

Tapio stuck a cork in each of the four jugs on the floor. Then he walked over to the counter and picked up one of the pistols. He took careful aim at an imaginary target on the wall. "Bang," he whispered, and then raised the gun as if it had fired. "Maybe I could keep one behind the bar in case there is trouble again."

"Which one of the Germans would you have shot Wednesday night?" Chops asked. "Because I promise, you would only have gotten one of them before they blew your head off and then killed everyone else in the room."

"Don't be so melodramatic, Chops."

"Well, what do you plan on doing with them?" Kaj asked. "Are you going to deliver them to the underground?"

He thought for a moment. Giving them to Olsen was out of the question. These guns were Chops' insurance policy, in case anything went wrong, and he wasn't going to give that away. Of course, Olsen would be angry if he found out, but only if he found out. Storing them was an added risk, and he did not want to keep them in his apartment. "I think we should keep them here. Smukke is right in the middle of town, so we can get to them quickly if we have to. Do you have someplace we can stash them, Tapio?"

"No secret compartments, if that's what you mean. But we can hide them in these cupboards. They'll be pretty safe."

"Pretty safe won't fly. What about my dressing room? Maybe we could pull up one of the floorboards. Better yet, we could hide them in the vent under my desk."

Tapio shook his head. "Store those bullets in a heating duct? That's using your head."

Kaj started to laugh. "That would be your luck, getting shot by no one in your own dressing room."

While the boy was speaking, Tapio dragged a stool to the corner of the kitchen and stood up on it. He pressed his hand on one of the ceiling slats, and it gave way easily. "How about here?"

"I thought you said you didn't have any secret compartments," Kaj said.

"It's not a secret compartment. This is how you get to the water pipes. They burst about every other winter, so you've got to be able to fix them without ripping out all the walls. Pass the guns up."

"Should we load them in case we need to use them in a hurry?"

"Why not?" Chops said as he began slipping the bullets into the clip. The brass shells were slick, and he had to press them straight down into the clip or else they would pop out and fall onto the counter. As he filled the clip, the spring inside gave more resistance and made it even more difficult to load. Finally, he had loaded all four guns, and he passed them to Tapio to store in the ceiling. Before coming down off the stool, he pulled the slat back into place.

"Well, that's taken care of," Tapio said with a sigh. "Who would have thought that I'd be storing guns in the ceiling of Smukke?"

"No one," Chops said. "That's the point. This is the first piece of real luck I've had in I don't know how long. Now let's hope that we don't have to use them." He looked around the kitchen.

Tapio nodded his head slightly. "I've been thinking. Does this have anything to do with Svenya? I mean, they said she was a spy when they took her. Is she involved with you?"

Chops shook his head. "Not as far as I know. She doesn't even know I'm connected."

"Any word?" Kaj asked.

"Well..." Chops knew if he showed them the letter they would want to know where he got it, but they were friends with Svenya as well, so he reached into his pocket and pulled it out. "I did get this."

Tapio took it and read it quickly. "At least she's OK. Guess that makes you feel better."

"A little."

"Lemme see." Kaj held out his hand and Tapio handed him the small piece of paper. He mouthed the words as he struggled through the small paragraph. "What does she mean, 'it hurts my hand to write'? Her hands are so strong she could copy the Holy Bible from back to front and not get a cramp."

"I don't know," Chops said, "but it's not good."

"Maybe she didn't write it, and the forger just said that to cover his tracks."

Chops shrugged. "It looks like her handwriting, and that's all I really know. I can't imagine the Gestapo using a professional forger to write a letter that doesn't say anything."

"Unless she's dead and they don't want you to know," Kaj blurted.

Chops swallowed hard and looked at the floor,

wanting to pop the boy in the mouth for saying something like that, but he knew eighteen-year-olds were brash by nature.

Tapio broke the silence. "Where did you get the letter?"

"I didn't say."

Tapio did not object.

"Do you need any more help around here? I've got some errands to run in town."

"The beer has to cool for a few hours before I can add the yeast, so there is really nothing left to do here. I was planning on cleaning the joint up so I can open tonight. Yesterday I was so tired that I couldn't push a mop, and I went to bed as soon as I closed the doors. You left right after you finished playing, I noticed."

"Yeah, everyone was pretty down last night, and I didn't want to stick around. I hope taking today off will make everyone feel better. If we keep playing like we did last night, we'll have to pay people to listen to us."

"You sounded all right."

"We were off, Tapio. That's all there is to it. Anyway, I've got to see about getting a bike. You have any ideas?"

Tapio thought for a minute before suggesting that Chops head to the square and see what he could find there. It was where he was headed anyway.

"Do you mind if I tag along?" Kaj asked.

"It'd be great," he said as he moved to the door. "Tapio, do you need anything while we're out?"

"No. Will you two be here tonight?"

"I will. How about you, Kaj?"

"Maybe. I've got to stop in the tattoo parlor and see if I've got to work. Mondays are usually slow, but the boss will probably be mad that I didn't show up last night. I just hope he doesn't fire me."

Chops knew that the boy depended on that job, and he hoped there would not be trouble. "We could drop by there right now if you wanted to."

"The boss doesn't usually show up until around five, so I've got a couple of hours to burn."

"You sure you don't need anything while we're out?" Chops asked Tapio before he opened the front door.

"No. You two get out of here so I can get some work done. I'll see you tonight."

"Later." Chops and Kaj walked out of the bar, up the icy steps, and onto the street. They headed north to the center of town, walking slowly and looking into the shop windows as they passed. A year ago the stores would have been full of new winter clothes, but now the selection looked thin.

If he noticed the lack of merchandise, it did not affect Kaj's spirits. He kept whistling, but Chops couldn't tell what song it was. "The ambulance driver sure did know what he was doing when the shooting started, didn't he. He didn't even stop to think before shooting out the lights. Bang, bang. Just like a cowboy. What did he say afterwards at the ambulance?"

Chops remembered most of what Olsen had said. He remembered almost getting into a fight with the man over whether to drive away or to look for Kaj. The spy had also accused Kaj of turning them in to the Nazis, although he found out later it had been the man who had stolen the ambulance. "Nothing," he said. "Just that we didn't have time to wait, although I'd been waiting for him along side of the road for a good fifteen minutes before he made it back to the rendezvous."

"He was probably behind the lines, knocking off Germans. How many do you think he got?"

Chops could see that the boy was idolizing Olsen, and it made him angry. Perhaps even a little jealous. Didn't he see that the spy had left him alone with the Germans without so much as a gun to protect himself? "He didn't say anything about shooting anyone."

"He probably got a dozen at least. Have you seen him since? Do you think he'll let me come on your next mission? Now that we've got some guns, we can do some real damage."

"Forget about the guns, Kaj. If that man comes to visit you, and it wouldn't surprise me if he did, don't say anything about them. Just say that a farmer brought you back to Copenhagen."

"If he's in charge, why don't we tell him about the guns?"

"He's not in charge of you, Kaj. And he's not in charge of me either. He hired us to do some work for him, and that's that. If I remember correctly, you still have some money coming to you. Wasn't that the deal?"

"Yeah."

"Then keep your mouth shut." Chops felt like he was being awfully hard on the kid. Instead of telling him how glad he was that he made it out of the woods alive, he was telling him to keep his mouth shut. He wanted to change the topic to something safe. "So what will you do with all that money, if you get your hands on it?"

"I don't know. I was thinking about maybe buying a jacket. You know, a spiffy blazer to wear out at night. All the clothes I have are just too boring. The kind of things you'd wear to church. I want something with some wow in it."

"Something to sweep the ladies off their feet, you mean," Chops said, nudging the boy in the ribs. Kaj cracked a smile but didn't say anything.

"Maybe you should pay more attention to the fine points of dress. The things a gal sees but doesn't recognize."

"Like what?"

"Like a sharp pair of shoes." He stopped and pointed to his black leather shoes. "Compare our shoes. You're wearing good, sturdy, Danish shoes. Heavy leather and thick soles. Keep you warm in the winter and last about thirty years. How long have you had those?"

"A couple of years."

"They'll last forever, but they aren't exactly what I'd call fashionable. Look here. What's the first thing you notice about my shoes?"

"They're black."

"Not just black, Kaj. Very black. Black and shiny. Just enough to make the cat standing in them look like he's dressed up tall. No one's going to look closely at the pointed toes or the slick uppers, but they all go in to make an effect. That's what you want, the effect. Don't worry about a new suit. The old one's fine. Get yourself a new pair of shoes. That's what I'd do if I were you."

"You really think so?"

"You bet."

"We'll see."

In just a few minutes they reached the town square. Ahead on the left was the tiny shop with an old rusted bicycle frame welded above the blue awning. Several new bicycles stood chained to a rack out front. The models varied only slightly. Some had wicker baskets mounted on the handlebars and others lacked bells and reflectors. Each carried a large paper tag on the frame with the price written in by hand. Chops looked at one, rolled his eyes, and showed it to Kaj.

"Three fifty?"

"That's what it says." Chops had only planned on spending half that, but he didn't want to waste his afternoon looking at all the stores in town.

"Are you sure you don't want to find something secondhand at the pier?" Kaj asked.

"These days, secondhand usually means stolen, and I can't afford to get picked up for driving a hot bike. Let's go inside and see what we can find." The store smelled heavily of oil and solvent, evidence of the workshop in the rear. People were spending more time making sure their old bikes kept working rather than buying new ones. Tires and spare parts hung on the cream-colored walls along with wrenches and pliers of various sizes. The bicycles inside seemed more adequately outfitted with mirrors, saddlebags, fur seats, and self-generating head lamps.

A middle-aged woman with a smudge of grease on her cheek walked out from behind the counter, wiped her hands on a cloth, and headed across the store to them. She had tied her hair back in a bun, and she wore soiled work clothes. "Can I help?"

Chops smiled and nodded. "I lost my bike a few days ago and I need another."

"Sorry to hear that," she said in a way that Chops believed she meant it. "Did you lose it to someone or all by yourself?"

"I guess someone decided they needed my bike more than I did."

The woman sighed. "I'm not surprised. Seems like a lot of bicycles are getting picked these days. You are the third this week that I've heard about, but I guess the police told you there has been a rash of theft."

Chops shrugged. He hadn't considered going to the police because he was afraid they would ask him too many questions, like where he was when the bike was stolen or what he had been doing that night. Walking into a police precinct was asking for trouble.

She waved her arm at the merchandise. "I don't have much to offer, but you're welcome to what I've got. I always have more in the spring and summer, and with the war and all, it's a miracle I've got anything at all. You're not looking for a tandem, are you?" She chuckled to herself.

Kaj looked up but didn't say anything.

"I was hoping to get something for less than two hundred," Chops said.

"Not these days. I guess everything has gotten more expensive than it used to be. The cheaper bikes are out front. Here, let me show you some." She headed to the front of the store and Chops and Kaj followed. Before they reached the door, Chops saw a man with a bandage on his ear walk by the window, and something clicked inside him. Although he only caught a glimpse of the man, he felt certain that he was one of the two thugs who had jumped him outside of Louisa's apartment. He didn't see his face clearly, but he remembered tearing the man's ear in the fight. Barely pausing to think, Chops grabbed a screwdriver from off the rack and slipped it under his jacket and into his belt. He told himself to stay cool. "I'm afraid I only brought two hundred Krone. I'll go to the bank and get some more. Come on, Kaj. Let's go."

He pulled Kaj by the sleeve and brushed past the saleswoman. He reached the street just in time to see the man turn the corner.

"You said you had the money," Kaj said.

"Forget the money. I just saw the cat who stole my bike."

"Are you sure?"

Chops did not answer. Instead, he headed down the street, walking quickly but not breaking into a run that might attract attention. He rounded the corner and saw the man about twenty yards ahead. A quick glance assured him that the street was empty, and he broke into a sprint. As Chops and Kaj approached, the man looked over his shoulder and began to run. "Nail him," Chops yelled, and Kaj took off past him like a war horse.

Five steps ahead of him, Kaj reached out, grabbed the man's coat by the shoulders, and pushed him into the brick building. The man grunted and pulled, but he was no match for the boy's strength. Kaj wrenched his arm behind his back in a hammer lock and pushed him hard against the wall a second time. The man went limp.

"Not here, Kaj. Drag him around the corner."

"Let me go, you son of a bitch," the man sputtered.

Kaj responded by pushing him forward and forcing him around the corner into a dead-end alley. Then he whirled the man around to face Chops. "Is this the guy?"

The man looked much smaller in the light, but it was he. Chops would not mistake his pinched-in face, and he knew that he had practically ripped off his ear in the fight. It was the bandage that gave him away. He resisted the temptation to belt the man senseless while Kaj held him. Instead, he relaxed and said, "How's the ear?"

"Fuck off, nigger-kike."

Chops paused a second, nodded, and then backhanded the man as hard as he could across the cheekbone. He followed with two quick upper-cuts with his left hand. Helpless in Kaj's grip, the man coughed and spat, and then looked up. All the color had drained out of his face, and a trickle of blood dripped from his lip.

Chops rubbed his knuckles and hoped they would not swell. Despite the chill, he felt tiny beads of sweat form on his forehead. Slowly, he pulled the pointy screwdriver out of his belt and stuck it against the man's throat, forcing his jaw upwards. "Should we kill him?"

Kaj's eyes widened, but he did not loosen his grip. The smell of feces crept into the air, and Chops knew the battle was over. Everything had happened so quickly that he had no idea what to do next. He didn't really want to hurt the man, but he wanted to know what had happened that night. He thought about what Wolf said, that the mugging probably hadn't been a random crime.

"Don't kill me, mister. It wasn't my idea."

"What did you do with my bicycle?"

"Tossed it in the harbor. That was the deal. Don't take it out on me. I just took the damned thing. You're not going to kill me for stealing your horn, are you?"

"What deal?"

"All I was supposed to do was steal your horn. And it was attached to the bike, so I took both of them. I got one hundred for the job, and the money's yours. I swear."

"Who paid you?"

"I never saw him before or since. Just some guy who said he didn't like your kind of music. That's all. Just some guy."

"German or Danish?"

"German."

"What did he look like?"

"He was...kind of... He was just a normal guy."

"What color hair did he have? What length?"

"Short. Blond. Average size. Maybe a little bigger."

"Tattoos? Scars? Anything?"

"Nothing special. I swear I've never seen him before. Please don't kill me. Please, God. I've got a wife. And a kid. I've got a kid, for Christ's sake." His voice had trailed off into a whimper.

He dropped the screwdriver and looked at Kaj. "Let him go."

"What?"

"Just let him go. Go on. Get out of here. Never let me see you again, understand?"

The man stood there for a moment and then began running down the street. He did not look back before turning the corner and disappearing. Chops' stomach began to turn, and he braced himself against the wall. Herr Wolf had been right. It wasn't the bike they were after. Someone wanted to silence his horn.

—

Chapter Seventeen

By the time Chops reached Smukke, his pulse had almost returned to normal. Roughly an hour had passed since the hood who had stolen his bicycle and cornet ran down the alley and disappeared on the Gammel Strand, and it had taken that long for the excitement to wear off. Fear always strikes after the fact. Chops did not hesitate when he was chasing a known criminal down a secluded alleyway. He stuck a screwdriver against the man's throat and threatened to kill him, remaining as calm as a spring morning, but after the incident, the fear gnawed away on his insides like termites.

Kaj's reactions were also delayed, but much more intense. "What the hell did you let him go for?" the boy demanded, shaking his fists in the air. Chops had never heard that tone in his voice.

"What would you have done? Killed him?"

"I wouldn't have chased him in the first place. But if I did, I wouldn't just let him go. He might go to the police, or the Gestapo, or just find some of his friends. Jesus, Chops, he thought we were going to kill him."

"We've got to get out of here," Chops had replied, cutting him off. They had walked down the street at a brisk pace, constantly looking over their shoulders to see if someone was following them. Although they recognized no one, they detoured up into the Konigstorv Square and then back down to the waterfront just to be safe. Kaj stopped arguing after about five minutes and walked the rest of the way to the tattoo parlor in a glum silence.

"I'll see you later," Chops said as they reached the tattoo parlor.

"Yeah."

From the waterfront it took about twenty minutes to reach Smukke. He surveyed the street as he approached the club, and he walked slowly, letting a young couple walking arm in arm pass him and turn the corner before he ducked down the stairwell and knocked on the door. As always, he used the code. Three soft taps and one hard. Morse code for V. V is for victory.

Tapio opened the door almost before Chops had finished knocking. Only his eyes and nose poked out between the brim of his crumpled tweed hat and the top of his cream-colored scarf, and his overcoat draped almost to the ground. "What are you doing here so early?" the bartender asked. "I didn't expect you here for another two hours."

"You were wrong," he said simply, easing himself through the door and shutting the latch behind him. He didn't like keeping the door open.

"Well, you're lucky you caught me."

"I thought you didn't need anything in town."

Tapio unraveled his scarf from around his face. "I thought so too. That was before I looked behind the bar and realized that we didn't have any coasters. If I had looked earlier it would have saved me a trip."

"Tell me the truth, Tapio," Chops said, hoping to sound jovial. "You just can't stand the smell of the beer brewing, so you thought you'd get some fresh air while you had the chance. Isn't that right?" Even though they were far away from the kitchen, they could smell the malt and the yeast from the beer.

"You've got it wrong. I love the smell of beer. That's why I run this joint." Tapio peered out the door and up the steps. "So where's your new bike?"

"Nothing worth having," Chops said. Some people liked to spread their news as soon as it happened, but he didn't like telling stories that did not have endings. He hoped Tapio would notice he didn't feel like talking.

"I'll be back in an hour or so," Tapio said. "If you leave, make sure and lock the place up. OK?"

"Sure."

As soon as the door closed, Smukke was completely dark except for one forty-watt bulb behind the bar. Dark and empty. The chairs were stacked on top of the tables and a light smell of aroma tried to cover the smell of old cigarette butts and fresh-brewed beer. Even in its best days, the room had never had good ventilation, and now that the small windows that peaked out onto the street were boarded up and the door stayed closed, fresh air never circulated.

Chops walked slowly to the back of the stage and stood there, cornet in hand, looking into the empty room. In a few hours dozens of people would be packed into the space, all moving and dancing and drinking and trying to forget the war. Or perhaps tonight would be another slow night. It was hard to say. He stepped to the toe of the stage, listening to the boards creak under his feet. Lightly, he fingered the valves on his cornet and listened to the felts tap against each other. These were empty-room sounds. Even the slightest chatter would cover them up. He did not finger notes, but rhythms, cadences; he was his own drummer, leading him into his private battle. The knuckles on his right hand had swollen from hitting the crook across the face, and they ached slightly. Ignoring the pain, he brought the horn to his lips and played one slow note, deep and full, letting the sound linger and then echo in the room.

Drawing the air deep inside his lungs, Chops played the first line to the chorus of a song he had learned as a child. *Are you from Dixie.* His father had sung that song to him often when he was young, and he could still remember sitting in his lap, looking up into his face, hanging on every note, every word a treasure unto itself. He could still smell his father's breath, heavy with onions and tobacco. Chops had not thought of that song since he was seven years old, and he did not know why it came into his mind right now. Suddenly he felt lonely. The words of the song ran through his mind as he played the notes, slow and somber although they were written upbeat. *If you're from Alabama, Tennessee, or Caroline. Anywhere below the Mason-Dixon line, then you're from Dixie.*

Everything came down to this. He was not in Alabama, Tennessee or Carolina. He was in Denmark, thousands of miles from home. Alone. That was the part that bothered him the most. He tried to pretend that it wasn't true, that he had found a home among the piers, but it was just a lie. Without Svenya he was a stranger. She made him belong. Together they made their own niche in the world, sheltering each other from the wind and the storms. As the trifles of daily life wore him down, she was there to listen and to care. And she had her own troubles, her dilemmas, which at times seemed trivial and at times monumental, but troubles are always lighter when they are shared.

Chops had to get her out.

Who paid the hood to steal his horn? He drew a deep breath and blew an F, attacking the note. Why had Svenya been arrested? A. This one he hit even harder. When would the deception end? C C C C C. He blew the high notes as hard as he could, spitting them out of his horn, hurling them across the room and splattering them against the far wall with ferocity.

Chops brought the cornet down from his lips. Blood was surging through his lips and making them burn. Of course he knew why they stole his horn. Most Nazis despised black people and jazz, and ripping him off served their hatred twice. Fortunately, Wolf had been able to help, and by doing that he also showed that he didn't know Chops was involved with the underground. The code had not been broken. By supplying Chops with a new cornet, Wolf showed that he suspected nothing. The secret was safe. Olsen always said that security was important, and he was willing to risk anything to make sure that everything was tight. Hadn't he suggested that Wolf might help? If Chops had been arrested, the spy would have disappeared and started his network somewhere else, in a different part of the city or the country. If this was true, it meant that Chops was no more to Olsen than an inanimate tool, a simple pawn which the spy could sacrifice on a whim.

And Svenya?

She had no value in the game at all. None at all. Hoping Olsen would help set her free was like hoping it wouldn't freeze in the wintertime. The Danish spy had practically said as much the first time Chops mentioned that she was in trouble, but he had wanted to believe otherwise. He had fooled himself. Pacing back and forth across the stage, his steps became attacks on the floor. The skin in his neck began to tighten, and he ground his back teeth together. His grip on the cornet tightened until the finger hook felt like it might cut into his flesh. How stupid he had been to think that the spy would help? Damn. Why would he? So far Chops had not made good on any of his threats to stop working with the resistance. In fact, he had worked harder and taken more risks than ever before.

Chops stopped and tried to draw a breath to fill his entire body. The pressure inside his skull had reached the point that he thought it would burst like an overripe grape. He closed his eyes and consciously asked his fingers to relax their grip on the cornet. After a moment they obeyed.

Olsen had miscalculated. Because Chops had acted like a puppy, the spy assumed he would continue to roll over and wag his tail. He didn't know that Chops had another alternative. Between the idle comments at the radio station, the dinner party, and finally the letter from Svenya, Wolf had made his offer clear. Give me someone from the underground and I'll give you your lover back. The leader of a spy ring in exchange for a viola player. It seemed like an easy trade for the German.

When she was free, they would slip on the next trawler and hide away in Sweden. Louisa could help with that. Chops had at least enough money to support himself and Svenya for a year, maybe two. If anything, working with the resistance would be lucrative. They could stay if they wanted, or perhaps even return to America. Everything told him to do it. Take Svenya and go home. Make the life you want.

And what would he be giving away? If only he were not helping the Germans. The Nazis. Their military machine rolled over Europe, forced jazz music underground, and preached racial superiority, and now Chops was about to give them exactly what they wanted.

Most people in Denmark could vividly remember every detail of the Nazi invasion, but Chops' recollection was sketchy. The armies had rolled over the border at dawn and headed straight for the capital city. Just about that time, Tapio and Chops had finished a bottle of gin and staggered out onto the dim and empty streets. As the German armored divisions were speeding towards Copenhagen, Chops was weaving his way home and pouring himself into bed. He heard some strange noises around noon, but pulled the pillow over his head and went back to sleep. Later he discovered that the entire Danish navy had left their moorings and scuttled in the harbor. The Viking pride sank itself in its home harbor instead of surrendering.

His first news of the invasion came around one o'clock, when he woke up and peered out of his window to see what all the commotion was about in the harbor. The sky was gray and foreboding, and on the dark horizon he saw a fleet of foreign war ships, with guns aimed at the city. The threat was very simple. Surrender or we bomb Copenhagen out of existence. King Christian had no choice.

Chops wished the question put to him were so simple. If A then B. Ergo if not B then not A. A logical relationship from which others could be determined. But instead of this mathematical simplicity, Chops found himself in a strange puppet theater where no one knew who held the strings and who was attached. Once again, Chops put the cornet to his lips. This time he played *Trumpet Voluntary*. Classical music always had a numbing effect, like an aural narcotic. Beautiful and vicious. As long as you played the notes exactly as they were written, varying neither in tempo nor intonation, the results were entrancing, but as soon as you tried to add a piece of yourself to the work, everything fell apart, and the loss felt like a cattle prod. So he marched in a historic line led by Bach and followed by every musician who ever played the notes, not worrying that classical music did not suit the image of the jazz renegade he had so painstakingly developed for the audience of the outside world.

After holding the last note and letting it fade away slowly, Chops lowered the cornet and felt that the anger and tension had faded away with it. If he really wanted to turn in Olsen, he had to consider all the angles. One miscalculation and he would lose everything. By pointing a finger at Olsen, he pointed a much clearer finger at himself. If the spy escaped the trap, Chops would fall into it. Even if Olsen did go to jail, there was no reason for the Gestapo to let him walk away, or for them to release Svenya. The more he thought about it, the more dangerous his plan became. If Olsen had any hint that Chops had switched sides, he would kill Chops immediately, just like he killed the man who sold him the ambulance. But he would never crack if the Germans caught him. He would immediately bite the cyanide button on his collar and welcome instant death because he was too professional to let them torture him. If that happened, another member of the resistance would track down Chops. Along the waterfront, Chops had heard too many stories of informants being dragged out of the harbor with their bellies sliced open and their insides pulled out and chewed on by crabs.

Chops would have to take Svenya and disappear immediately. If he couldn't make sure that he could get away, the plan would be suicide. But Louisa could help. She had been around so long that no one would question her if she said she needed to get someone to Sweden. He would go to Kakadu and ask her. If she said yes, then he was in business.

The trickier issue was with Wolf. How could he be certain that the German would keep his side of the bargain? Chops had learned much from Olsen, but the most important lesson was that no one could be trusted. For every additional person involved, the risk increased geometrically. The danger would never go away, but perhaps he could minimize it. As Chops stared into the empty bar room, the possibilities became even more convoluted, but he knew that there must be an answer. What was it?

Maybe Wolf could put up some sort of collateral. Or better yet, Chops could threaten to testify against him if everything did not go smoothly. He imagined how the dialogue would go. Seated in the corner office of the radio station, Wolf would clear his throat and ask, "What if I didn't live up to my side of the bargain? I might even have you arrested."

The smile would not fade from Chops' face. "In that unlikely event, I would have to tell my interrogators that you had known about the resistance ring for months but had chosen not to do anything about it."

The color would slowly drain from the German's face. Or perhaps Wolf would see the threat for what it was and laugh. He might arrest Chops on the spot and let the Gestapo torture him until he unveiled everything he knew. The only certainty was that once he put this plan into action, he couldn't stop it again. No second chances.

Second chance.

Second chance. Chops repeated the words out loud several times, knowing that he had just found the missing piece, but he couldn't quite make it fit the puzzle. Second chance. Perhaps he would offer Wolf a second chance. A second installment. Of course, that was the answer. He would promise Olsen as the first of many, a gift in good faith. Once the Gestapo let Svenya out, he would show them supply dumps, decipher Allied codes, turn in corrupt officials... The list of promises went on and on. He could make a very tempting offer. As soon as Svenya was out of jail, they would slip away to Sweden and renege on the bargain. Never before had Chops made a deal he planned to cheat on, but it didn't bother him.

Some noise on the street above caught Chops' attention, and he thought that Tapio might have returned. He rolled his eyes, knowing that he wouldn't be able to leave for another hour—longer if Tapio had heard about him and Kaj chasing down that hood. The sooner he spoke to Louisa, the better he would feel about his plan. Gradually, the footsteps faded and Chops realized that Tapio had not come back from town.

Quickly, Chops slipped his cornet back into the case and slid it under the side of the stage. If he still had his old horn, he would have carried it with him or at least hidden it under the table in his dressing room, but now he was in a rush and it just felt like someone else's horn, someone who he didn't like.

His overcoat lay on a barstool next to the door. After putting it on and turning out the light, Chops opened the door, twisted the knob to make sure it was locked, slipped outside, and scurried up the stairs. Although the sun was low and casting long shadows on the street, it seemed unusually bright. Leaving the darkened cellar had the same effect of walking out of a movie cinema in the middle of the day.

The clear, cold air bit at his skin, and he pulled his collar around his neck. The only people on the streets seemed to be the seamen who docked their ships early in the fall. Chops walked east, past the Glypotec and the castle. He walked quickly, not paying attention to the stately architecture or the cyclists who sometimes rode on the sidewalks. He had hoped that everything would feel lighter somehow, now that he had made his decision to betray Olsen, but he could taste a thread of doubt, large enough to make him gag but small enough not to choke him. How much was he prepared to sacrifice for Svenya? If he left Copenhagen, he could never protect his friends, and the Germans might crush Smukke under their boots. They might do that anyway.

Chops turned the corner and walked under a high stone arch. "Fourteenth army blocked in Algeria" called the paper vendor half-heartedly from under his black fisherman's cap. Chops watched his stubby jaw and the brown teeth moving up and down. Would Chops turn in this man in exchange for Svenya? Yes. Yes, he would, he thought as he walked past. He would take one of the Colt .45's hidden in the ceiling at Smukke and blow the man's head off if it would save Svenya.

It was just before five o'clock when Chops arrived at Cafe Kakadu, and from the street he peered through the large glass panes and saw that most of the tables inside were empty. These days, Kakadu did most of its business at breakfast and in the mid-afternoon, although before the war it saw its busiest hours between midnight and two. He watched Louisa wipe off the counter top with a gray rag and then check to see how much coffee was left in the bin. For Chops, this was not a social visit. He came to ask a friend a favor, and although he knew that she could get him to Sweden without any trouble, he felt uncomfortable about asking her. Everything was different after spending the night with her last night, or was it?

Walking through the door, he caught Louisa's eye and walked up to the counter.

"Hello lover," she says in a way that could have been bitingly sarcastic or vaguely endearing, and Chops couldn't decide which. He did not comment. What could he say? He felt like he did in junior high school, when he decided that kissing the principal's daughter had been a mistake.

She smiled and he saw her as she was last night. Remembering how she dug her fingers into the small of his back and bit his shoulder made blood rush to his cheeks. He tried to act normal. "How are you?"

"Tired. Not much sleep last night. And yourself?"

"Been thinking."

"Oh shit," Louisa called, much louder than she needed to. "Sounds like trouble."

Chops perched himself on one of the stools and dropped his elbows onto the counter. "Maybe so. Maybe not."

"Do you want a cup of coffee or anything? Glass of juice?"

"Cafe au lait."

"It'll just take a second," she said as she turned away.

Chops reached into his jacket pocket and pulled out a pack of cigarettes. Lighting one, he wondered why he was surprised that Louisa was acting awkward, something he had not counted on. Of course he had not been alone in the bed last night, and she must have some mixed feelings as well. She wasn't just a crusty middle-aged woman who landed in a shabby dive in Copenhagen out of sheer chance. Maybe she hid her emotions and fears so she would get along better on the streets, but they were there, and this was the first time in eight years that she had ever shown them. Maybe just a little, but they were there.

She returned and set the cup down on the counter. Pointing to his cigarette, she asked if she could have one. Without a word he picked up the pack and shook one out, and as she put it to her lips he cracked open his Zippo lighter. Exhaling a billowing cloud she asked, "So have you come to any conclusions?"

"I've decided to take your advice."

"That's the scariest thing you've ever said," she replied with a smile. "What advice?"

"I'm going to leave Copenhagen. With Svenya." The words hung in the air like they were stuck in a spider's web. Chops surprised himself with the conviction behind the simple sentence. The finality. He was going to leave. He picked up his cup and sipped the creamy coffee.

Louisa's face went blank, but Chops didn't know if it was out of fear, anger, disappointment, or pure confusion. "Did I miss something?"

"I'm going to get her out."

"How?"

Chops took a long drag on his cigarette and set it down on the ashtray. This plan was too dangerous to tell anyone, although he could use all the help he could get. But perhaps if he were vague enough it would be all right. "I'm going to make a deal."

"With the Gestapo? You are a prick." Louisa grabbed a sugar jar and slammed it down on the counter with a crack. She leaned forward and stared at him. "After all the Germans have done, you are going to make a deal with them? I can't believe it. What are you going to do, lead a raid on Smukke and get all your friends put in the slammer? Super. Those people trust you. Hell Chops, they worship you. And you just pulled the wool over everyone's eyes. Including mine." Chops had thought she might turn and walk away, but instead she just stood there and stared at him with her reddening eyes.

"Nobody's gonna raid Smukke," he said calmly. "In fact, part of my deal is that they continue to turn their backs until the war is over. The Germans don't care about Smukke. If they did they would have shut it down long ago. They want to shut down the resistance."

"What do you know about the resistance?" Her eyes narrowed, and Chops considered asking her the same question. If he was wrong about Louisa, if she were also involved, then he had just made a deadly mistake. He looked around to make sure no one was watching. Even though the place was almost empty, he lowered his voice. "I've got something the Germans want, and I'm going to make a trade."

"In exchange for Svenya?"

Chops nodded, and Louisa began to laugh. "That's the most absurd thing I've ever heard. I mean, who would have ever thought you were working with the resistance? I don't know what you have up your sleeve, but you've lost your mind. What makes you think the Gestapo will release her when you've given them what they want?"

"Because I'm going to promise them more. I'm

going to promise them a whole army of saboteurs. After I get through with them, they will think there are twenty legions of well-trained Danes, ready to throw the Germans out of Copenhagen at a moment's notice. Suicide troops. People in the army. Even some of their own who are secretly against Hitler. They will do anything I say in return for that."

Louisa shook her head. "Why should they believe you?"

"The Germans are so paranoid, they will believe anything I tell them."

"One more question."

"Shoot."

"What's going to happen to you when you can't produce this army of saboteurs?"

"Nothing. Because by the time they figure it out, I'm going to be in Sweden with Svenya."

"And you want me to find you a place in the hull of some ship headed to open waters?"

"I want you to find us a place. Can you do it?" Chops asked her the question although he knew the answer. The real question was would she do it.

"Yeah, I can do it. It won't be cheap, but I can do it. When do you want to leave?"

"Friday morning."

"That's not much notice."

"Not much time for word to leak to the Germans. That's how I see it."

"I'll give you the details tonight at Smukke. Tell me, Chops, if your plan doesn't work...if you can't get Svenya out of jail, are you still going to go to Sweden?"

"No. I'll be dead."

Chapter Eighteen

Chops sat alone at the small square table in Hviids Vinstue. He looked at the grandfather clock across the room and then at his watch to see if the two agreed. They did. Three forty-five. He had arrived on time, and Herr Wolf was fifteen minutes late and counting. Most elegant, downtown pubs were empty at this time of the day, and he had assumed Hviids would be too, but to his surprise, almost every table was filled with men in business suits and men in uniform—both German and Danish. Chops told himself that on another day he would not have felt uncomfortable in this old-boy, upper-crust atmosphere, and that the tension in his stomach was due purely to his mission alone. Wolf's tardiness did not help.

Yesterday, right after Louisa had agreed to help him escape to Sweden, he had telephoned Herr Wolf at the radio station to arrange a meeting. "Why don't we meet tomorrow around three-thirty at Vinstue Hviids," Wolf had suggested. Chops would have preferred to meet sooner, but he agreed because he didn't want to sound harried. He had never been to this particular wine cellar before, although it was one of the oldest and most famous in Copenhagen. The slate floor, the walnut paneling, the multi-colored, blown-glass windows all blended together to create the atmosphere of well-preserved elegance. Some of the drawings and certificates on the walls dated back three centuries, and nothing had been added to the decor in seventy years. The waiters seemed to have been there just as long.

Chops sipped from his Tuborg beer, savoring the crisp, bright taste. He held the glass up to the light and marveled at the clear, golden color and the thin layer of foam. No stores had stocked any beer in six months. Those who worked at the Tuborg factory sold bottles on the black market in small numbers, but management kept strict watch over the kegs. Rumor had it that ninety-five per cent of the beer made in Denmark was exported to Germany, and by now Chops had gotten used to drinking the cloudy, cidery beer he and Tapio brewed in Smukke. He hadn't seen Tuborg in a bar in months, but he did not usually frequent places that catered to such a select clientele. As soon as he walked through the door, a host stopped him and asked his name.

"Chops."

"Do you have reservations?"

"I'm meeting an associate," Chops said without trying to cover his resentment. He had never heard of a bar asking for reservations, especially in the middle of the afternoon.

"His name."

"Klaus Wolf. He is the director of Danish National Radio."

The expression of the host's face transformed from grumbly displeasure to unbridled welcome. "Why yes, of course. Herr Wolf mentioned that he would be meeting someone this afternoon. Sit at any free table, and I'll point him to you when he arrives."

Chops looked at the old grandfather clock again. Three fifty-one. He decided he would stay until four o'clock, four-fifteen at the latest, before assuming that Wolf had gotten tied up with something and would not make it. Gazing around the room, Chops saw no one under fifty years old. Everyone looked like businessmen or representatives from parliament, with their thinning hair, sagging eyes, and three piece suits. Among the military men he saw only officers, and there wasn't a woman in the house, not even a waitress.

Chops would have felt better, if he could have met Wolf in a more private setting, but this was the German's suggestion. It made sense. The radio staff might start rumors if they had met in the station, and Wolf wouldn't risk going to the waterfront, although this place was nothing more than a white-collar Kakadu. If you wanted to pay to smuggle stolen porcelain out of Denmark, you would go to Kakadu. If you wanted to have the export laws altered in your favor, you would come to a place like Hviids Vinstue. Here people had contacts. Chops' stomach went cold when he realized that Olsen might have contacts here too. It was a risk he had to take.

Looking up, Chops saw Herr Wolf coming through the arched doorway to his left. He looked distinguished in a blue suit with a medal pinned on his left breast. When he reached the table he did not sit down. "Good afternoon, Chops. How are you?"

Chops stood up and offered his hand. "Fine. And you?"

"Excellent." He looked around and motioned to an empty table in a small alcove. "Why don't we sit over there?"

"OK," Chops said, and they pushed across the

room and sat down at a table so small that their noses almost touched, but the niche provided a touch of privacy for which Chops was grateful. "What is that medal you're wearing?" he asked.

Wolf did not look down. "It's the service cross from the great war."

"I didn't know you fought in the First World War."

"Come now, Chops. Everyone my age fought in the First World War. I was in the signal corps, so I was spared from the worst of it—the trenches, the mustard gas, but you didn't come here to talk about ancient history, did you?"

Chops hesitated. "A friend of mine was arrested by the Gestapo last week. Her name is Svenya Hjorth."

Wolf nodded. "I understand she is a spy."

"She's not."

"Then you have nothing to worry about, do you?"

Wolf's reply followed as quickly as a fencer's rapier, and Chops reminded himself to be careful. The rules were the same as at the dinner party but the stakes were much higher. "I wish I had your faith in the Gestapo's sense of justice. Or their willingness to administer it."

"These are difficult times, Chops. Everyone is concerned about security, and we can't let people accused of treason continue to roam freely, regardless of how circumstantial the evidence."

Chops chewed on the word "accused". Had someone really pointed a finger at Svenya, or had the Gestapo itself passed the verdict on her? Either way, it was preposterous. Or was it? If he led a secret life with Olsen and the resistance, it was possible that she did also.

A gray-haired waiter came to their table and

asked if they would like something from the bar. Without looking to Chops for approval, Herr Wolf ordered two beers.

When the waiter was gone, Chops asked the question outright. "Can you get her out?"

"Yes."

"Good." Chops had not expected such a direct answer. In two minutes with this man he had accomplished more than he had in a week of bargaining with Olsen. More and more he felt that he had found the solution to his problem. "The question now is will you."

"That is the question," Wolf answered, reaching into his pocket to grab a box of cigarettes. Chops wondered if he was stalling for time, trying to decide how to proceed. After lighting a cigarette for himself and for his guest, Wolf continued. "As I said, everyone is concerned about security. When we came into Denmark, everyone believed that Germans and Danes could coexist peacefully, and we did for several months, relatively speaking. However, recently we have begun to feel a certain amount of, shall we say, unrest amongst the population, and my superiors are becoming uneasy. You see, Chops, we don't know the scope of the situation here."

"We?"

"High command. I'm really an outsider when it comes down to it."

"Oh," Chops replied, although he wasn't sure he knew what that was supposed to mean.

"If things had gone my way, Denmark and Germany would have agreed on the present protectorship agreement without the rather bullish display of force that we used. Recently, the Gestapo has arrested several suspected agitators, hoping to ferret out the resistance before any real

harm occurs. At this stage, it would be rather difficult to reverse the process."

"But you said you can get Svenya out."

"I would have to offer something in return."

"Like what?"

Before Wolf could answer, the waiter returned
and placed two glasses of beer on top of cardboard
coasters on the table. "Fifteen Krone, please."

Chops and Herr Wolf both reached for their
wallets, but Wolf said, "Let me invite you to this
round." He handed the waiter a fifty. When the
waiter was gone, he said, "What can you tell me
about the resistance?"

Chops took a sip of beer. "If we were in America,
I would refuse to answer on the grounds that anything I said might incriminate me."

"But we are not in America. And this is not a
court of law, but simply two friends drinking a glass
of beer and trying to solve a problem. Nothing said
here will leave the table."

Chops remembered Olsen hammering the rake
into the tree above his head and saying that Wolf
could not be trusted. He was on dangerous ground,
but he saw no choice but to proceed with caution.
"I know a lot of people on the waterfront. I hear
things."

"Things that you might pass along?"

"I might."

"I see. Unfortunately, a pledge that you might
pass information along is not enough to warrant
the release of a known agitator. The Gestapo would
require something more concrete. After all, you
could be lying."

Chops paid careful attention to Herr Wolf's
nuances, the way he said the Gestapo would require more and not that he, personally, would require more. And that his reliability was in doubt.

He smiled, knowing reliability was his trump suit.

"Last Sunday, an RAF Mosquito bomber flew over a farm north of Copenhagen and parachuted two canisters containing small arms and ammunition, plastic explosives, blasting caps, rations, and other supplies. This was intended for the resistance, but your men intercepted it. That was the seventh shipment from the Royal Air Force, six of which were received as planned." Chops carefully mixed the lie with the truth, hoping that Herr Wolf would believe the entire parcel.

"You know where the rest are stored?"

"I might."

"Such information would be very useful to the Gestapo. It might be enough to ensure the release of your friend."

Measuring the look in the German's eyes and the tone of his voice, Chops knew that he had taken the bait. It was just like watching the audience from on stage to see how they were reacting to different songs and styles of play, one of the tricks he had learned as a young man and perfected over the years. However, he had to be careful not to promise what he couldn't deliver. "I'm not sure how useful that information would be. Of course, the Gestapo could grab the stuff, but Denmark is a big place. Your boys couldn't stop more from coming in."

"But if there were no one to receive the parcels, our problem would be solved."

Chops shook his head. "Too many cats in the alley, if you know what I mean."

"You are implying that the situation is much worse than we feared."

"Downright unpleasant."

Wolf took a minute to digest this. He sipped his beer, smoked his cigarette, and played with his coaster, so much so that Chops had the feeling he was overacting. "What would you suggest?"

"Now I'm no expert in anti-sabotage, but if I wanted to disable an army, I'd start by knocking off the general. Then maybe everything would fall apart on its own."

After a moment Wolf said, "Forgive me, Chops, but I must say I'm not at all sure how to read you. Sometimes it seems you are nothing more than a street-wise kid, and sometimes I sense something much more."

"I am—after all—an associate professor at the University. Or I was."

"Yes, of course. And you have managed to stay out of jail under a regime that openly denounces Negroes, along with Jews, gypsies, and all the rest. Besides all that, you are a well-known jazz musician, and the country of your birth is at war with Germany. You must say it is rather remarkable that you've stayed out of trouble this long."

"It helps to have a Danish passport."

"Ah yes. Your late wife."

Chops wondered if he had told Wolf about Marie. Perhaps he had mentioned it at the dinner party, but he wasn't quite sure. Even if he had not, it would not be a difficult piece of information to obtain. "We seem to have strayed from the point."

"Yes. You said the way to crush an army is to eliminate the general. Am I to understand that you could deliver this general to the Gestapo?"

Chops finished the last third of his beer in one draught. A trickle escaped and dripped down his chin, and he wiped it off with a napkin. "Anything's possible."

"This sounds promising."

Chops looked at Herr Wolf. He was a rather refined man, well-dressed and comfortable. Yet something did not add up, but Chops could not pinpoint exactly what. "Just out of curiosity, what's in it for you?"

"The same as for you: protection. The radio station has been under fire ever since I came to work there. My superiors think that I stray too far from the party line, for example, by broadcasting the Thursday Night Exchange. No matter what I call the show, everyone knows it is jazz and that jazz is frowned upon. In return for this general, as you call him, I would secure my position and never again would I encounter resistance from above regarding what I play, or even how I live. Did you know what a risk it was for me to invite you to dinner? Everyone in the occupation government is under some degree of scrutiny. If headquarters knew that I entertained a musician at my house, I might have to answer some uncomfortable questions. If they knew that you brought me a contraband bottle of wine, I could get sent back to Germany. However, if I helped destroy an organized resistance ring that is as large as the one you describe, I would be beyond reproach."

Chops nodded. He had not even considered that Wolf, too, must watch his step. The rumble of multiple conversations in the bar had not decreased, and Chops looked around to make sure that no one was listening. He lowered his voice. "This general is the head of the only organized resistance ring in Denmark. He has direct communications and supply routes to London. He might not be able to throw you out of Denmark, but if he continues his work he will be a real pain in your ass. I'll bring him in, but not until you get Svenya out of jail."

Wolf laughed in a cynical way. "The Gestapo would never agree. When he is behind bars, then the girl goes free."

"What if he is shot while trying to escape?"

"That is the Gestapo's problem. They are professionals, and they won't let that happen. Bring him to us, and you get the girl."

"That's not all I want." Wolf raised an eyebrow, and Chops continued. "I need assurances that you won't just arrest her again the next day. Or me either, for that matter. And to pull off this exchange, I will need to expose some of my friends to the Gestapo. They must be protected as well."

"Can you be a little more specific?"

"My band plays almost every night."

"Yes, I know. At an underground club called Smukke on Puggards Gade. It's run by a gentleman named Tapio Brocks, and that is where your friend was arrested. I know all about it."

"That is where everything will come down. I'll arrange for this general to arrive at a given time, and you can be waiting for him. Promise me that your boys won't arrest everyone in the club and shut it down. That joint has nothing to do with the resistance. People come there to drink and to dance. That's it. You have nothing to fear from them."

"That can be arranged." The German spoke very slowly. "But if anything goes wrong, if the Gestapo walks into a trap, if your man doesn't show, anything at all, then they'll mail your head to Germany, and I won't be able to do a thing about it."

"I'll pull it off."

"I'm sure you will try, Chops. However, I'm not so convinced that you will succeed. After all, this man has been operating right under our noses. What makes you think that he will just walk into a trap? Does he trust you?"

Chops shrugged. "No. Not me or anyone else.

But I'm not going to be so obvious as to invite him for a drink. In fact, I'm going to demand that he doesn't come near the club. But he will." Chops smiled, savoring the plan that would deliver Olsen into the German's hands and free Svenya from the hell of Gestapo interrogations. "Oh yeah, he'll be there. Just make sure you're ready for him."

"When?"

"Thursday. After the show. I'll arrange for your boys to get into Smukke early so they can be ready. As soon as we finish playing, you and me will go to Smukke, and he'll show up. I guarantee that."

"I'll pass that on. Give me a call at the station tomorrow."

Chops pushed out his chair and then hesitated. "Before I go, I want to tell you a story. When I was about ten years old and living in New Orleans, a raccoon found his way into our garbage can, dumped it over, and spread the trash all over the street. Not just once. He got into our trash every night for a month, and every morning my mother sent me out with a broom and a dust pan to clean up his mess. Every day I got madder and madder until I decided that the time had come for me to do something about that raccoon.

"The next night I laid a trap for him. I turned the trash can upside down and propped it up on a stick. When the raccoon came, he knocked over the stick, and the trash can fell down on top of him. There I was, hiding on the porch. I ran up, slipped a board under the can and turned it right side up. When I looked inside, I saw his eyes glowing like little moons in the bottom on the trash can. They scared the hell out of me, but I didn't stop. I put a laundry bag over the garbage pail and dumped that old raccoon into it. Tied it up tight and headed off to the Mississippi where I was going to drown my troubles for good."

Chops leaned forward over the table so his face was only inches away from Wolf's. "The problem was, that old raccoon wanted to live as much as I wanted to kill him. As I was carrying the bag down the street, he dug his teeth into my back, right through the canvas bag and through my shirt. Pain shot through me like I've never known before or since, and I dropped that bag. But the coon held on for another second, and he hung there by his teeth in my back like a fish hook. When the bag finally hit the ground, it was soaked in blood, and it was jumping around like crazy." Chops sat back in his chair and let the story sink in.

"Did he get out?" Wolf asked.

Chops shook his head slowly back and forth. "I had tied it up tight. I picked up that bag and flung it against the ground as hard as I could. I smashed it on the streets ten or twenty times until there was no life left in it. Then I sank it in the river just like I had planned, and I washed the blood off my face and arms on the bank. But no matter how hard I killed that old raccoon, the cut on my back kept on hurting. It pained me for weeks. Still hurts sometimes," he said.

"So what's the moral?" Wolf asked.

Chops finished his beer and stood up. "You Germans are funny. Always looking for morals when there ain't no moral to be found."

Chapter Nineteen

The last song on the Ma Rainey album faded away, and the speaker crackled as the needle reached beyond its groove. The walls of Chops' apartment seemed to contract when the music ended, as if the strength of Rainey's voice alone held them out beyond their angles. Chops surveyed his work. On the desk lay five sheets of paper, the result of two hours of meticulous problem-solving. Letters, key signatures, notes, scales, meaningless doodles and harmonic progressions covered the first three pages—failed attempts at encoding Peder Olsen's message that London's Radio Security Service would unravel after tonight's broadcast.

On the fourth page he had successfully encoded PACK RECEIVED, although he had sworn he wouldn't play the notes if the spy did not help Svenya.

The wall clock said six thirty. It was time for him to pack up his cornet and leave for the radio station. The tram stop was only five minutes away, but he had to ride it across the canal, into the heart of the city, and then change cars at the Nykonigstorv. Missing his connection would make him late for the seven o'clock radio show. He had been certain that Peder Olsen would contact him before tonight's performance, but it looked like the spy was not going to show. Was it just a thin hope that he would see Svenya without betraying Peder Olsen? It was true. As much as he disliked the man, he felt uneasy about denouncing him. But as Olsen said, "This is war." History would not change. The war would be won or lost somewhere else, in Russia, North Africa, or perhaps on a second front in France, but not in Denmark. The Viking kingdom was merely a sideshow.

But Olsen thought it was important, important enough to return to Denmark after the occupation and risk his life to establish a working resistance. If it was that important, why hadn't he lifted a finger to help Svenya? Did he think Chops was bluffing?

He wasn't.

On the fifth sheet of paper, Chops had encoded the message he would send tonight. Instead of playing PACK RECEIVED as Olsen had demanded, he would broadcast the truth, PACK NOT RECEIVED. When he realized that Chops had deliberately disobeyed him, he would be furious, perhaps to the level of carelessness. Olsen would know to track him down at Smukke because the Backbeats always played a midnight set there after the Thursday Night Exchange. When he arrived, the Gestapo would be waiting for him. He would not have a chance. In exchange for the leader of the resistance; they would free Svenya.

Chops knew the chances of success were slim. Perhaps Olsen was in another part of the country right now. He might not react tonight, or he might somehow detect a trap. Something as simple as not knowing the password to Smukke could botch the entire plan, and Svenya wouldn't get this chance again.

282 OGLESBY

Only the last link in the chain was steady. Louisa had taken care of her end of the deal, like she always did. Around lunch time, Chops had been to Cafe Kakadu. The little coffee shop was filled with workers on their afternoon break, and Louisa didn't have any help at the counter. She could not step outside to talk in private, so he sat down in the corner, lit a cigarette, and waited. After a few minutes she walked over to his table, flung down a cafe au lait which he hadn't ordered, and whisked to the next table before he could say a word. The cup clinked against the saucer, and some of the dark liquid spilled over the rim. On the coffee-soaked napkin he read her message. "Passage for two aboard the GARM. 4:00 a.m. Don't be late."

"How much for the coffee?" he called, folding the napkin and placing it in his pocket.

"It's on the house," she replied without looking up.

If everything worked right, he and Svenya would be together on a boat headed for Sweden before sunrise. How much had a week in Gestapo prison changed her, he wondered. Beatings, interrogation, solitary confinement, all of these things would scar her forever. In the past eight days, he too had changed. He had killed four men, threatened a perfect stranger, and betrayed the Danish spy he had worked with for months. But they had survived. Tomorrow they would leave for Malmo. For them, the war would be over, and they could spend months healing their wounds.

Starting a new life in Sweden would be difficult, he realized. For the two of them, he took only his cornet, a pocketful of cash, and the picture that he had taken out of her apartment of them standing together in the Tivoli gardens. She would

appreciate that. Chops could not risk that someone would see him leaving with a suitcase, either
a German—for certainly the Gestapo had posted a
sentinel to report his movements—or a neighbor,
who might casually say something to the wrong
person, or Peder Olsen himself, responding to
Chops' threat that he would not broadcast the code
unless the spy brought news of Svenya's release.

Chops read the fifth sheet of paper again.

PACK NOT RECEIVED.

F D E C
E-flat E E
A G F-sharp E F-sharp B-flat B F-sharp F

Encrypting the code had been difficult and
time-consuming because the relationship music
had with mathematics did not exist with grammar. Words simply did not fit into acoustically
meaningful melodies. If he could have dedicated a
separate song to each note, the task would have
been simple, but having only a thirty-minute show
to work in, Chops decided to squeeze all fifteen
notes into three songs. It wasn't easy.

The problem occurred not with the distant letters like the P and A in PACK, but with adjacent
notes, the F and F-sharp needed for the ED in
RECEIVED. Such "half-steps" only existed between
the third and fourth notes in a scale and between
the seventh and first, forcing Chops to choose between the awkward keys of C-sharp and F-sharp.
No one wrote in those keys. Chops could not ask
the Backbeats to transpose their music in their
heads, not into such unusual key signatures and
not without offering some explanation. He had to
find a solution.

He tried to come up with a different message with the same content, NO PACK RECEIVED, PACK NOT CAUGHT, PARACHUTE LOST, but he inevitably found similar problems. Finally, Chops decided on three different key signatures, F, G, and its related minor, E minor. The only sacrifice to musical integrity was beginning a solo on the flat seven, E flat in the key of F.

Earlier today he had warned Tapio.

"I don't like it, Chops," the barkeeper had said when Chops told him the plan. He had pulled up a stool and sat down, resting his elbows on the bar. "What's going to happen to you?"

"Everything goes right and I'm out of here."

"For good?"

"Looks like it."

"I don't like it," he repeated, shaking his head. "What will become of this place once you're gone? No band, that's for sure. The Backbeats couldn't agree to wear underwear without you to kick them in the pants. No band means no dancing, and that means no Smukke. It'll just be another hole-in-the-wall, and people will lose interest after a while."

Chops smiled at his friend's naiveté. "You're way off. Smukke made me. Not the other way around. It's not a club. It's a belief. An affirmation of free will. People don't come here to listen to music or to dance or to drink. People come here to be what they can't be outside, to do what they can't do outside. If the Backbeats fall apart, somebody will put another band together. Or maybe a poet will come along...or a playwright. Smukkies will always find an excuse to dress up and come here."

"Maybe." He looked around the bar as if it were already a thing of the past.

"Things might get a little out of hand tonight," Chops said after a moment. "I want to take one of the guns we put up in the ceiling."

"I thought you said using those was a bad idea. What made you change your mind?"

That Colt .45 was his ace in the hole. The Germans had confiscated all the weapons in Denmark shortly after the invasion, and they would never expect him to have one. He would only use it if something went wrong, and even then it might not help. But it might. On the other hand, he did not quite trust himself. As deep as the anger, the frustration, and the loss scared him, he was worried that his temper might flare, and then anything could happen. "I got no idea what's gonna happen tonight, but if it's gonna be a shooting match, I'm gonna have a gun. I might take one myself, if I were you."

"If they find it on you, you'll go to jail for sure. Who will that help?"

"They won't find it. We'll put it behind the stage, and I'll get it before we start playing. It will be fine."

"Do you know anything about guns?"

"Just what I've seen in the cowboy movies," Chops said with a smile. "Point and shoot."

"Don't get wise, Chops. Drawing a gun is a serious move. If lead starts flying in here, a lot of people will be hurt. There's only one exit and no place to hide. And bullets will ricochet off these stone walls. This is a bad place to fire a gun."

"I'm going to take it," Chops said flatly. "Come on around back and help me take one down."

Together they walked to the kitchen and removed the guns from the ceiling. Tapio took two of them and the extra ammunition and stuck them behind the bar as Chops hid his in the muffler in Sticks' bass drum. They met at the bar in silence.

"So when do you leave?"

"Tomorrow."

"We probably won't have any time tonight to have a shot in peace." Tapio reached behind the bar and pulled out a bottle of bourbon and a couple of glasses. Chops took the one that Tapio poured for him. He held it up, watching it refract the light as he swirled, watching the droplets cling to the side of the glass and crawl down leaving a thin trail behind.

"We've had one hell of a time, haven't we?"

"Yeah." They clinked glasses and tossed back the drink. "Thanks, Tapio. I gotta blow this joint." That had been the only bit of nostalgia that Chops had permitted himself, and it burned more than the whiskey in his throat. He had been around long enough to know that, between coming and going, the former is the one you celebrate. As they said in New Orleans, "The only good-bye party worth going to is a funeral."

Chapter Twenty

"This is the first time we've been cold together," Svenya had said to Chops seven weeks ago as they walked arm and arm beside the pond in Orsteds Park. The air was fresh and crisp and smelled vaguely of wood smoke from the neighborhood chimneys. Large snowflakes had settled on the fur-trimmed hood that made her look like some Arctic animal with a woman's face. The small lake had begun to freeze around the edges, and the ducks and geese who lived there squawked and swam in small circles, as if they were confused by the change in their house. A large, brown terrier barked at the birds, standing with his front paws on the ice but not trusting himself to go any further. Svenya made Chops promise he would go skating with her as soon as the ice was deep enough. He agreed, and when they kissed he felt a beautifully cold pressure against his lips.

The winter of 1942 had come to Denmark over night, blowing away the moderate autumn air and covering the trees, bushes, and ground with a hard frost that crunched under their feet. Although he had wanted to stay in bed, Svenya insisted they spend the morning playing in the park. She was a child of the ice, adept at making snow castles and at home on skis, whereas Chops was reared on the bayous and back streets of New Orleans. For him, ice belonged nowhere outside a glass of tea. Svenya had showed him the glory of winter for the first time.

Pausing on the front steps of the radio station, hand on the doorknob, Chops savored the tiny pellets of sleet biting into his face and clicking on the ground like a distant drum roll. He turned his face into the wind and breathed in, letting his eyes water and his cheeks numb. The tiny crystals dropped out of the darkness into the cone-shaped spotlight of the overhead lamp. He knew this was his last moment of calm before the evening's treachery began, so he took a deep breath before pushing himself through the door.

Chops scraped his feet on the mat before he walked into the entrance hall. The warm, stale air immediately made him sniffle, and he wiped his nose with his handkerchief. The regular guard was not sitting behind the desk. Instead, there were two Gestapo guards, both large and chunky, yet not brutish. One wore glasses. Both had crew cuts. They seemed well-fed and pleased about their assignment in Denmark, as most of the occupying Germans were.

"Excuse me, sir," one man said as Chops approached the desk to sign in. He stood up and looped his finger through the handle of the cornet case.

"Yes?"

"Please raise your hands."

Slowly Chops released his grip on the cornet case and raised his hands in the air. He watched carefully as the guard placed the case on the table. He ran his hands down Chops' sides, then down both legs and both arms. He was both polite and efficient, treating Chops like a diplomat while remaining thorough.

"New procedure?" Chops asked. Never before had he been searched in the studio.

"Following orders, sir." He stepped back to the table.

"No problem." He closed the case and headed to the staircase, concentrating on keeping his steps even. Once inside the stairwell, he sighed and then started the climb. He congratulated himself for making it through the unexpected search without losing his cool. He told himself that if he remained calm through the rest of the evening, tomorrow he and Svenya would arrive in Sweden. He had never been there before. He wondered what it was like. By the time he reached the top landing, he was breathing hard. Had he been smoking more than usual? Svenya had always warned him about cigarettes.

Inside the studio, the band was huddled around the piano, talking quietly. He walked over and placed his hand on Dragor's shoulder. "How are they hanging?"

"You're late."

"Ain't life grand?" He opened his case and pulled out the cornet. Dragor had developed an attitude that Chops recognized, because it had happened to him many years ago. Having matured as a musician, he was tired of being led. He wanted to lead. That happened to musicians just like birds. The young stay in the nest until they get cramped. Out they go, and the sooner the better. Some fall to the ground and others take to the air, and nobody could tell which way it would go. By fleeing to Sweden, Chops would avoid the imminent confrontation with his lead clarinet player. As a child, he had learned always to leave his house in order, and this might be his last chance to pull away the curtain that had fallen between him and the rest

of the Backbeats. "Did you guys get a special greeting when you walked in tonight?"

"Frisked up against the wall, if that's what you
mean," Grena said.

Chops bent over and raised his index finger.
"No sailor's exam?"

Dragor's mouth dropped open. "They
didn't...did they?"

He smiled. "Just checking."

Sticks pointed to the control-room window. "I
don't know what's going on tonight, but the gun
makes me nervous."

Chops glanced through the large window into
the control room. In addition to Herr Wolf and the
two usual technicians, an armed guard stood behind the desk. He was a big man, blond with broad
shoulders and a pointy chin, and he wore a black
Gestapo uniform. A machine gun hung menac-
ingly from his shoulder. Chops had not thought
that the Gestapo would be in the studio, but it
certainly meant they were planning to arrest Peder
Olsen later on.

Had Herr Wolf believed his story about inform-
ing on more resistance leaders in the coming
weeks? If not, they might make two arrests tonight.
Of course they knew he was involved with the resistance, but only as a minor player. If they had
cracked the code, they might not let him stay on
the streets, but then they wouldn't give him the
chance to play tonight either. Unless they figured
it out tonight, he was safe. Chops looked at Sticks.
"Forget the prick."

Behind the glass, Herr Wolf looked up and
waved. Chops had never seen him dressed up like
that before. His tailor had done a good job on the
double-breasted tuxedo and the white rose on his
lapel set it off just right. He looked like he belonged

at a fancy charity ball, not in a radio station. From his outfit, no one would suspect he had contacts in the Gestapo.

"Your sugar-daddy's calling," Dragor said.

"Who cares as long as he dishes out the cash?" Chops answered. "We've got a good set tonight."

"What's up," Christoph asked.

"*A Tuesday Dance, Sweet And Slow, Polka Dot Stomp, Volcano, Oh Grandpa,* and *Do Nothing 'Till You Hear From Me.*" The last song was his own private message to Svenya, although he knew she would not hear it.

"Who's the bimbo?" Sticks asked, and Chops turned to see what he was talking about.

Anna Schadling had just come into the studio. She, too, was dressed for the prom in a red silk dress with a short, ballooning skirt that showed off her legs. Chops had forgotten that, at the dinner party, Wolf had offered to let her come to the studio to see the band play. Did he have to be polite to his friends on a night like this?

Chops walked over and offered his hand. She looked at it for a moment before shaking. "Good evening, Mr. Danielson."

"Please. Everyone's informal here. Call me Chops."

She did not respond.

"Herr Wolf said you were going to sing a song with us tonight," he said jokingly. "What will it be? Billie Holiday? Memphis Minnie?"

"Herr Wolf was mistaken."

She showed no inflection of friendliness and, for a moment, Chops wondered if this was the same lady he had met at the Wolf's dinner party. Where was her sparkle and her conspiratorial air that made him believe they had somehow connected? "Did you have fun at dinner?"

"It ended early."

"My, aren't you the clever one? Hopefully tonight will provide better entertainment."

She nodded. "I'm sure this will be a very special evening. I've been looking forward to it for quite a while."

What did she mean by 'special'? "Where's your husband?"

"Oh, he had some business to take care of."

"Business?" Chops repeated. "I thought you were here on holiday."

"Nothing is purely vacation." She looked towards the control room. "I must join my host and let you prepare for the show. Excuse me." She turned away from him and walked into the control room.

Chops moved to the center of the room and the band gathered around him. No one said anything, and from the despondent look on Stick's face he realized that something was wrong. It worried him because jazz thrives or perishes on energy, and it wasn't there. Perhaps the search in the lobby and the armed guard had scared them. He smiled. "It's an easy show tonight, boys. No reason for our Aryan guest to get nervous. Dragor, stay out of the top register and don't play any chromatic runs. In fact, stick to the diatonic as much as you can. We don't have anything to worry about as long as we play cool. Next week we can blow the roof off this house, but tonight we stick to basics. Grena, no chord substitutions. If the score says F minor, you play F minor, not F minor seven flat five. Is that clear?"

"Sure."

"What about you?" Dragor asked Chops. "Are you going to stay out of the fourth register?"

"If I don't, kick me in the butt until I drop an

octave. We'll start off with Earl Hines' *A Monday Date*. I'll play the standard walla-walla interlude and then pass lead to you, Dragor. Keep it short, one verse and twice through the chorus. We'll end on the flair, as written."

"What about the short-count I came up with?" Sticks asked, referring to the slight adjustment he made to the original score, ending the piece abruptly between the third and fourth beats of the last cadence. That added a little bit of pizzazz to the old standard.

Chops motioned to the guard standing behind the glass. "Let's keep it simple tonight."

Grena shook his head. "I'm with Sticks. The flair makes me want to puke."

"Fuck the Krauts," Dragor said. "They've wanted us to play boom-click-click all along. I don't see why we should start now."

Chops had always known why people called jazz musicians "cats." You couldn't control them, and you couldn't teach them anything they didn't already know. They liked the night and took affection when they wanted it. They came and went as they pleased. In general, they were a pain in the neck, but somehow you just didn't have the heart to shoot them. Even if you did, they had nine lives. Two years ago, Chops had taken a bunch of average Danes, guys who liked to be comfortable and who did as they were told, and he formed a band. Sometime in the last twenty-four months they had become cats through and through. Fuck the Krauts, indeed.

Chops raised his eyebrows and said, "Well, if you insist. Let's blow the pants off that sausage-head."

"Won't make any difference to you," the clarinetist said with a thin smile. "You couldn't hit the fourth octave if you tried."

"Right. Let's tune on B-flat."

Grena played the note on the piano and let it hang for a second.

Chops took a moment to listen to the tone, to let it sink in. He hummed it, letting it fill him and displace any thoughts he might have about Svenya or Olsen or the arrest. Now there was only music. Music and the code. After blowing some warm air through his horn, he fingered the B-flat and adjusted the slide until he was in pitch.

As the sweep second hand approached its zenith, Chops wedged his cornet between his legs, pulled two spoons out of his breast pocket and slid them between his fingers. The ON THE AIR sign, which had malfunctioned a week ago, lit up, giving him comfort and courage enough to break the one cardinal rule Wolf had laid down, that English never be spoken over the airwaves. Instead of simply clicking off the tempo, he tilted his head upwards towards the microphone and said, "Whip them cymbals, Pop."

He began beating the spoons against each other and against his free hand in a controlled frenzy. For two measures, he rapped out complex rudiments, double paradiddles and flamimaques, using the convex side of the spoons for a fleshy snap and the concave side for a hollow pop. After the eighth beat, the rest of the band came in with the eight-bar introduction to daniel Foster's *A Tuesday Dance*.

"Oh yeah!"

From the first note, Chops could tell that his small act of defiance had energized the band even more. No longer were they concentrating on the Gestapo guard in the control room or his dull black machine gun. All their energy went to producing jazz, sweet and unadulterated. He slid the spoons back in his pocket, brought his horn to his lips, and joined the band in the third measure of the intro.

Chops had not chosen to start the show with *A Tuesday Dance* simply because he liked the tune. The structure of the score made it perfect for concealing his code. Each verse had three sections: vocals, instruments mimicking the vocals, and out and out solo jams. Since he wouldn't dare sing the English vocals, the cornet played them straight through and took solos afterwards, giving him twice the opportunity to encrypt his message.

The men at the Radio Security Service in London would listen to the song and record the first solo note he played after a rest. That became a piece of the code. This worked particularly well with *A Tuesday Dance* because the phrases of the vocal melody constantly pushed the beat. It drove the song, starting a phrase just before a listener would expect it. This necessitated a slight rest before the phrase, making the beginning of every phrase a part of the code. In addition, the song was written in the key of F major, which contained all seven notes required for PACK NOT if you include the E flat required for the letter N. That flat seven was fair game in every jazz arrangement.

The band finished the introduction, and Chops played the melody with conviction. REST—*Don't forget the Tuesday dance...* REST—*You promised me last Wednesday.* The first two letters of the code were already under his belt, and in the control room Herr Wolf was swaying with the tune like a cradle in the wind. The system worked just as Chops had told Olsen it would. Given enough time to pick the right songs, he could encode the Declaration of Independence, and the Germans would never know it.

He finished the verse as written in the seventh measure of the phrase, and Dragor slipped up behind him with a solo and resolved the melody in the eighth measure. This pattern was called "catch as catch can" and it made Daniel Foster the most famous jazz composer of his day. The melody preceded the harmony by one measure, providing a seamless but tricky way to pass the solos from one musician to the next.

Dragor mimicked the melody, spicing it with crescendos and trills. Listeners could sing along with him, but he provided his own accompaniment as well, playing off the long, swelling notes of the bass and the cornet. To this playful song he added a touch of arrogance, as if he were saying, *If you resist my Tuesday dance, I'll have fun with your best friend on Wednesday.* He ran up and down the scale, each time daring himself to go one note higher and he never failed. Chops was tapping his feet and thinking of his next solo as he listened to the clarinet go. Dragor was hot.

One of the reasons the composer, Daniel Foster, had trouble keeping his bands together in the early thirties, was that "catch as catch can" provided an arena for intense competition among soloists. The theory was for the soloist to bow out in the seventh bar and let his successor claim harmonic resolution, but to the musicians' egos, that amounted to letting someone else sign their masterpiece. Playing through the eighth bar would shatter etiquette because it would dismiss the harmonic intent, so crafty musicians found a better way to torpedo their would-be successors. They would simply resolve the melody in the seventh measure, making the eighth harmonically superfluous. The successor must begin his solo on a harmonically irrelevant chord.

This was exactly what Dragor did, and Chops saw it coming.

There were three ways to overcome this situation—none of them graceful. He could give up, re-resolve the phrase, or say "the hell with it" and blow the fool out of his horn. This was called showboating.

Chops knew Dragor expected him to mimic his cadence on top of the tonic chord. To do this and not sound like a child who can only copy other people's riffs was a difficult feat. Normally Chops would re-resolve the melody by inverting the notes, descending to the root if his predecessor climbed to the dominant note or vice versa.

But tonight Chops couldn't do that. He had to start the phrase with a low E—a note that made no sense except to a few highly trained cryptographers in London. He paused for half a beat, hit the E, the F, the G, the C, and continued up the major pentatonic in triplets until he hit the high F, which he held for two full beats. The low E did not belong in the scale, but it sounded like a launching pad.

As he played the rest of his solo, Chops watched Dragor out of the side of his eye. The clarinet player was standing with his knees straight, rocking from side to side as if he were riding a boat on open water. He was gloating and Chops knew it. But he had taught Dragor to play "catch as catch can," and the clarinetist might as well enjoy his little victory.

Sticks followed Chops' solo with a drum solo that shook the room, and Christoph joined in with a walking bass solo that was built to dance to. From then on, Chops and Dragor exchanged solos, passing the lead back and forth like jugglers.

No one at the station even raised an eyebrow as Chops hid three more of his magic notes. Afterwards, the whole band came in and played two repeat choruses, ending on the short count that Sticks had come up with. In the control room, Wolf was still clicking his fingers three beats after the band had stopped.

Chops pointed a finger at Dragor. "Where'd you learn to play like that," he said, just loud enough that the microphone would pick it up, and everyone in Denmark would hear.

He nodded to Sticks, and the drummer counted off a quick four, setting the pace for *Volcano*, an old Count Basie tune. In that blazing piece Chops encoded the R-E-C-E, and in the Fats Waller arrangement that followed, he finished the I-E-V-E-D. Within the first half of the show, Chops sent the message PACK NOT RECEIVED, telling London the truth about the botched parachute drop and deliberately defying Olsen's orders. If that wouldn't make the spy show up at Smukke tonight, nothing would.

In the last half of the broadcast, Chops showed that he could play sweeter, slower, higher, and faster than Dragor ever dreamed of. When the set was finished, he realized he might have played the best show of his life. Not even when he practiced every day with the Guy Sherman band had he ever put so much into a performance. Even if he never touched a cornet again, he would be content as long as tonight's jam freed Svenya from her cell.

"Did you eat some vitamins this morning or did you get laid last night?" Grena asked Dragor as he closed the lid on the piano, and the clarinetist just shrugged.

"You got anything left for a midnight set at Smukke?" Chops asked as he ducked behind the piano. He paid no attention to the answer as he opened his case and slid his instrument inside. He mopped his forehead with the light-blue towel and then he closed the case. As he straightened up, he noticed Herr Wolf in the control room motioning for him to come inside. He nodded, set the cornet case on top of the piano, and walked to the control room door.

"What's that all about?" Dragor asks as he put his hand on the doorknob.

"After a show like that, I think we deserve a raise. What do you think?"

Dragor shrugged. He had never liked the idea of playing on the radio in the first place, and he did not respond to the compliment.

"What time does the next trolley leave?"

"Seven-fifty."

"Let's hope I come out of the lion's den before then," Chops said as he opened the door. One of the technicians was reading the news into the microphone; the cold snap would continue, another German victory in Africa. The same old routine and no one believed a word of it. He took the opportunity to look around the control room. He was surprised at how large it was. Most of the time only one or two people were in there, yet it was almost as large as the studio. Shelves of albums lined the walls from the ceiling to the floor, but he doubted many of the disks would suit his taste. He glanced at the knobs, sliders, meters, and buttons that somehow took his music and put it into thousands of homes. They looked complex.

"Don't touch," Anna said in a low voice, stern and steady.

Chops' stomach began to tighten. Those two words displayed a quality of controlled authority found in school principals and police lieutenants.

More unsettling than the tone, was the expression itself, "Don't touch." The French love to touch things, to toss in the air, to fiddle with, and to caress. "Don't touch" was a particularly German expression.

"You played very well tonight, Chops," Herr Wolf said after the news had ended. "I've never seen the trick with the spoons before. How did you come up with that?"

"I learned as a kid. One you've got it, it never goes away."

"Fascinating. Anna, have you ever seen that before?"

"No."

"Excuse me, Herr Wolf," the young technician said from his seat. "I'm not quite sure how to log that last news clip under the new system. Does it belong on the seven o'clock sheet or the eight?"

"Let's see. Excuse me," he said as he walked over to the control board, leaving Chops and Anna Schadling alone by the door.

At first they said nothing, cautiously avoiding eye contact, but the discomfort grew with every second. Even the clothing he was wearing became uncomfortable. "Would you like a cigarette?" Chops asked, pulling the pack of Lucky Strikes out of his jacket pocket. He pulled two from the pack, stuck one in his mouth, and held the other out to her.

"I don't smoke American cigarettes," she said. "It's against the law."

"That law's one of my favorites," he replied, lighting the cigarette. He blew a big cloud of smoke into the air and smiled. She had seemed so nice at Wolf's party the other night. Intelligent. Beautiful. French. Earlier tonight her unfriendly behavior confused him, but now she was beginning to irritate him. "Did you like the show?"

She nodded. "Your clarinet player is very good. It's rare to find a woodwind player with both speed and tone outside the orchestra. I assume he is classically trained."

Chops looked through the window at Dragor, who was standing next to the piano talking to Grena. How much did he suspect? "Yeah. Been playing since he was a kid."

"It shows. He has confidence, especially in the upper register. But for someone who has been playing for so long, I'm not sure why his solos consisted only of two scales. The pentatonic is amiable but gets boring quickly, so every few measures he would run up and down the chromatic. Doesn't show much of a grasp of harmony, does it? But perhaps he is simply constrained by form."

Who was this woman to complain about Dragor's lack of harmonic expertise? Herr Wolf hadn't said that she knew anything about music, but she had a concrete grasp on harmonic theory, or maybe she was just faking it. "Swing is one of the most unconstrained forms of music ever created, not only in rhythms but also in harmony. In fact, if I remember correctly, the solo I played in *Volcano* was completely in Dorian mode."

"Yes, I know the modal scales. I just didn't hear that in your solo. Perhaps it was too subtle...for me."

"Perhaps."

She held up her index finger, as if an idea had just occurred to her. "The one thing that stuck out in your solos was that they always began with a slight rest followed by a bright bell-tone. I liked it the first time, but after that it became old. Almost like a pattern...a habit you've developed. Some of the best trumpet players slowly crescendo into their solo and then hit the bright notes, but not you. You only exploit the dynamic range in the body of your solos."

He chuckled. What was the word she used? Pattern. She had just put her finger on the code, but did she know it? "Some people call that style, Mademoiselle."

She smiled for the first time of the evening. Thin and mischievous. "I guess I just don't know enough about jazz."

He took another pull on his cigarette, and the ash almost burned his finger. He dropped it on the carpet and crushed it with his foot, wondering just how he had been duped. "There's always time to learn."

Herr Wolf straightened up from the control panel and looked at the clock. "Not much time left. Chops, is everything set on your end?"

He nodded.

"You're sure?"

"Yeah."

"Good. Lieutenant Asch, pull the car around front. We'll be down in just a minute."

"Yes sir." With a fluid motion, the tall, uniformed guard adjusted his leather machine-gun strap so the weapon hung flush against his side. It disappeared under the blue and gray plaid overcoat he took off the rack. After wrapping a muted scarf around his neck, he placed an old English bowler on his head, and he looked just like a civilian, the kind of guy who sat next to you on the tram every morning and read a novel or a magazine. No military hair cut. No uniform. No gun. The Gestapo guard saluted and walked out of the room.

Were they planning on taking Peder Olsen with just one man? At least a half dozen soldiers had stormed Smukke the night they arrested Svenya, and she was a harmless infant compared to the Danish spy. There was no way they could simply slip a pair of handcuffs on him without a struggle. Herr Wolf's cavalier attitude confounded Chops, but he had seen the Gestapo in action before, and he trusted their ability as much as he distrusted their intentions.

When the door closed, Wolf said, "Anna is in charge, Chops. Do exactly as she says."

"Anna," Chops said in amazement.

"She'll pluck your eyes out and eat them like oysters. She came all the way from Berlin for this. She is the best the Gestapo has to offer."

Chops tried to laugh, but it came out like a snort. He couldn't make sense of this revelation. Obviously the vacation with her husband had only been a cover, but the timing still did not fit.

"No one will pluck out your eyes, Chops," Wolf said. "It's just an expression."

Chops told himself that he was still on stage and that this was one more performance, the most important one he had ever given. Something was not right, and he knew that if he lost his composure the curtain would close forever. Fortunately, Frau Schadling began talking, and he concentrated on her words.

"In just a few minutes the three of us will drive to Smukke and get into position. You will take the tram with the rest of the band to keep from arousing suspicion. We will wait in the building across the street from Smukke which we've already occupied. When your contact arrives, tell him that you need to speak to him outside. When you walk out the door, we'll arrest him. It should all be very easy."

Chops smiled and threw a curve ball. "What makes you think my contact is a man?"

"It's just a figure of speech," she said without missing a beat. "Is your contact male?"

"It doesn't matter. Your plan is not tight. There will be resistance."

"We are prepared."

"Maybe. The problem is Smukke has its own watchdog. They pay a kid to keep an eye on the street. If any soldiers appear, he sounds an alarm and everyone inside makes a break for it. You run the chance that something will go wrong in the confusion. If someone starts shooting, it will be a slaughter."

"We'll take that risk."

"Why? The resistance strategy is to force the German army to suppress the people, so there will be widespread uprising. Then you have to bring real troops in to keep the peace, weakening your forces on the eastern front. If this causes Denmark to explode, then the resistance has achieved its goal. Your best bet is to take my contact quietly."

Anna Schadling and Herr Wolf looked at each other for a moment. Then Anna said, "What do you suggest?"

"Smukke only has one door. If you arrest my contact inside, he has nowhere to go."

"But if we have to open fire inside, you know that innocent people will be killed. It will be like shooting fish in a barrel."

Tapio had made the same observation, and Chops had considered it carefully. "Not if you arrest him in my dressing room. It will all be very simple. When he arrives, I'll say I want to speak to him in private, and we'll go back to my room. Once he's inside, you slap the cuffs on him and bring him out quietly."

"Anna, he has a point," Wolf said. "Even if something goes wrong, your men are still across the street. He won't get away."

"I don't like the idea of being cooped up in a back room. Then we're in the barrel with the other fish."

"But they don't have guns," Wolf said. "I don't think we have too much to worry about."

"It's a bad idea, Klaus," she said.

"We don't have time to argue. He could be at Smukke right now. We've got to go."

"Is the password still 'V is for Viking?'" Anna Schadling asked.

Chops hesitated. How did they know so much? "Yes. And the knock is still three soft and one hard. Morse code for V."

"Clever." She looked at her watch. "It should take us about half an hour to get in position. What time does the bar usually close?"

"It depends. Usually it stays open until about three, but people have been a little nervous since the last raid." For some reason he thought he was saying something that she already knew.

"OK. We'll wait until three o'clock."

"And then?"

"If contact is not made, I will arrest you as an enemy of the state."

Chapter Twenty-one

As Chops and Sticks walked down Puggards Gade, the sounds emerging through the thick oaken door to Smukke increased in intensity, like sneaking up on a honey-bee hive. A shrill laugh topped the din and then faded into the sea of voices. Even a little music came through the door, a slightly blemished song pounded out by some drunk patriot on Grena's piano. When they reached the stairwell, even the words became clear. A faceless ensemble belted out the chorus that marked the cornerstone of the Danish resistance. The song that couldn't be taught in school and that every school child knew. Denmark's Freedom Song.

Gaa til Modstand
alle danske,
alle Mand som en
og gor Danmark frit

"They shouldn't sing so loud," Sticks said. He and Chops had walked together from the train station, and the rest of the band would follow in ten or fifteen minutes. Two small groups walking down the streets of Copenhagen after dark would get much less attention than a group of five, although

Chops knew that tonight the procedure was in vain.

He glanced over his shoulder at the buildings lined up across the street from the night club. Shops and office buildings, some with cheap apartments on the top floor or in the attic. Behind one of those dark windows watched a team of Gestapo soldiers, waiting for Anna Schadling's command.

"Smukkies come here to sing songs like this," Chops said. He banged on the door as hard as he could. Three hard and one harder.

The slat in the door opened almost immediately, and more of the noise from inside escaped. Tapio's face appeared in silhouette.

"V is for Viking."

The barkeeper opened the door, and a rush of warm and fragrant air assaulted the musicians. It smelled like life: cheap perfume, bathtub gin, smoke and sweat. The potpourri was heavy and vaguely sexual. Tonight it smelled like a teenage love affair. Beautiful, naive, and dangerous. As the boisterous crowd sang the Freedom Song of Denmark, Herr Wolf, Anna Schadling and an armed Gestapo guard lurked in Chops' dressing room behind the stage, waiting to arrest the keystone of the resistance.

Svenya would be free tonight.

"Big crowd tonight, eh?" Tapio said, after he closed the door. "Drinking a lot, too, Chops. I hope we don't give out of gin."

"You're always worried about the hooch."

"I'm surprised so many people come for the short set," Sticks said.

"Shrink your head a little bit. They've been here all night. I brought out the radio and we listened to the show. Usually the reception is no good, but yesterday I ran an antenna up on the roof. I disguised it as a weather vane, but as long as no one notices that it doesn't turn, I think we're in good shape. You played a good show, by the way."

"Thanks," Sticks replied. "I'm going to put a new skin on my snare before the set." He walked away.

Chops looked around, scanning the crowd for incongruous clothing and solitary strangers. The chance always existed that the Gestapo had infiltrated Smukke, or more likely that they paid a regular to keep his eyes open. If Olsen's arrest was important enough to bring a Gestapo specialist from Berlin, they would certainly take some extra precautions. He lowered his voice. "Did my guests arrive?"

"Oh yeah. I picked them. I might not have noticed, especially since they had a lady in the group, but the tall guy forgot to change his shoes before he came. Standard German officer issue. Pointed toe and raised heel. They were even shined for inspection. You didn't tell me they would have a lady with them. She threw me off for a second. She's a looker. A real minx."

"More like a ferret," Chops said. "Did they mingle with anyone, order drinks at the bar, or anything like that?"

"No. They just said they would wait for you in your dressing room. They came in about twenty minutes ago, and I haven't seen them since."

Chops rubbed his chin. Just because Wolf didn't speak to anyone in the bar didn't mean that he didn't have help hidden in the crowd. A Gestapo agent could have come in earlier, or perhaps the secret police had paid a regular to keep his eyes open a little wider than normal. Informants invariably landed at the bottom of the Copenhagen harbor, but the Germans never seemed to run out of them. "Anyone else unusual around?"

"Chops, look around. This place is packed, and I can't possibly keep track of everyone. Even at the door it was difficult keeping people straight. Too many tonight."

Tapio was right. The crowd was as thick as Chops had ever seen it. People moved, turned their backs, covered their faces with their hands as they lit cigarettes. It would be almost impossible to spot someone in this dark, smoky room.

"Everybody's begging for booze. I've got to get back to the bar. Good luck tonight. If you get into trouble, you know where I'll be."

"Go get 'em, champ." Chops patted Tapio and watched him disappear into the crowd. The bartender was a small man, and it was hard to imagine how he could help if something went wrong with the arrest. The anticipation crept up on him like it always did before he went on stage, but it was deeper, more internal.

He eyed the wall of people standing between him and the stage. It might be easier to backtrack to the door and then walk beside the wall, but if he pushed his way through he would have a better chance of seeing anyone that didn't belong. Positioning his cornet case in front of him like a battering ram, Chops plowed through the sea of couples standing on the dance floor. A couple of familiar voices said hello and complimented him on the radio show, but he did not stop and chat like he might have on another night.

"Give me a hand with this, would you, Chops?" Sticks said as Chops climbed up on the stage. He was bending over his drum set, holding a tom-tom in one hand and a wrench in the other.

"What's up?"

"My tom is clicking. Here, hold it like this." Sticks positioned the drum at just the right angle and height so the head faced him with the correct slant but the bottom rim did not rest on the bass drum and make the unwanted clicking sound when he played. Chops held the drum and Sticks tightened the bolt with a groan.

"You're gonna strip it," Chops warned.

"If it's not tight, it will slip for sure. OK. Let go for a second." He stepped back to look at his work. He sat down and started playing, stomping hard on the bass drum and alternating sextuplets between the snare and the tom-tom. Within six measures the tom had slipped down and begun clicking against the bass drum. "Damn."

"Keep your cool, Sticks," Chops said. He pulled the towel out of his cornet case, clamped it between his teeth, and tore off a two-inch strip, which he folded into a nice pad. He knelt down and wedged it between the drums and said, "Try that."

As soon as Sticks began to pound on the drums, Chops slipped his hand inside the open bass drum and grabbed the Colt .45 he had hidden there this afternoon. He jammed it into his belt at the small of his back and hoped no one had seen him. He stood up.

"No rattle at all," Sticks said when he was finished.

"It's not elegant, but it will do the trick until you can find a new bolt."

"I was going to try that next," he said.

"I know."

Chops clasped his hands behind his back, a casual pose that allowed him to touch the gun he had slipped into his belt. Colt .45 Automatic, fully loaded, safety off. If he stood slightly sway-backed, his jacket hung straight down from his shoulders like a curtain from a rod, completely concealing the weapon. As long as he didn't bend over, the

Colt was secret.

He was surprised to see Kaj and Louisa chatting as they approached the stage. He stepped down to meet them. On a couple of occasions Chops had taken the boy to Cafe Kakadu, but this was the first time he had seen the two together by themselves, and they seemed to be enjoying themselves. Louisa was smoking a cigarette and listening attentively as Kaj spoke, waving his thick arms up and down. She spotted Chops, placed her hand on the boy's shoulder to quiet him and then stepped towards the musician. She wrapped her arms around him and kissed him on the cheek. Alcohol wafted from her lips like fog off a river, and the expression in her eyes flickered when she accidentally nudged the gun he had stashed behind his back. "Your stiffy's on the wrong side tonight, Chops. It's usually up front."

"Only when I want to shoot," he replied with a grin. He accepted her levity as a blessing that kept him from thinking of the danger around him.

"What's been keeping you busy, Kaj?"

"I worked all afternoon in the shop. Nothing special, you know."

Louisa shrugged. The ruffled emerald dress looked good on her. Her hair was pulled back and held in place with a comb made of mother of pearl. Standing next to Kaj, the athletic teenager, she looked rather elegant, like an heiress on the Riviera. "Are we going to do the big dance tonight?" she asked Chops, raising her voice over the crowd.

"You bet your sweet one we are. The biggest."

"Is it true, what Louisa told me?" Kaj asked.

Chops nodded. He had meant to tell the boy that he was leaving but had never found the right time. Now he didn't know what to say. Did it look like he was trying to sneak out of town without a word to his only faithful student? Reaching into his pocket, Chops pulled out the keys to his apartment and tossed them to Kaj. "There are six hundred and twenty-eight records in my apartment. Most of them are pretty good. Make sure you're the first to get to them."

"What?"

"You can learn something from them, boy. Take your lessons straight from Louis and the Duke. You don't need me in the middle."

"I can't believe you're leaving," he said a little bit too loudly.

Louisa grabbed the short hairs on the back of his head and pulled him down towards her. At first, Chops thought he would lift her off the ground, but he bent over complacently, almost apologetically.

"Watch your trap," she whispered. "You don't want everyone to know that, do you?" She winked at Kaj before letting him go, and Chops thought perhaps he saw the boy blush.

"OK."

"You two go over to the bar and have something to drink while I set up with the band. We'll be swinging in ten minutes or so."

"What are you playing?" Kaj asked.

"You'll find out soon enough," he answered. Having spent all his time planning the "Thursday Night Exchange," Chops had neglected to work out a show for the late set. Ten minutes in his dressing room with the band would have helped, but that was impossible with Herr Wolf and company there. The Backbeat's performance would be a little off the cuff, but this wasn't the first show in his career that he had faked.

"Buy me a drink, sailor," Louisa said, grabbing Kaj's arm above the elbow and scooting next to him. He looked at Chops and shrugged, as if to say "How could I say no?" He turned and she followed him through the crowd, moving effortlessly in his wake.

Chops stepped up onto the small platform they called a stage, careful not to hunch over and expose the gun under his coat. The stage's two-foot elevation brought it much closer to eye level, but Chops knew that when people watched the band, they started at the instruments and they watched from the front. Only the band could possibly see the gun behind his back. He still wished that the gun weren't in his belt. He always sweat when he played, and the moisture might cause the gun to slip. What would he do if it fell out of his belt and dropped down his pant leg as he was playing?

He looked into the crowd for anyone unusual or slightly out of place. Nothing. An arm-wrestling match between two sailor-types was progressing at one of the side tables, and a crowd had formed and started making bets. At first, the two arms did not move, as if they weren't playing yet. Then they began to quiver, and sweat beaded on their heads. As the peak of arms slowly began descending to the right, the hushed voices began to murmur. The loser collapsed with a thud and people cheered. Money passed back and forth, and when the two men stood up, the loser refused to shake hands. He walked away.

Dragor, Christoph and Grena moved through the crowd towards the stage, talking to people here and there. They must have come in while Chops was watching the arm wrestling, and he realized he couldn't keep his eyes on the door all night. Peder Olsen could slip in or out without him knowing it.

"Let's go in the back and talk about the set," Dragor said, as he stepped up on the stage.

Chops shook his head, although he too would have liked a chance to get things together. "This crowd wants music and I want to give it to them. Snap your ax together and let's jam."

"C'mon Chops," the clarinetist continued. "What difference is five minutes going to make? No reason for us to sound like a garage band that can't decide on a set."

"*On the Sunny Side of the Street* is up. Now put your reed in your mouth and let's blow."

"You're the boss," Dragor said with a sarcastic tone.

"Never forget it," Chops replied.

Two minutes later, the Backbeats began their set, and the couples flooded to the dance floor. They moved like whirling dervishes, fast and furious, spinning and dipping, clicking their fingers and swinging their hips. Chops crammed all of his anxieties in the mouthpiece and blew them out the bell. His cornet was a rifle, and he stared down the barrel and took aim at the dancers, punching out rapid-fire accents. Kaj and Louisa danced together in his cross hairs, holding hands and gliding across the floor with fumbling grace. What they lacked in technique they made up for with momentum, and their fellow dancers gave them space. Had he ever seen Louisa dance without a drink in her hand before?

Sweat began to wet Chops' face, but he did not let up. He kept his solos high and fast, giving Smukke everything he could find. When he lowered the cornet for the piano break, his lips felt like overripe fruit. With the remains of the towel he swabbed the sweat from his face, and he wished he had brought a glass of beer or water on stage with him. He felt good after the break, and played the coda a perfect fifth above the score.

"Harmony in the coda?" Dragor said with a sideways glance.

"Yeah," Chops replied. "It's like using adjectives in a sentence."

Before Dragor could rebut, Sticks counted off the tempo for *Twelfth Street Rag*, and both men slipped in without missing a beat.

As the song progressed, Chops edged to the tip of the stage and arched back. The heat from the audience enveloped him, and he swayed with the rhythm, joining the dance. In his mind he channeled all the energy in the room into his cornet, controlling it, taming it, sculpting it into melody. Yet he always kept one eye on the crowd. Did they like the high notes? Were they ready for a slow tune or a popular song they could sing along with?

Peder Olsen sat at the bar. He had not been there long, but Chops hadn't seen him sit down. Perhaps he had missed him because of the cleft tweed hat he wore tilted over his left eye. The Danish spy nursed a drink and spoke to no one. Legs crossed on one of the high stools, he nodded when he caught Chops' eye, and the cornet squealed. He was only minutes away from the end of the game. Peder Olsen had walked straight into Chops' trap, and Svenya would be his reward.

Years of training kept Chops from staring at Olsen for too long, because on stage he belonged to everyone. Turning to his right he played a few measures to the people standing on the wall, single men who came to meet ladies but didn't quite have the gumption to move. Perhaps attention from the stage would give them the courage they needed, but Chops did this out of instinct. He did not care who went home alone. This night was his.

When his gaze returned to the bar, Olsen was gone.

A familiar-looking, dark-haired girl sat on the stool, smoking a cigarette and talking to the guy next to her. Chops placed her. Ingy, short for Ingrid. She worked in the steno pool at the University and came to Smukke at least once a week. She looked like she had been sitting there all night, but she hadn't.

Chops looked to the front door but it was closed. Had Olsen already slipped out, content just to let the priest see him in the holy of holies? Perhaps the spy knew the Gestapo would arrest Chops if the plan failed, and he had come only to taunt. No. He could not have found out about the plan. He must still be somewhere in the room, here in response to the broadcast, mad as a wet hornet, and until now, Chops had not considered how his anger would manifest itself. Shoot first and ask questions later? Chops did not much like the way he smiled from the bar. He had never seen the spy lose control before, not even when he surprised him in front of his apartment, but if broadcasting the code sent him over the edge, he was a wounded tiger stalking through the jungle of casual forms. It seemed doubtful. If he were intent on hurting Chops, why would he have shown himself at the bar or come to a public place? More likely he just disappeared to make Chops nervous and put him on the defensive at the beginning of the argument. Well, he had a surprise coming. But maybe he wasn't hiding at all, and the crowd just made it seem that way.

"What's next?" Christoph called.

"*One and Two Blues*," Chops replied.

Without another word, Christoph started off with a walking bass line, slow and sultry. An eerie hush descended on the club, and the couples came together on the dance floor like magnets. Chops chose this old Bessie Smith tune because it was based on the most rudimentary twelve-bar blues progression. Mediocre musicians loved to play songs like this because they were easy to fake, and Chops loved it for the same reason. While trying to figure out where Olsen had gone, he didn't want to try to keep up with sophisticated chord changes.

"Where are you?" Chops' cornet called out over the hollow sounds of the double bass. "Where are you hiding?" He relaxed and drew out his phrasing, as if to say "I've got all night to find you, Mr. Olsen." In all his encounters with the Danish spy, this was the first time he had really been in the briar patch. His friends danced below him, not paying any attention to anything except what they found in their ears and their arms, wrapped up in one another, cheeks on shoulders, bellies rubbing, legs intertwined. A few couples were even kissing in the back. It was just like a slow dance should be.

Olsen was standing right at the foot of the stage when Chops looked down. His attention had been in the center of the crowd, and he had overlooked the spy. Although he was dressed like everyone else in the crowd, wearing a double-breasted, pinstripe suit and a white ascot that suited him rather well, his rigid posture kept him from blending in with the crowd, like an iceberg in a sea of motion.

Chops did not stare. As anxious as he was to close in for the kill, as it were, he strung out his solo an extra twelve measures, playing long, relaxed phrases, keeping the spy barely in the bottom of his vision to make sure he did not disappear again.

The song ended with a twelve-bar bass solo, so as Christoph played the final measures, Chops walked to the back of the stage and put his cornet in its case. He looked out over the crowd. The slow music had quieted them down. The couples were still holding hands, looking to the stage, moon-struck.

Chops nodded to Olsen, and the spy headed towards Chops' dressing room. "Call it a night," he said to Dragor as he walked to the edge of the stage.

"After three songs?"

"Yeah."

"What?"

"I've got to go."

"You've lost your mind."

"Great." If one of his musicians said that to him, he would have belted him, but this was his band, and he could do what he wanted. The Backbeats were a page in history, a thing of the past. Chops vaguely felt sorry for Dragor, Grena, Christoph, and Sticks. Their band had just evaporated and they didn't even know it. Perhaps this was the opportunity Dragor was looking for. Maybe he could keep the band together, but it did not seem likely.

As soon as he walked off the side of the stage, Olsen grabbed his arm, clenching like a vice. Their eyes locked. "Do you have any idea what you did tonight?" Olsen spat.

With a quick twist, Chops freed himself from the spy's grip. "Let it wait, Olsen. People can hear you. Security is important, right? We can talk in my dressing room." That was one of the things he had learned from working with the resistance. How much had he really learned, he wondered.

Chops and Peder Olsen walked silently to the dressing room, and Chops fought hard to keep his excitement from showing on his face. The Gestapo waited on the other side of the door, and when they had made the arrest, they would free Svenya.

He grabbed the door knob.

It turned easily.

"After you," he said as he opened the door. The light inside the dressing room was off, but Olsen stepped inside without hesitation.

Chops followed and slammed the door as hard as he could. Olsen was trapped. He reached for the light switch and turned it on.

The Gestapo driver stood in the corner with a machine gun out. Wolf and Frau Schadling sat on the desk. As soon as the light came on, they both leapt off the table and snapped to attention. Their knees locked, back straight, stomach in, chin out.

"Sieg Heil!" Herr Wolf barked, throwing his right arm up in the Nazi salute. Frau Schadling and the driver followed in unison.

"Sieg Heil," Olsen responded, casually flipping his right hand up. He smiled. "Good evening, Major Wolf."

Wolf did not relax. Gone was the laid-back man who bent the rules and who swayed back and forth as the Backbeats played. He had become a model officer of the Third Reich. "Congratulations, Colonel Olsen. It seems your operation has been an unprecedented success."

Chapter Twenty-two

Chops' vision disintegrated to a blotchy gray-black field, and a heat wave flashed through him. Tiny beads of cold sweat began to form on his forehead and cheeks. The muscles that held his frame upright went limp, and he feared he would spill onto the ground in a puddle. His lungs froze. Gradually, shadows formed on the edge of his vision and slowly solidified into figures as the black cloud collapsed into itself. The hole in his vision shrank until it reached the size of a dime, and Chops realized he was staring down the barrel of an MP 40 submachine gun.

"Relax, Chops," Olsen said, pulling the straight-back chair out from under the dressing table, but the words sounded as if they came through a thick pane of glass or through water. "Sit down. You're a little wan. Here, have a drink." He turned to the guard. "Lieutenant Asch, you can put the gun down."

As Chops fell backwards into the chair, the Danish spy, or whatever he was, reached into the bottom drawer and pulled out the bottle of whiskey that Chops hid for special occasions. No one knew about that bottle. Olsen twisted off the cap and handed it to him.

Without thinking, Chops grabbed the bottle by

the neck and took a slash. Fumes rose as the whiskey burned its way down his throat, and he latched onto the familiar feeling. It grounded him. Here he was. In his dressing room. With Peder Olsen. With Herr Wolf. With Anna Schadling and a Gestapo guard, and none of these people was who they seemed to be.

"You never suspected, did you?" Olsen asked.

"What about Svenya?"

"She's fine," Wolf said.

"She'd better be."

"Relax, Chops. Have another pull from the bottle and I'll explain everything."

"I prefer a glass," Chops said as he reached across his dressing table. He grabbed the tarnished silver-plated Old Fashion glass that he used as a pencil holder and dumped its contents onto the floor. He poured three fingers and took a sip without even wiping off the rim. Inside he had collapsed, but his stage facade remained intact, and he instinctively rode on it. He reached into his breast pocket and pulled out his cigarettes. He shook two out of the pack, stuck them both in his mouth and lit them. Blowing a massive cloud of smoke from his double-barreled habit, he said, "Are we going to play twenty questions, or are you just going to tell me just what the hell's going on?"

"I work for them."

"You're a traitor."

"A traitor?" Olsen paused, raised his eyebrow, and looked at Chops as if amused. "That's an odd word coming from your lips, only moments after you betrayed the leader of the Danish resistance. Right after you delivered into the jaws of the Gestapo the only man you knew who you judged capable of helping the Allies, your own country included, to 'liberate' poor helpless Denmark. Then you call me a traitor. No. I'm not a traitor. I've never switched sides."

Chops drew his eyes away from Olsen, looking for an ashtray on his desk which was littered with sheet music and record sleeves. A pad of paper listed awkwardly, and he flipped it over. His ashtray, overflowing with old cigarette butts, was underneath. He tapped his cigarettes into it and put them back into his mouth.

"National Socialism is the future of Europe," Olsen continued. As he spoke he paced back and forth, but he never took his eyes off Chops, and the musician knew he was looking for a reaction. "I've believed it all along. A strong leader rises in Germany, and the people join together around him. The country becomes strong because the people become strong. The same thing can happen to nations. Nazi Germany is Denmark's only hope. Who else can protect us? Our own sea-warring Vikings are long dead.

"You didn't switch sides either, did you Chops? You're not a traitor. You never chose sides to begin with. You proved that tonight. Why should you care whose messages you broadcast as long as you have a full plate and a warm bed to sleep in? You're an opportunist, and that's why I like you. It's why you're still alive."

Chops knew he was being provoked, and he fought hard to keep his eyes level and his face unreadable. Olsen's condescending little speech infuriated him because his words rang true. He had tried to stay out of the political sphere, but it was supposed to be only a facade, a survival tactic. Had his true face changed to match his public mask of a devil-may-care musician? No. Now, more than ever, his anger told him that he did care. He could not play a part in the Nazis' aggressive transformation of sensibilities, and for a moment he thought about going for the pistol stashed in his belt, but the dull-gray machine gun kept him from moving. One thing was certain. He would not let them arrest him. If that was their plan, he would fill the air with lead so fast they wouldn't have time to blink. But not yet. He might still have a chance to fight, but this was not the time. He couldn't drop the curtain yet. "Keep talking."

"I didn't know the Germans were going to invade, but when they did I knew exactly what to do. I fled to England, knowing I'd come back as an Allied spy. I was very coy about accepting the mission, of course. They asked every male refugee if they wanted to form a reserve division to fight for the Allied cause and, as a patriot, I agreed. Basically that meant working with the civil service, keeping trains on schedule and so forth, demeaning labor, but I did not object. It was all a part of my plan.

"After close observation, they asked one out of every hundred volunteers if they would continue their work with the special operations executive, and I was on the top of their list. The SOE recruiting officer and I had several long conversations, because I did not want to seem too eager to risk my life, but eventually I let them convince me.

"They locked us up in Lord Montagu's Beaulieu Castle and trained us in the art of sabotage. I'd spent some time in the Danish army, but the British methods were relatively advanced, especially with explosives and timed detonators, and they taught me a lot. We weren't supposed to know what our mission was, and we talked about it among ourselves after hours. We knew. Training happened in stages, and every time we found out a little more. At the same time they pried into our pasts, trying to uncover anything that may make us a bad risk. They threw out one man because he was homosexual, although I'm not sure what that has to do with spying. Naturally, I met every qualification.

"After six weeks, they told us everything. We were to return to Denmark to meet up with the fledgling resistance here. Our task was to organize and train them in acts of sabotage so we could light the country on fire from the inside out, but Chops, of course you know all that. We've been over it a hundred times."

Chops remembered the pep talks Olsen had given him, especially in the beginning. The speech about the German army being stretched like a rubber band echoed in his ears. Back then he had thought it sounded exaggerated, but he had chalked that up to cynicism. Would he ever learn to obey his instincts?

"The mission was very dangerous because of the quality of the counter-intelligence division of the Gestapo, but I survived. Naturally I had some help in high places." He motioned to Anna with his thick, broad hand. "The Gestapo made sure no one looked at my papers too closely, and they warned me about all the raids and roadblocks. Eventually I spotted you, and together with Frau Schadling and Herr Wolf, we came up with this plan to filter information to London."

"But why?" Chops said. "I thought you wanted to keep information away from the English."

"Not entirely. Sometimes we give away our secrets, the small ones, the ones they would discover anyway, like certain large troop movements or minor scientific advances. This way we build their trust and steer them away from anything significant. It is critical that we know what they know. Important information is useless if it is not a secret."

Chops thought hard about this, and in its own perverse way it made sense. "You know that they know, but they don't know that you know that they know?"

"Precisely. The occupation of Denmark is a lot more strategic than anyone has yet realized. Of course, we said we only wanted to secure our supplies and to capture a land bridge to transport troops to Norway, but that was only part of the story. We control the information flow."

Anna turned around and looked at the pictures on the wall. She quickly ran her finger across the framed photo of Bessie Smith and checked it for dust. She didn't straighten the picture afterwards. Obviously she had heard Olsen's speech before.

"However, nothing says the British believe what they hear. This is where spying becomes the most interesting. Armies react with mathematical simplicity. Two tanks defeat one tank. A well-fed soldier defeats a cold and hungry one. But the real turns of the war depend on individual decisions, often not much more than hunches. How much of this information will Winston Churchill believe?

"It is difficult to say. It's a matter of trust, a judgment of human nature. It depends completely on whether or not he believes me, with you as my mouthpiece. He is in a difficult position, as are all heads of state, because he received contradictory information from his spies. We're not his only spy, you know. Think of all the sources of information he really has.

"By leaving the Danish government intact, along with most of its military, we know certain information will make its way across the Channel. More dramatically, they have the report of every Dane who left the country. The great majority of these came over right after the invasion, so the English knew exactly which armies we used and which airborne divisions. How many ships. These informants were carefully scrutinized, and many were arrested, not for fear of getting bad information, but on the chance that they were in fact German spies who would send information back to the continent after they were established in their communities. It is the risk a country runs by accepting refugees in wartime, and they are beginning to pay the price."

"But that's just the beginning. All Axis POW's are interrogated. Radio broadcasts are intercepted. Codes broken. Officers bribed or blackmailed. The amount of information is staggering, much of it contradictory, but the final decision always comes down to one thing. Whom do they believe?" Olsen paused, as if for dramatic effect.

Chops knew it was a rhetorical question, but he answered it just to interrupt the script. "I don't know. Who?"

"They believe you, Chops. Me and you. We are the jewel in the SOE's crown. I wouldn't be surprised if they were planning on knighting us after the war. The idea of broadcasting messages via your cornet solos was so creative that, in the beginning, the boys in London never thought it would work, but it did. We made sure. Today your messages get top priority on Baker Street. We never dreamed it would be this successful. Who would have thought that they would be supplying us with arms and explosives?"

A picture of that snowy night blitzed through Chops' head. He saw the flash of muzzle fire, felt the branches as they scraped his face and hand, heard the screams of the German soldiers after the hand grenade he threw exploded. He listened to the silence that followed.

"You planned the ambush? I killed four men that night, four German soldiers. What kind of animals are you, to send your own men into a suicide mission? What could it possibly have accomplished?"

Anna put down the old wine bottle that had served as a candle stick. "Don't be absurd. This kind of thing is too volatile to attempt a stunt like that. There are too many variables as it is, but even the most well-planned operation has its grand snafu, and the RAF parachute was ours. We did not think we'd recover. You see, this whole operation has been run straight from Berlin. High command here in Denmark did not even know about it. Like Colonel Olsen said, the British have spies throughout the government here in Copenhagen. We could not risk that word would get back to them that you were actually working for us. That would have been disastrous."

Peder Olsen took off his hat and tossed it on the table. "The counterintelligence team here in Denmark is very good. They found out about the parachute drop on their own."

"From the man who gave you the ambulance."

"Unfortunately," Olsen said.

Anna Schadling pointed at Chops. "However, the actual troops involved were not as good as their superiors expected. You and Colonel Olsen evaded them on your own. That was real. Frankly, I'm surprised that you survived, but you did."

"The whole fiasco did have one positive outcome," Wolf added. "High command of special operations was quite impressed that you made it out of the woods alive. Snuck right out from under a German ambush. They heard the whole story the next day from one of their people in the army. That is why it was so important that you told them the truth tonight. Lying to your superiors would have tarnished your image, but you stuck your chin out and told them the truth. The British can't help but love the combination of honor and heroism."

"But how did you know I would change your message? You were adamant that we lie to the SOE so they would continue to send supplies. Were you so sure I would disobey orders?"

"It was a calculated risk. We had a contingency plan in case you followed orders."

Three hard knocks on the door silenced the conversation in the small dressing room. The guard took a step back and pointed his machine gun at the door, and Olsen shook his head. "Get rid of them," he whispered.

"Beat it," Chops yelled.

"You want a drink?" Louisa's voice sounded strong, even through the wooden barrier.

"Go home, I'll see you tomorrow," he called, relieved that someone was checking up on him, grateful for the moral support. "Don't worry," he said to Olsen. "Everyone knows better than to come in when the door's closed."

"Good." Anna reached into her pocket and pulled out a piece of paper. She unfolded it and handed it to Herr Wolf.

He placed a pair of wire-rimmed glasses on his nose and read the text, mouthing the words as he went. His nod to Anna Schadling told Chops that they had been planning this for a long time. Holding out the paper, he said, "This is your next message."

Chops reached forward and took the note. The weight of the message bore down on him as his eyes scanned the simple sentence.

52ND ARMY TO STALINGRAD

Living in an occupied country, Chops constantly heard news of the war in the east. The front stretched from the Arctic to the Black Sea, but throughout the fall, everyone had their eyes on an industrial town on the Volga River. Stalingrad. The assault had begun in August, and even now, in mid-November, the city was still under siege. "What?"

Peder Olsen lifted his leg and placed his foot on the arm of Chops' chair. He bent forward, bringing his face within inches of Chops' own. He smelled vaguely of the white soap flakes that the Germans had been rationing in the city. "Hitler has decided that Russia is his single most-important objective. He wants Stalingrad, and he wants it now, so he's willing to take troops out of Norway to do it. You have the historic privilege of leaking this information to the SOE. This is the most important intelligence that London could hope for. They will be ecstatic."

"He's sending more troops to Russia? Didn't he learn his lesson last year when so many soldiers froze in their tanks?"

"That's the point. He wants to capture Stalingrad before the winter sets in. The 52nd Army is 100,000 strong, and they are well-seasoned from the fighting in Norway. With their help the city will fall in a week."

"Why are you telling this to London?"

"We're not telling London. They are stealing the information. Of course it's not true, but everything else you have told the SOE has been. Your credibility is established."

"You're feeding lies to the Allies." Chops said it softly, almost afraid to utter the words. The plot was as subtle as it was sinister, and only now did he begin to grasp the implications.

"Exactly. The point is, we need the 52nd in Norway and in Russia. So how can we have the same army in two places at once? Simple. We lie. You see, our intelligence services have learned that the Russian General Rokossovsky is planning a counterattack in Stalingrad. They want to cross the Don River from the northwest and surround our Sixth Army. It will be a massacre."

Anna Schadling stepped forward. "The Fuhrer doesn't believe they can cross the river, since all the bridges are down. It is, in his words, a natural barrier."

"But the river will freeze," Chops said. "Then they won't need bridges."

"That's what we're afraid of. However, if Stalin thinks he'll have to face the 52nd, he won't risk the assault. He'll surrender Stalingrad and pull his troops back to defend Moscow."

"Why are you telling me? Have you ever considered that I might not play along?"

"Oh, yes. We were very worried about that. We considered keeping you in the dark and just giving you more messages to encode, but I was afraid you would figure it out. You are not stupid. You had to be told, and we did not know how you would react. But now we know."

Olsen stood up and waved his arm at Wolf, Schadling, and the Gestapo guard. "Without regard to the military implications, you've just betrayed the head of the Danish resistance. All we did is arrest your friend..."

"And gave you a few subtle hints," Wolf interrupted. "Granted, paying someone to steal your cornet wasn't exactly subtle, but it did get you moving in the right direction."

"You managed the rest on your own. You contacted the Gestapo, via Herr Wolf. You broadcast the wrong message, knowing I would react, and when I did, you made sure the authorities were here to arrest me. It was a very well-conceived trap."

"What?" Chops said, finally beginning to understand what had been happening over the past week. They had manipulated him like a child. "You arrested Svenya to get control over me. Why didn't you just say so last week? Just say, 'These messages are lies and if you don't broadcast them, it's lights out for your friend.' Why go to all this trouble?"

"No, no. You've got it all wrong. It was a test, not a power play. You, of all people, are much too volatile to act like a puppet on a string. It may have worked for a week or a month, but we try to think long term. We needed to make sure you were on our side, or at least not on theirs. The question was how deep your allegiance to the Allies went, and that's not the kind of thing you can casually ask, is it old boy? Over and over again you asserted that this was not your war. You had left America and left her for good, et cetera, et cetera. You must have given that speech a thousand times. Herr Wolf believed you, but I wasn't willing to take the risk. I needed to know for certain if you would continue playing your magic notes if you knew their real purpose."

Wolf walked over and stood next to his double agent. Compared to Olsen he looked small, elderly, and treacherous. "I pointed out all the advantages you get from the show and from knowing it has official license. The first is safety. Never again would you have to worry that someone will crack the code."

"We did, by the way," Anna Schadling said. "One of our transmission monitors, who knew nothing of this arrangement, figured it out the very first night. We gave him a promotion and told him to keep his mouth shut. He knew better than to ask any more questions."

Olsen continued. "Not only that, you just got a raise. A big one. Three weeks ago, London asked me to make sure you were paid enough. They like keeping their spies happy, and I told them I thought you needed more money. Enough to move out of that slum you live in and into a nice flat down town, the kind of place befitting a full-tenured professor at the Conservatory. The Dean was pleased when he heard you would be returning in the spring.

"Despite all we could offer, I wasn't convinced. A spy with convictions is dangerous to the enemy. Mixed loyalties make him a danger to himself. But a spy with no loyalties...that is a prized possession. We had to come up with some way to test your allegiance."

"So you arrested Svenya."

"Exactly. And after a few subtle hints, you came up with a way to free her. You betrayed the resistance and had me arrested. If that doesn't say which side of the line you're standing on, nothing will."

Something about the conversation confused Chops. Part of him felt like they were explaining a puzzle that he had failed to solve on his own, a riddle that they had created, and that they were savoring their own brilliance, but he could taste the air of a door-to-door salesman. And then that of a job interview or a subtle cross-examination. He had to say something. "So the whole damned thing was to prove what I'd told you again and again, that I don't care who wins this war? It's a little extreme, don't you think?"

"Maybe, but security is always important."

"Do you finally believe what I've been saying all along? That I don't give a damn?"

"Absolutely. We just outlined for you one of the most important disinformation assaults of the war. Would we have told you all of this if we didn't trust you? You're like a full partner."

"Major Schadling will also provide direct access to Berlin, if it goes that far."

She nodded reluctantly.

"And now you're going to release Svenya," Chops said. Somehow he had managed to play his cards right. Despite the turns and deceptions, he had done just enough to get her out without inflicting any real damage on the Allies. Tomorrow, after he and Svenya arrived in Sweden, he could send a message to London and warn them about the plan. They might not believe him at first, but he knew enough to convince them.

Chops noticed an odd silence in the room, and he could hear what was happening in the bar. The crowd was thinning out early because the music had ended, and there wasn't much else to keep their attention. Smukkies wouldn't hang around and drink deep into the night, not when most of them had to go to work in the morning. Binges were reserved for the weekends. The silence in the dressing room was awkward, almost embarrassing, like when a teenage girl, accidentally pregnant, says "You'll marry me, right," and the man has decided to split. "You are going to let her out, aren't you?" Chops said.

"Of course," Herr Wolf said in a saccharine voice. "But...we can't do it immediately." He hastened to add, "Of course we will transfer her out of Gestapo headquarters to Grey's Prison for Women. It's the regular Danish facility, run by Danes and well-known for superb treatment of inmates."

"You said you'd let her go."

"Of course, and we will. But not quite yet. We

can't completely let her out of our grasp. You might have a change of heart."

Chops said nothing. As he stared at Wolf with hard eyes, he wanted to draw his gun and to make these lying bastards pay for their deceit, but he kept his hand still.

Wolf took off his glasses and placed them in his jacket's inside pocket. "Come now, Chops. Don't be so naive. Everyone hedges their bets. We all have our little insurance policies in case things don't go our way. What would keep you from disappearing tomorrow? Then we would have to revert to older means of getting our information to London, and we can't have that. Keep a stiff upper lip. Grey's Prison is a lot better than a Gestapo detention cell. You know that. It's almost like living in a dormitory. Clean sheets. Regular meals. They even have visiting hours. And if things continue to go well, perhaps even a weekend furlough. She might even get out under house arrest, although it depends on her behavior. We have some influence over these things."

"What's to keep you from putting her back into Gestapo prison?"

"You are. As long as you continue to broadcast the code on a weekly basis, everything will be fine."

"And if I refuse?"

Anna Schadling and Herr Wolf exchanged a quick glance, and Chops knew he had said the wrong thing. "Why would you refuse? You're on our side, right?"

Anna Schadling took a step forward. "Refusing would be a bad idea, Mr. Danielson. As we said, we will get our messages to London. The SOE believes Colonel Olsen. He is the key. You merely provide an interesting channel of communication. Others could be arranged if you became indisposed. What would your execution achieve?

"We would be forced to deport your friend to a German concentration camp. The camps are very humane, but certainly not as comfortable as Grey's Prison for Women."

"Just checking."

"I'm sure."

"Tell me this. There won't be any more running around at night and getting shot at, will there? That's not my style."

Olsen shook his head. "That was a bad situation, I admit. No, there will be none of that. Just the code."

"I'll do it." Chops said, gauging his words very carefully. "But I want to see Svenya. As far as I know, you've already shipped her off to some concentration camp."

"You'll see her tonight. As a gesture of good faith, we've decided to transfer her to Grey's Prison right away. We can pick her up at the Dagmar House and drive her to the other facility. It's a fifteen-minute drive out of the city, so that will give you some time to catch up. But Chops, it would be dangerous for her if she knew anything about our arrangement. You won't tell her anything, will you?"

"I won't tell her anything."

Chapter Twenty-three

Chops stubbed out his cigarette, his ninth since climbing into the German staff car with Olsen, Wolf, Anna Schadling, and their driver. It was his twelfth since leaving Smukke. During their drive to Gestapo headquarters, the smoke had escaped through the cracked window, but now that they were parked, it just lingered in the back seat like a bad idea. He lit another.

"I was hoping that was the last one," Olsen said from the front seat.

"It wasn't." Chops inhaled deeply and continued to look out the window across the Radhus Platzen. The red-brick city hall with its tall tower and its statue of Bishop Absalon, the charismatic twelfth-century leader, dominated the square, but Chops concentrated on a smaller, less imposing building, the Dagmar House, which had been constructed in the thirties to house a light industrial firm called Kampsax. Today, it headquartered the Gestapo, and Svenya was somewhere inside, probably in a cell in the basement.

The minutes had crept by. Determined not to seem impatient, Chops kept himself from looking at his watch and gauged the time by the trams that moved in and out of the square. Radhus

Platzen was the main hub on the transportation net and even at eleven o'clock at night a tram would pull in and out every ten minutes or so. He counted four: the One to Kongens Nytorv, the Thirty to Sundbyvester, the Two that usually dropped him off three blocks from his house, and the Sixty-eight to Utterslev. A handful of passengers climbed on and off the trams or waited under the three-sided shelters, but in general it was a slow night. At the Dagmar House nothing moved. He had not even seen a guard patrolling the Gestapo headquarters, but even the Danes weren't brave enough or stupid enough to cause trouble here.

Before they had walked out of Chops' dressing room in Smukke, Wolf had warned him that transferring a prisoner would be difficult and time consuming at this time of night. The warden on duty would have to get permission from his supervisor, who would have to sign papers and alert Grey's Prison.

After Wolf explained the procedure, the five of them had left Chops' dressing room and pushed their way through the crowd without saying a word. Most everyone had left, including the rest of the Backbeats, and those that remained looked like they would stay until Tapio kicked them out. As the entourage moved past, Chops thought that he heard a murmur following them like a shock wave, but it might have been his imagination. Louisa, Kaj, and Tapio were talking together by the bar, and his instincts told him to walk right up and join the conversation. Those days had passed. Louisa had told him that she wouldn't be at the waterfront when his ship sailed, so his last good-bye was a slight nod as he passed. He bit his lip and wished that they had left already.

Once outside, the Germans had led him quickly

and confidently through the back streets. This was once his domain, but now he was behind the lines. The jagged shadows mocked him, those thick curtains of darkness where once he could relax and watch the world unfold or squeeze Svenya's hand and kiss her. Where were the hidden eyes? Chops could not find them. All the windows were dark and the doors closed, but he knew if he made a wrong move, hidden Gestapo guards would strike like a nest of vipers.

As they turned onto Bryghusgade, Chops saw the Gestapo staff car half a block away. Although the motor pool had removed the swastikas and replaced the military license with civilian plates, the black Benz radiated Gestapo airs. Without a word, the driver opened the doors and they climbed inside. The engine turned over on the first try and purred softly as they headed off to Radhus Platzen.

The smattering of one-way streets and unmarked dead ends stretched the trip out to ten minutes, and Chops almost remarked that it would have been quicker to walk. During the drive, Wolf explained that when they arrived at Gestapo headquarters, he and Anna Schadling would go inside and wade through the bureaucracy. Svenya would be released into their custody, and from there they would drive to Grey's Prison for Women, fifteen miles outside of the city.

Chops hated waiting, loathed it even more because he was cooped up with Peder Olsen. At least the smoking irritated him. He lit another. The rain started again, and its light drumming on the steel roof of the car was slightly hypnotic. Different possibilities of how the night could unfold ran through his mind, and every realistic scenario ended brutally. He didn't have a chance of freeing Svenya by force. What if he simply opened fire on Olsen and

Wolf as they sat parked outside of Gestapo headquarters? One Colt .45 against a trained officer
with a machine gun? And Olsen was probably
armed as well, and then there were the troops inside the building to worry about.

The trip to Sweden would have to wait.

The thought struck him like a stone. From the
moment that the Gestapo arrested Svenya, Chops
had asked how he would get her out, not if he
would. Between his connections with the black
market, the resistance, and the radio, he should
have been able to pull a rabbit out of a hat somehow, but he had blown it. What had he done
wrong? Maybe he should have strong-armed Olsen
from the very beginning or tried the official chan-
nels, although that might have meant his depor-
tation.

Could he come up with another plan or would
he simply play the lackey? Perhaps he could bribe
someone inside the prison or even arrange an old-
fashioned jail break, but no...what good had his
plans done him, or Svenya, so far?

At last, the front door of the Dagmar House
opened, and Anna Schadling and Herr Wolf stepped
out. Svenya followed with a guard behind. Silhouetted by the interior light, she looked frail and vulnerable.

Chops pulled up the door handle.

"Stay put."

"I'll be back," he said as he stepped onto the
curb. He paid no attention to Anna Schadling or
Herr Wolf when he approached the group, but focused on her. He winced. How had he expected
her to look after eight days of interrogation? Her
left eye was almost swollen shut, and he could tell
by the angle that they had broken her nose. Svenya
looked at him and smiled thinly for a moment. One

tooth was chipped. Hers was an expression he had seen before on New Orleans kids whose parents drank too much. The smile of vague and groundless hope. Then her expression became as blank as the gray prison smock she wore. How had he expected her to react?

He broke through the curtain of mist between them, and reached down to take her hands, although they were bound in cuffs. Her fingers were cold and lifeless, as if they had been soaking in a bucket of ice water. He took off his overcoat and draped it around Svenya's shoulders. "Everything will be all right," he said, and he wished he believed it.

She leaned forward and placed her face against his chest. Automatically his arms wrapped around her, pulling her head tight against him, and his fingers clasped her hair. He could feel her breaths, short and shallow, and they rocked him like giant waves of anguish and fear. She did not cry. Tears might have flowed the first or second day in detention, but by now her ducts were barren.

She looked up at him and blew a loose strand of hair out of her face. "I look like hell, don't I?"

Chops chuckled. "Yeah."

"So do you." She placed both hands under his jacket and felt his chest. "Haven't changed your shirt since the show. It's still sweaty. Your eyes are sagging, too. When's the last time you slept?"

"It's been a while."

"What's happening to us?"

"It's all a big mistake, but everything will work itself out. Everything will be OK." It was all he could think of, and he felt inadequate and vaguely dishonest. If Wolf and Schadling weren't watching them, he would have confessed everything, but they stood there next to the black staff car and they had told him to keep his trap shut.

"It's no use pretending, Chops. I'm in big trouble. They haven't told me much, but I've gathered the basics. They'll keep me in Grey's for a long time. A very long time."

"I tried, Svenya. I really tried." This was his confession, and as brief as it was, it told everything—that her arrest was his fault and his responsibility, and that he had failed. He had let her down.

She looked up at him, and he lost himself in her eyes, those oceans of strength and sorrow and resignation. "I know you did, but what could you have done? I love you, Chops. Don't forget that. Not ever."

Slowly he bent forward, bringing his face towards hers until he could smell her subtle fragrance. She closed her eyes, and then he hesitated, just for a moment. Their lips touched. He had imagined that their first kiss would make them transcend the present, that Olsen and Wolf and Schadling would disappear, as if they had been a trick with smoke and mirrors. He and Svenya would have been alone, lifted above it all, hovering on a cloud of togetherness, a journey away from fear and oppression.

But it was just a kiss.

The wind in front of Gestapo headquarters still blew the tiny raindrops sideways against their faces, and their feet remained in puddles. Her lips were cold and chapped, and his own mouth tasted like soot from the half-pack of Lucky Strikes he had smoked. Because her hands were chained together, their embrace was awkward and uncomfortable, the kind even an adolescent would not have willingly endured. And precisely because Olsen, Wolf, and Schadling did not disappear, they kept on kissing.

As Chops ran his fingers through her hair and pulled her towards him, he felt a subtle warmth of conspiracy, the glow of playing music that was just a touch too spicy for the current taste.

The engine of the staff car started, and the driver revved it a couple of times. It was like the school bell sounding, the signal that recess was over and they had to come inside to endure their keeper's devices. Like the belligerents they were, they ignored it, forcing Anna Schadling to tap Chops on the shoulder and say, "It's time to go," forcing her to intrude, to break protocol and propriety, to be rude.

Without a word, they walked to the car and climbed in. Chops held the door and followed. It was cramped inside, with Svenya wedged between Chops and Wolf. Olsen sat by the window up front. The driver put it in gear, and they headed through downtown, past Tivoli and the train station. The familiar sights ran past the window. Svenya did not look out the window. She kept her eyes straight ahead as if she did not want to see the city; the streets that she would not be able to walk down, the shops she could not go in, the coffee houses and butcher shops and other icons of civilized, normal, free life. Chops did not blame her. He dreaded seeing the walls of the prison.

The only sound was the wind passing outside and the hum of the engine. The silence was not comfortable, but what could he say? I promise I'll write and visit when allowed? Of course he would do these things. Anything he might have said would have sounded banal, so he contented himself by sitting next to her and resting his hand on her leg. This was not the silence of spent lovers, but a clumsy and needy one, one that needed to be broken.

"Cigarette?"

She nodded quickly, and Chops reached into his breast pocket and pulled out his pack. Seven left. He pulled out two and placed one in Svenya's hand. She brought it to her lips using both hands because they were chained together.

"Can she take these off?" Chops asked as he flicked his Zippo and held the flame up for her.

"Not till she's inside," Herr Wolf replied.

"My hands are lethal weapons, didn't you know, Chops?"

"That's supposed to be a secret."

"They are professionals. They knew it all along." She rolled her eyes in her head.

Chops lit his own cigarette, enjoying the small jab Svenya made at Wolf's expense. Her voice barely edged on sarcasm, and Chops could tell that she had given her interrogators a hard time. Good for her. Wolf was helpless against her banter, and it occurred to him that the head of the radio station, too, was a victim of this ordeal. How would Wolf react if he drew the gun, he wondered. Would he simply remain silent or would he make a move?

Now he could not get the gun out of his head. It pressed into his back and chafed as the car went around turns, begging Chops to draw it. Why didn't he? He could force the driver to take them to the waterfront, or just shoot them all and dump them on the side of the road. If he started shooting in the car, Svenya might catch a bullet by mistake, and if he plugged the driver, the car would certainly wreck. At fifty miles per hour a collision could kill everyone, and with her hands in the cuffs, Svenya wouldn't have a chance. But those were not the thoughts that kept his hand still. It was Olsen. He was the most dangerous individual Chops had ever encountered, and he terrified

Chops more now than ever before. Even if he fired the pistol into the back of the double agent's skull at point-blank range, something would go wrong. He would come back from the grave.

They had left the city behind them and the residential outskirts as well, and now they were driving on the two-lane highway that led to the prison. The road curved in and out between small farms and orchards, and then headed into the woods.

"Get off my tail, you jerk," the driver muttered looking into the rear view mirror.

Chops glanced over his shoulder and two bright headlights blinded him. They floated all over the road, coming within inches of their rear bumper and then sagging back, swaying right and left across both lanes. The car belonged to the Danish Army officers' pool. Usually it was the German soldiers who got drunk and started trouble, but sometimes it was the Danes, and when the two groups came together, fights often broke out. One Danish soldier was killed in September.

Honking wildly, the Danish car pulled out in the right-hand lane and shot past them on a blind curve. A hand stuck out of the tinted window and gave them the finger as he passed. It eased back into its lane and increased its lead, so its tail lights became two faint red dots, fang-marks on the road, then disappeared around another curve. "Drunken bastards," the driver snapped.

As they headed around the bend, Chops noticed something in the middle of the road. Without warning, a blinding light assaulted them from the front, and Chops realized that the Danish car had spun one hundred eighty degrees and waited to turn on its head lamps until it was too late to avoid a wreck. The driver shaded his eyes with one hand while he wrenched the wheel to the side and stomped on the brakes. Wheels screeched like crows as the car fish-tailed out of control and headed towards the ditch on the side of the road. Chops wrapped his arms around Svenya, trying to protect her. Motion stopped suddenly and momentum hurled them against the back seat. Chops had turned just soon enough to avoid planting his face in the seat in front of him, but his shoulder hit hard. He bit his lip and tasted blood. The front fender crunched like a tin can, and the windshield cracked where Anna Schadling's head smashed against it.

Without asking if everyone was OK, the driver grabbed his machine gun and lurched out of the car.

"Lieutenant," Anna Schadling said, but the driver acted like he hadn't heard.

First he walked to the front and inspected the damage in the beam of the one headlight that was still working. He kicked the grillwork. Then he looked at the Danish car, cocked his weapon, and marched towards it screaming, "Raus. Raus aus dem Auto. Raus." Get out of the car.

As soon as he put his hand on the front-door handle, a bulky figure emerged from the opposite rear door and pointed a gun at the soldier. "Drop the gun, fuckhead."

Chops recognized Kaj's voice immediately.

The guard did not move. He stood still, frozen in shock, not even looking around for help. Inside the car, no one breathed. If not for the constant drizzle, Chops might have thought that all time had stopped. "Drop it," Kaj repeated, and slowly the man lowered his weapon to the pavement.

Chops heard a rustle in the front seat, and then a click. Peder Olsen had just cocked his .9mm Luger, the one he had pointed at Chops earlier in the week. Obviously, he would not go on a mission like this unarmed. Slowly, carefully, professionally, he raised the gun, using both hands to keep it steady. He tilted his head to the right, taking aim at Kaj from inside the car.

Without thinking, Chops reached behind his back and grabbed the Colt .45. He jammed it into the back of Peder Olsen's head. "Do you want to die like this?" he spat.

A moment passed. Then two. Three. What had he done? He placed his free hand on Svenya's knee, hoping to calm her and himself as well. She smiled. From the corner of his eye, he tried to see Herr Wolf's reaction, but Svenya obscured his view. She blocked his line of fire as well.

Peder Olsen spoke, his words even, unabrasive and confident. "Congratulations, Chops. I am truly impressed. What about you, Klaus? Are you impressed?"

"Very."

"Shut up." He tried to think of what to do, but his mind went blank. Everything inside of him said he should pull the trigger and never ask any questions. To leave this man alive for one more second was begging for disaster. Even with a gun at his head he seemed in control and invincible. Chops tried to squeeze the trigger, but his fingers wouldn't obey. He couldn't do it. "Put the gun down."

Olsen complied.

They watched the scene unfolding outside. Louisa climbed out of the driver seat and picked up the guard's machine gun. She slung the strap over her shoulder and pointed the barrel from her hip. "Hands on your head."

The guard obeyed.

"Shoot this fucker if he blinks," she said to Kaj, and then headed over to the staff car. She walked with an assurance that Chops had never seen before, certainly not on a woman. She yanked open Chops' door.

"You look good with a gun in your hand, Chops."

"He's armed," he said, not moving the gun from the base of Olsen's skull.

Without hesitation, Louisa reached through the front window and Chops stifled a scream. He had expected Olsen to bite her arm or kill her instantly with a jujitsu blow, but she pulled the pistol out of his hand like it belonged to her. She stuck it into her waistband. "Everybody out of the car. Nice and slow. No sudden moves and no tricks." She took two steps backwards and watched carefully as they climbed out of the car.

Chops breathed easier when both of his feet were firmly planted on the ground. Although he was a bit bruised and shaken up by the collision, nothing was broken, but his neck was becoming stiff and his shoulder ached. He reached inside to help Svenya out of the car. "Are you OK?"

"I'll be all right."

He looked around in incomprehension. The Gestapo staff car was totaled on the side of the road, both front wheels pointing in because the axle was broken. Kaj and Louisa were herding the Germans into a line on the side of the road. They did not speak.

"Where'd you come from?" Chops asked.

"I stood outside the door to your dressing room and I heard every word they said, including where they were taking her. I knew just where to intercept you. I've been to Grey's before."

"We hot-wired this heap of scrap metal. What should we do with these worthless sods?" she said, pointing the gun at the Germans.

"Who's got the keys to the handcuffs?" Chops

asked. He wanted to get Svenya out of chains as soon as he could.

"They're in my pocket," Peder Olsen said. "I'll have to take my hands off my head to give them to you."

"Just one," Kaj said, cocking his .45 and stepping past Chops and Svenya.

"And move very slowly." He held the gun level at the double agent's chest and walked right up to him. Chops knew that he could not have acted as self-assured as the eighteen year old for one simple reason: he was afraid and the boy was not.

Peder Olsen unclasped his hands and very quietly inched his arm down to waist-level. He stared straight into Kaj's eyes the entire time, and neither blinked. He slowly unfastened the lowest button on his overcoat, and then the second.

Kaj tilted the gun towards the double agent's chin.

The drizzle increased to a sprinkle. Peder Olsen edged back his jacket and slipped his fingers into his pants pocket. They stayed there a moment and then began to reemerge. The keys to Svenya's handcuffs glistened in the headlight as he held them out to Kaj, never breaking eye contact. Kaj held his hand out palm up, and Olsen's moved forward.

The keys dropped to the ground.

For the briefest moment, Kaj's eyes followed their descent, and then it was too late. Olsen grabbed his wrist, jerking it upwards, forcing the boy off balance. The gun fired wildly into the air as Olsen spun under his arm and then yanked it down, banging Kaj's completely extended elbow against his shoulder. Chops heard the joint crack, and the gun fell to the ground.

Chops pointed his Colt .45, but could not find a target. The sights trembled as he stared down the barrel, and Kaj and Olsen were so close together they were touching. If he pulled the trigger, he would be tossing a coin as to whom he would hit.

After firing his elbow into Kaj's rib cage twice, Olsen bent his knees, lowering his center of gravity, and tried to heave Kaj over his shoulder. The eighteen year old pulled back, and Olsen could not quite bring him off the ground. Stepping forward with his right foot, Kaj grabbed the agent's hair and used his own head as a twelve-pound sledge, smashing the spy right behind the ear. He cranked the agent's face around and hammered into the bridge of his nose. Then he straightened up and shoved Olsen, who staggered backwards in a daze.

Bang.

The shot echoed in the woods. Kaj's eyes widened, and a small trickle of blood appeared from a bright-red hole in his temple. He did not make a sound; he simply took one step backwards and fell shapelessly to the ground.

Chops turned his head and saw Anna Schadling, her arm outstretched, smoke rising from the barrel of her derringer.

The bullets tore into the woman's flesh before she heard the explosions from the sub-machine gun Louisa had slung over her shoulder. Her face grimaced and she turned her head to the side, but nothing could save her. Herr Wolf screamed as the bullets pierced his throat, and although the driver tried to dive to the ground, he was dead before he landed. His body convulsed on the ground as lead flew into it.

Louisa stood, slightly crouched, legs planted firmly like a boxer's, spraying bullets back and forth in waves. She held the gun steady against the recoil, and did not take her steel eyes off the targets. Even when the clip expired and the last shell had hit the ground, she did not move. Click. Click. She squeezed the trigger again and again, but nothing happened. "I got 'em, Chops. I got 'em good."

He turned to Svenya. The rain had matted her hair against her head, and she shivered under his overcoat. She stared at the carnage and nodded slightly, perhaps only rocking her head because her neck was tired—Chops did not know. She was alive, and that was enough to begin again, to close the doors to the past.

"Shut your eyes," he said as he placed the barrel of his gun on the chain between her wrists. He fired, severing the link, and she immediately wrapped her arms around his neck.

"I'm cold," she said.

"I know you are," he said. He wanted to comfort her, to receive her comfort, to hold her forever, but it was impossible. "Go on and get in the car. Someone expects us at the prison and they're gonna come looking. We can dump the car in the channel and make it to pier 32 by the time the boat leaves for Sweden, but we don't have much time. Louisa, climb in."

She looked at him and then pointed the gun at the ground. In that motion she seemed to melt from a statue of hatred. "Should we bring Kaj?"

He nodded. He had so much to say about the boy, about the years they had spent together as teacher and pupil—and as friends—that it was best to say nothing at all. He walked around to the rear of the car. Then he realized...

Peder Olsen had disappeared.

Epilogue

Svenya did not sleep peacefully. Her hair was still damp and matted across her forehead like old hay, her breaths short and shallow. Every few moments her face twitched. Chops had not taken his eyes off of her since he laid her down on a makeshift mattress of folded sails and covered her with his overcoat only minutes after the old trawler set sail. She was safe.

She had said nothing in the car as Louisa drove them to Cafe Kakadu, and Chops had practically carried her inside. He grabbed one of the chairs off a corner table, and she carefully lowered herself onto it. "What's happening?" she said in a hollow voice.

"We've got to get out of here. We're going to Sweden."

"When?"

"Soon."

Louisa walked behind her and began rubbing her shoulders. "What day is it, Svenya?"

No response.

"Huh, Svenya? Tell me what day it is?"

She sank her head in her hands. "Today is...it's...Saturday. Is it Saturday?"

Chops shot Louisa a horrified look.

"It's OK," Louisa said, more to Chops than to Svenya. "She's in a little bit of shock. You'll be all right. You just need to rest a little bit and you'll be fine." She turned to Chops and spoke in a calm but stern voice. "Get rid of the car. Drive to the Knippels bridge and put it over the side. Get back here as soon as you can."

Chops didn't move.

"She'll be fine, Chops. Go on."

"What about Kaj?" He had not thought to take the boy's body out of the trunk.

"Burial at sea."

He had been extra careful driving to the bridge, keeping on the empty back streets. When he was halfway across, he pulled on the emergency brake, climbed out, and released it. Slowly the car made its way to the edge, teetered, and then plunged into the black waters below. It landed with a muf-fled splash, floated for a moment, and then sank into the Inderhavn. He watched the waves ripple out in circles and he said good-bye to Kaj, as good a friend as he'd ever had. Chops had tried to utter a short prayer, nothing more than "Lord, into your bosom I commit your servant," but tears welled up in his eyes and he couldn't get the words out.

On his way back to the cafe, Chops milled through the back streets he once thought he owned, keeping his eyes out for anything moving, his hand ready to go for the Colt .45 in his belt. He wanted to pass by Smukke, to go inside or simply to look down the staircase at the oak door, but that would be the first place they would look for him. Kakadu was safe.

The rain did not let up and by the time he reached the cafe he was soaked, and he shivered, not from the cold but from the fear. Peder Olsen was out there, somewhere.

Chops could hear the wind blowing waves against the ship's hull, and the candle flickered, casting deep shadows across Svenya's face. The boat's cargo bay was damp and cold, and he looked for something else to lay over her to keep her warm, but there was nothing but a few crates and some mooring line. He wished he had thought to bring blankets or some food, but there had been no time.

He stroked Svenya's cheek, and her face was warm with fever. She moaned softly and turned away. Would she ever recover? No. Not completely. Her scars would last forever, as would his, but at least they were together. That's what he had been fighting for, wasn't it?

They had said very little as they waited in the old cafe. Louisa fixed a pot of coffee, and they drank it in silence. Nothing moved outside. Once, a car drove by but it did not stop. At three thirty Louisa said it was time to go. As they walked to the door, Louisa said, "Hey Chops. Aren't you forgetting something?"

He shrugged.

She walked behind the counter and pulled out his cornet. "I took it out of your dressing room after you left."

"Thanks."

From there Louisa led them to pier 32 where the GARM was ready to sail. The boat was an old trawler, once rigged with a mast and sails, but from the fumes he could tell she burned diesel now. As Chops and Svenya waited, Louisa boarded the ship, and the captain came out of the cockpit and met her. He was a bearded old man that Chops did not recognize. He could not hear what they were saying, but when Louisa nodded, Chops and Svenya came aboard.

"You'll come home after the war?" she asked.

"Yeah," Chops said.

"Take care." She reached out, touched him on the shoulder, and smiled thinly. Then she turned around and walked down the gang plank, steadying herself on the rope hand rail.

The dark welt across Svenya's sleeping face hurt him to look at. "It will be OK." He sat on an overturned trunk, and his back and legs ached from being cramped in the small space. Hoping that the salt air would clear his head, Chops pulled his coat up over Svenya, grabbed his cornet, and climbed the ladder to the deck.

The rain had stopped, but the sea was still rough. Chops leaned over the rail and looked at the ocean below him. He closed his eyes and thought about happier times, listening to Svenya practice the viola, playing hot jazz in Smukke, watching his friends come and go in their best clothes. He prayed they would be safe, but it was difficult to believe. He remembered talking to Kaj about tattoos and clothes, giving him advice on his love life, teaching him to play the cornet.

His thoughts drifted back to something an old man in New Orleans had told him years ago. "Jazz comes down to one thing, and one thing only. When you're happy, blow happy. And when you're sad, blow sad."

As the boat rocked back and forth, Chops took his cornet from the case and put it to his lips. Closing his eyes, he began the saddest song he had ever played.

* * * *

If you are ever fortunate enough to visit Copenhagen, spend an hour or two along the waterfront. Walk along the Gammel Strand and drink a cup of coffee in one of the cafes on the Nyhavn. Stroll through the side streets and you might pass by a set of stairs leading to an old oak door. Then take the midnight ferry to Sweden and stand on the upper deck. Listen. Above the waves crashing against the hull and the wind whipping across the bow you might hear it still, a silver Bach cornet, crying in the darkness.

The End